Darcy, Knight Errant

Part of the Elizabeth and
Darcy True Love Multiverse

By Jaime Marie Lang

Book Cover by Jaime Marie Lang

Editing by Bailey and Bloom Ink

Contents

Dear Reader,

I HAVE LONG BEEN fascinated by the "what if" of *Pride and Prejudice* variations. There is just something about imagining the possibilities if just one unexpected event were to occur. What if there was a slight change in the story? How would it alter the outcome? As a fan of sci-fi movies, I was inspired to peer into a multiverse of Elizabeths and Darcys, where their love story took on different twists and turns, yet always led them to each other. The only real question is, how will it happen this time?

Within the *Elizabeth and Darcy Multiverse*, the possibilities for their love story are boundless, offering endless excitement and intrigue. Time travel, epic battles, unexpected character arcs, and enchanting fairy-tale crossovers could all be part of their adventure together. Almost anything could happen when you are dealing with a multiverse. Well, anything but Elizabeth and Darcy being denied their happily ever after.

While writing *Darcy, Knight Errant*, I asked: What if Elizabeth met Georgianna first? How might that change the story? I hope you find pleasure in the narrative I discovered while reflecting on this particular "what if."

Chapter One

Elizabeth sighed and shook her head, utterly perplexed by the situation. For two weeks now, Elizabeth had watched a young lady come in to help at the charity with her companion, and every time Elizabeth saw the young Miss Darcy, she seemed all too morose. Though the girl's clothes spoke of wealth and privilege, and she appeared to be enjoying the typical good health of youth, it seemed as if she was incapable of joy. Elizabeth couldn't shake the feeling that something was troubling Miss Darcy, prompting her to wonder about the unseen burden she carried.

From across the room, she observed Miss Darcy sitting next to her companion, patiently guiding the youngest attendees in the art of sewing a proper hem. Even before the enthusiastic and well-mannered girls she helped, the young lady seemed to wilt. The urge to act grew within Elizabeth. She could not leave the poor thing so miserable without at least trying to help. Maybe it was the older sister in her. Miss Darcy looked slightly older than Lydia and if Lydia had behaved in such a way, Elizabeth would never hesitate to step in.

Not one to enjoy plain sewing, Elizabeth assisted another set of girls and young women in learning to read. Once her lesson for the day was complete, Elizabeth normally took tea with some of the other volunteers, and she was determined that today she would get Miss Darcy to join her for a cup or two.

A young voice pulled her out of her introspection. "Miss Bennet? I do not understand this one."

"What are you struggling with?" Elizabeth smiled down at the girl and, kneeling next to her, looked at the page she had been given. "Which word is giving you trouble, Beatrice?"

The young girl pointed to the page and Elizabeth studied the small nursery rhyme she had given Beatrice to study. As Beatrice had expressed interest in becoming a nursemaid, Elizabeth had given her "Rock-a-Bye Baby." The word that Beatrice was struggling with was bough. Instead of simply giving the thirteen-year-old the answer, Elizabeth asked, "Have you tried sounding it out?"

"Yes, that is why I am so confused. It has an end like dough for making bread, but when I say it with a B, it sounds like a bow for my hair and that does not make any sense. Why would a bow break and how would that make a baby fall?" Beatrice gazed at Elizabeth, her mouth twisting for a moment before saying, "I do not think I like this story."

"I can certainly understand why you are so frustrated. 'Rock-a-Bye Baby' may be a sweet lullaby, but it does not make much sense when you think about it. The word you are struggling with has more of an *ow* sound than a *dough* sound."

Scrunching her nose, Beatrice mouthed the word a few times before asking, "So when it says the bough breaks, they are talking about a tree limb?"

Elizabeth nodded and exclaimed, "Yes, exactly." She was so happy to see how hard Beatrice was working to sort out not just the words, but the meaning behind them. Although she did not have the best circumstances, she was a very intelligent girl.

It only took a moment before Beatrice's mouth fell open in horror. Jerking her head around to stare at Elizabeth, she sputtered, "Why would anyone sing to a baby about falling out of a tree?!"

Pressing her lips together to suppress a giggle at the girl's exasperation, Elizabeth managed to shrug. "That I do not know. Though I will say my cousins never seemed to mind when I sang it to them." Standing, Elizabeth brushed off her skirt and forced herself to concentrate on her charges for the rest of their allotted time together. She truly enjoyed helping others discover the power of the written word.

Soon enough, a melodic bell chimed, alerting everyone that the morning's lessons had concluded. Her students expressed their gratitude and departed, their footsteps fading away. Elizabeth hurried to Miss Darcy's side before she could slip away, as she often did once she fulfilled her duties. Reaching out, Elizabeth grasped the edge of her sleeve as she began to turn towards the exit. When the young girl turned back, her eyes wide, Elizabeth smiled sheepishly. "Miss Darcy, I hope you will forgive my boldness, but I have wanted to speak with you for some time."

With large blue eyes round as saucers, Miss Darcy stared at her briefly before uttering, "Me? Why would you want to speak with me?"

Smiling at both Miss Darcy and her companion, Mrs. Annesley, Elizabeth continued, "Though I am rarely in London for very long, I enjoy volunteering while I am here. Most of the volunteers I meet here are older married women. I am delighted to know that there is another young lady volunteering as well. I would love to have a friend as like-minded as myself while I am in town visiting family. They have a lovely little sitting room available for the volunteers to take tea here. Would you be willing to have a cup of tea with me before you go home for the day?"

As Elizabeth patiently waited, she couldn't help but be intrigued by the bewildered look on Miss Darcy's face as her eyes flickered towards Mrs. Annesley, a perplexed crease forming on her forehead. The poor girl appeared painfully self-effacing and shy, causing Elizabeth to hope that she would be open to forming a friendship. After a moment, Mrs. Annesley nodded to Miss Darcy with a smile. At that, Miss Darcy turned back to Elizabeth and, though looking down at her pretty boots, she finally replied, "It would be lovely to enjoy a cup of tea with you, Miss Bennet."

Elizabeth's instinct was to take the younger girl's arm in hers and walk together to the sitting room, but she did not want to overwhelm her. Instead, she only said, "Splendid! I will lead the way."

GEORGIANNA STILL DID NOT know what was going on. Even at her school, she had never encountered someone so genuinely eager to be her friend. Of course, there had been several young ladies who had pretended to offer friendship, but they had all shown themselves to be less than sincere. They had not acted as friends long before Georgianna had discovered the truth—they had all merely wanted access to her very wealthy and handsome older brother. This young woman, however, showed none of the telltale signs she recognized so well.

As she followed Miss Bennet, it occurred to Georgianna that the only other person who had ever been so bold was Miss Caroline Bingley. Not that Miss Bingley would ever show her face at a charity. No, Miss Bennet was a conundrum, and she would simply have to wait and see what she wanted. After all, no one ever wanted Georgianna just for herself. Any attention shown to her would only be for her connections or her money. That was a hard-earned lesson gifted to her by George Wickham.

It had been difficult to discover that she was seen as a mouse of a girl with no defining qualities. In a heart-wrenching moment, the man she believed loved her shattered her self-worth with hurtful words, declaring her undeserving of love or friendship. The sting of his words lingered, haunting her every waking hour. While her brother and Mrs. Annesley assured her that his words were untrue, she could not help but feel their continued power over her. So Georgianna watched with confusion—and admittedly, a little awe—as Miss Bennet ushered her into a little room of pleasant colors and comfortable-looking chairs.

Miss Bennet walked to a little alcove near a window after nodding to one of the serving girls to request tea service. Turning back to smile at Georgianna and Mrs. Annesley, Miss Bennet said, "I have always enjoyed sitting here by the window, though if you prefer, we could sit elsewhere."

Shaking her head, Georgianna found herself sitting down on a well-stuffed settee and responded by softly saying, "This is lovely, thank you."

Georgianna watched carefully as Miss Bennet, who was still smiling at her, sat down. Though appropriately demure, her smile did not just stop at her lips. It seemed to envelop her entire face, almost as if her smile was shining forth from her very being. Settling her skirts, Miss Bennet said, "I am so pleased that you were both willing to overlook my forward behavior. I have been assisting at the London Ladies Society for the Betterment of the Female Poor for quite some time, and it is rare for me to encounter someone who is even remotely close to my age. So I am, of course, thrilled to be given the opportunity to chat with you both. If you do not mind my asking, do you reside in London? Or, like me, are you only here part of every year?" There was just something about Miss Bennet's enthusiasm that was uplifting and infectious, and Georgianna felt the corners of her lips turning upward, if only slightly.

After looking at Mrs. Annesley for approval, Georgianna murmured, "I reside in London much of the year, but I always cherish returning to my family's estate in the country." It was common enough to have a country estate, so Georgianna felt no compunction about mentioning an estate. She never revealed the name of that estate as Pemberley to anyone anymore. Despite calling one of the nation's largest and most-esteemed estates home, she had no desire to flaunt it or be showered with excessive flattery.

"I always love returning home to the country after a time in London," exclaimed Miss Bennet. Then, seeing that the tea service had been brought, she asked, "How do you both take your tea?"

Miss Bennet made quick work of dispensing their tea exactly as requested, and Georgianna was envious of how well she managed it all. Any time she attempted to pour, Georgianna always made a hash of it, clattering things about with shaking hands. For a time, there was silence, but somehow Miss Bennet carried her cheer over into the quiet moment with her convivial attitude. For the first time in what seemed like forever, Georgianna actively contributed to a conversation by asking, "Where do you call home, Miss Bennet?"

"My family's estate is in Hertfordshire, near the small town of Meryton. Though my family estate is neither large nor as prosperous as some, Longbourn has been in the family for the last eight generations." Elizabeth took a sip of her tea, and a smile spread across her face, causing her cheeks to plump and her eyes to sparkle with delight. "I love walking the trails there as I visit the tenant families. While I enjoy the parks here in London, there is just something about the land around my home that calls to me."

Leaning forward, Georgianna remarked, "I know exactly what you mean. I never feel so myself but when I am walking the well-worn paths that twine about the rosebushes near my home. Even in winter, when it is bare of all its normal beauty, those paths call to me." Once she finished speaking, Georgianna sat back, suddenly aghast at her forward behavior. She never allowed herself to get so carried away, especially not with a practical stranger. Looking over at Mrs. Annesley, she expected to see her frowning at her forward behavior, but was met with a smile.

With what Georgianna had come to think of as her motherly smile, Mrs. Annesley said, "I think the place we call home often brings a sense of tranquility to most people, whether it's the picturesque garden path or the idyllic countryside. Yet, for just as many, the soothing ambiance can be found indoors, amidst the shelves of a library or the harmonious melodies of a piano."

Nodding, Miss Bennet acknowledged the truth of Mrs. Annesley's words. "You are right. My father would certainly never find peace about the estate. He is happiest amongst his books. My younger sister Mary, on the other hand, is happiest when she is practicing the piano."

Finding herself inexplicably drawn in, Georgianna said, "I have always wished for a sister. Not that I have been ungrateful for my brother, mind you—he is the best of men. It is only that I have always supposed a sister would be more of a friend and confidant."

Laughing lightly, Miss Bennet said, "I can attest to the veracity of your supposition. Among my four sisters, I have cultivated deep friendships, but we have also had our fair share of conflicts and squabbles. So, though I will always support the idea of having sisters, it is not without caution. On the other hand, I have always wished for a brother."

By the time they finished tea and separated for the day, Georgianna had shared more of herself with Miss Bennet than she had ever shared with anyone else before. Not even with her brother had she expressed herself so freely. That was not to imply that she spoke rashly, rather that she embraced the freedom to express herself. Miss Bennet lent such an air of compassion and interest that Georgianna's responses felt natural. Riding home in the carriage with Mrs. Annesley, Georgianna felt strangely hopeful.

DARCY WATCHED HIS SISTER from across the table as she ate. As usual, the meal was quiet except for the slight sounds of their cutlery. He hated how incapable he felt around her. Their interactions were scarce during his time at Eton, and it wasn't until he graduated from Cambridge that they reconnected. His normally reticent disposition had not helped matters, but he had worked hard to build a relationship with the little sister that he loved. But then their father had died, and he was no longer a brother, but her guardian.

He found it difficult to navigate the position he found himself in. Unlike caring for Pemberley, caring for his sister was not something he had been prepared for. The fact that she almost eloped served as further proof that he was not well prepared to direct the life of a teenage girl. He could only hope that his faith in Mrs. Annesley was better founded than it had been in Mrs. Younge.

He had made many blunders in the early days after Ramsgate, mistakes that ended in his sister crying. In those days, he couldn't seem to go a day without uttering words that would bring tears to his sister's eyes. It left him hesitant to say anything and yet he knew his sister would not speak unless prompted. For all of this, Darcy knew he was mostly to blame, and it gutted him.

Squaring his shoulders, Darcy mentally castigated himself as the silence dragged on. Darcy was a twenty-eight-year-old gentleman, and he could not be such a coward. It was merely a conversation with his sister; he was not facing Napoleon. Darcy searched for something benign to say and finally settled on, "Did you have a productive day at the charity today, Georgianna?"

Looking up from her plate, eyes wide, Georgianna swallowed before saying, "Yes, Brother, Mrs. Annesley and I worked with some of the youngest girls on their needlework."

Mrs. Annesley added, "Miss Darcy has a fine hand with a needle, and I believe the girls gained a lot from her kind attention." She smiled warmly at Georgianna before taking a bite of her meal.

Darcy saw how his sister perked up at the older woman's motherly expression and praise. He silently watched the interchange, wishing all the while that he had the ability to bring such a smile to Georgianna's face. Unwilling to give up though, he pressed forward, still trying to draw Georgianna out. "Are you enjoying yourself there?"

This earned Darcy an enormous smile. Georgianna practically bounced in her chair when she said, "Yes, very much. I met a girl who might even want to be friends. We had tea together."

Keeping his mouth closed with difficulty, Darcy glared at Mrs. Annesley. Was she or was she not supposed to be protecting his sister? Any number of people there could be trying to take advantage of Georgianna. This whole volunteering at a charity had been something he was uneasy with at the start. If he was being honest, he still felt uneasy with the idea. The world had already been so cruel to his sister. Why continue to expose her to how ruthless life could be? He wanted to shelter Georgianna from everything he could, but Mrs.

Annesley had been firm in her belief that Georgianna needed wider exposure to the world, not less. Now he worried that he should have insisted it was a bad idea. Just who was this girl his sister had met? Was Mrs. Annesley allowing his sister to be ensnared by a perfect stranger?

Turning to his sister, he tried to keep his tone light as he said, "My dear, places like women's charities for the poor are no place to find friends." His sister's wide eyes and trembling lip hurt Darcy, but he felt the need to get his point across. He continued, "If you are truly longing for companionship, I am certain Lady Matlock would gladly invite you to one of her elegant teas, where you could meet young ladies more suited to your social status. Young ladies who are less likely to befriend you for personal gain."

Tears gathered in the corners of Georgianna's eyes as she took in his words, and they ate at his heart. He wanted so desperately to see Georgianna happy, but he could not relax his guard for a moment. The last time he let his guard down, he almost lost her. It was better for her to be safe than happy with some friend who would only use her.

Pushing her seat back, Georgianna stood, her shoulders hunched. She stood there for a moment, only looking down at her plate before dropping her serviette and turning her back to the table. At the doorway, she stopped and said, "I know you are the great Mr. Darcy of Pemberley, but do not suppose you know everything." Then she was gone.

Turning his frustration to Mrs. Annesley, Darcy said, "I wonder, Madam, what you thought you were doing when you let my sister become involved in such an unsuitable entanglement."

Setting her fork down, Mrs. Annesley calmly stared back at him, unruffled. "Unsuitable, sir?" she asked.

"Yes, unsuitable!" Pushing back from the table, Darcy paced, hoping to get his anger under regulation. Turning back to Mrs. Annesley, he cried, "I went along with your belief that helping people in need would give Georgianna a sense of worth and accomplishment, not so that she could befriend some poor chit destined to be a shopgirl or nursemaid. No matter how kind they may appear, someone like that would inevitably befriend her for her wealth and connections, if only because they needed to."

Mrs. Annesley did not shrink back at his anger. She stayed calm and only asked, "Who exactly do you think volunteers at the London Ladies Society for the Betterment of the Female Poor?"

Confused by her response, Darcy froze. He had never considered who might volunteer at a charity. He assumed good Christian ladies who wanted to help their fellow man volunteered at the charity, but Mrs. Annesley's question implied that he was missing something. The question was, what was it?

Chapter Two

Biting back a sigh, Mrs. Annesley looked at the clueless man across from her with compassion. Her question had completely caught him off guard. He might be a man of twenty-eight, but he did not know the first thing about women. She almost pitied him for the rough road he would travel when he fell in love.

Mr. Darcy could not understand that it was her cloistered situation that had left Miss Darcy vulnerable to the Mr. Wickhams of the world. She did not need to be protected; she needed to be taught how to recognize evil and how to combat it. Miss Darcy needed to know that yes, there were wolves in the world, but there were also friends, and she needed to be able to recognize the difference.

Not one to be intimidated by a tantrum—regardless of the age of the one misbehaving—Mrs. Annesley set herself to educate the man. She only hoped for his sister's sake that he would take her wisdom to heart. "Mr. Darcy, I know that you only want what is best for your sister, but I believe you are operating on some misconceptions that are hindering your endeavors."

She could tell that she had caught him off guard once again by his change in stance and the tightening of his shoulders. With his hands firmly clasped behind his back, his narrowed eyes conveyed a sense of determination as he replied, "Well then, Mrs. Annesley, enlighten me."

Mrs. Annesley nearly laughed at his pomposity. It was clear that he thought her wrong and possibly ignorant, but he would, wouldn't he? Men had surrounded him for most of his life. Having lost his mother at a young age, he lost the softness and understanding she might have lent him. It was probable that he would take everything about women at face value and that, combined with his evident prejudice, left him unable to truly help and understand his younger sister. He could not understand the underhanded and petty way women of his sphere interacted with one another and the world.

Tapping one of her fingers against her leg under the table, Mrs. Annesley maintained her cool regard as she said, "Let us start with the fact that you told your sister she might find a friend at one of your aunt's teas."

Shifting his weight from one foot to the other, Mr. Darcy gestured with a nonchalant flick of his hand. He huffed, "Yes, there would be plenty of young ladies and women there that would love to befriend a sweet girl like Georgianna without the risk of an unequal friendship."

Now Mrs. Annesley did smile, though only faintly, as she asked, "Have you ever attended one of your aunt's teas?"

"No, though I have greeted the ladies there on the way to visit with my uncle and cousins. They all seemed to be well-mannered and kind—the perfect friends for my sister." Crossing his arms, Mr. Darcy waited for her response, though his posture told Mrs. Annesley he was becoming less certain of himself.

Tapping her finger a few more times, Mrs. Annesley replied, "It is apt that you used the word *seemed*, Mr. Darcy, and this is where the first important lesson about women comes in. While you may grasp the notion that women have less power in our society, you cannot grasp the ways in which they wield the power they do possess." Tilting her head slightly, Mrs. Annesley decided an example was necessary for Mr. Darcy to better understand. "If I told you that Lady Penelope said the riding outfit your sister wore the other day was quite singular, and she wondered where she could have possibly gotten it, what would you say?"

Mrs. Annesley watched as Mr. Darcy pondered her question. He was not a stupid man; he just did not have all the pieces to the puzzle before him. After only a moment, he said, "I would think she was complimenting her outfit and was interested in getting her own."

Pressing her lips together before she spoke, Mrs. Annesley said, "You think that way because you are a male and do not fully understand the way women operate. The comment was *meant* to offend, and drawing rooms are rife with similar subtle jabs. Women are told that regardless of what they are underneath, they must always appear gentle and demure. So, it has developed that their insults follow suit."

Rigid, Mr. Darcy groused, "Surely not all women behave in such a manner."

"No, but a drawing room is not generally the place to find people of a better caliber," Mrs. Annesley answered, shaking her head.

Frowning, Mr. Darcy asked, "Then where can my sister safely find the companionship she obviously wants and needs?"

This time, she allowed her smile to widen before she said, "Don't be fooled by your misconceptions; charities offer an ideal environment to bond with other kindhearted young women."

Moving back to his chair, he slumped down into it, and after running his hand through his hair, he said, "I still need for you to explain why to me."

At least his thinking was moving in the right direction. Mrs. Annesley was more than happy to explain everything to him. "Because while it is popular to help the poor, for the most part, the cats of society do it from a distance by donating money. The women who volunteer are mostly good and kindhearted people. Your sister would benefit more from finding friends at the London Ladies Society rather than with your aunt, where all the ladies are focused on jockeying for position."

Resting his head in his hands, Darcy said, "That may be true, but Georgianna cannot befriend the people who are there for aid. They cannot have anything in common and besides, society might very well shun her for such a friendship."

Tapping her fingers on her leg in a fast pattern, Mrs. Annesley hoped he was finally going to realize where he had gone so wrong. Looking him in the eye, she asked, "Mr. Darcy, did your sister ever say she was hoping to befriend one of the poor girls she was teaching?"

"No, but what other girls are at the charity? I thought the volunteers would all be elderly widows whose children had left home and were bored with too much free time." Mr. Darcy suddenly sat bolt upright in his chair and stared at Mrs. Annesley. "Are there other girls volunteering at the charity?"

"Not many, but Miss Darcy has met a young woman not that much older than her who teaches reading. And I know you are about to ask about her family and connections, so I will tell you what I know about her." Mrs. Annesley leaned back in her chair and revealed what she had learned before encouraging Georgianna to be friendly with the young woman. "Your aunt and her aunt, Mrs. Gardiner, both serve on the board of the London Ladies Society. While Mrs. Gardiner is the wife of a tradesman, she is also the granddaughter of a baron and both she and her husband are known to be refined and well-mannered. I will admit that the young lady in question is not of the first circles, but she is the daughter of a gentleman with a modest country estate. In all my years, I have never encountered someone as friendly, kind, and genuine as that young woman. The way your sister positively beamed during their interaction was truly heartwarming and you spoiled that by reprimanding her for trying to make her first ever true friend."

Once again, he had said the wrong thing and hurt his sister. Would he ever learn? It had been hours since Mrs. Annesley had excused herself to go comfort Georgianna, and for most of that time, he had been pacing in his room.

How had he not known how complicated a world his sister was facing? Darcy felt as if he should have known better, but really, how could he have known? Only now was he realizing how different their two spheres of the world were, and it was not as if he had a wife or a female cousin who could have warned him beforehand. In reality, ever since he had come into his inheritance, he had spent most of his time around women avoiding their company altogether.

After his father passed, eye-fluttering ladies who clung to his arm like limpets besieged him. Two separate attempts at compromise taught him early on to be cautious around young, eligible women, and their mothers, for that matter. Developing a hard, unapproachable mien kept all but the most determined women at bay. Sadly, the only thing he had gained from all his knowledge of women thus far was that he was determined Georgianna would never be the sort of woman who would attempt to gain a husband in such a way. Though, in hindsight, he might have done better to go over the *right* ways to gain a husband. The problem with that was that he still did not know how to gain a wife. He was basically clueless when it came to the concept of matrimony.

Halting his pacing, he massaged at the knot that had developed in his neck, knowing that if he did not stop fretting soon, it would lead to a full-blown megrim. Darcy blew out a long breath before making his way to the large wingback chair in the corner of the room. He knew that obsessing would get him nowhere. Ever the orderly thinker, Darcy decided to come up with a few mental lists of what he should do.

The foremost problem was that he felt as if he was failing Georgianna and that they were slipping further and further apart. Obviously, he would have to apologize to her for jumping to conclusions. His gut told him that he should explain how difficult this all was to him, as it would surely help them bond. It would go against all his father had taught him about standing strong and never showing weakness or emotion, but that approach was getting him nowhere.

Truth be told, he was lonely, and never showing weakness was exhausting. He was only human, after all. Was it too much to want to rely on more than just himself? Darcy hoped that he could be forgiven for allowing his sister to know more of what he struggled with. Georgianna was so kindhearted that he could not imagine she would think less of him if he showed weakness.

Running his hand down his face, Darcy gathered the energy to stand. He had the first step of his plan formulated and finally felt as if he could rest. So what if he already felt embarrassed at the idea of allowing Georgianna to know of his worries, faults, and foibles? Nothing of any importance was easy, and his relationship with his sister was the most important thing in his life.

GEORGIANNA REPRESSED THE DESIRE to bounce in her seat as she rode with Mrs. Annesley towards the London Ladies Society. She knew that Miss Bennet was always there on Tuesday mornings, and she could not wait to see her. Her anticipation for a true friend was so intense that she could feel the excitement bubbling up inside her, ready to burst forth at any moment.

Across from her in the carriage, Mrs. Annesley smiled at her indulgently. "I should probably tell you to settle, but I am thrilled to see you so happy, Miss Darcy. You have been so much brighter the last several days."

"To be truthful, I feel brighter and certainly less downtrodden. Ever since my brother and I spoke, I feel as if so much has changed." Looking Mrs. Annesley in the eye, Georgianna confided, "He apologized, you know."

"I had hoped he would," said Mrs. Annesley with a smile.

Brushing at a speck of lint on her dress, Georgianna continued, "We ended up talking for hours—really talking. I have always viewed my brother as this cold, austere figure who was not only perfect, but untouchable. I am sure that it has not helped that he is so much older than myself and not only my brother, but my guardian."

Eyes kind, Mrs. Annesley commented, "No, that could not have made it easy for either of you."

"You know, I had never considered how difficult it was for William to take on a much younger sister. Would you believe he admitted to being completely clueless to the ways of women, or at least women of worth?"

"Women of worth?" questioned Mrs. Annesley.

Georgianna huffed angrily, "William confessed that twice women have attempted to trap him in compromising situations, and he only barely escaped." Puffing out a breath, Georgianna paused before saying, "Now that I think of it, my brother has spent most of his adult life fighting off or hiding from women. It is no wonder that he does not understand them. For the first time, possibly ever, I actually feel close to my brother."

Mrs. Annesley tilted her head. "It is not uncommon for gentlemen in your brother's position to be the object of pursuit by women of the ton. Your brother's method of dealing with being hunted seems to differ from most gentlemen I know, and not necessarily in a better way. I don't mean to insult your brother, but rather acknowledge the hardships he faces."

Looking out the open carriage window, Georgianna pondered her next words before looking back at Mrs. Annesley and saying, "I am realizing that my brother is in as much need of companionship and support as I am, despite him being so much older. It may not be easy, but last night I decided that I am determined to do my part by inviting him to socialize with me more. My constant hesitation to overstep has left both of us isolated and lonely. In retrospect, my brother may face the same issue—always hesitating out of fear of offending me—leaving our conversations stilled and awkward. But I am not a child anymore. Drawing closer to William is something I can and should do, as it will benefit us both in the long run."

Smiling at Georgianna, Mrs. Annesley said, "I am glad your relationship with your brother has improved and will continue to do so. Though I wonder if there is more to your joy than just the improvement to your relationship with Mr. Darcy."

A few moments of introspection had Georgianna nodding as she said, "Somehow, knowing that William is not perfect and learning that he is floundering as badly as I am helped me forgive myself for my past errors. Then, too, knowing that a lady like Miss Bennet might want to be my friend is helping me put Mr. Wick—that man's words behind me." Hesitating, she looked at Mrs. Annesley with concern. "You do believe Miss Bennet is genuine, don't you?"

Leaning over, Mrs. Annesley patted Georgianna's knee. "I believe Miss Bennet cannot help but being genuine. I have never met another young woman with such a *joie de vivre* about her."

Relieved, Georgianna relaxed back into the cushions of the carriage. "William said that I may invite Miss Bennet to tea this week if I wish. I hope she is available."

In no time at all, Georgianna found herself helping various girls with their lessons with a needle and thread. It was difficult to concentrate, as she often watched Miss Bennet across the room as she worked with her own group. At times, they caught one another's eyes, and both women smiled.

Georgianna was putting supplies away when Miss Bennet appeared at her side. Turning to her, Georgianna could not help but smile widely. Returning the smile, Miss Bennet said, "Miss Darcy, I was hoping to see you here today. Do you have time to have tea with me?"

"Not only do I have time," Georgianna started with a growing smile, "but I was hopeful for it."

Miss Bennet's response was an enthusiastic, "Splendid!"

It only took a moment for Mrs. Annesley and Georgianna to finish putting away their supplies before they were accompanying Miss Bennet once again to the pleasant little sitting room from before. Two matrons of middling age were chatting quietly across the room from them, the sound of their voices barely reaching their ears. This time, Mrs. Annesley offered to pour the tea, giving Georgianna the opportunity to chat more freely with Miss Bennet. Feeling quite bold, Georgianna said, "Miss Bennet, I want to thank you for wanting to have tea with me today. In fact, I cannot tell you how much I enjoyed our time together last week."

Accepting her tea from Mrs. Annesley with a grateful smile, Miss Bennet replied, "I enjoyed our time together as well. Though I enjoy my time in London, I often spend time with others not at all close to my age. It's delightful to be in the company of someone like yourself." Pausing to take a sip, Miss Bennet continued, "While it seems we both enjoy helping others here, I am curious to know what you enjoy doing while you are in town."

With a smile, Georgianna answered, "Going to concerts with my brother is something I genuinely relish, as he is not always available to escort me. Really, I take pleasure in anything musical, and though I know it may sound trite, I do enjoy shopping. What do you enjoy while here in London?"

"While I enjoy music and concerts, I think I might prefer the opera and the theater myself. It must be lovely to have a brother who might escort you to concerts. My Uncle Gardiner takes me when he can but is not always available. I especially like it when he or my aunt can take me to one of the museums or Hatchards. Unlike most young ladies, I would rather shop for a new book than a new hat or fan."

Though she was not opposed to a new novel, Georgianna would certainly prefer shopping for clothes to a book. She studied Miss Bennet while Mrs. Annesley commented on the most recent play they had seen. Feeling the oddest sort of sensation, Georgianna pondered her new friend. She was intelligent, liked the opera, plays and reading, not to mention the museum. Georgianna couldn't help but draw parallels between Miss Bennet and her brother William, despite their contrasting personalities. Georgianna wondered idly how they would get along with one another once they eventually met.

Chapter Three

"IF YOU'D LIKE, I can bring your items up to your room for you after I drop off the rest at the kitchen, miss," the maid suggested with a warm smile.

"Thank you, Annie. Could you take these too?" Elizabeth handed over her gloves to the maid.

With a smile and a bob, Annie left, her arms full of the items that Elizabeth had procured while they were out that morning. Immediately, Elizabeth took to the stairs, going to her aunt's sitting room.

She found Madeline Gardiner reclining on her chaise lounge, sipping tea. For all that she was pale and wan, she perked up when Elizabeth entered the room. "Did you have a good day at the Society, Lizzie?"

Settling herself in the chair closest to her aunt, Elizabeth answered, "I had a splendid time. I had the chance to take tea with young Miss

Darcy once again. She seemed happier today somehow and I am glad for it." As she spoke, Elizabeth studied her aunt. She seemed better, but then she always seemed better in the afternoon.

She had come to London to help her aunt handle things while dealing with a difficult lying in. More than with any of her other four children, she had been unwell. Elizabeth hoped that being there to manage the household and take her place at charities and the like would help her aunt to recover her strength.

Setting down her teacup on its saucer, Aunt Madeline said, "I am glad your day went well and that you could take tea with Miss Darcy."

"As am I. I enjoy being able to chat with her. I think she enjoys my company as well. She asked me to come to tea tomorrow at Darcy House. I told her I was available, though if you need me, I can always send a note round to reschedule." Elizabeth took the moment to pour herself a cup of lemonade. She was thirsty after a busy morning and her aunt always had some waiting for her when she returned.

With a tired yet warm smile, Aunt Madeline replied, "I can manage a few hours without you, and you know it. The staff is capable of caring for the children and managing any other issues that come up in your absence. You have my blessing to go visit with Miss Darcy as long as you bring Annie with you. If Miss Darcy is who I think she is, I knew her mother, you know."

Surprised, Elizabeth sat up straighter, exclaiming, "I did not know that. I have not wanted to push and ask too many questions until she feels more comfortable with my friendship. I do know that she is from Derbyshire and her only sibling is an older brother."

"Then she is most likely exactly who I thought. There are very few Darcys, after all." Picking up her cup of tea once again, Aunt Madeline took a sip and Elizabeth waited patiently for her to continue. It was only after a second and third sip of the helpful ginger tea that her aunt continued. "You know, I grew up in Lambton. My father was the rector there and one of the closer estates was called Pemberley. Even though they often went to services at the Kempton chapel, I did often see Lady Anne Darcy at the shops in Lambton. I was only a girl of sixteen the last time I saw her, but I remember her being not only beautiful, but kind as well. I think she died not long after young Miss Darcy was born."

Elizabeth sighed as she sat back in her chair. "The poor thing. To lose her mother before she ever had the chance to know her? I know that I often complain of my own mother, but to have never had a mother cannot be any easier."

Shaking her head sadly, Aunt Madeline said, "No, I imagine not having a mother around was not easy for her or her older brother. I believe he was only twelve when she died. He went off to Eton shortly after her funeral, and I couldn't help but imagine the immense loneliness he must have felt, attending school so soon after losing his dear mother."

"So much loss for a pair of siblings so young," Elizabeth commented, empathizing with the loneliness that must have permeated their lives. Georgianna, raised by a succession of servants, and her brother, sent away to school to be educated by unfamiliar faces.

Lips compressing into a line, Aunt Madeline said, "Sadly, their loss did not stop there. Miss Darcy's older brother had been only a year past his majority when their father died."

It struck Elizabeth to her heart to learn of the Darcys' multiple losses. Despite never having met Mr. Darcy, she felt an overwhelming sense of compassion towards him. Elizabeth helped her father run much of Longbourn as well as sharing the mistress responsibilities with Jane, but to be forced to handle it all would be too much. He must have felt like Atlas holding up the sky! Frowning, she questioned, "Do you know if they had any extended family to rely on?"

Elizabeth watched as her aunt stilled, looking off at nothing for a moment before shaking her head. "Old Mr. Darcy was an only child of an only child, so they are all that is left of the Darcy line, I am afraid. As for their mother's people, they have several family members there, if I am remembering correctly. Lady Anne was sister to the current Earl of Matlock, though I am uncertain how close they remain to them."

Elizabeth reflected on everything she had just learned and realized she was even more grateful for the time, although brief, that she had spent with Miss Darcy. "I hope Miss Darcy gets support from some female relatives, otherwise she will have a difficult time of it. It is no wonder she seemed so glum. I guess her to be around sixteen, possibly between Lydia and Kitty in age. That is such a hard time for a girl—not quite a woman, but no longer the girl you once were." Shaking her head, Elizabeth pondered her difficulties from four summers ago. "I can vividly remember the summer I turned sixteen. There were many days when I was moved to tears, although I could only sufficiently explain it to Jane. I think that is the summer Father began to wash his hands of me. He said that I was too much of a silly girl for his taste and certainly too much like my mother to be bothered with."

So much had changed around that time. Her mother had forced her out into a society that she was not comfortable with, and her emotions were in turmoil most of the time. It did not help that her father, the one steady aspect of her life, had seemingly abandoned her. Shrugging, Elizabeth tried to look at the good in the situation. At least he had not cut off her access to his library of books, even if he had stopped wanting to discuss them with her.

Her desire to regain her father's affection had led her to taking over responsibilities of the steward after the man was let go when it was discovered that he had been embezzling. She had hoped her father would realize that she was, in fact, not a silly girl. Even though his attitude had not changed, Elizabeth found she enjoyed the work. It was fulfilling to know that she was helping the tenants and the prosperity of her home. A new steward was eventually appointed, and she took it upon herself to forge a strong working relationship with him, since her father was uninterested in doing so.

Elizabeth found herself eager to reach out to Miss Darcy and be a comforting presence. Now that Georgianna had settled more comfortably into herself, it was easy to sympathize with someone who might very well be suffering as she had. Taking another sip of her lemonade, Elizabeth smiled. Yes, she was quite looking forward to visiting Miss Darcy tomorrow.

Darcy smiled as he watched Georgianna chat happily with Mrs. Annesley. Pondering over the weekend had helped him to realize that he needed to learn to trust both her and Mrs. Annesley. Trust came hard, but if his sister was going to move confidently through life, she would have to learn to make her own decisions. And if she was going to be able to make those decisions, he would have to give her more freedom and support.

After finishing his last meeting, he sought her out to fulfill his commitment to being more involved in each other's lives. It was easy to see how much her spirits had lightened, and he was left wondering if it was from her association with her new friend or his opening up to her. He would like to think that he could take at least a little of the credit for her cheerful smile.

Knocking lightly on the open door to Georgianna's sitting room, Darcy smiled when Georgianna saw him and quickly rose to her feet to approach him. Out of the blue, she pulled him into a hug, and he relished the unexpected outpouring of affection that had been absent from his life for so long. As he hugged her back, memories of his mother embracing him flooded his mind. She had often hugged him before she passed, and it had been so long that he had almost forgotten.

Pulling back from him, Georgianna asked, "How did your meeting go?"

Surprised that she was interested in his day, he replied, "I managed to negotiate a better price for the wool Pemberley produces for next season, so I suppose it went well enough. I am happy to be home, though."

"I am happy you are home as well. Would you..." Georgianna hesitated, then set her shoulders and asked, "Would you like to join us until we are called to dinner?"

It was not something he would normally do, but he found it was something that he wanted to do. Habit left him alone in his study until dinner. Then afterwards, he would have an hour or so with his sister or Mrs. Annesley playing the piano or quietly reading. It was what families in high society did. It was what the Fitzwilliam side of the family did, but it was not what he wanted to do anymore.

He smiled down at his expectant sister and said, "Yes, I would love to join you." Taking a seat in the chair near where she had been sitting, he asked, "How was your day at the charity?"

"Though I suppose I will always enjoy helping the young women and girls," Georgianna admitted with an infectious smile, "I think I look forward to spending time with my new friend the most."

"I am glad you have found a friend there." After speaking with Mrs. Annesley and Georgianna a few days before, he felt guilty for his previous reaction at her attempt to make a friend. She deserved not only to have a friend but to have the ability to choose that friend. Darcy could remember his father getting upset when he befriended Bingley, yet all these years later, Bingley was still his closest and most loyal friend. Despite the effort he had been putting into it, he was still just as awkward with people, though Bingley did not seem to mind. Even with his sister, he was awkward, but as they grew closer, he believed there was potential for improvement.

Darcy glanced at Mrs. Annesley, where she sat doing something with yarn and needles. She nodded encouragingly at him and with her support, he continued, "Did you get the opportunity to invite her to tea here at Darcy House?"

Sitting up straight, Georgianna exclaimed, "I did. Lizzie is coming tomorrow. I have already spoken with the cook, and she is going to make the most divine delectables." Clasping her hands together, she beamed at him.

"Lizzie?" he asked, certain that could not be the proper name of the girl his sister had met.

"Yes, she said that I may call her Lizzie, as that is what her friends and family call her." Looking at him from the corner of her eye, she remarked, "I wish to ask her to call me Georgie. Do you think that might be fitting?"

It seemed that she was becoming closer to the girl more quickly than he thought possible. Happy to reassure her, he replied, "Yes, allowing her to call you Georgie is perfectly acceptable."

"I am glad." Then, grinning at him, she added, "You know, Brother, Lizzie is very much like you."

"Oh?"

Attempting a serious mien that slipped when she smiled once more, Georgianna said, "Yes, we discussed what we both prefer to do while in London, and while she enjoys attending the opera and going to the museum, she does not enjoy shopping unless it is a visit to Hatchards."

Eyes widening, he said, "Indeed, she seems quite singular." He had, in fact, been wondering about what the young lady was like. Mrs. Annesley said she was the daughter of a gentleman of modest estate and her aunt was on a charity board with his aunt. Thus far, they were equal, but he was still curious about her character.

"Yes, she is unlike the majority of the young ladies Aunt Matlock has introduced me to. In truth, she surpasses them in every way. She is proving to be much kinder and more widely read."

"Widely read?" That was not a phrase often used in regard to young women. Was this "Lizzie" a bluestocking?

Wrinkling her nose, Georgianna said, "She must be if she quoted both Shakespeare and some Roman named Suetonius when we were discussing the play *Julius Caesar,* which we had both seen."

Leaning back in his chair, Darcy tried to take in the information his sister had just shared. Suetonius was Caesar's biographer and while Darcy had read his work, he only knew a few other gentlemen who had. His writing was not even translated into English from the original Latin. If this young woman had truly read his writing, she was more than simply well-read.

Before he could think of a response, his sister was saying, "I can't help but wonder how you'll interact with each other. You are both so similar, but also so different."

"I am sure we will meet at some point if the two of you are friends," Darcy replied. "In fact, the way you described the young lady has left me intrigued, and I must admit, motivated to meet her in person."

GEORGIANNA ADJUSTED THE VASE for the third time before standing back to view it from a different angle. Yes, it definitely looked better that way. Smiling, she turned when she heard footsteps approaching.

Mrs. Annesley stood just inside the entrance to the drawing room. Looking around at the changes Georgianna had made for their coming guest, she smiled. "Everything looks lovely, Miss Darcy. I am sure Miss Bennet will especially love the arrangement of flowers."

"Thank you for the compliment. I so much want everything to be just right. This is the first time I have ever invited anyone to tea at Darcy House, or anywhere else, for that matter." Looking back at the arrangement of fresh flowers, Georgianna smiled. "Miss Bennet strikes me as someone who would be fond of fresh flowers."

"Yes, I believe you are probably right," Mrs. Annesley replied.

In an effort to not pace around the room, Georgianna sat down, but could not help her fidgeting. The clock on the mantel said that Miss Bennet would not arrive for another ten minutes or so. With as excited as she was, it seemed like an eternity.

It gave her the time to worry that Miss Bennet would eventually find something about her that would cause her to turn away in disgust. The worry gnawed at her, threatening to cause her to blurt out her recent disappointment just to relieve the tension and waiting. Because then, the lingering expectation of disappointment would be put to rest.

She had just started to fold her handkerchief into even smaller sections when William walked into the room. He was certainly a welcome distraction. Standing, she said, "William, how wonderful to see you. I thought you had already left."

William sighed. "I should have left some time ago, but I took longer than expected to finish my correspondence. I am sure Bingley will understand if I am a little late meeting him at the club." He ran his hand through his hair, and Georgianna was careful not to laugh at the way his hair became disheveled. Despite not being as close to her brother as she desired, she was well aware of his strict adherence to punctuality and timely communication. Having them in conflict with each other was resulting in the ruination of his valet's hard work.

Eager to comfort her brother, Georgianna said, "I doubt Mr. Bingley would ever notice if you were late. He is consistently either early or late, never on time. Are you sure he even owns a watch fob?"

Chuckling, William shook his head and replied, "He should. I gifted him one two years ago." Leaning in, he kissed Georgianna's forehead before adding, "I just wanted to tell you to have a good time with your new friend. I will be home well before dinner tonight."

Telling him to take care while he was gone, Georgianna returned to her spot on the settee, glad that the ten minutes had been at least halved. Thankfully, Mrs. Annesley had not commented on her nervous anticipation of the coming visit. There was little conversation between the two of them while they waited. When Darcy House's butler finally entered the room to announce Miss Bennet, Georgianna jumped to her feet, suppressing a squeal. Mrs. Annesley, on the other hand, rose from her chair with much more dignity and went to stand beside Georgianna.

Coming into the room with a smile, Miss Bennet curtsied, and Georgianna rushed forward to clasp her hands. "I am so glad you have arrived."

Miss Bennet, in a tone that Georgianna thought matched her own, replied, "And I am so happy to have been invited into your splendid home."

CONTEMPLATING THE YOUNG WOMAN his sister was visiting with, Darcy sat in his carriage, the steady clip-clop of the horses' hooves filling his ears. He had barely started to pull away when her carriage arrived, and she was assisted down by a well-dressed footman. Oddly curious, he turned to watch her as she entered his home. Her outfit was composed of muted colors and clean lines, reflecting a preference for a more understated and elegant style. Just before the door closed, he caught sight of a flash of chestnut hair peeking out from under her hat. His sister's new friend unaccountably fascinated him. Shaking his head, he tried to put her out of his mind. With the knowledge that he would meet her eventually, he dismissed his curious thoughts as insignificant and redirected his mind to the upcoming meeting with Bingley.

Chapter Four

IF ELIZABETH HAD NOT previously guessed from Miss Darcy's wardrobe that she was wealthy, walking into her London home would have certainly informed her. With every glance, she saw elegance and carefully restrained opulence. Beautiful rugs dotted the well-polished floors, while ornate vases were full of fresh, hothouse flowers. She saw at least one painting that was done by a well-known artist.

With her uncle involved in the importing business, Elizabeth had the opportunity to regularly explore his warehouses. Not only did she appreciate the fine craftsmanship held within Miss Darcy's home, but she also had a good sense of the likely price for such unique items. To support such an expense, Miss Darcy's home estate, at the very least, had to be two to three times larger than Longbourn.

This all fled her mind when Miss Darcy approached her and clutched her hands in greeting. Returning the greeting, she said, "And I am so happy to have been invited into your splendid home."

Gesturing to the pleasingly arranged settee and chairs, Miss Darcy exclaimed, "Please sit down and I will ring for tea."

Elizabeth noticed the precision in Miss Darcy's speech and gestures and realized that she must be struggling with a certain amount of nervousness. This prompted Elizabeth to try to make her feel at ease. Taking a seat on the settee, Elizabeth said, "I am uncertain if you changed anything for my visit, but I cannot help but compliment it all." Smiling, she gestured at the flower arrangement. "I have always been excessively fond of displays of fresh flowers. Did you arrange them yourself?"

Blushing as she sat, Georgianna answered, "Yes, I did. I have long been fond of flower arranging. There are so many fresh flowers available from the gardens at Pemberley that when I am at home in the country, I have a lot to work with. I hoped you might appreciate the fresh blooms. How is your family? I know last we spoke you said that your aunt had been feeling unwell?"

Pleased that Miss Darcy would remember her comment about her aunt, Elizabeth explained, "Aunt Madeline is doing better this morning. She is having more good days than bad at this point, which I am glad for. She had been doing so poorly that I was worried she would still be unwell when I had to return home."

With a frown, Miss Darcy asked, "When do you suppose you might be returning home?"

Elizabeth was about to answer when the maid brought in the tea, accompanied by a tray of various delicious-looking cakes and finger sandwiches. It took a moment for Miss Darcy to pour the tea and see to everyone getting a bite to eat before Elizabeth responded, "Sadly, I will go home before the end of the month. Despite my usual aversion to staying in London during the summer, I couldn't refuse my aunt's plea for help when she fell ill during her confinement. I was needed to step in and take care of the household and help with the children. But she is doing better and with the time for harvest approaching, I would like to be home to help with everything." Taking a sip of her tea, she suppressed a shudder as she considered what Lydia and Kitty might be getting into without her there to help supervise.

Seeing Georgianna's genuine interest as she sat patiently next to her, Elizabeth decided to confide in her and share her concerns. Giving a wry smile, she added, "Besides, I am afraid of what trouble my younger sisters are getting into while I am away. My older sister Jane is a good role model, but she is not always stern enough to keep them in line."

Mrs. Annesley set her cup down in its saucer on one of the conveniently placed tables before saying, "It seems as if you have a life full of responsibility for one of your age, Miss Bennet. It is something to be admired. Though I wonder how you are able to maintain such a positive viewpoint through it all. I have known many who have taken up responsibility at a young age who have allowed it to affect them adversely."

Tilting her head, Elizabeth considered the companion's words. She supposed that with all she did, she could become weighed down. In fact, she often was if she could not get out and walk for an extended period of time. What was it that gave her the ability to see the bright side? She had never really thought about it before. Covering her hesitation with another sip of her tea, Elizabeth said, "I have always been especially fond of nature, and I often go for daily walks, especially when I am home at Longbourn. There is just something about seeing the sunrise paint the morning mist in a golden glow or watching a swirl of scarlet leaves propelled by the breeze that lifts my spirits. When things like that exist in the world, it's as if all the bad things, or the heavy things that I must deal with, suddenly don't seem so terrible. More than that, though, I also try to only look at the past as long as it brings me pleasure in remembering it."

Sighing, Miss Darcy said, "That is a lovely sentiment. One I wish I had, actually. I must admit that I struggle sometimes with past choices and things that had not gone as I had hoped."

With a warm smile, Elizabeth tried to reassure Miss Darcy by reminding her, "You need to keep in mind that I have a good four years of life experience on you. When I was sixteen, I was often weepy and out of sorts. You would not recognize me as the girl I was before." Watching Miss Darcy's mouth drop open into a little O, Elizabeth continued, "Give it time and you will find that you have gained strength from your experiences. If it helps, I think you are building on a good foundation."

Reaching out, Georgianna clasped one of Elizabeth's hands with her own. "Thank you for being so willing to visit me. I understand I may not have much to offer in terms of friendship, as I am just a silly girl, but your willingness to spend time with me despite your many responsibilities is something I am truly grateful for."

Carefully setting down her teacup in its saucer on the nearby table, Elizabeth focused her attention on Miss Darcy. She had spent enough time with her sisters to know that there was something weighing on her behind her words. It was as if Miss Darcy did not see her own value and Elizabeth was determined to help her recognize it.

MISS BENNET LOOKED GEORGIANNA straight in the eye and she wondered what Miss Bennet could intend with such seriousness. "It is not a chore to spend time with and get to know someone as pleasant as yourself. You do yourself a disservice in thinking that it might be so. I would call myself honored to have a friend such as yourself." With a tilt of her head and a discerning glance, she continued, "I am certainly gladdened that any small attentions I have paid you might have helped you, though."

Georgianna blinked away tears. For so long, she had believed Wickham when he had told her that no one would ever want her just for herself. Georgianna now knew he was a womanizer, gambler, spendthrift, and a liar, but still she had believed him when he had said she was unlovable. Why had she been so foolish to believe him?

In an instant, Miss Bennet closed the gap between herself and Georgianna, her hands reaching out and her voice filled with regret. "I'm so sorry. I didn't mean to say anything to upset you."

Offering a tremulous smile, Georgianna tried to reassure her by saying, "No, it was nothing you said. I was simply reminded of something someone said to me not that long ago."

Miss Bennet wrapped her arms around Georgianna's shoulder, offering a comforting embrace. "What could they have possibly said to bring you to tears?" she asked, her voice filled with concern.

Georgianna whispered, "When I refused to elope with him, he told me I would never—could never—be loved or even liked for who I was. That I would only ever be tolerated for my connections and wealth."

"Well, whoever said that was most likely a bitter fool trying to hurt you. You would do well to ignore their words, though I can imagine it will be difficult. I struggle with dealing with unkind words myself." Miss Bennet squeezed Georgianna's shoulder for a moment before saying, "Whatever *he* said, I want to make it clear that my motivation to be your friend is purely based on sincerely liking you and the enjoyment we find in each other's presence, with no ulterior motives."

Georgianna leaned back somewhat so that she could face Miss Bennet. "Are you sure you do not want to know more about what happened? I mean, most proper young ladies would never have even considered eloping."

Tilting her head, Miss Bennet said, "Only if you want to. Your happiness is the only thing I care about, so unless it's related to that, I am unconcerned about your past. Obviously, if you need a shoulder to lean on in order to unburden yourself, I am here. But remember what I said before—it is my philosophy to try to only look at the past as long as it brings pleasure to me in remembering it. You may not remember the villain with much pleasure, but you can be happy that you have learned from the situation."

When Georgianna looked at Miss Bennet, she knew her face could not help but show her confusion. What had she learned from the situation besides grief and humiliation? As if noticing her confusion, Miss Bennet asked, "Would you ever consider eloping again?"

"Of course not!" exclaimed Georgianna.

Smiling ever so softly, Miss Bennet prompted, "Why?"

Georgianna pondered for a moment, glad that Miss Bennet seemed willing to wait while she thought. What had she learned from the disaster earlier in the summer? "If a gentleman respects me, he will seek my brother's permission to court me. If he does not, then I know he has less than honorable intentions." She saw Miss Bennet and Mrs. Annesley both nod at her comment. It only took another few moments of contemplation before she added, "I now know that a man's worth extends far beyond a handsome face and empty flattery."

Mrs. Annesley commented, "That is a hard thing for most young ladies to learn. Good looks and a gentlemanly demeanor can mask a hidden, villainous side. It is very easy for heads to be turned by flattery. It is always nice to think a handsome gentleman thinks well of you, but we all must stop and question why he is saying such things."

"I have had little experience with compliments from anyone, let alone handsome gentlemen, but what you say, Mrs. Annesley, makes sense," commented Miss Bennet with a nod.

"Yes, Mrs. Annesley, I am very grateful for your sound advice as well." Pausing, Georgianna admitted, "Though I have decided that I am not yet ready to take on the responsibilities of marriage. Most importantly, I need to trust my instincts and ask someone I trust if I am uncertain about my course of action."

Swallowing after taking a bite of one of the little cakes, Miss Bennet said, "I think that is a good choice, Miss Darcy."

After a moment of hesitation, Georgianna said, "I would love for you to call me Georgianna, or even Georgie, Miss Bennet."

Smiling, Miss Bennet said, "I would be more than happy to call you Georgie, but only as long as you remember to call me Lizzie and let go of all your worries about that villain."

"Then I will endeavor to forget that villain's words and be determined to be the best of friends with you, Lizzie." Georgianna was so glad that Lizzie was proving such a true friend. She had even brought up her greatest mistake, and it had not changed Lizzie's view of her in the least.

Enveloping Georgianna in a warm hug, Lizzie said, "And I will be the best of friends with you, Georgie." After a moment, she leaned back and asked, "Now what say you we come up with a plan to go shopping together before I have to leave in two weeks?"

"Does that mean we will go to Hatchards?" Georgianna asked with a giggle.

"Well, perhaps we can go to several stores you like with a trip to Hatchards somewhere in the middle and end with a visit to a tea shop?" Lizzie commented with a snicker.

Turning to Mrs. Annesley, Georgianna inquired, "What say you? Do you think we can fit in two shopping trips before Lizzie has to leave?"

ELIZABETH WAS RELIEVED THAT she had maintained her cheerful demeanor until her uncle's carriage arrived. It had not been easy with her anger simmering just beneath the surface. Now she collapsed back into the seat of the carriage despite the concerned look Annie was giving her. Her mind was just too overwhelmed to maintain a facade.

Annie pressed her lips together for a moment before asking, "Are you well, Miss Bennet?" Like a good maid, Annie had been in the room when she had been talking with Georgianna and Mrs. Annesley. She had been sitting in the corner working on some sewing, close enough to watch but not near enough to overhear, so Elizabeth did not need to worry that she had overheard anything. She did, however, did not want to worry the girl.

Sighing, Elizabeth sat up straight before answering, "Yes, Annie, thank you for asking. I only just remembered something that is disturbing, but I am fine." Resisting the urge to rub her forehead, Elizabeth smiled at Annie. She needed a brisk walk to Oakham Mount, but she would not get it.

"That is good, miss," Annie replied with a nod, though Elizabeth suspected she was still worried.

Aware of Annie's quiet presence, Elizabeth tried to maintain at least a level of composure despite the way her mind was spinning. All she could think about was how some villain had tried to prey on poor Georgianna. It was obvious that she would possess a sizable dowry, and with Georgianna's status and beauty, she would be a remarkable lure to fortune hunters. That alone would be enough for any girl to deal with once she came out, but whoever it was had not even waited for her to reach her majority or to have her bow before the queen. She was practically still a child.

Sometimes she doubted men had any redeeming qualities. Of course, she knew that there were sterling examples of the species like her uncle, but there were so many others that fell short. Somewhere out there in the world was a man who had used all his appearance of good to hide his evil intent. Not only had the man tried to persuade a girl who was practically a child to leave her family and elope, but when he had failed, he had lashed out in an attempt to crush her spirit. Elizabeth may not have been there, but she was clever enough to understand why he would tell her she would never be loved for herself. The villain had wanted revenge for his failure.

Georgianna would not have been moved if the man had shown his true colors, so it was fair to assume that he had courted her most assiduously. The comment about Mrs. Annesley having been with her only for a few months made more sense now, as Georgianna's previous companion had been let go. The woman had obviously been a poor example of a companion if she had allowed anyone to woo such a young girl who was not even out.

If even a wealthy girl like Georgianna was such an easy target, despite having a companion, an older brother, and an uncle who was an earl, what chance did she or her sisters stand? The best description she could come up with for her father would be idle. He was also negligent and sarcastic, but besides that, he would never put forth the effort to protect and shepherd his five girls. Protecting his daughters would never take precedence over his books. Elizabeth didn't hold out hope that her father would make any effort to investigate potential suitors for her or her sisters. Frequently, she had overheard her father expressing his wish for a quiet life and complaining that it would only be possible if her mother could find unsuspecting men to foist his daughters on.

Somehow, she had always known she could only depend on herself when it came to finding a husband. It was one reason she would jokingly say she was going to end up a spinster. It had always seemed that the worst that would come from her father's inattention was a life without a husband and children. Now that she saw the danger that was truly before them, she wondered how she could ever possibly protect herself and her sisters. Broken hearts and betrayal were just the beginning. If a scoundrel would try to run away with an heiress, what would they do to a dowerless nobody?

She wanted to declare confidently that she would be impervious to the advances of a scoundrel, but doubt had crept in. She would never agree to an elopement because she knew the consequences her family would face because of such an action. Despite this, Elizabeth was concerned that without the knowledge gained from her meeting with Georgianna, the sweet words of flattery could have easily influenced her to lose her heart.

She was often overlooked at home, and it was no better away from home. The young men of Meryton would dance with her, but mostly she was just Jane's younger sister. It did not help that she was better read and unwilling to back down when someone else was wrong. She had heard, "You are just a girl and cannot possibly know of what you speak," more than a few times. For all her knowledge and competence in running a household or an estate, it scared Elizabeth to wonder what would happen if someone arrived in town and paid her kind attention.

Pulling a deep breath into her lungs through her nose, Elizabeth held it there for a few moments before releasing it in a long steady stream through pursed lips. Fretting was doing nothing. Squaring her shoulders, she muttered, "*Praemonitus, praemunitus.*" When she was twelve, she had read it while her father was teaching her Latin, and it had long stayed with her. *Praemonitus, praemunitus* loosely translated meant forewarned is forearmed. Her father had been more than happy to discuss the phrase with her, but ever the intellectual, he had no care to apply his learning to his own behavior. Elizabeth, however, thought it might be time to apply it to her life.

Chapter Five

Sometimes Darcy wondered how people like Bingley could exist. He had more energy than any three other men and, at times, seemed to vibrate with it. Of course, that could have something to do with his odd attachment to always drinking coffee. Darcy might have enjoyed a cup of the brew in the morning while he reviewed reports, but Bingley was constantly drinking the stuff night and day.

Despite Bingley's invitation to discuss something important, he knew not to expect Bingley to be concise. So they played billiards and eventually ate, but still Darcy did not know why he was there. At least they were at his club. It was always preferable to meet at their club rather than either of their homes because of Bingley's sister.

Twisting his wineglass on the table in front of him, Darcy said, "So, what was so important that you needed to see me today?"

Putting his cup of coffee down with a slosh, Bingley leaned forward and exclaimed, "That's right. I asked you here to talk to you about the property!"

"What property?" asked Darcy.

Grinning, Bingley announced, "I found a property outside of town. It is about a morning's ride from here and I leased it for the year, starting... Well, I cannot remember at the moment when I take control of it, but I leased it!"

Letting go of his glass, Darcy forced himself not to just react and instead ask questions. He had learned recently what jumping to conclusions could do. So he asked, "When did you view the property?" All the while, he hoped his friend had actually seen the place before leasing it.

Fidgeting in his chair, Bingley replied, "Three days ago. While I know that Caroline will complain because it is not London or Pemberley, I found the place to be all that is pleasant." Bingley stopped to take another sip of his coffee before saying, "I wanted to agree to leasing it on the spot, but I remembered what you said about contemplating important decisions. So I told the man I toured the place with, a Mr. Philips, that I would give him a reply the next day. I thought it over all night and the next morning and by noon, I had sent off an express to Mr. Philips asking him to start the process of leasing the estate. As of this morning, everything is in order, and I am hoping to get you to come along with me and help me learn the process of becoming a landed gentleman."

Resuming the twisting of his wineglass, Darcy tried to digest all that his friend had said. He had always known that Bingley had wanted to obtain an estate. Darcy had even suggested to him to start off by leasing an estate. But Bingley also wanted a matched set of bays and a white dog for some reason, and he had yet to acquire either of those. On the one hand, it seemed odd to Darcy that he would make such a big move without consulting him, but on the other, he was slightly encouraged that Bingley was finally making decisions on his own.

There was a reason his cousin had called Bingley *the puppy* for so long. Bingley had had the tendency to trail after Darcy ever since his first days at Cambridge. He was always asking his opinion and asking for advice before acting on anything. It was possible that this was the first move towards independence. If that was the case, Darcy certainly wanted to support such an endeavor. "When are you planning to go there and take possession of the place?"

After finishing off his coffee, Bingley gestured to the silent man in the corner of the room. Soon enough, someone refilled his cup and offered milk and sugar before Bingley responded with, "It is mine as of Michaelmas, or some time around then and it comes fully furnished with staff in place. So I hope to arrive as soon as I may. Please say you will come with me."

Darcy considered his eager friend's smile. Besides his cousin Richard, Bingley was the only person he was close to. He knew many people could not puzzle out their relationship, as he was always dour, and Bingley was gregarious. Despite their differences, Bingley was a staunch friend. He saw through Darcy's fierce scowl to the man who had never learned to travel easily through the sea of humanity. Bingley had consistently come to Darcy's aid when he felt overwhelmed at social gatherings. The cheerful man had a knack for deflecting the debutantes and their mothers, a skill that Darcy lacked when he felt like a fox being chased. Of course he would help his friend as he tried to learn estate management.

With a nod, Darcy said, "I will be there. Though I tell you now that I will not ride in a carriage with your sister." Darcy could not help shudder, remembering the last time he had ended up in a carriage with Caroline Bingley and her sister, Mrs. Hurst. Normally he was better at warding the woman off, but through some contrivance that resulted in him having to let someone go for taking a bribe, she had ended up in his carriage. She spent the whole time *accidentally* falling against him when the carriage would hit a bump in the road.

"Still sorry about that, by the way. I have talked with her on more than one occasion about her behavior towards you. I have told her flat out that you will never marry her, but it has not seemed to help." Shaking his head, Bingley took several gulps of his coffee and Darcy tried to remember if it was his third or fourth cup since they had arrived at the club. With a chuckle, Bingley added, "I have just told Caroline that I will take the place in Meryton, and that Louisa has agreed to be my hostess. I know Caroline would want to do it, but I am afraid that she would drive the staff away within a week with her ostentatious demands. I have also told her we may not do any redecorating. She would paint everything in that horrible burnt orange that she thinks is all the rage this season and I cannot abide the color."

Darcy could not help wince at the thought of a parlor or a sitting room full of such a horrid shade. He knew that one of the leading ladies of the ton had cruelly told her the shade was in style so that she could joke about Miss Bingley behind her back with her gossiping friends. It had also been his guess that the lady had told Miss Bingley that she was one of the few ladies who could pull off the color because she wanted to spot her in the room so that she could avoid her annoying presence.

Dismissing Miss Bingley from his mind, Darcy asked, "What is the estate called?"

With his eyebrows raised in excitement, Bingley replied, "We will be going to Netherfield."

To Elizabeth, it felt as if time was flying towards her departure from London. Already she was enjoying her second shopping trip with Georgianna. They had gone through several shops looking at various bits and bobs and had even stopped at Hatchards. All told, Elizabeth had found something to gift each of her family members.

Now she and Georgianna, along with Mrs. Annesley, were on their way to Gunter's Tea Shop for a special treat.

"I simply cannot believe you will leave for your home in two more days. I have become so accustomed to having your company that I do not know what I will do with myself once you are gone," Georgianna sighed.

Wrapping her arm around Georgianna's slender shoulders, Elizabeth said, "Neither of us live in London year-round. If it was not me leaving, it would be you. Besides, you know your brother has given you permission to exchange letters with me. I fully expect to get a letter from you once a sennight or once a fortnight, if you find yourself truly busy."

Giggling at Elizabeth's comment, Georgianna took a moment to respond. "I suppose I will have to be satisfied with letters until we can contrive to meet again. Though I cannot picture myself so busy that I could not write you, Lizzie."

Tilting her head in apparent consideration, Elizabeth tapped her chin with a finger before saying, "I do not know, Georgie. Your brother just arranged for you to have lessons with Master Rossini, and I know how fixated you get when you are learning a new piece. Besides, I know Mrs. Annesley said she was going to help teach you how to handle household accounts, along with Darcy House's housekeeper."

Hugging Elizabeth back, Georgianna replied, "I may be busy, but I will always have time to write you, and you have promised to reply no matter how busy you get helping at your family's estate."

"Yes, I promise to write to you at least as often, possibly more. Now no more of this morose thinking. We are going to Gunter's—we cannot be sad when we are about to have ices!" Looking across the carriage at the kindly woman, Elizabeth made a point to draw her into the conversation. "Mrs. Annesley, you must tell me what flavor you will be trying."

Mrs. Annesley smiled before saying, "I have always been fond of the fruit flavors they have. Last time I think I enjoyed bergamot, but I do not know what they might have this time. What about you, Miss Bennet? Do you enjoy any flavor over the others?"

Looking back and forth between Georgianna and Mrs. Annesley, Elizabeth remarked, "You have found me out. I cannot help trying the oddest flavor I see. It is a failing of mine, I know, but I cannot fight the impulse to try flavors I could not have previously imagined."

Covering her mouth to stifle her sputtering laugh, Georgianna's attempts to hide her amusement were in vain. Unable to contain herself any longer, she burst out and asked, "What is the worst thing you have tried?"

Biting her lip, Elizabeth pondered the many flavors she had tasted over the years. "Definitely brown bread," she finally replied, wrinkling her nose.

Shaking her head, Mrs. Annesley asked, "Why not just stick with something you know you will like? You had to have tasted many flavors that were not so enjoyable."

With a shrug, Elizabeth said, "But what if there is a flavor out there that I could absolutely love, and I never find it because I did not try it?"

Still giggling, Georgianna asked, "Have you at least tried some flavors that you have enjoyed?"

Nodding, Elizabeth listed them off on her fingers as she said, "Green tea, blackberry, and oddly enough, burnt filbert. Though I have tried many flavors that were fine, those three have proved to be my favorite."

Glancing out the window, Georgianna exclaimed, "I wish we were closer to arriving. I am impatient to see what flavors of ices they will have today! For some reason, I find I am inspired to try something new." She glanced at Elizabeth with a smirk.

Elizabeth was happy to see Georgianna exhibiting such cheer. So much about her demeanor had changed in the three weeks they had been in close association. Of course, the girl might continue to struggle with melancholy thoughts and regrets, but the fact that she could laugh with her was remarkable. While it was not Elizabeth's obligation to assist Georgianna in rediscovering her smile, she found solace in knowing that her attempts to befriend her had not been fruitless.

Then, too, the relationship had not been one-sided. Elizabeth had learned about the dangers of men, like the one they only referred to as the villain. With stories of his deceit and manipulation echoing in her mind, Elizabeth felt better prepared to protect herself and her sisters moving forward.

At one point, she had worried Mrs. Annesley would take issue with all that Georgianna was saying. However, Mrs. Annesley had been remarkably compassionate, explaining that she felt Georgianna needed to purge the pain the villain caused from her system and having an understanding friend who accepted her despite knowing all would certainly help matters. Elizabeth felt a deep sense of honor knowing that Mrs. Annesley had entrusted her with such an important role.

With the slowing of the carriage indicating they had arrived, Elizabeth asked Mrs. Annesley, "Will you join us in trying a new flavor, Mrs. Annesley?"

Had Mrs. Annesley not been a companion and tasked with always displaying proper comportment, Elizabeth thought she might have rolled her eyes at her question. As it was, she wrinkled her nose and said, "The thought of not fully relishing my treat is enough to prevent me from taking any risks in choosing my flavor. Though I might pick a fruit flavor I have not yet tried." Elizabeth could not help but chuckle at the way Mrs. Annesley stood her ground.

When the door opened and the footman helped Georgianna down, Elizabeth followed with a smile on her face. She was glad that her Aunt Madeline had encouraged her to spend extra time with Georgianna before she left for Longbourn. Making friends was a truly delightful endeavor. Up until that point, Elizabeth was only truly close to Jane and possibly Charlotte, but now Georgianna, and even Mrs. Annesley, were turning into the best of friends a young lady could have.

THERE WAS SOMETHING VERY reassuring about watching her charge and Miss Bennet chat about their ices. Mrs. Annesley had been worried about drawing Miss Darcy out of her reticence. She had tried several things that had not worked, but meeting the cheerful Miss Bennet had done wonders. Now Miss Darcy was actually smiling in public and laughing when at home. Not only that, but she was gaining more confidence in herself and her interests. Oh, she might always be quiet with strangers, but Mrs. Annesley no longer feared for the girl.

Taking a small bite of her lemon ice, Mrs. Annesley let it melt on her tongue, enjoying the burst of flavor. Her choice left her feeling quite satisfied. She could not imagine trying Parmesan the way Miss Bennet had. No, she would stick with her fruit flavored ices, thank you very much.

"Oh, my dear Miss Darcy! What a pleasure to see you here." The rather cloying voice that came from behind Mrs. Annesley was one that she recognized. Turning, she saw both Miss Bingley and Mrs. Hurst approach. Taking a deep breath to fortify herself, Mrs. Annesley studied Miss Darcy, waiting to see how she would handle the latest confrontation with Miss Bingley.

Eyes widening for a moment, Miss Darcy glanced briefly at Miss Bennet and Mrs. Annesley before facing Miss Bingley and saying, "Hello, Miss Bingley, Mrs. Hurst."

Miss Bingley shook her head in a way that sent the dyed ostrich plumes in her turban twitching. Stepping even closer to Miss Darcy, she prattled, "I was just telling my sister that we should come by and visit you. We tried to see you last week, but your butler told us you were not at home. Isn't that right, Louisa?" It did not escape Mrs. Annesley's notice that Miss Bingley was entirely ignoring Miss Bennet and herself. Mrs. Annesley had grown accustomed to this behavior from the social climber. Miss Bingley was of the opinion that you did not speak with staff unless absolutely necessary and she felt Mrs. Annesley's role as a companion put her firmly in that category.

As for ignoring Miss Bennet, that was another of her failings. Miss Bingley always assumed that unless she knew a person, they were of no consequence. And if they were of no consequence, they were better off ignored or possibly derided. The companion in Mrs. Annesley wanted to help her correct the issue before she destroyed her reputation by snubbing the wrong person, but the human in her could not wait for it to happen, and she hoped that she would be there to see it. As Miss Bingley never asked for advice and rarely acknowledged her presence, Mrs. Annesley assumed that Miss Bingley would bring about her own downfall at some point or another. Really the only question was how soon it would happen. As it was, Miss Bingley only hovered on the edges of society because various ladies liked to use her for the gossip she acquired and to make themselves look better by comparison.

Growing tired of waiting for Mrs. Hurst's reply, Miss Bingley resorted to stepping on her older sister's foot in a rather unladylike manner. Faced with Miss Bingley's attack, Mrs. Hurst could only let out a timid squeak and demurred, "Yes, Sister." Then, turning away from the table, she continued to eye the displays of treats that had apparently garnered her attention.

Miss Darcy glanced her way, and Mrs. Annesley understood her confusion. Miss Darcy faced a dilemma as Miss Bingley had not posed a clear question, making it challenging for her to respond truthfully without appearing rude. It would be impolite to say that she wasn't home because Miss Darcy had explicitly told the butler that she was never at home if Miss Bingley was calling.

Rescuing Miss Darcy from Miss Bingley's expectant gaze, Mrs. Annesley said, "You forget that Miss Darcy is not out and, as such, she would not be home to callers."

Miss Bingley flashed a glare at Mrs. Annesley before she could control her expression. "Oh, but surely, as such a close friend, silly rules like that need not apply to me. Isn't that so, Georgianna?"

Reaching out, Miss Bingley attempted to lay her hand on Miss Darcy's arm, but Miss Darcy moved out of reach by reaching out to stir her cup of tea.

Where a month ago Miss Darcy might have frozen at such a display by Miss Bingley, now she handled it with grace and even a little fire. Looking up at Miss Bingley, Miss Darcy said, "Oh, but it is so important to pay attention to society's rules, Miss Bingley. I would have imagined your education at that ladies' seminary would have covered such topics."

Smothering what appeared to be a smile behind her serviette, Miss Bennet watched as Miss Darcy looked at Miss Bingley, her expression guileless. Miss Bingley, on the other hand, seemed to develop a twitch that once again set the feathers in her turban fluttering about. After a moment, her expression cleared, and she said, "You are correct, Georgianna. Following society's dictates is an important habit to follow. You are so wise for someone so young. In fact, I think you are an example to young ladies everywhere. I think that might be why my brother is ever so fond of you."

Mrs. Annesley knew that Miss Bingley wanted to appear to be closer to the Darcy family than she was, so she often tried to use Miss Darcy's familiar name while in public. It was not a habit Mrs. Annesley would allow without censure, so she said, "It is *Miss Darcy*, Miss Bingley." She waited for Miss Bingley to look her way before explaining, "You addressed Miss Darcy as Georgianna, but you do not have permission to do so. It is another one of those pesky rules that we all must follow if we are to participate in society."

Mouth in a hard line, Miss Bingley nodded her head before saying, "You are too good to remind me, Mrs. Annesley. It must come so easily to you, having learned it well in your role as a companion."

Shaking her head, Mrs. Annesley replied, "No, that was a lesson I learned long ago from my mother, Lady Clare."

Two bright spots of pink suffused Miss Bingley's cheeks as she turned back to Miss Darcy. "It is always such a pleasure to spend time with you no matter how briefly, Miss Darcy, my dear, but my sister and I must go." With only a nod only to Miss Darcy, she turned to leave, dragging her protesting sister with her. Apparently, Mrs. Hurst had been looking forward to enjoying one of the many treats being offered at Gunter's.

They all finished their treats rather quickly after that before making their way to the carriage. As they pulled away from the curb, Miss Bennet burst out laughing. Soon they were all laughing, though after a time Miss Bennet said, "I thought her feathers were going to flit right out of her turban."

Chapter Six

It suddenly occurred to Darcy as he made plans for his trip to Netherfield with Bingley that he had been going about several things all wrong. While he had been proceeding along as normal, things were not, in fact, normal. Things had changed when he started developing a closer relationship with Georgianna. His normal way of doing things when heading somewhere ordinarily included making plans for Georgianna, but somehow that seemed wrong now. Wasn't it a little heavy-handed to not even ask her opinion on matters?

Putting down the correspondence he was reviewing, Darcy pushed back from his desk and went to seek his sister. Not only was he growing ever closer to her, but he was realizing just how remarkable a young lady she was becoming. It was probably time to allow her some input in directing her own life.

He found her in the library looking at an atlas with Mrs. Annesley and asked, "Hello ladies. May I ask you what you are looking for?"

Georgianna looked up at him and smiled. "We were attempting to find the places that were referenced in *The Morning Herald's* report on the latest battles and skirmishes with Napoleon's forces."

While Darcy knew that Mrs. Annesley was trying to expand Georgianna's horizons, he had not known that would include the war in Europe. Drawing closer, he replied, "I did not know that you had been following the war on the continent."

With a nod, Georgianna said, "Sometimes Richard mentions places he has been, and Mrs. Annesley recommended I familiarize myself with Richard's whereabouts in order to feel closer to him." Glancing down at the atlas, she touched a spot on the map somewhere in Spain before saying, "Once I could locate where Richard was, I became curious about what he was facing and, well, one thing led to another."

Darcy knew that most people thought that women should be protected from the realities of war, but he was changing his mind about how to protect his sister. "That is certainly one way to learn about the world. Have your studies expanded beyond the area affected by the war?"

Shaking her head, Georgianna answered, "Not yet, but we were planning on studying where our favorite teas and spices come from next."

Looking at Mrs. Annesley, Darcy nodded to her. He was very much impressed. He asked, "Mrs. Annesley, do you mind if I borrow my sister for a few minutes?"

"Not at all, Mr. Darcy. Take your time," she answered.

Walking to one of the alcoves with Georgianna, he was pondering how to bring up his trip in a few weeks when she asked, "What are you worried about, William?"

Startled, he asked, "How did you know I was worried?"

With a knowing smile, Georgianna said, "I have come to realize that you get a little notch between your eyebrows when you are worried."

"I should have known," Darcy admitted, not bothering to smother the chuckle that escaped him. "Richard has said something similar in the past." Sitting down on the settee that was placed just so to catch the light for reading, Darcy patted the spot next to him. Once Georgianna sat down next to him, he continued, "I have been invited to go with Bingley to the estate he leased. At first, I was just going to plan for you to have extra tutors while I was gone, but then thought I should ask you what you wanted to do. Though I had originally thought to have you stay in London, I am sure Bingley would invite you."

The sight of his sister's beaming smile caught Darcy off guard with its contagious energy.

It had been a very long time since he had seen such a smile on her face—not since the first time he had come home from Cambridge and she had greeted him after such a long absence. Apparently, asking her for her input had been the right thing to do.

Smile never leaving her face, Georgianna asked, "May I presume his sisters shall be there?"

Grimacing, Darcy answered, "Yes, they will."

"I certainly can understand why you would hesitate to ask Mr. Bingley to invite me," Georgianna replied with a giggle. "Thank you for trying to protect me from Miss Bingley's grasping ways, Brother. That is very gallant of you." Then, losing the laughter in her voice, she said, "As much as I have enjoyed spending more time with you, I have committed to lessons with Master Rossini for another eight weeks, so I could not come until sometime in November if I chose to come at all. Where is this estate that Mr. Bingley has leased?"

Proud of the responsible young lady his sister was becoming, Darcy answered, "The estate is called Netherfield and apparently is outside of a small town called Meryton. It is only four and twenty miles from London. I can come back to London if you ever have need of me in practically no time at all."

For some reason that Darcy could not decipher, Georgianna's eyes twinkled mischievously, though she only said, "Once I am done with my lessons under Master Rossini, I would be delighted to join you, provided you can endure Miss Bingley's company for that long."

Tilting his head in confusion, Darcy tried to comprehend why Georgianna would readily agree to accompany him to a small town and up until Bingley's announcement, an unknown estate. Without a doubt, he knew she had a low tolerance for Miss Bingley, and her civility towards her was merely a matter of etiquette. Realizing that the more he learned about his sister, the less he understood, he gave up. It was possible that he would gain understanding in due time, but for now, he opted to savor the happiness that came from their growing closeness.

Impulsively, he reached out and gave Georgianna a brief hug. "Knowing that you will join me will give me something to look forward to. I won't keep you any longer so you can return to your study of the atlas. I still have several things I need to take in hand before I leave with Bingley after Michaelmas."

Georgianna could not help bouncing on her toes as she stood next to Mrs. Annesley and looked down at the atlas. She knew that Mrs. Annesley had spotted her joy as she said, "Though I am glad you are growing closer to your brother, I am curious to know why your brief conversation with him has you so enthusiastic."

Knowing her voice could not help but convey her excitement, she exclaimed, "William said that he will leave soon to go help his friend Mr. Bingley learn estate management. He admitted that at first, he was just going to plan for me here in London, but then realized I might want to be given the opportunity to choose to go with him or stay here." Georgianna was no less excited about that than where her brother was going. The fact that he welcomed her input on a matter was heartening.

Nodding sedately, Mrs. Annesley smiled. "To be asked your opinion on something is always a good feeling."

Georgianna felt her cheeks stretch as her smile widened. Looking at Mrs. Annesley, she said, "I have told William that I would like to join him once my lessons with the master are complete, and he agreed to the plan." Then, bouncing some more, she added, "And that is not even the best part!"

"What is the best part?" Mrs. Annesley asked indulgently.

Leaning over, Georgianna flipped through the atlas. She stopped at the page that held the part of England where they lived and pointed to where Meryton lay not that far outside of London. "My brother and Mr. Bingley will be staying at an estate outside the town of Meryton."

"Meryton...isn't that where Miss Bennet lives?"

Clapping her hands, Georgianna beamed, "Yes! I have enjoyed the idea of being able to exchange letters with Lizzie, but if all goes well, I will see her again when I visit."

Drawing her brows together, Mrs. Annesley questioned, "Did you tell your brother about the fact that Miss Bennet lives outside of Meryton, too?"

"I told him where she lived in one of our conversations. It is not my fault he has already forgotten where my new friend is from." Georgianna rolled her eyes at her brother's lapse in memory. If he did not remember where her only friend lived, she would let him find out the hard way.

"He never ended up meeting Miss Bennet, did he?" Mrs. Annesley looked carefully at Georgianna before continuing, "What exactly are you thinking, Miss Darcy?"

"I have always thought that the two of them have so much in common that it was a pity that they weren't, at the very least, friends," Georgianna admitted with a smile.

Shaking her head, Mrs. Annesley said, "But Miss Darcy, though they both like many of the same things, their personalities are quite different. In contrast to Miss Bennet's vibrant and cheerful nature, your brother carries himself with a reserved air and can be seen as excessively proud. Aren't you worried they might not get along?"

Biting her lip, Georgianna considered the problem that Mrs. Annesley had brought up. It was likely that her brother would meet Lizzie while he was staying with Bingley. It was also very likely that her brother would blunder the introduction. Just the day before, he had confessed that his aversion to attending balls stemmed from his tendency to become so anxious that he often ended up offending someone before the night was over.

While acknowledging the high chance of things going awry, she had a strong intuition that they could also unfold amazingly. Considering the positive impact Lizzie had on her life, it was only logical to believe she could also help William. Perhaps if Georgianna provided a little help, it might smooth things over.

"YOU HAVE NO COMPASSION for my poor nerves, Lizzie!" This was followed by the fluttering of Mrs. Bennet's handkerchief before she continued, "You spent months in London and wasted the opportunity to capture a husband. How dare you tell me you did not attend a single dance?"

Elizabeth diligently kept her attention on the reports from the steward that she was studying. She knew that catering to her mother during her fits of nerves only made things worse. More than that, she was trying to see how much damage her absence had done to the state of Longbourn. At least the steward was competent. The only real problem was that her father often could not be counted on to approve repairs or aid for tenants without prompting, and Elizabeth was the only one bold enough to force the issue.

From the chair next to the table where Elizabeth sat, Jane spoke up by saying, "Mama, you know Elizabeth was in London to help care for our aunt and your brother's household. There were more pressing matters at hand than finding a husband."

Mrs. Bennet turned to her oldest daughter, her eyes at first widened in shock and then narrowing in anger. "There is never anything more important than catching a husband!" Clutching at her chest, Elizabeth's mother called, "Hill! My salts! I need my salts!"

Slumping in her chair, she fanned herself, moaning, "I do not know why I have been cursed with so many ungrateful daughters. Your father will die, and we will all be thrown into the hedgerows when that hateful heir arrives to take our home. If your baby brother had lived, he would have shown me the proper respect. He would have loved his mother as a child should. Unlike all of you girls." Then, glaring at Jane, she added, "For all my efforts, even you, Jane, have failed me and cannot understand my plight."

Jane was rarely the focus of their mother's anger and therefore she did not handle it well. She became pale and looked down at the embroidery hoop in her hands, hunching in on herself. Shouting at Jane was too much. It seemed that her mother had worsened in her absence. Castigating her oldest daughter for defending someone was not something their mother would normally do. Had something changed in her absence?

Across the room, Lydia and Kitty stared at their mother openmouthed, while Mary frowned. Setting her papers to the side, Elizabeth stood. Smiling at Mrs. Hill as she bustled into the room with a vial of her mother's salts, she said, "Mrs. Hill, it seems my mother has overset herself. Thank you for arriving so promptly." Turning to look at all of her sisters around the room, Elizabeth added, "My sisters and I will withdraw to allow her to regain her equanimity in peace."

Kitty and Lydia looked back and forth between their mother and Elizabeth for a moment before standing and walking out of the room. Mary did not even hesitate. She closed her book of Psalms and walked out without a glance at their mother. Then, taking Jane by the shoulders, Elizabeth propelled her from the room.

Pausing in the hall, she asked a passing maid, "Could you have a tea service sent up to the schoolroom?" Only waiting for the girl's nod, Elizabeth continued up to the sisters' refuge.

Mrs. Bennet, who had received little education herself, didn't think her daughters needed a governess. With no use, the schoolroom sat empty until Elizabeth and Jane took it upon themselves to convert it into a relaxing sitting room for the sisters to enjoy. It was now an odd amalgamation of mismatching furniture that they had pilfered from the Longbourn attics with the aid of Mr. Hill and a stable boy or two. It served as the perfect haven for the Bennet sisters in times of distress.

Once they were all settled in their preferred chairs, Elizabeth said, "While I know mother has always been fractious, this is something new. Did something change while I was away?" Glancing first at Jane and her unusually glum demeanor, Elizabeth looked to her younger sisters for information.

Mary looked at Jane with a similar concern before saying, "It all started when Aunt Phillips told us that a young single gentleman was coming to view Netherfield and possibly lease it. Mama demanded that we all go into Meryton, hoping to spot him."

Finally, Jane sighed and looked at Elizabeth, her eyes sad as she continued the tale. "As we strolled along the shops, we spotted the newcomer emerging from Uncle Phillips's office, accompanied by our uncle. They started walking towards us and just when it seemed that they would greet us, I felt Mama shove me in the center of my back. I would have fallen into him, and probably landed on top of him, if Mary hadn't caught my arm. We both went down in a heap, but at least the gentleman was still standing."

"Mama tried to compromise the two of you in front of everyone in town," Elizabeth grumbled, shaking her head. She rose quickly and started pacing, unable to keep still. "I do not know why I did not expect her to resort to such matters. She is desperate to marry any and all of us off, hopefully to a wealthy gentleman who will provide for her when our father dies."

Jane cried, "Oh, Lizzie, it was so embarrassing! The gentleman was so kind he helped Mary and I both to our feet and was very cordial about it. I was so humiliated that I could not tell you in a letter."

Kitty piped up with, "He was very handsome too, with reddish hair and smiling blue eyes."

"Ever since then, Mama has taken every opportunity to scold Jane," added Lydia, her voice angry.

Elizabeth looked at her youngest sister with kindness. She might be livelier than what was proper, but she vehemently protected her sisters and those she believed were mistreated. When she was younger, she had received an unfair amount of their mother's spleen. Mrs. Bennet had somehow blamed Lydia for the death of her twin brother as a newborn. As if it had been Lydia's fault that she was born healthy and her brother frail. Nor was it her fault that Mrs. Bennet had been told that she would never have any more children after such a difficult birth.

It had been left to a wet nurse and, to a lesser extent, Jane and Elizabeth to care for little Lydia. It was only when Lydia had turned fourteen and their mother finally noticed how much she resembled Jane that Mrs. Bennet had forgiven the girl for living when her brother had not. She talked about how Lydia would be sure to catch a husband where so many of her sisters could not. At only fifteen, Lydia was "out," and their mother often spoke of how Lydia would save her from the hedgerows.

Sitting back down with a sigh, Elizabeth reasoned, "We will have to do all we can to prevent Mother from trying something like this again. A marriage based on compromise has little hope of happiness. I would think that she, of all people, would know better." Unbeknownst to many, their mother held a secret—she had compromised their father. It was through comments made by their parents that the sisters discovered the roots of their parents' animosity, which only fueled their determination to avoid the same mistakes that had plagued their family and to hopefully find happiness in their own marriages one day.

Chapter Seven

That night, Elizabeth sighed as she sat at her dressing table. It had been a hectic day. Besides convincing her father to do something about the drainage area near the far fields, she also had to coordinate the replacement roofs for two of the tenant cottages. Despite her father giving her the money for the roofing materials, it was disheartening to think that he hadn't given a second thought to the Wheeler and Marsh families, who had undoubtedly experienced untold days and nights of being damp and cold. It was no wonder that Mary told her the Marsh's youngest child was once again sick.

Then there was her mother. Now that she had crossed the line into underhanded behavior, Elizabeth was worried about protecting her sisters and herself. One misguided act by Mrs. Bennet could ruin all their reputations and destroy any chance they had of having happy lives and marriages. For now, they had agreed to always go places in groups in hopes that they could protect each other from their mother's machination. If their mother got worse, well...well, that would have to be a problem for another day.

Rolling her head back and forth with a grimace, Elizabeth tried to loosen the knots in her neck and shoulders. Giving up after finding a modicum of relief, Elizabeth reached into her pocket with a smile. She had received a letter from Georgianna and had waited all day for the opportunity to read it.

Carefully, she loosened the seal and smoothed out the letter from her friend. She had only been back home for a few days, but she already missed her visits with Georgianna. After enduring a tumultuous day, Elizabeth's weary heart yearned for a glimmer of joy to uplift her spirits.

Darcy House, London

Dearest Lizzie,

I know that you have only been gone for a short time, but I already miss you. I went to the London Ladies Society this morning and though all my students were as bright and receptive as always, it was simply not the same. There was another young woman I did not recognize in your group of girls and, of course, we did not have tea.

I continue to grow closer to my brother, and I couldn't be happier about it. We have been talking more after dinner and trading confessions and opinions on many things. We have more in common than I had ever thought. I have long known that I was painfully shy and now I know it is something that my brother struggles with as well. Would you believe my brother admitted he gets flustered at gatherings and balls? I have often feared my come out because I have worried I might suffer similarly!

I had thought that his reserved demeanor was just his disapproval of me, but now I know better. I learned from him that our father was always disapproving if he showed any emotions. So after being constantly upbraided for his unseemly displays, as our father called them, William just stopped showing his emotions. Even to this day, he admits that expressing emotions is a challenge, despite strongly disagreeing with our father's demands. It fills me with gratitude that my brother treated me differently, but it also brings a tinge of sadness to think about the experience he had.

Well, enough of me and my brother. How are you? How is your family? What about the tenants that you were worried about? Mrs. Annesley said that when we return to Pemberley, she will help me come up with a schedule to go visit our tenants. I have even started sewing small garments because you spoke of how you and your sisters would gift the tenants' children with clothes. I suppose with as many tenants as Pemberley has, what I make will surely fit someone's child.

We spoke a lot about all of your sisters while you were here, so I almost feel like I know them. I hope they endured your absence tolerably well. Please send them my warm greetings. It is only now as I write to you that I realize we never much spoke of your parents, though I know that unlike me you are not an orphan. I do not quite know what to make of that, but I will leave it up to you to explain or not as you wish.

I hope your family appreciates your presence there because I certainly miss your presence here. If they ever prove themselves unequal to the wonderful person I know you to be, I beg you to return to London. It would bring me great joy to welcome you as a guest, whether it be here or at Pemberley. Please write to me as soon as your schedule will allow. I intend to keep the post service very busy with our letters.

Your Friend,

Miss Georgianna Darcy

Placing her chin in her hand, Elizabeth contemplated her friend's letter for a moment before she folded it up and blew out the candle. She would hopefully have time to write Georgianna back the next day. Though she was unsure what she would write, she supposed something would come to her. She certainly did not want to write of her father's indolence or her mother's attempt at compromising Jane with a complete stranger. Elizabeth hesitated to disclose what her parents were like.

Though to be fair, Georgianna had shared quite a bit about her brother. It seemed that she was not the only one with difficult parents. It was such a pity that Georgianna's brother had been scolded for simply showing natural emotions as a child. She could easily see how that would affect a young man into adulthood.

Sliding under the covers, Elizabeth worked at becoming comfortable while she pondered both her situation and poor Georgianna's brother. No matter one's position in life, parents could be a burden to their children. Yawning, Elizabeth fell ever closer to sleep as she realized she had never once met Georgianna's brother. She wondered what he looked like.

GEORGIANNA BARELY KEPT FROM squealing when she saw Elizabeth's letter on the silver platter being brought to her by the footman. While she was enjoying her lessons with Master Rossini and everything else she was working on with Mrs. Annesley, most of her idle thoughts were on Meryton and the goings on there.

She was grateful that Mrs. Annesley had yet to come down to break her fast, as it meant that Georgianna could read the letter right away. Taking up the letter, she thanked the footman and opened it. As always, Elizabeth's handwriting was even and precise, and in no time at all, Georgianna was reading her tale of Longbourn.

Longbourn, Meryton

Dearest Georgianna,

I cannot tell you how pleased I was to receive your letter. It was a restoring breath of fresh air after a long day filled with stress. Now I know you will worry about me, but do not. As you know, I am capable of handling most any situation, even if it seems like some days are quite trying.

As I feared, my father showed little initiative to do much while I was away. While I am grateful that we have a capable steward, there are just some things that he cannot do without my father's approval and the funds only he can provide. So, I dedicated most of my first several days back home to catching up on what should have been done in my absence. But now at least I have gotten my father to agree to the new roofs for two of our tenant families and the work needed on the drainage in a few fields by a creek.

I regret that the Jones and the Wheelers had to suffer with leaky roofs while I was away. At least they were the only ones to receive roof damage after the large storm that had gone through the area over a month ago. For all that they endured, they were still so grateful when they learned I was getting everything taken care of.

While all of that was going on, there was also my mother to redirect. She is upset that my older sister Jane is still unmarried at twenty-two. While I was gone, she even attempted to force the issue by shoving my sister at an eligible gentleman, hoping there would be a compromise. Thankfully, my middle sister Mary was there to prevent catastrophe. Because of her failure, my mother has been even more prone to fits of nerves, as she calls them.

If circumstances continue to deteriorate, the thought of escaping to London with my sisters becomes increasingly appealing. However, I must warn you that if I were to bring an entire household of ladies, your decision to host me might be one you regret. I am only joking, though. Or at least I am mostly joking. If it came down to protecting one of my sisters from my mother's machinations, I would send her to London in a heartbeat. So it is a good thing that I can handle my mother for the most part.

At first, I was unsure about confiding in you about my troubles, but then I remembered how you had shared the challenges your brother faced, and the hardships caused by your father, so I thought it was only fair. I am glad to hear that you are becoming ever closer to your brother. The joy I experience in my relationship with my sisters is immense, and I cannot imagine my life without them. So it is good to hear that you will enjoy something similar.

How are your lessons going with Master Rossini? I expect you're already wonderful and planning to impress me thoroughly the next time we see each other. What of learning to handle the household accounts? While I do not dislike the math required, it is rather tedious after a while. I am grateful that my sister Jane handles the household accounts so that I need only pay attention to the estate ledgers and deal with the tenants.

I look forward to hearing from you again as soon as you may write.
Your affectionate friend,
Miss Elizabeth Bennet

Putting the letter down on the table next to her plate, Georgianna frowned. Elizabeth was such a cheerful person that Georgianna never would have assumed that she had such concerns in her life. Lizzie practically vibrated with enthusiasm and good cheer. Hadn't she been there for Georgianna, guiding her through her own struggles and leading her towards equanimity and cheer?

Georgianna found it unfair that Elizabeth had to shoulder so much on her own. Well, maybe not on her own. She had her sisters there to aid her, but it still seemed that Elizabeth carried the greater burden. It made Georgianna wonder how Elizabeth had become such a remarkable person.

She would visit the area soon. Could she possibly lighten her friend's load in any way? Looking up, Georgianna spotted Mrs. Annesley coming into the room and said, "Good morning, Mrs. Annesley. I trust you slept well."

"Yes, I slept very well," answered Mrs. Annesley before moving to the sideboard and making herself a plate of toast and eggs, along with a cup of tea. Sitting down, she asked, "Is everything well, Miss Darcy? You seem distressed."

Setting down her teacup, Georgianna sighed. "I received a letter from Lizzie that disturbed me. She shared a few details about the situation at her home, and it became apparent that she is facing a heavy load. She is just such a nice person. I don't think it is fair that she must suffer so."

Putting down her teacup, Mrs. Annesley commented, "Miss Bennet is quite mature for her age, as well as being compassionate. I have noticed in the past that often occurs when people must take on responsibility at a young age."

Crumbling a piece of toast into bits, Georgianna huffed, "I just wish that I could help Lizzie in some way. I mean, despite all my mistakes, so much of my life is easy."

"Did she ask for your help?" questioned Mrs. Annesley.

Tilting her head, Georgianna said, "No, she did not ask for help with anything. She just told me of the issues she was dealing with."

Buttering her toast, Mrs. Annesley asked, "Have you considered that your friendship and willingness to listen, so to speak, could be a tremendous help to her?"

Wiping her hands on her serviette to get rid of the buttery crumbs stuck on her fingers, Georgianna said, "I had not thought of that, and I will always be there for Lizzie, but it still does not seem fair."

Mrs. Annesley, the corners of her lips turning down slightly, commiserated with Georgianna by saying, "Unfortunately, one of life's bitter truths is that life is not fair."

SNEAKING AWAY FROM THE chaos that was a houseful of sisters who were unregulated by any authority, Elizabeth took a deep breath of the crisp autumn air. She tried to remind herself that Kitty and Lydia were still young. It was likely that sisters might always fight over the fact that someone had borrowed an item of clothing without permission. It did not help that their mother always supported Lydia, saying that Kitty should give way to her prettier younger sister because she was much more likely to catch a husband than Kitty was.

The snap of a twig had Elizabeth spotting Jane behind her. Wincing, Elizabeth said, "I am sorry for abandoning you to the chaos, but I simply could not try to break up another one of their fights."

Smiling, Jane dismissed her apology with a wave of her hand. "Think nothing of it. You know it will end the same as it always does—Mother will assert that Lydia should keep the ribbon because of her superior beauty, leaving Lydia feeling remorseful. Eventually, she will apologize to Kitty and return the ribbon. I would be concerned more myself, but I think Lydia is good at heart, despite everything. She hates to hear mother disparaging her sisters as much as I do."

Nodding, Elizabeth agreed. Lydia might have trouble restraining herself, but she cared about those around her. Elizabeth felt it was because of Jane spending so much time around Lydia as she grew. Who, when offered Jane as a shining embodiment of goodness, could actually go down the wrong path? Pulling Georgianna's letter out of her pocket, Elizabeth said, "I will come back in once I have had the chance to read Georgianna's latest correspondence."

"Take your time. You rarely have a moment to yourself besides the long walks you take in the morning, and even then, you have a footman following you about," encouraged Jane.

Sitting on the nearby bench, Elizabeth unfolded the letter and began to read.

Darcy House, London

Dearest Lizzie,

I am sorry to hear about your struggles at home and though I trust you will handle it in the very best way, I wish you would not have to. It seems as if you at least have the estate matters handled. As for your mother, I do not know what to say. I do, however, want to assure you that I'll always be here to listen, or rather, read your concerns.

I would be more than willing to host you and your sisters if the situation ever arises. If the situation becomes dire, I trust you will do as you should and find your way to me, no matter where I may be. Here at Darcy House, there are several guest rooms and as for Pemberley, well, there are enough rooms to house your sisters many times over.

For myself, I have exciting news. Or rather, it is news of my brother. One of his closest friends has invited my brother to help him learn estate management at a place called Netherfield. I assume that you have heard of it as it is outside of Meryton. Who would have thought that my brother would have missed meeting you so many times in London only to meet you in Meryton?

On a separate matter, I feel I must warn you of some additional unpleasantness that is headed your way. Do you remember that horrid woman who attempted to latch herself onto me at Gunter's? I am sure you cannot but remember her, if only for the poor feathers attached to her turban. Sadly, it is her brother that invited William to Netherfield, and she is to be his hostess.

I can only imagine how horrible she will presumably be to the poor people of your town. As you might have supposed, she mistakenly believes that her time at her seminary and her dowry of twenty thousand pounds make her superior to most everyone she meets. In all honesty, she holds the belief that only those connected to nobility as her social superiors and treats everyone else horribly, despite the fact that her family obtained their money in trade and none of them have ever owned property. I expect her to treat the staff horribly and to look down her nose at everyone.

I have saved the best news for last. While I am currently having my lessons with Master Rossini, I have already received a gracious invitation to visit Netherfield once they conclude at the end of October. I truly cannot wait to see you once again. I will count down the days before you and I can once again have tea together.

Your friend,

Miss Georgianna Darcy

Remembering the haughty woman who had tried to fawn over Georgie had her grinning to herself, while the caring words Georgianna had gifted her at the start of the letter had Elizabeth blinking away tears. Not only was Georgianna not put off by her family's issues, but she was also supportive.

More than supportive, she was willing to offer shelter from the storm that was her mother and father. Only her Aunt and Uncle Gardiner had been so gracious as to tell her she could always come to them in a time of need. Not even Charlotte had said something like that. Elizabeth couldn't help but feel an immense sense of gratitude for stumbling upon such a wonderful friend during her stay in London.

Beyond all that, she had information that even her Aunt Phillips did not have. She knew about the guests at Netherfield, but should she share what she knew? She was not one to engage in gossip, and she had no intention of doing so now. The last thing the gentleman needed was for everyone to discuss them, making it difficult to settle into the neighborhood. That would happen enough already with only the speculation of the community. Besides, she had never met either of them in person. And if she did not reveal what she knew about them, she could not disclose what she knew about Miss Bingley.

Elizabeth's eyes widened as she remembered something. Georgianna had confessed that her brother was shy and awkward. She had even written that his uneasiness at balls often led to him inadvertently insulting people, and there was an assembly scheduled for the following week. It would be intriguing to observe Georgianna's brother at the assembly, and she found herself wondering just how awkward he could be.

Chapter Eight

IT WAS VERY WELL possible that Darcy's teeth would shatter before the end of his stay in Netherfield. As it was, his whole jaw ached horribly from gritting his teeth while in the company of Miss Bingley. Being confined in the carriage with her on the way to an assembly had made the evening even worse.

It had seemed silly to ride his horse when everyone else was riding in the carriage. The gathering was not twenty minutes away, and yet it seemed like the torment would not end. At least she had not tried to fall across the carriage towards him. Though her perfume was so potent in the confined space, she might as well have been sitting in his lap. He was going to arrive at the assembly with a pounding head and a stomach churning with nausea.

Closing his eyes in the shadowed interior of the carriage, Darcy tried to relax the muscles in his neck and jaw. In the last week or so, he had gotten a lot accomplished with Bingley. He had to admit, if only to himself, that they had mostly accomplished so much because it had given him the opportunity to stay away from Miss Bingley. While he was out surveying a poorly draining field or checking the tenant cottages for needed repairs, the harpy that was Miss Bingley could not corner him.

He had explained to Bingley more than once that he would never offer for his sister and his friend understood, even if his sister was in denial. Darcy's valet, Chambers, had several safeguards in place just in case she got it into her head to compromise him. Not that he would bow to her wishes, but why cause a scandal if he did not have to?

He had been dreading the assembly the whole week. He only rarely attended the assemblies near Pemberley and only attended balls in town when he absolutely had to. The very notion of all the gossip floating around the room regarding his ten thousand a year made him extremely uncomfortable.

Before he was ready, Darcy was stepping down from the carriage and making his way into the hall. He would have preferred to arrive early, or even on time, but of course Bingley's sisters seemed incapable of showing up anywhere on time. So now all eyes were on him, weighing him and his worth. Darcy struggled to not swallow convulsively as the rest of the party came up behind him.

In no time at all, a very gregarious gentleman was introducing his group to those about the room, but Darcy was so consumed with trying to put distance between himself and Miss Bingley that he paid not a whit to anything the man said. Darcy managed to keep her from clutching his arm like a limpet by clasping his hands tightly behind himself.

When another guest caught Miss Bingley's attention, Darcy finally slipped away and took refuge in a poorly illuminated corner of the room, hoping if he just held still enough, she might mistake him for an oddly shaped potted plant. Despite his efforts at camouflage, Bingley approached him with a grin lighting up his face.

"Come, Darcy," said Bingley, "you really cannot hide this way. I would prefer to see you enjoying yourself. Join the merriment and dance!"

Shaking his head with a grimace, Darcy grunted, "I shall not. You know I detest dancing when I am unacquainted with my partner, as I never know what to say, and trying to come up with a response to conversation makes me lose my step in the dance."

"Come now, this is the country. It is not as if they will gossip about a few missteps. There are so many pleasant girls and several of them are uncommonly pretty."

With a nod to the pretty blonde, Darcy said, "You are dancing with the only handsome lady present."

While tracking the woman with his eyes, Bingley said, "Oh! She is the most beautiful creature." Then he smiled and continued, "Her sister is sitting just behind you, and she is also rather pretty, and I dare say she is very agreeable. Let me ask my partner to introduce you so you may dance."

Turning to follow Bingley's gaze, Darcy spotted the young lady his friend was looking at. He was at first surprised that she looked so different from her fair sister, but then he noticed her smile. Her smile froze him with its warmth, and he could do nothing for several heartbeats, but then he remembered how easily young ladies mistook his kindness for something more. He did not want another *misunderstanding.* He found himself saying, "She is tolerable, but not handsome enough to tempt me; I am in no humor at present to give consequence to young ladies who are slighted by other men."

Wincing, Bingley looked at the young lady and tugged at his cravat before chuckling weakly and saying, "You always make the worst jokes, Darcy. What have I told you about your sense of humor?" Then clapping Darcy on the back, Bingley gestured to the far wall where there was a line of ladies chattering. "My sisters are here, somewhere. Dance with one of them."

Glaring at his friend, Darcy said, "Bingley, Mrs. Hurst has retreated to the card table in search of her husband, and as for Miss Bingley, I have already told her I will not dance with her this evening. It is time for her obsession with me to stop. I will no longer feed it by dancing with her or being seen talking with her in public." Then, rubbing at his aching forehead, Darcy added, "With all the perfume she is wearing tonight, dancing with her would certainly not be something I could enjoy. It would be a punishment. The headache I received from the carriage ride with her is already causing me great discomfort.

I know you enjoy dancing, and you want me to be happy, but it simply will not work for me."

GEORGIANNA HAD BEEN RIGHT—HER brother was obviously uncomfortable at the assembly. He had even said something quite insulting. If Elizabeth had not been observing his face, she would have missed his grimace once the hurtful words left his mouth, and she suspected that he might not have truly meant what he said.

When he continued speaking with Mr. Bingley, she found herself feeling sorry for the gentleman. Elizabeth had, after all, only spent a few minutes in the company of Miss Bingley, and he was having to live with her. It did not surprise her that he had developed a headache. Searching in her reticule, she found the headache powder that she always brought in case she or one of her sisters fell ill. She found a servant and entrusted them with the powder, requesting that it be delivered to Mr. Darcy, accompanied by a cup of soothing peppermint tea.

Having completed her quest of goodwill, Elizabeth went in search of her sisters. Catching sight of Jane with Mr. Bingley and Lydia, Elizabeth walked in their direction.

Once she arrived, Mr. Bingley turned to her with an obvious wince and said, "Miss Elizabeth, I apologize for my friend's words. I should have known better than to try to goad him to dance when he was already feeling unwell."

Shaking her head, Elizabeth replied, "Think nothing of it, Mr. Bingley. I could tell he was out of sorts. It is not uncommon for someone to speak out of turn when feeling unwell. I can't criticize him for speaking in a way he may regret later, as I have made the same mistake myself in the past." While she stated her forgiveness, Elizabeth couldn't shake the lingering doubt that perhaps her knowledge about the man influenced her forgiveness. It was not something she wanted to dwell on, however.

Ever compassionate and concerned for others, Jane asked, "Is Mr. Darcy unwell?"

Sighing, Mr. Bingley said, "My sister's copious amounts of perfume have given him a headache. Which, in turn, has made his unease in the presence of strangers worse."

Reaching out, Elizabeth squeezed Jane's hand and explained, "I have asked a servant to bring him some headache powder and peppermint tea." Hopefully he would be well enough to survive his trip back to Netherfield intact.

"How kind of you to help him in such a way," commented Bingley with a touch of surprise tinting his voice.

Jane was quick to inform Mr. Bingley. "My sister is always looking out for others. Your friend Mr. Darcy is not the first person she has aided with one of the many things she keeps inside her reticule." Glancing at Elizabeth with a smile, she added, "She works hard to anticipate and plan for any eventuality that could affect those in her vicinity adversely."

Elizabeth hoped that the warmth in her cheeks would be mistaken for something besides a blush. The hall was quite warm, after all. The rare occasions when she received even the slightest compliment always left her feeling awkward. Fortunately, those moments were few and far between.

By the time she felt she had herself back under regulation, she realized the next dance was starting, and Johnathan Lucas was coming to collect her. Having been out for several years at that point, it was quite easy for her to follow the pattern of the dance and even chat lightly with Charlotte's younger brother.

Mrs. Bennet had at one time tried to contrive a match between the two of them, but quickly realized that it was a hopeless case. For one, Elizabeth and her intelligence overwhelmed the poor boy. For another, they saw each other as siblings and nothing more. When Mrs. Bennet tried to get Lady Lucas and Sir William on her side, they refused.

It had been odd to see the normally jovial Sir William become stern and unmoving in the face of her mother's persistent whining demands. He had put his foot down, saying that he would never, under any circumstances, permit such a match. However, he had kindly approached Elizabeth afterwards when her mother was not present and reassured her that his decision was not because he did not think well of her. Unlike her parents, he had higher aspirations for his children's love lives—he wanted them to not only find a partner, but to be truly happy and fulfilled. He knew she and Jonathan did not suit one another, so he had acted in both of their best interests. Elizabeth had been grateful that someone—anyone—wanted what was best for her.

The resulting argument between their two families had put a kink in the friendship between her mother and Lady Lucas. And even two years later, her mother did not fully approve of her friendship with Charlotte and Johnathan, and the name Lucas was never uttered at Longbourn with kindness.

At the end of the dance, Elizabeth curtsied to Johnathan and thanked him before she went in search of her two youngest sisters. Without a parental figure present to guide them, Elizabeth, Jane, and Mary always liked to keep a careful eye on them at the assemblies whenever possible.

Lydia was the easiest to find. She was laughing with the Long girls and Maria Lucas. Walking up to the group, she asked, "What has you all so merry this evening?"

Lydia smiled in response and linked her arm with Elizabeth. "We have been talking about the newest arrivals to Meryton—the ones who are staying at Netherfield."

"Yes, Miss Elizabeth, you would not believe their behavior!"

"Whose behavior?" asked Elizabeth. She hoped no one had seen Mr. Darcy's faux pas earlier in the evening.

A chorus of giggles answered her inquiry before Helena Long tittered, "The woman with the turban dressed to attend a ball with the Queen."

Understanding the giggles more, Elizabeth said, "I believe her name is Miss Bingley."

Lyda said, "Since her arrival, Miss Bingley has made it a point to complain about and shoot disdainful glances at everyone and everything here." Looking at her sister with her eyebrows raised, she added, "We may all be *nobodies from the back of beyond*, but at least we know it is not good manners to speak of our dowries and the annual income of the gentlemen we know as much as she does."

"She has been talking about money?" asked Elizabeth in shock. Yes, she knew the woman was pretentious, but she did not know she would be so without basic manners as well. Looking at the woman standing nearby with her nose in the air, Elizabeth shook her head.

Nodding, Maria Lucas added, "Yes, her sister even tried to get her to keep her voice down, but she said there was nobody here who knew anybody important, so it did not matter who heard her."

Sighing, Elizabeth watched Miss Bingley criticize all her neighbors. Elizabeth knew they might not all be lords and ladies, but they were mostly good people. None of them needed the derision of a small-minded woman. One thing was certain: she would have a long letter to write to Georgianna in the morning.

GEORGIANNA STUDIED THE MENU for the week before handing it to Mrs. Annesley to look it over. She was enjoying making up the menus at Darcy House, even if she was only picking what she and Mrs. Annesley were having. She had progressed as far as making up a few menus for a time when William would be back with them, and even a menu for if they were to host a dinner party for friends. Though besides her cousin Richard and Elizabeth, she did not know who else would ever be in attendance.

Nodding, Mrs. Annesley said, "You have thought of everything. You even have well-matched wines listed to go with each course. I expect that once you return to Darcy House with your brother, you will have acquired the skills to entertain small groups."

"Do not get carried away, Mrs. Annesley. I do not have enough people I would feel comfortable hosting to host multiple dinners." Tilting her head, Georgianna considered the possibility of having Elizabeth over often. That would certainly be enjoyable. Smiling, she said, "Though I suppose I could just invite all the same people over repeatedly."

"You know that is simply not how entertaining is done," Mrs. Annesley chuckled. "Though I am sure that by the time you are out, you will have plenty more friends and acquaintances to arrange dinners for."

Georgianna considered her words with Elizabeth in mind. Before she had met Miss Bennet at the charity, Georgianna had thought she would never gain a genuine friend. Too many of the people that approached her were like Miss Bingley—snide and full of cruel gossip. Now that she had one excellent friend though, it seemed possible to find others.

A footman entering the room interrupted her thoughts as he brought her the day's mail. Thanking him, she sorted through the stack. There was a missive from her aunt, Lady Catherine, most likely commanding her to spend more time practicing the piano and chastising her for imagined misbehavior. She would read it later, or possibly have Mrs. Annesley read it in case there was something of genuine import. Georgianna no longer wanted to cater to the cantankerous woman.

There were also letters from her brother and Elizabeth. With just a hint of hesitation, she carefully unfolded William's letter, reserving Elizabeth's for later. She read it with a smile on her face, only for Mrs. Annesley to ask, "What does your brother have to say that would put such a smile on your face?"

Giggling, Georgianna explained, "It is not a long letter—mostly it tells of his arrival at Netherfield and how he has spent the last week helping Mr. Bingley survey the property. He also speaks of hiding from Miss. Bingley and asks for any suggestions to keep her at bay. He ends by stating that there will be an assembly he will have to attend, or else Miss Bingley has said she would stay home and keep him entertained." Shaking her head, Georgianna looked at Mrs. Annesley and added, "I believe the only way Miss Bingley will ever leave him alone is if he tells her he has taken up gambling and has lost his fortune and Pemberley. Or perhaps he could say he has had a calling from God and would like to teach the heathens in Africa, then ask her to join him."

Mrs. Annesley smiled at Georgianna's comment, then with a shake of her head she said, "It's a shame that Miss Bingley is so focused on pursuing Mr. Darcy, as she could use this time to find a husband who truly values her. Surely there is someone out there that shares her tastes, or at least needs her dowry for their estate. As it is, she is nearly a laughingstock among the ton as they watch her ever worsening antics."

Georgianna only shook her head before unfolding Elizabeth's letter.

Longbourn, Meryton

Dearest Georgianna,

There was an assembly last night in Meryton and you will never guess who I finally saw. Or maybe you can guess because he is visiting. I saw your brother last night, though we never spoke directly to one another. He avoided being introduced to me and even insulted me when he caught me smiling at him. Though he said, "She is tolerable, but not handsome enough to tempt me; I am in no humor at present to give consequence to young ladies who are slighted by other men," be assured that I am not offended.

To be fair, he told his friend, Mr. Bingley, he was suffering from a headache from his sister's perfume. She was wearing far too much of the stuff. If I had not known of him through you and your letters, I might have thought him proud or contemptuous. However, knowing what I did, I could see that he was just as you said—shy and uneasy. I am sure that being in pain did not help him. I managed to surreptitiously provide him with headache powder and some peppermint tea to help him somewhat.

The person who was contemptuous was Miss Bingley. That woman—I will not call her a lady—insulted everyone and everything present at the assembly. Her attire was more befitting of a grand ball with royalty in attendance than a casual country dance. An even more ornate feathered turban was present, if you can believe it. While she might have thought that her appearance was gaining notice because of her sense of style, it most certainly was not. Most of the ladies and gentlemen there were agog at her horrible use of feathers and burnt orange.

The one benefit of the evening was that my youngest sister, Lydia, did not get into any mischief because she was so busy watching Miss Bingley be an example of all the wrong things to do. I am at least reassured that Lydia is aware of what poor manners look like. At only fifteen, she has no business being out, but my mother is so terrified of what will happen to us when my father dies, she has demanded all of us be actively trying to catch husbands.

I could continue telling you of last night for several more pages, but I must get downstairs for a walk before breakfast. I will need all the serenity that nature has to offer to handle my mother's complaints of a sore head and her incessant gossip about what she heard and saw last

*night. Suffice it to say, the party at Netherfield will be at the top of her
list to discuss.*

Your loving friend,

Miss Elizabeth Bennet

Georgianna set Elizabeth's letter down with a huff. She was glad to
hear from Elizabeth, but she was very put out with her brother. How
could he insult a young lady in such a way while at a public assembly?
If Elizabeth heard his ill manners, of course others could have. What
was he thinking?

Pushing back from the table, Georgianna paced the room. She had
made a single circuit and began another of the room when Mrs.
Annesley asked, "What in Miss Bennet's letter could have you so
upset?"

"He called her tolerable! That addle-brained brother of mine said
that she was tolerable but not handsome enough to tempt him
to dance with!" Going back to the table to pick up the letter,
Georgianna read aloud the second part. "He said, *I am in no humor
at present to give consequence to young ladies who are slighted by other
men.* He calls himself a gentleman and yet he said that at an assembly,
loud enough to be heard by everyone. William said it loud enough to
be heard by Lizzie.*"

With a wince, Mrs. Annesley admitted, "That was very badly done
by your brother. What are you going to do?"

Sitting down, Georgianna took up a sheet of paper. "I am going to
write him a letter. He helped me after my near disaster at Ramsgate.

The least I can do is help him see the error of his ways, even if I must pound it into his head word by word."

Chapter Nine

The library at Netherfield was sadly lacking enough books to really be called such, but it was one of the few places Darcy had hidden from Miss Bingley successfully. It was possible she did not know the small room on the second floor existed, which suited Darcy just fine. He had spent more than enough time hiding in his room with the excuse of completing correspondence.

Ever since the assembly, Miss Bingley had gotten worse, claiming to understand how much he disdained the people in the country town for their lack of style and manners. He refrained from contradicting her because it would be rude to dispute his hostess, but if she did not stop, he would be compelled to intervene soon.

The one good thing about the library was that it had at least most of Shakespeare's best works. So, for now, he was sitting on one of the two chairs in the library reading *The Merchant of Venice*. Amid the loan negotiation between Shylock, Bassanio, and

Antonio, Chambers burst into the room, abruptly interrupting Darcy's reading. Knowing Chambers would only search him out if it was important, Darcy asked, "Is something amiss, Chambers?"

In his usual formal manner, Chambers presented a letter to him, bowing slightly as he said, "Sir, an express has arrived from Darcy House."

Putting his book to the side, Darcy sat up in a rush, exclaiming, "Are they waiting for a response?" Taking the letter, Darcy noticed it was from Georgianna, and he could not help but worry.

"No, sir. Though I have arranged for him to get a meal below stairs," answered Chambers.

Glancing out the window, Darcy took in the sun low in the sky and said, "Chambers, if he doesn't have any pressing matters, can you arrange for him to stay the night? It's too late in the day for him to make it back to London safely before it gets dark."

"Of course, sir, I will speak with Mrs. Nichols." With a nod of his head, Chambers left the room. Opening the letter in a rush, Darcy began reading.

Darcy House, London

Brother,

I will first tell you that all is well at Darcy House. You do not need to worry about me or anything going on here in London. Everyone here is well, though at the moment I am quite put out with you.

Before I can fully explain my fury, I suppose I should clarify something. Though I know I told you, I do not think you realized that my dear friend Lizzie's home estate lies near Meryton. She returned to her home, an estate named Longbourn, shortly before you journeyed to Netherfield.

I must admit that I did not remind you that you would be in close contact with my dear friend. I saw it as my own little joke that you might happen upon her in some manner, and you might become acquainted only to realize the prior connection. Never in my wildest dreams could I have imagined that you would dismiss and insult her.

I know you are uneasy at assemblies, but that does not give you the excuse to be cruel. Is this truly how you protect yourself? If I had written to you about overhearing two gentlemen talking about me, with one of them commenting that I was only tolerable, what would your reaction be? I think your reaction would be quite dramatic. My friend has no brother to rush to her defense as I do, but that does not mean she should be insulted without consequence.

Miss Elizabeth Bennet is one of the best people I know. In our brief span of acquaintance, she has been my rock, providing me with comfort and solace when I needed it. Her kind attention has been a catalyst for bringing joy and confidence back into my life. And yet you insult her? I am ashamed.

As someone who understands the difficulties of shyness, I know firsthand some of the challenges you face. However, lashing out is not the solution. You need to find a more effective strategy to safeguard yourself from individuals who may exploit you for their own benefit and improve your ability to distinguish between allies and enemies.

Despite your behavior, Lizzie states your words do not offend her. In fact, she saw to it that you received peppermint tea and headache powder. I expect you to apologize to her at the earliest opportunity.

I love you, William. I write these things to help you become the man I believe you aspire to be—the kind of gentleman I know you have the potential to become—just as I am aware of your willingness to support me in my journey to become the best gentlewoman I can be. No matter the challenges, I have faith in your ability to remain the kind person I know you to be.

Your loving sister,

Miss Georgianna Darcy

Collapsing back into his chair, Darcy ran his hand through his hair. How had he tangled matters so badly? While he had briefly felt guilty for what he had said after he had said it, he had never thought of apologizing. He saw that the young lady had heard what he said, but she had not appeared hurt, so he thought nothing of it after a few minutes.

Since when had he seen insults as a way to prevent people from trying to trap him in unwanted marriages? Was it sometime after the third compromise attempt? To protect himself, he considered any young lady or matchmaking mother who continued to pay him attention, despite his scowl, as a target of his defensive measures. In town, most people were pursuing his wealth, leaving him with no genuine sense of remorse. Georgianna was correct, though, and had someone said the same thing about her, he would have rained fire down upon the perpetrator. Had anyone tried to condemn his actions in the past?

He could remember one or two brothers who had tried to take him to task for his statements. It was to his shame that he had waved off and ignored them, usually by saying that his statements could not have truly hurt the young ladies, as he had seen no one cry. Or that it was their own fault for eavesdropping. He had often pointed out to himself that his friend Bingley had never corrected his cruel behavior, but he wouldn't, would he? Bingley looked to him as an example of all that was ideal in a gentleman. He was not only failing himself and his sister, but Bingley as well. How had his behavior fallen so far from the mark?

ELIZABETH GNAWED ON HER lower lip in agitation as she looked out the window towards Netherfield. Her mother had once again tried her hand at matchmaking, having sent Jane off on horseback to Netherfield to have tea with Mr. Bingley's sisters. Jane had barely left when a powerful thunderstorm arrived, trapping her sister at Netherfield and likely soaking her on her journey.

Elizabeth had seen the clouds in the distance and said that Jane should take the carriage, but her mother overruled her. Worse, her father found the struggle between Elizabeth and his wife humorous. He ended up supporting her mother by asserting that they needed the horses on the farm and prohibiting Jane from using the carriage. Elizabeth suspected he was still put out that she had taken him to task on her return from London for having let so much slide in her absence.

Now, with the sun rising above the horizon, Elizabeth wondered how her sister was managing her stay with Miss Bingley. Elizabeth knew Jane was not like her. She always attempted to see the best in people and frequently experienced disappointment when they let her down. Having met Miss Bingley before and knowing more of her from Georgianna, Elizabeth worried about her Jane. Fretting was not useful though, and so Elizabeth went to break her fast with her family.

Having lost her appetite from worry, Elizabeth nibbled on a roll. Across the table, Mrs. Bennet crowed to them all as she cut up her ham. "I knew just how it would be when I saw those clouds. My plan went perfectly. The weather trapped her there for the night and now she would have her choice of two wealthy gentlemen. If she does not come home at least courting, then she is not my daughter."

Elizabeth caught Mary's eye, and they shared a look. They both knew their mother's hopes were preposterous, but there would be no point in saying so. The family continued eating, and mostly ignoring her mother's chatter, until a footman brought Elizabeth a missive. Opening it immediately, Elizabeth read it:

Netherfield, Meryton

My Dearest Lizzie,

I find myself very unwell this morning; I suppose due to being so thoroughly wet through on my ride to Netherfield yesterday. Despite the best intentions of my friends, Miss Bingley and Mrs. Hurst, who insisted I stay close to the roaring fire to dry off, I couldn't seem to rid myself of the chill that had taken hold. When they realized I was decidedly ill this morning, Mr. Jones was sent for. Do not be alarmed—I suffer only from a sore throat, headache, and slight fever. Might you arrange for additional clothing to be sent? I hate to be such a bother and continue to borrow Mrs. Hurst's clothes while I am unwell.

Yours, etc.

Upon realizing what the message contained, her father's laughter echoed through the room, a mix of amusement and sarcasm. With a further chuckle, Mr. Bennet reassured his wife, "Don't worry, dear Mrs. Bennet. Even if our daughter dies of this illness, you can take comfort in the fact that it was all in the pursuit of a wealthy gentleman."

Waving her husband off, Mrs. Bennet said, "She has nothing more than a cold. People do not die of trifling colds." Then, with a brilliant smile, she added, "This is even better. Before, Jane would only have the time it took her to break her fast to win over one of the gentlemen, but now she can stay there recovering from her illness for as long as it is convenient to my cause."

Pushing back from the table, Mary said, "I shall go gather some of Jane's clothes to send back with the servant who brought the message."

Calling after her, Mrs. Bennet said, "Be sure to pack several of her best dresses. Jane must look her best while there."

What little of the roll that Elizabeth had eaten felt like lead in her stomach. Both Jane and Kitty, with their delicate constitutions, often battled lingering coughs as their colds settled into their chests. Angry beyond her current ability to keep silent, Elizabeth said, "Mother, if Jane is ill, she will be staying in her room in bed, not flirting with either gentleman at Netherfield."

Looking at Elizabeth with scorn, Mrs. Bennet replied, "That, my dear, is why you will never marry. You simply do not know how to catch a husband." Her statement had Mr. Bennet laughing once again.

Turning to her father, Elizabeth threw down her serviette and stood. "I am so happy I have been able to provide for your entertainment. After all, you only mock my happiness while my mother seeks to undermine my sister's health. I will be going to Netherfield to check on my sister."

Despite her mother's screeching, she remained focused on her task and, although she felt guilty about leaving her younger sisters to endure their mother's fits of temper, she remained determined. There was no telling how sick Jane truly was. Jane was often one to minimize her suffering, not wanting others to worry when they should. Then, too, Elizabeth worried if Miss Bingley and Mrs. Hurst would put forth the effort needed to take care of her ill sister.

She put on an old pair of boots that would help her manage the wet and muddy landscape and gathered her pelisse and reticule before heading to the stillroom. She did not know what powders and nostrums the Bingleys might have available, so she took some of all that she thought Jane might need. In practically no time at all, she was off. Hopefully, the three-mile walk would cool some of her ire before she reached Netherfield. It would not do for her to arrive still in a snit of frustration.

WHEN THEY SHOWED THE subject of his ruminations into the room, Darcy struggled not to choke. It was as if the power of his thoughts had made Miss Elizabeth appear. Their eyes met briefly, and in that instant, a strange connection seemed to form before Miss Bingley's strident voice shattered their moment.

"Miss Elizabeth, things must be more different in the country than I was led to believe if guests may show up at one's house whenever they choose." Miss Bingley glanced briefly at Mr. Darcy before turning back to Miss Elizabeth and adding, "I did not know that I was to expect you."

Though Miss Bingley's tone was cutting, Miss Elizabeth did not seem to be in any way intimidated and that intrigued Darcy. In fact, the only reaction she had to Miss Bingley's attack was to raise one of her eyebrows ever so slightly. Miss Elizabeth was obviously worse for wear and appeared to have traveled a long distance on foot. Several strands of her hair had worked their way loose and there was mud on her hem and boots. Darcy was so busy studying Miss Elizabeth that he almost missed it when she said, "I have come to see to my ailing sister, Jane."

Bingley turned to his sisters, concern etched on his face, and exclaimed, "Miss Bennet is here? And she is unwell?"

Darcy and Bingley, along with Hurst, had dined with some of the neighborhood gentlemen and returned late because of the storm. They knew that Miss Bennet had been invited to tea, but there had been no mention that she had remained or that she had fallen ill. Though it did not surprise Darcy—Miss Bingley would have wanted to keep the young lady away from him and her brother.

Taking a sip of her tea, Mrs. Hurst sighed but did not speak. On the other hand, Miss Bingley waved off her brother's question with a snort. "Miss Bennet arrived at tea thoroughly wet through from the storm. Really, Charles, she was foolish to attempt the visit by horseback. I had hoped to see her gone by now, but she has apparently fallen ill. I have summoned the apothecary they have in these backwoods to see to her, and I am sure he will suggest she recover at home. There is no need to concern yourself."

Bingley's mouth hung open at his sister's cruel dismissal of their ailing guest for a moment before it snapped shut and he stood. Gesturing to the maid standing by the wall, Bingley said, "I am sure that our maid can show you to your sister, Miss Elizabeth. Please reach out to me or Mrs. Nichols if you should need anything. When the apothecary arrives, please inform me if there is anything that can be done to assist your sister's recovery."

Smiling large enough that the power of it reached her eyes, Miss Elizabeth said, "Thank you, I will." Then, giving a curtsy, she left the room, following the young maid.

Bingley looked down at his sister as she spread jam on her toast with a glare. Bingley cleared his throat and announced, "I apologize, but Caroline and I need to excuse ourselves for an important discussion."

"Really, Charles, we have nothing to discuss. Besides, I am eating." As if to prove her point, Miss Bingley looked away from Bingley and took a bite of her toast.

In a move that Darcy had never seen before, Bingley's voice turned hard, and he barked, "Caroline, put down the toast, and accompany me to my study now!" Eyes wide, Miss Bingley did as commanded and followed her brother out of the room.

Once they were gone, everyone ate in silence. Darcy could not help but imagine what sort of conversation was taking place in Bingley's study. Part of the problem was that Mrs. Hurst's personality was too subdued when compared with her stubborn sister. Mrs. Hurst may have officially been the hostess, but Miss Bingley was directing whatever she wanted to the apparent detriment of others.

Taking a sip of his coffee, Darcy stared at the door Miss Elizabeth had only recently passed through. The lady's presence once again brought to mind his recently realized failings. There was an ache in his heart thinking about how cruel he was to the young lady who had gone out of her way to be kind to his sister. More contemplation only left him to understand that, in all reality, he should be regretful for having been cruel to anyone. His position in life granted him many privileges, but being cruel was not one of them.

Once upon a time, he had thought that his father's dictates and comments about him had been cruel. Darcy could remember thinking that when he grew up, he would never use his words to cut as his father did. Yet here he had fallen into the habit himself, if not for the same reasons. The former master of Pemberley seemed to take delight in using his language to put people in their place. Maintaining the distinction of class was of utmost importance to his father, and he insisted on receiving the deference he thought he deserved, whereas Darcy had used words and insults as a defense against those who would use him.

Regardless of how it came about, it was wrong, and he was going to work diligently to change his ways. He had already written to his sister to apologize for insulting her friend and he promised her he would work to do better. Darcy had planned to apologize to Miss Elizabeth at the gathering held by Sir William Lucas, but the heavy rain that evening had made it impossible for him to attend. Hopefully, while she was in residence, he would get the opportunity to amend his behavior and prove to her, and himself, that he was indeed worthy of the gentleman title.

It made sense that she would have arrived to see to her ailing sibling. A lady who was compassionate enough to note the sore disposition of his sister's heart and do something about it would certainly journey across fields to minister to a sick sister. The state of her boots had certainly suggested such endeavors. While Miss Bingley would be sure to harp on her appearance, Darcy found that the exercise had rendered her quite beautiful.

Chapter Ten

Elizabeth struggled not to yawn as she walked down the stairs. Mrs. Nichols arrived early that morning to check on Elizabeth and her sister. Seeing how exhausted Elizabeth was, she urged her to leave the room and suggested she take a walk to refresh herself, demanding that she eat and drink something. Elizabeth hurried off to partake in a quick meal and a cup of coffee, so she could promptly return to her sister's side.

The sight of Mr. Darcy sitting at the table, holding a teacup with steam wafting from it, took her by surprise. She did not know why, but she had supposed the Netherfield party would be abed at such an early hour. Her surprise made her hesitate in the doorway, though the smell of food and coffee made her stomach rumble. It had been a while since she had enjoyed the bread, cheese, and tea that were sent to her the evening before.

Upon seeing her, Mr. Darcy put his cup down and jumped to his feet. "Miss Elizabeth, please sit down and I shall fetch whatever you may wish to partake of." Having said as much, he pulled a chair from the table for her in a gallant fashion which amused Elizabeth despite how tired she was.

"Would you prefer coffee or tea, Miss Elizabeth?" asked Mr. Darcy as she sat down.

Sighing, Elizabeth rubbed at her forehead and replied, "I normally prefer tea, but this morning I feel I will need the coffee."

Frowning momentarily, Mr. Darcy walked over to the sideboard and poured Elizabeth a cup of coffee, inquiring, "Would you prefer cream and sugar?"

Smiling at his thoughtfulness, Elizabeth answered, "Yes, thank you."

There was a steaming cup of coffee in front of Elizabeth in short order and she happily took a sip. With both hands wrapped around the cup, she smiled, relishing the way the cream and sugar had tamed the coffee's bitterness. She knew it was not the most ladylike way to hold her cup, but she was too tired to care.

Putting a plate of various breakfast items before her, Mr. Darcy sat back down. After taking a sip from his own cup, he asked, "How is your sister, Miss Elizabeth?"

Elizabeth put down her coffee and studied the pastry, ham, and eggs on the plate before her. Then sighing, she looked at Mr. Darcy's concerned face before remarking, "Not well, Mr. Darcy. As the night progressed, her fever became worse. I spent most of the night replacing the cool cloths on her forehead to bring the fever down. Just as she was resting more peacefully, Mrs. Nichols barged into the room and promptly sent me away, claiming that I needed to eat something to keep my strength up."

Looking down at her plate with a sigh, Elizabeth broke off a piece of the pastry and popped it into her mouth. The flaky goodness that filled her mouth was quite surprising. Something about the subtle flavors was familiar, and she wondered idly if the cooks at Longbourn and Netherfield shared recipes. The flavor on her tongue was so familiar that it brought tears to Elizabeth's eyes, forcing her to take slow, steady breaths to regain her composure. She had a sense that her overwhelmed state resulted from her exhaustion. She was just so tired.

Mr. Darcy's soft voice drew Elizabeth's attention when he said, "At the risk of cultivating your ire, I believe Mrs. Nichols is correct. Though I applaud your sisterly love, you must care for yourself, Miss Elizabeth. You cannot care for her if you fall sick yourself or collapse from exhaustion."

Taking another fortifying sip of her coffee, Elizabeth nodded before saying, "While I understand that on an intellectual level, it is hard to follow through when I see my beloved sister so ill."

Elizabeth watched as Mr. Darcy nodded. It struck her that he had his sister's eyes. Not only were they the same blue, but they were just as expressive and compassionate when he was not shielding himself from the world. She wondered if that was the reason he had lashed out. Did someone hurt him before, causing him to want to protect his soft heart from pain?

Clearing his throat, he said, "I understand your struggle. Two years ago, Georgianna was afflicted with scarlet fever, and I was beside myself with worry."

Elizabeth gasped. She had known of several tenants in the area who had died of scarlet fever when she was a child. Elizabeth knew he would have done everything he could to aid Georgianna, as she was all he had of his immediate family. "I can well imagine how hard that would have been for you, considering she was all that remained of your family. Georgianna has said that even though you were not always as close as you are now, there has always been love and affection between you." Pressing her hand to her trembling heart, Elizabeth murmured, "Thank God Jane does not have such an illness."

They both sat in silence while Elizabeth nibbled on her meal and Mr. Darcy continued drinking his own coffee. Eventually, he said, "There was talk of an apothecary being summoned?"

"Yes, they requested Mr. Jones's attendance on Jane, but Mrs. Nichols let me know he said he could not come until sometime today. Apparently, he was dealing with some sort of carriage accident outside of town that left several individuals badly injured." Rubbing at her forehead once again, Elizabeth explained, "It is Jane who is truly skilled at caring for the ill, not me. Despite that, I brought what

I could from the Longbourn stillroom to care for her. I will be glad when Mr. Jones arrives to provide some direction."

They lapsed into a comfortable silence, and Elizabeth took another sip of her coffee, feeling a renewed sense of energy coursing through her. Hopefully, the coffee would help to combat the headache that was taking hold. She studied Mr. Darcy. From his hesitant expression, she wondered if there was something he wanted to say. If he was as shy as Georgianna had been, he might find conversation difficult, so she said, "It surprised me to see anyone else awake. Are you an early riser, Mr. Darcy?"

With a smile, Mr. Darcy answered, "I am a country gentleman at heart. I have never adapted to town hours, and I am usually up with the sun. Yesterday, when you arrived and I was eating with the others, was an aberration. Bingley and I had ridden out to check on one of the fields after the storm as we were worried about flooding. We had only returned to break our fasts shortly before you arrived."

Elizabeth found that she quite liked Mr. Darcy's smile. His even, white teeth stood out amongst his slightly tanned skin and Elizabeth wondered if he often inspected the fields about his estate while visiting tenants. It would make sense, as the Darcys must have a rather large and prosperous estate. Hoping to maintain the flow of conversation, Elizabeth interjected, "We have that in common, then. I often walk a considerable distance, returning home before my family even stirs from their beds. It really is the best way to commandeer some peace in a household of women."

Chuckling, Mr. Darcy said, "While I have difficulty imagining living in a household of women, I easily relate to taking solace in nature. Though I prefer riding to walking." Elizabeth watched as Mr. Darcy's smile seemed to fade. Then, hesitating, he added, "I know that this might not be the best moment, but while I have the opportunity, I want to express my deep feelings of regret and apologize for what I said at the assembly."

Tilting her head, Elizabeth took in his bent posture and down-turned mouth. He appeared truly apologetic for his choice of words at the assembly, so it was easy for her to say, "Although there was no offense taken, Mr. Darcy, I appreciate your apology and accept it. You may put the incident out of your mind. Though I will reserve the right to remind you if I see you misspeak again."

Although Elizabeth's initial inclination to forgive him was based on her friendship with Georgianna, the more she discovered about him, even if it was only a glimpse, the more she desired to unravel his mysteries. After all, for all that he had been cold at the assembly, he had been nothing but solicitous this morning. Elizabeth, who was accustomed to taking care of everyone, found herself captivated by Mr. Darcy's attention to her needs. It was unusual for Elizabeth to be cared for, but she couldn't deny the pleasant feeling it brought her.

DARCY FELT HIS BROW wrinkle as he watched Miss Elizabeth leave the room. She had not taken a very long respite from caring for her sister and was quick to return to Miss Bennet's side. He had rarely met someone so selfless in society. Regardless of the relationship, many people he knew would have passed on the responsibility of caring for the ill individual to the servants.

It was no wonder Georgianna had so many good things to say about her friend. She was certainly unlike any ladies of the ton that were constantly being paraded before him, which only made his comments at the assembly worse. Yet she had willingly forgiven him without hesitation. He lacked knowledge of Miss Elizabeth, which prompted him to feel the need for further study.

For some time, he had dismissed Georgianna's comments about her friend *Lizzie* as mere exaggeration. After all, she had gone most of her life without a close friend. Of course she would think well of the girl. No gentleman's daughter would truly study tomes in the original Latin or truly dislike shopping for fripperies. But after meeting Miss Elizabeth, he realized she was all his sister claimed her to be.

Pushing back from the table, Darcy went to Bingley's study. Hopefully his friend was up, and they could talk. If not, he could hide from Miss Bingley for as long as he was able. Entering with the slightest of knocks, Darcy was happy to find Bingley at the desk, reading from a stack of papers.

Bingley put the stack of papers down only to pick up his coffee and take a sip. Thus fortified, he said, "Good morning, Darcy. I've followed your recommendation and now, by waking with the sun, I'm accomplishing so much more." Taking another sip of coffee, he added, "It certainly helps that I can work while my sister is still abed and less likely to barge in and waylay me."

"Yes, I had a feeling you would accomplish more whilst your sister was incapable of disturbing you," Darcy replied with a laugh as he sat down in one of the armchairs facing the desk. "Actually, speaking of Miss Bingley, I was curious to hear of how things lie between you at the moment. We did not get a chance to discuss matters yesterday."

Bingley set down his coffee cup and ran his hand through his hair, turning it in to a riot of curls that would probably give his valet fits. Frowning, Bingley said, "I am at my wit's end with Caroline. It seems that when Miss Bennet arrived soaked from the rain, the only consideration she gave her was to allow her to sit closer to the fire. She did not offer to allow her to dry herself or even offer a change of clothes. It is no wonder that Miss Bennet fell ill. I know I am new to running an estate, but that cannot be the way you see things run."

Darcy could not hide his disgust. "That she looks down on the gentry of Meryton—who have been the stewards of these lands for centuries—while she is the daughter of a tradesman is utterly abhorrent. I do not think your sister truly understands what it means to be genteel or even a proper hostess. Regardless of rank or position in life, we should always see to the comfort of guests and offer them every courtesy."

Slouching in his chair, Bingley groaned, "I do not think anything I said had any effect on her. What is worse is I made Louisa my hostess, but she cedes to Caroline in all things. I am tempted to send them back to London and try to manage on my own, but you know how social I am. I had wanted to hold dinners and the like."

"You know that if your sisters were to have the local families over, they would spend the whole time sneering at them," Darcy cautioned. "It would do you no favors. Frankly you would do better sending them back to town."

"Would you believe she did not see it as her responsibility to see to Miss Bennet's care?" Bingley said with a huff. "I found out that it was only Mrs. Nichols's oversight that a room and maid had been assigned to her. When Mr. Jones could not come yesterday, Caroline wanted to send Miss Bennet home despite her fever. Miss Bennet, from what I know of her, is kindness personified. She does not deserve such spite."

"Neither does Miss Elizabeth," added Darcy.

Taking a gulp of his coffee, Bingley stared at the empty cup before saying, "I am only glad that Miss Elizabeth took a tray in her room last night and was not present to hear my sisters talk about her."

"You will have to do something about your sister. Her arrogant behavior and judgmental nature will alienate the kindhearted people of Meryton. She will make it nearly impossible for you to settle in as a new landowner. If she was not your sister, I would have cut her long ago." Rubbing at his forehead, Darcy thought about how his friendship with Bingley had prevented him from treating Miss Bingley as she deserved to be treated. Meanwhile he had been treating who knew how many young ladies with undeserved derision.

Getting up, Bingley poured himself more coffee from the waiting carafe. Looking at Darcy, he said, "Yes, and I appreciate your forbearance, though maybe it is time to treat her differently. Asking her to behave as I wish to has done nothing. Frankly, I wish I could send her back to the schoolroom with a strict governess."

WITH A CONTENTED SIGH, Georgianna sank into the chair by the crackling fireplace in her room, and wrapped a snug shawl around her shoulders for added warmth. Despite the damp and rainy day, Georgianna was quite excited. She had received a letter from Lizzie, and she could not wait to read it.

Having received the letter shortly before her lesson with Master Rossini, she had already had to wait long enough. She marveled at how she maintained her focus on the smooth black and white keys, despite her eager anticipation. As much as she would have liked to be in Meryton with her brother and Lizzie, Master Rossini had been a tremendous boon to her playing. He had been amazing at helping her imbue the music with more feeling. That afternoon, Master Rossini had even commended her on the improvement that she had shown.

Georgianna broke open the seal with a sigh. She had only recently received William's very apologetic letter and hoped to learn of his apology to Lizzie in her letter. At least he had better have apologized. If he had not yet apologized, then she would find a way to go confront him.

Netherfield, Meryton

Dear Georgianna,

Yes, you have read the address correctly. I am currently residing at Netherfield. I know you must be full of curiosity regarding my stay here with the charming Miss Bingley. Do not worry; I will tell you how this came about, but first it will take me going back a bit.

Three days ago, Miss Bingley invited my older sister Jane to tea at Netherfield while also informing her that the gentlemen would be out. I suspect that Miss Bingley only invited her in order to gain information with which to disparage my family. My sister Jane would never suspect such underhanded motives, though I warned her to keep her guard up.

The problem arose when my mother realized that it looked like rain. She demanded that Jane ride on horseback and refused her the use of the carriage. My father thought his wife's antics comical and supported her, getting a good laugh in the process. While I would have refused to go in such a situation, Jane is very obedient and went on horseback as directed.

So my poor Jane arrived at Netherfield wet through, having made her way to Netherfield in a thunderstorm. The storm prevented her from returning home that evening and by morning, she was quite ill. Sadly, my mother was quite happy to receive the news that Jane was ill because she felt this would give her the opportunity to capture either your brother or Mr. Bingley. I have journeyed to Netherfield to help look after Jane, as I do not trust Miss Bingley to lift a finger for her care.

By now you must be wondering at my mother's attitude. It would take pages to fully explain my mother, but I can sum it up by saying that my mother is the very worst sort of matchmaking mother. If I am being honest, though, it is not entirely her fault. She is of mean understanding and instead of helping her understand, my father enjoys mocking her and watching her fail.

Have I told you that our home is entailed away from the female line? As it stands, a cousin several times removed named Mr. Collins will inherit when my father dies. He is some twelve years older than my mother and she worries incessantly that this cousin will throw us from the house the moment he comes to take Longbourn on my father's death. Because my parents have never attempted to save money for such a predicament, my mother's fears are entirely justified. However, you and I both know that dressing my sisters in expensive lace and throwing them at anyone in pants won't solve the problem. Every time I attempt to explain the flaws in her strategy to save us, she turns a deaf ear and dismisses my concerns.

I really must end my letter now. Jane looks to be rousing, and I must get her to drink as much as I can while she is awake. I will try to write to you again soon.

Your friend,

Lizzie

Georgianna looked over her letter from Lizzie a second time with a frown. Though she would never wish illness or Miss Bingley on anyone, Georgianna was happy that somehow Lizzie had ended up at Netherfield. Wanting her brother and Lizzie to develop a friendship, she saw the importance of having them in proximity to each other. She hoped that despite Jane's illness, they might speak occasionally. Although Lizzie had not mentioned an apology, her preoccupation with caring for her ill sister was clearly visible.

While she felt a certain amount of happiness knowing that Lizzie would be closer to her brother, learning about Lizzie's mother took her by surprise. Georgianna had always known that she was privileged, but it had never truly occurred to her just how much so. It was outrageous that Lizzie's mother had sent her daughter into inclement weather, hoping it would help her catch a husband. But then again, the woman seemed to be terrified of the genuine possibility of being made homeless, along with all of her daughters.

The blatant favoritism towards men was never more evident to her than in that moment. The sheer audacity of an unfamiliar man asserting his dominance and displacing women who had resided in a home their entire lives, all because of his gender and personal desires, was nothing short of disgraceful. Yet it was apparently the law of the land. Mrs. Annesley was right—life wasn't fair.

Chapter Eleven

ELIZABETH WAS RELIEVED WHEN Jane's fever broke shortly before Mr. Jones arrived. The kind apothecary had arrived shortly before midday and assured Elizabeth that Jane was through the worst of it. He advised she might return in two days if her fever did not return. Mr. Jones left Elizabeth with more tea made with feverfew and birch bark and advised that Jane should drink it with honey several times a day to help with her lingering sore throat. Elizabeth was truly happy to see her sister was more like herself, though it would have been nice to use Jane's illness as an excuse to take a tray above stairs and avoid Miss Bingley and, to a lesser extent, Mrs. Hurst.

As she approached the parlor where the Netherfield party gathered to wait for dinner to be announced, Elizabeth took a deep breath and straightened her shoulders. She had dealt with her share of ladies who were determined to make her see her place in the world during her time at the Ladies London Society. This was no different, though someone as supercilious as Miss Bingley had never confronted her. After all, she was, in fact, the daughter of a tradesman, and thus she would never be above Elizabeth in the eyes of society, whatever her dowry.

With each step closer to the room, she could hear more of the ongoing conversation. Despite the closed door, Miss Bingley's voice carried easily, its stridency reaching Elizabeth as she said, "I still do not see why we must open our home to the Bennets. I only invited Miss Bennet for tea, and to my surprise, she had the audacity to feign illness. As for Miss Eliza, she was not invited at all."

Pausing before the door, Elizabeth debated if it was best for her to enter or wait until Miss Bingley finished complaining. Before she could decide, she heard Mr. Bingley's response. "Caroline! That is completely out of line. This is exactly why I refused to allow you to be my hostess. They are guests in my home. It is not your place to speak so poorly of them. Besides, we all know that Miss Bennet is truly sick and not pretending. Perhaps Miss Bennet would be better off if you and Louisa had seen to her needs when she arrived wet. And if Miss Elizabeth came to minister to her sister, you are the only one to blame. After all, your behavior since we have arrived at Netherfield would not reassure her into thinking that you would care for her sister adequately."

The soft murmur that followed could only be Mrs. Hurst, who rarely raised her voice and reminded Elizabeth of Kitty. She seemed to be more of a follower who went through life in the wake of her younger sister's dynamic though vindictive personality. Just as Elizabeth was about to enter the room, she heard the faint sound of footsteps approaching from behind her.

As she turned around, her eyes met Mr. Darcy's as he approached her. Before she could utter a word of greeting, Miss Bingley's voice rose once again, "You are blind, Charles! You cannot see how they are only here in a ploy to entice you and Mr. Darcy with their arts and allurements. They are graceless nobodies who I have heard have very little in the way of dowries. They must be desperate to escape this backwater town, and you and Mr. Darcy are their means to do so."

Mr. Bingley was quick to respond by saying, "Keep your voice down, Caroline. Any minute now, Miss Elizabeth will grace us with her presence, and I do not want her to hear your nonsensical ramblings."

Elizabeth, though not embarrassed, was at a loss as to what she should say. Mr. Darcy, on the other hand, smiled kindly before saying, "As much as I enjoy spending time with my friend Bingley, I find it is best to wait to come down until just before they announce dinner." Offering her his arm, he added, "Shall we brave them together? At least that way we can defend one another should the need arise."

Taking his offered arm, Elizabeth smiled up into Mr. Darcy's blue eyes and said, "I would be more than happy to defend you, kind sir, though I wonder what exactly I am to protect you from?"

Eyes dancing, Mr. Darcy said, "Our host's sister has the habit of gripping my arm like a falcon attacking its prey the moment she sees me. Beyond that, she presumes to declare how I feel about things, and I have not the ability to refute her without insult."

Struggling to suppress a giggle, Elizabeth responded, "Taking a gentleman's arm is a skill that sadly all not all ladies can acquire."

Quirking an eyebrow, Mr. Darcy asked, "Do you think not?"

"Miss Bingley is proof of not being able to learn the skill."

"True." Smile widening, Mr. Darcy continued, "Do you have any tips I can pass on to my sister? I would hate for her not to learn the skill."

"Well, first she must know that you only take a gentleman's arm when it is offered," explained Elizabeth.

Nodding, Mr. Darcy said, "After that, what recommendations should I provide to Georgianna?"

Careful to keep her hand softly on his arm and nothing like what she had observed of Miss Bingley, Elizabeth said, "She must never clutch at a gentleman's arm. Instead, you let your hand glide gracefully and rest there. Always like a dove gliding to her perch, never a falcon seeking prey."

They were both laughing as they entered the parlor and Mr. Bingley asked, "What are you talking about that has you both so jolly?"

Elizabeth caught Mr. Darcy's eye for a moment and her eyes crinkled in mirth before she answered, "We were discussing birds."

Face screwing up in confusion, Miss Bingley huffed, "Really, Miss Eliza, birds? I cannot have you bothering my guests with such inconsequential drivel."

"You forget, sister, Mr. Darcy is my guest, not yours," asserted Mr. Bingley. Then, looking at Mr. Darcy and Elizabeth, he added, "Besides, it does not appear to have disturbed Darcy to discuss birds in the least."

Mr. Darcy escorted Elizabeth to a seat while Mr. Bingley was remonstrating with his sister. She had just sat down and was thanking Mr. Darcy when someone announced dinner. Smiling, Mr. Darcy once again held out his arm to Elizabeth, only to have Miss Bingley come streaking across the room in an attempt to grasp his arm. Turning his glare on the presumptuous woman, Mr. Darcy exclaimed, "I was offering Miss Bennet my arm, Miss Bingley, not you."

Miss Bingley froze, and Elizabeth watched as her flushed cheeks took on a vermilion shade that clashed with both the burnt orange of her dress and her carrot-colored hair. Though she felt slightly bad that the lady had been so embarrassed, Elizabeth felt that there was a lesson she learned from the situation. Then, ignoring the woman altogether, Elizabeth focused on Mr. Darcy, who once again offered her his arm. "May I escort you into dinner, Miss Bennet?"

Laying her hand on his offered arm, she answered, "Yes, Mr. Darcy, you may."

As Darcy made his way into the dining room, he was quick to notice that there were place cards, and someone placed him between Mrs. Hurst and Miss Bingley. Knowing he would not survive another night surrounded by their inane chatter, he quickly switched some cards around and put Miss Bennet next to him. Holding the chair out for her, he couldn't help but notice the mischievous glint in Miss Elizabeth's eyes and the playful curve of her smile. It seemed she had caught his subterfuge and approved. Darcy knew he could not hide his glee at his subtle jab at Miss Bingley's pretensions, but found he enjoyed sharing it with Miss Elizabeth.

He sat, smiling slightly as everyone else finally entered, and he wondered if Bingley had needed to calm his sister before they came into the dining room. Though everyone else came in and sat without issue, Miss Bingley once again froze, realizing that her plans had been thwarted.

She opened her mouth, most likely to complain when her brother cut in by saying, "What are you doing standing there, Caroline? Come sit down so that we can be served. I am hungry."

"But the seating arrangement," sputtered Miss Bingley.

The normally silent Hurst complained, "There is nothing wrong with the arrangement. Sit down or leave. I am hungry as well."

Marching to her newly assigned seat, Miss Bingley threw herself down with a disgruntled huff. As the dinner progressed, Miss

Bingley became increasingly upset. None of the dishes met her expectations—the sauce was either overly salty or lacking in flavor, and the meat was dry and overcooked. She found reason to complain about anything and everything.

Engaging in lighthearted conversation with Miss Elizabeth, Darcy realized how much more enjoyable it was when compared to the relentless gossip and complaints he had learned to disregard while seated next to Miss Bingley. Darcy tried to ignore the glares that Miss Bingley was shooting at him and Miss Elizabeth from across the table. Miss Bingley pounced when Miss Elizabeth commented on how much she enjoyed the simple way the roasted vegetables had been prepared.

Frowning, Miss Bingley said, "It is such a pity that you have not been able to know the truly good food produced by a French chef. You cannot know what you are missing stuck out here in the wilds."

Miss Elizabeth smiled unaffectedly and asked, "Is it your belief that those with a sophisticated palate can only be satisfied by a French chef? What about the individuals who delight in the flavors of English fare, meticulously prepared by their English chefs?"

Shaking her head, Miss Bingley's tone became condescending as she said, "Miss Elizabeth, no one of note has an English chef. It is simply not done. I tried to convince my brother to replace the chef already employed at Netherfield, but sadly he said that, per the lease, we could release none of the staff."

Turning to Darcy, Miss Elizabeth said, "Mr. Darcy, what is your favorite dish prepared by your French chef in town?"

Did Miss Elizabeth know he did not have a French chef? Darcy watched Miss Elizabeth's green eyes dance as she waited for his reply and struggled not to smile as he answered her. "While I do not have a French chef at Darcy House, I quite enjoy the spare rib my English chef prepares on occasion, and I believe Georgianna prefers her vegetable pie."

Across the table, Miss Bingley's mouth dropped open, but Miss Elizabeth ignored her. "While I understand everyone has their own preference and tastes, I have never been fond of the heavy sauces found in French cooking. What is your opinion of the current fashion of preferring a French chef?"

Enjoying the playful conversation with Miss Elizabeth, perhaps more than he should, Darcy answered, "I agree with you. I much prefer being able to taste a good cut of meat rather than struggling to find it under a heavy sauce. As for the trend of having French chefs, I have never found that it made sense to choose your cook by what is popular rather than your own tastes. While there are undoubtedly people who genuinely appreciate French cuisine, I think just as many people choose it solely to satisfy their pretentious inclinations with a French chef. I doubt I will ever have a French chef at either Darcy House or Pemberley."

After that, Miss Bingley spoke little and merely poked at her food. When the meal was coming to a close, and the women were rising to leave, Miss Elizabeth politely excused herself, informing everyone that she had promised her sister to bring a book from the library to read aloud. After making his own excuse, Darcy made his way to the library, the scent of old books filling his nostrils as he entered the quiet space.

He watched Miss Elizabeth run her slender finger down the spines of a few books before clearing his throat. She turned, startled at first, but when she saw it was him, she smiled. Encouraged, he said, "I wanted to thank you for such an enjoyable dinner, Miss Elizabeth. Miss Bingley so often dominates the meals here, so it was a pleasure to see you be able to hold your own."

Playing with the book she had been looking at, Miss Elizabeth said, "I enjoyed the meal more than I thought I would. Though I feel slightly guilty for having so confounded Miss Bingley. She may be difficult to get along with, but that does not give me the lease to be so mischievous."

"If someone constantly spews forth prejudice and small-minded opinions, eventually it will come back to bite them," Darcy reassured her. "Miss Elizabeth, you did nothing wrong. You simply defended yourself from the attack of a small-minded woman. She should not only know better but also do better, considering you are a guest in her home."

Miss Elizabeth watched him for a moment, head tilted, before she said, "Thank you for defending me, Mr. Darcy. It is not often that I have witnessed a gentleman willing to do so. Many men prefer to overlook the actions of women, believing they are too elevated to be bothered by such trivialities."

Darcy knew what she meant. There was a time not so long ago that he might have just tuned out Miss Bingley's nastiness without a thought for the person she was attacking. Once upon a time he had thought that as a Darcy, he was above such petty sniping, but he was trying to be better than that now. Sighing, he said, "At one point, I might have been as you say, but I am trying to journey down a path of self-improvement. Something Georgianna said when she took me to task for insulting you has made me think of the tales of chivalrous knights. At one point, gentlemen patterned themselves after knights, striving to be honorable and free from ignoble actions and self-centered motives. However, regrettably, as a whole, we are straying from the ideal we should strive for."

Blushing delightfully, Miss Elizabeth cried, "I had no intention of Georgianna bringing you to task. I am so sorry."

Darcy stepped forward slightly and reached out his hand, wanting to comfort her in her distress. "Don't be. I needed to hear it and to have my eyes opened. Hearing my worth bandied about always unsettles me, but that does not mean I may injure others. I have always believed that I upheld the good principles I grew up with, but I have only now realized that I let my pride and conceit, which I was long exposed to, guide my actions. I want to do better, and to become the chivalrous man I always thought I was."

"Then I wish you success on your journey of improvement. I have learned for myself that it is a lifelong journey, and one must always continue to strive to do better or there is a risk of deviating from the goal." Miss Elizabeth smiled at him before turning back to the shelf and selecting a book and moving to leave. She paused in the doorway as she left the room, a look of concern on her face as she did so. After only a slight hesitation, she said, "You might wish to know that from the moment Miss Bingley arrived at the assembly, she proclaimed that as a man of ten-thousand pounds a year you could have no interest in such a plebeian gathering in the backwoods of nowhere. She did not modulate her voice or attempt to hide her contempt for everyone and everything. She even went to the extent of proclaiming that her brother's wealth and her dowry made her superior to everyone there. You might consider if the dances you attend with Miss Bingley are the ones where people discuss your wealth. I believe she might be the source of at least some of your troubles. It might help you view my neighbors better if you knew they were mostly gossiping about her bad manners and what she said and not your monetary value."

Thus speaking her piece, Miss Elizabeth quit the room, presumably to once again minister to her ill sister. Darcy did not rejoin the party as he had previously intended. Instead, he collapsed onto the nearest chair and thought of all that Miss Elizabeth had revealed to him that night.

Chapter Twelve

Riding back to Longbourn in the carriage provided by Mr. Bingley, Elizabeth kept a careful eye on her sister. Jane was healthy enough to return home to finish recovering, though she was by no means completely well. Their mother had once again refused them the use of the carriage in a ploy to force them to remain, but feeling that staying any longer would be inappropriate, Elizabeth had asked for the use of Mr. Bingley's carriage to return home.

Surprisingly, Elizabeth had enjoyed the stay at Netherfield. Despite the weight of caring for her sister and worrying over her, she carved out moments in the morning to enjoy breakfast with Mr. Darcy. During these stolen moments, she discovered his skill as a captivating conversationalist and debater. She quickly learned that they had enjoyed many of the same books, though they did not always hold the same view on those books.

It had been several years since her father had been willing to discuss what she read, and so Elizabeth had thoroughly enjoyed the opportunity she found with Mr. Darcy. They had even attempted a game or two of chess. While Miss Bingley derided her manly interest in chess, Mr. Darcy was quick to defend her. She would miss the opportunity to spend time with him, but Mr. Darcy assured her that there were already plans in place to call on the Bennets as soon as propriety would allow.

Still easily tired, Jane laid her head on Elizabeth's shoulder before saying, "Do you think Mama will be angry that we did not stay at Netherfield for the entire week as she demanded?"

Sighing, Elizabeth thought back to her mother's response to her request for the carriage to return home once Mr. Jones said that it was safe for Jane to travel. Her mother had said by all means Elizabeth could return, but she would not send the carriage. Since Elizabeth had walked there, she could walk back. As for Jane, their mother had said that Jane should play the invalid and extend her stay, being sure to stay in Mr. Bingley's company to capture his attention and not come home until she had contrived at least a courtship from the man.

Patting Jane's hand, Elizabeth consoled her. "Mama will not be angry at you, especially if you tell her Mr. Bingley wants to call on us as soon as may be. No matter what Mama wants, neither of you know each other well enough to enter into a courtship. Frankly, I spoke with Mr. Bingley more than you did while we were there. Though

I can tell you now, I have no interest in his courting me. Not that Mama would ever encourage such a match."

Looking at Elizabeth, Jane asked, "Why wouldn't you want to be courted by Mr. Bingley? He is everything that is good, and his happy manners are quite appealing."

Smiling at her sister's quick defense of the man, Elizabeth answered, "He is also very agreeable and handsome, and I give you leave to like him if you choose to, but he is not for me. I yearn for someone who can challenge me and is of a more responsible disposition. I do not want a gentleman I could so easily direct about. So I give you leave to fall in love with Mr. Bingley as long as you take your time getting to know him."

At that, they both giggled happily, finishing the ride to Longbourn in merry chatter about nothing. When the carriage stopped and one of the footmen opened the door, Jane, well wrapped in two shawls, descended the stairs with his help. Elizabeth easily followed and was quick to wrap her arm around her sister's waist as they walked towards the entrance to Longbourn.

Sadly, they had not made it far before their mother descended upon them. "What have you done, you hateful girl! I told you that you should come home, not that you should take Jane away from Mr. Bingley. Have you no compassion for my nerves? How can Jane catch Mr. Bingley if she is here and he is there?"

Elizabeth ignored her mother's rant, and instead she moved with Jane into the house. It was cold outside, and she did not want Jane relapsing. She knew from her experience that her mother did not want her to defend herself, so she did not.

Jane, however, hated it when their mother berated any of her sisters, so she said, "Mama, Mr. Jones said that it would be best that I return home to finish recovering. Elizabeth's priority was my well-being, and it would have been impolite to stay after Mr. Jones suggested I go back home."

This turned Mrs. Bennet's attention to her oldest daughter. "I cannot believe that your sister was seeing to you as she should if this is how you look. Your beauty has all but faded. There is no bloom in your cheeks and your hair has lost its shine. We must get you inside at once. We cannot have anyone seeing you like this." Pulling Jane away from Elizabeth, Mrs. Bennet rushed her into the house. Calling back over her shoulder, she said, "Do not dawdle, Elizabeth. Your father said that his horrid cousin is coming to Longbourn this afternoon. Since I will be responsible for your sister's care, I trust you will make all the necessary arrangements."

Elizabeth shook her head as she watched her mother bustle into the house with her sister, the Bingleys' carriage crunching on the gravel behind her as it left. She knew it was wrong of her to want to turn around and walk away from all that was her life at Longbourn, but in that moment it was all she wanted to do. Drawing a deep breath of air into her lungs, Elizabeth trudged toward her home.

She was not at all surprised that her mother had foisted the arrangements for their last-minute guest on to her. Ever since Jane was fourteen, and she was thirteen, the true mistress's duties for Longbourn had been theirs. Their mother only indulged in the parts of being the mistress of an estate that she enjoyed, such as hosting elaborate dinners to impress their neighbors.

Instead of retreating to her room to rest as she wished, Elizabeth sought out Mrs. Hill to discuss the progress made on behalf of the Longbourn heir. Among the many guest rooms available, Elizabeth was determined to find one that would both impress him with its elegance and put him far away from her and her sisters. Regardless, she was going to have a footman stationed in the hallway where she and her sisters resided. She did not know what kind of man he was, and she was not about to leave them unprotected.

BETWEEN HIS PREOCCUPATION WITH Miss Elizabeth's departure, and Miss Bingley's unending chatter, it was difficult for Darcy to read. No matter how he tried to concentrate, he could not make his mind focus on the words before him. Part of the problem was that Miss Bingley was incessantly harping on the people of Meryton and Miss Bennet and Miss Elizabeth, in particular.

As she flipped through the pages of a ladies' magazine, Miss Bingley leaned over to Louisa and said, "I overheard some gossip at one of those dreadful social events we attended, claiming that she is regarded as one of the area's jewels. Jewels? She came uninvited with her petticoats six inches in mud. It just goes to show how provincial these people are."

"No, Miss Elizabeth is nothing like any ladies we associate with from town." Darcy noted that while Mrs. Hurst seemed to agree with her sister, she also said nothing that was not true.

Miss Elizabeth was not anything like the women they associated with. She was not petty, and certainly not like many of the harpies in town. Despite having only known Miss Elizabeth for a few days, he couldn't help but miss her, and found he was drawn to her kindness, capability, and intelligence. This was an uncommon occurrence for him.

Darcy debated the wisdom of curtailing Miss Bingley's mean-spirited comments. Miss Bingley was the sort of woman who would not be curbed by any criticism on his part. More than that, he feared that if he defended Miss Elizabeth, it would only paint a target on her back in Miss Bingley's eyes. It was for those reasons the Darcy kept his peace, but Miss Bingley would not stop.

After studying one of the fashion plates in the magazine for a time, she turned the page again. This time she said, "While Miss Bennet's beauty is unquestionable, Miss Elizabeth cannot hold a candle to her older sister. I suppose her teeth are white and even, but really, I can find nothing in her countenance to recommend her." Then, tittering in a way that ground against his nerves, she added, "I heard it said that she meets with Longbourn's steward about the care of the tenants and various other issues. She even goes to the tenants' homes to provide aid to those in need. Can you imagine, Louisa? Going to one of those hovels?"

Unable to fight his inclination any longer, Darcy said, "I am happy that you have finally realized that you are not suited to being the mistress of an estate. When will you be returning to London in your search for a husband?" Pausing, he pretended to consider something before adding, "I hear that second and third sons who have taken up law or trade are often looking for brides with large dowries."

Mouth gaping, Miss Bingley stared at him in horror while across the room, Mr. Hurst had sat up, proving that he had, in fact, not been asleep on the settee. Bingley looked back and forth between his sister and Darcy as if waiting for someone to make the next move in a deadly game. Miss Bingley came out of her stupor in a rush and cried, "What are you saying, Mr. Darcy? I can plan dinners and throw balls. The best masters have trained me on both the piano and the harp exquisitely. I would make the perfect mistress of an estate."

Closing the book that he had not been reading, Darcy stared at Miss Bingley, determined she would hear him. "The mistress of an estate is not a mere ornament, there to hold entertainments and feed people. The mistress of an estate visits the tenants and sees to their needs. She coordinates the care of the dairy and the home farm and the herb garden. In the stillroom, she makes lotions and soaps and unguents. She makes sure everyone under her preview is healthy, warm, and well-dressed. That includes the tenants and servants and, sometimes, the poor of the closest town. If necessary, she sews their clothes herself."

Miss Bingley had listened to him, her eyes widening with every word. When Darcy stopped, she whispered, "You must be joking with me, Mr. Darcy. Surely you would not want your wife mingling with people so beneath her. There must be someone else who sees to all of those things."

"No, I am not joking. No wife of mine would ever believe herself above other people how you imply. Even my dear mother, the daughter of an earl, rode out regularly to check on the tenants and dispense aid to those in need. In even the smallest of estates, the mistress is required to see to the tasks that I named. All of which are tasks Miss Elizabeth carries out without complaint. Deriding her shows only your ignorance." Shaking his head, Darcy wondered if he was going too far. He had only recently promised himself that he would not be cruel. But wasn't it better to make her realize that all her aspirations would not get her what she wanted? Then, too, he wanted to be chivalrous, and wasn't defending a lady the epitome of chivalry even if he was protecting her from another woman?

Sighing, he added, "I do not want to hurt you, Miss Bingley, but we will never suit. I have hoped you would come to an understanding of this on your own, but you are going too far. When the Bennet sisters visited Netherfield, you failed to extend them even the basic courtesies of hospitality that I would expect of the mistress of my estate. Gossip, fashion, and all things popular in society are not to my liking. I hope you can comprehend that we are not a good match. You would be better off in town, where people focus on the petty matters that seem to captivate you."

Finally, looking away from Miss Bingley's pale face, Darcy noticed Hurst's smile. It seemed that his speech was at least approved of by one person. He still felt as if he should apologize to Bingley for speaking out of turn, though not a word he had said was untrue.

Miss Bingley, still pale, glanced around the room and, eyes landing on her brother, said, "Charles, say something to Mr. Darcy. Tell him that his is wrong."

Frowning at his sister, Bingley said, "I cannot Caroline, he is right. I have been trying to make you understand he is not the right person for you and that he lacks any interest in you."

Spinning back around, Miss Bingley glared at Darcy before fleeing the room. Darcy watched her go before turning back to Bingley and apologizing. Bingley only shrugged and replied, "Caroline has not listened to me. It needed to be said, and you needed to be the one to say it. It was time."

Hurst laughed and said, "It was long overdue," from across the room.

Miss Darcy giggled as she read her brother's latest letter, causing Mrs. Annesley to look up from her embroidery. Smiling at her charge's joy, Mrs. Annesley asked, "What do you find so humorous in your brother's letter?"

Eyes dancing, Miss Darcy said, "Although it's good news that Lizzie's sister is well enough to go back home to Longbourn, I believe he's regretting their departure from Netherfield. William writes of how much he has enjoyed coming to know Miss Elizabeth, as he calls her. Her wide range of knowledge and her ability to debate competently over differing opinions has surprised him." Pausing, her expression lost some of its joy as she continued, "I know I told him they had much in common. Do you think he did not believe me?"

Putting down her embroidery hoop, Mrs. Annesley said, "Consider the women he knows. Even those who claim to enjoy reading would never dare express an unpopular opinion. If someone questioned them on their beliefs, they would be completely incapable of supporting their views in debate. Miss Bingley, for example, would immediately change her views to match your brother's. It might not be so much that he did not believe you, but that he underestimated the truth behind your words."

Fidgeting with the edge of the letter in her hand, Georgianna responded, "I suppose you are right. If all the women he knows are like Miss Bingley, Lizzie would come as a pleasant shock. I can only hope that he enjoys spending time with her so much that he will want her spending more time with us as a family." Folding the letter back up, Georgianna grinned and picked up her own sewing project.

As Mrs. Annesley observed Miss Darcy, her eyes narrowed, and she couldn't help but notice the telltale blush that appeared on Miss Darcy's cheeks as she averted her gaze. "Miss Darcy, are you hoping that something develops between your brother and Miss Bennet?"

Blush intensifying, Miss Darcy smiled before she confessed, "I think Lizzie would be the very best of sisters. She would be a wonderful mistress to Pemberley, and I think my brother would be happy to have a wife he could talk to intelligently."

Sighing, Mrs. Annesley said, "You know, finding a marriage mate is more complicated than finding someone you can debate with."

"Yes, yes, I know. But I can hope, can't I?" chirped Miss Darcy.

Taking her embroidery hoop back up, Mrs. Annesley acquiesced, "Yes, you can hope, but don't forget that you have another week of lessons before we can go to Meryton."

Concentrating on the rose that she was currently trying to embroider, Miss Darcy said, "I am already planning on what to pack so that we can leave first thing the next morning."

Chuckling, Mrs. Annesley worked on her own project. It would be interesting to see Miss Bennet and Mr. Darcy interact with one another. As sweet as Miss Bennet was, she did not have the best prospects, and it would be a wonderful thing if she caught the eye of a man like her employer. There were certainly many worse options.

Chapter Thirteen

Elizabeth was not a tall woman. She was the shortest of all her sisters, not that this bothered her. In fact, it was a boon as it meant that she could borrow any of her sisters' dresses with just a slight alteration to the hem. As the tallest of the girls, Jane could not borrow from her sisters, though being their mother's favorite, she had more dresses than any of her sisters save Lydia, so it was not an issue.

So it was a surprise to Elizabeth when she greeted her father's cousin and had to look down to look him in the eye. Or attempt to look him in the eye. It was disconcerting to realize that his gaze had fixated quite a bit below her face. Fighting the desire to cross her arms in front of herself, Elizabeth cleared her throat, drawing his attention away from her chest.

Mr. Collins had a narrow face with dark eyes set close together and a notable overbite. It was peculiar how his body didn't align with his head; it appeared there was an excess weight that contradicted his small size and narrow face. Elizabeth suppressed a shudder as she met the man's eyes, sensing the unmistakable lust behind his beady gaze. Glancing at her father, who stood beside her, Elizabeth hoped to see some anger at his heir's actions or at least irritation, but she found none. He only shrugged and said, "Welcome to Longbourn, Mr. Collins."

After bowing in a subservient fashion more fit to greet a royal, Mr. Collins glanced along the line of Bennets and frowned. Looking back at Mr. Bennet, Mr. Collins said, "I was told, cousin, that you have a wife and five daughters, but I only see four young ladies present. Why have you not commanded everyone to come greet me, your heir and future master of Longbourn?"

Elizabeth could hear Mary gasp from beside her and Lydia, at the end of the line, giggle as she did when she became nervous. Her father coughed, and Elizabeth wondered if he was attempting not to laugh outright at his heir. After clearing his throat, Mr. Bennet replied to the presumptuous question. "My oldest daughter is currently getting over an illness, and her mother is tending to her care. Therefore, at the moment, you will only meet those of us present here."

Nodding his head, Mr. Collins replied, "That is wise of you. It would be the rudest action to expose me to an illness. It would not do for me to return to my patroness, Lady Catherine de Bourgh, carrying contagion. Her daughter, known as the rose of Kent, has fragile health and it would be unforgivable to expose her to illness."

Elizabeth thought he had finished speaking when he stopped to take a breath, but he continued on. "I want to assure you all that my stay here as I view my future property is more than incumbent. I am also here, granting an olive branch. The rift that formed between our two branches of family and the subsequent injustice that unfolded will remain unspoken. Only know that I will not seek to punish you for your ancestor's misdeeds. Like my omniscient patroness, I am magnanimous in my decisions and my gifts of mercy."

He would have most likely continued if not for Mr. Bennet simply turning and walking back into the house. Mr. Collins watched him go, mouth agape. When a gust of icy wind had Kitty and Lydia huddling together for warmth, Elizabeth put an end to all the nonsense by saying, "Mr. Collins, it is a cold autumn day, and I am sure that you are tired from your journey. Mrs. Hill, our housekeeper, has a bath ready for you so that you may refresh yourself after your travel."

Smiling, Mr. Collins said, "Thank you for such attention, cousin, but I only bathe once a month."

Elizabeth ignored the gasp that came from one of her sisters and, thinking quickly, said, "You would refuse our hospitality, Mr. Collins? I would not think that someone connected to such a great personage as Lady Catherine de Bourgh would be so inconsiderate."

Eyes bulging in his weasel-like face, Mr. Collins was quick to say, "You are right, cousin. Though it is not my way, it would be rude of me to refuse your hospitality."

"I am glad you agree, Mr. Collins. After all, cleanliness is next to godliness, or at least that is what I have always believed at Longbourn." Forcing herself to smile even as his glance seemed to slip south of her face once more, she gestured for him to enter the house ahead of her and added, "We will partake of dinner in two hours. If you should choose to rest, I am sure a footman will show you into the dining room."

Mr. Collins seemed to perk up at what he perceived as his honor to walk a head of them. He strode into the building without looking back. Linking arms with Mary, she shepherded her sisters into their home and told them she would meet them in the schoolroom. She sought Mrs. Hill and made sure she knew of Mr. Collins's arrival, asking that they have a footman available to cater to his every need. At all times.

Raising an eyebrow, Mrs. Hills face turned hard as she asked, "He is that sort of man then?"

Sighing, Elizabeth rubbed at her forehead. "It was all I could do not to shudder at the way he was leering."

Mrs. Hill, ever the mother hen to the women and girls at Longbourn, said, "I will make sure that the maids work in pairs if they must help him or clean his room. As for providing him a footman to help him, I think I will have Marcus and Johnathan aid him."

Elizabeth gasped, followed by a giggle. "They should be able to handle him with ease. My father's heir is at least a foot shorter than both of them."

"Charles, I am decided it is time for me to return to London. I have wasted far too much time here among the country savages. It seems Mr. Darcy is not the man I thought he was. If I am to marry and establish my place among society, I need to return to the marriage mart as soon as possible." Having said what she wished, Miss Bingley looked at her brother in expectation.

She had come into his study without knocking after having been gone from the family for most of the day. Darcy wondered if she had even seen him sitting in the wingback chair by the fire. Sitting behind his desk, Bingley studied his sister for a moment before asking, "What would you have me do, Caroline? I have no interest in returning to London. Even if I did not want to court Miss Bennet, I have made commitments here at Netherfield. I cannot flit about. I have responsibilities now."

Miss Bingley had none of her normal cloying mannerisms when she proclaimed, "If you want to tie yourself to that horrid family, I no longer care. I have my own future to see to. Louisa and her lout of a husband have agreed to return to town with me so that I can join the little season. I am determined to accept someone within the year and I do not want to make things more complicated. Please allow Mr. Hurst to approve any requests for courtship or proposals for my hand in marriage. Additionally, I request you permit him to sign my marriage settlement."

Bingley nodded in understanding. "If that is what you wish, I will do so. I want you to be happy, Caroline, and you have not been happy here." Miss Bingley turned to leave, but her brother called after her. "Please choose the man you will tie your life to with care. I would not want you to regret your decision, Caroline."

She looked at her brother for a long moment before smiling faintly and shutting the door behind her. Darcy almost felt like holding his breath while waiting to see what Bingley's reaction would be. Bingley's laughter surprised him, so he asked, "Bingley, are you all right?"

"Do not fret, Darcy, I am fine. I have been trying for the last day to find a way to ensure that my sister does not interfere with my attempt to court Miss Bennet and here she has excused herself from the problem. The only issue is that I can no longer host a ball like I wanted."

For himself, Darcy was happy to be rid of her. "I am glad it has turned out as you wanted. Though I will say that I did not know that you had decided in favor of courting Miss Bennet. While you have often found yourself attracted to ladies you have met in the past, you have never attempted to court any of them."

Moving to pick up his cup of coffee and take a sip, Bingley replied, "While I've had a tendency to be inconsistent with women in the past, this situation is different."

"How so?" asked Darcy.

Putting his cup back down and fiddling with it, Bingley said, "Miss Bennet is different." Looking away from Darcy and instead retreating into his mind, Bingley mused, "Before when I spoke with a young lady, our conversations went nowhere. Everything was superficial and soon enough, I became bored with the fact that not only did I know nothing more about her, but she had no wish to know anything more about me. Miss Bennet was quick to abandon the inconsequential nothings and talk about more substantial things."

"I have often gotten tired of young ladies talking about nothing but the latest on-dits and the weather," sighed Darcy. He hesitated to say that he had once thought that Miss Bennet was the sort of lady who would talk of nothing but bland subjects. Her placid smile had always made him doubt her depth or sincerity. It appeared he did not know as much about the lady as he had once thought. Brows drawing together, Darcy said, "Between both of your cheerful smiles, it seemed like you were engaged in a lighthearted conversation about puppies and other joyful subjects, rather than delving into anything profound. What is it you were talking about?"

Leaning back in his chair, Bingley crossed his arms and asked, "Did you ever think that we were smiling because we enjoy each other's company and not because we were discussing puppies? We have seen each other socially maybe four times and I already know more about her than any other lady I have met. We have spoken of things from what we like about autumn to our worries about our respective siblings." Downing the last of his coffee, Bingley looked at the bottom of his empty cup with a frown.

Putting his cup down, Bingley added, "Would you believe that Miss Bennet and I have discussed the difference and similarity of managing a business and running an estate? She has an uncle who has done very well in trade and so knows something of both. She cares not at all about a suitor's connection to trade. If it meant finding a husband who genuinely loved and respected her, she would gladly settle for one who actively worked in trade."

Bingley's revelations astounded Darcy, but he couldn't deny the happiness he felt for his friend's discovery of such a remarkable woman. Sitting forward, he said, "If that is the case, I am happy for you. I never considered the possibility that you would find a lady so suited to you in the country."

A bark of laughter from Bingley caused Darcy's eyes to widen. Bingley only said, "Darcy, even though I believe you have a romantic soul, you remain blind to love because you never anticipate its presence. You have become cynical about the inherent goodness of people and skeptical about the existence of true love because of the many betrayals you have experienced. When you do finally find love for yourself, it will blindside you."

"WHAT I CANNOT DISCERN is if he is a heretic or merely absurd," complained Mary.

After dinner, all the Bennet sisters had come to Jane's room, where their mother had insisted she convalesced and regain her looks before Mr. Bingley came calling. Jane, unable to spend any time with the sole relative from their father's side, tried to stay optimistic and remarked, "I'm certain he can't be that awful."

This elicited laughs from both Kitty and Lydia. The bolder of the two, Lydia said, "Oh, he really is. His eating habits are atrocious, he spent half his time staring at Elizabeth's bosom, and he said that he only had baths once a month. Though Elizabeth convinced him that he must bathe if we offered it, or he would reject our hospitality."

Elizabeth blushed, knowing her sisters had seen his unnatural fascination with her person. Jane looked at her with wide eye while Mary said, "I did not think it was possible for a man who had dedicated his life to studying and serving God to be so utterly ridiculous. I was most bothered by his saying that his patroness was omniscient. His reverence for her surpasses even that of almighty God."

Rubbing her temple, Elizabeth sighed in frustration as her headache worsened. "I am not as concerned with his absurdity as I am with the way he stares inappropriately. I have asked that one of our footmen stay in his vicinity day and night. Please, I want you all to promise that you will be aware of your surroundings while he is here. Never allow yourself to be alone with him."

Elizabeth studied her sisters and their varied responses to her statement. Mary's eyes had widened and then hardened. Within their parish, there were women who faced constant mistreatment from the men in their lives. Mary took it upon herself to support and care for these women, tending to their injuries and offering a listening ear. Of all her sisters, Mary had seen more of the darkness in the world and was more capable to face it if necessary.

Kitty scooted closer to Mary, eyes wide, but seemed reassured when Mary put her arm around her. Lydia nodded, looking angry, but then leaned over and patted Kitty's hand, sensing her older sister's fear. Jane, still pale from her recent illness, looked sad. Shaking her head, she pleaded, "You cannot think he would be so cruel as to harm one of us. We are family and he is a man of God. Surely, he would never stoop to such wicked deeds."

Taking Jane's hand, Elizabeth looked into her wide eyes and said, "While I would hope not, I will not put my faith in his ability to behave as he should. While he is technically our cousin, it is a very tenuous connection from three generations ago and sadly, not all men of God are good. I would rather we practice caution now than be sorry later." Jane nodded, but still looked sad that such precautions had to be taken.

"Lizzie, do you know what he was talking about when he mentioned our family wronging his?" Kitty asked, confused.

"I think four generations ago a second son of a Bennet married a woman named Miss Collins and changed his name in order to inherit her family estate, but poor investments and mismanagement caused them to lose the estate. For some unknown reason, his son came to Longbourn when his grandfather Bennet died, thinking that because he was the oldest grandson, he should inherit Longbourn."

Huffing, Lydia complained, "Even I know that is not how inheritance works."

Chuckling softly, Elizabeth said, "No, that is not how it works. Still, Mr. Collins was extremely upset. He viewed himself as a gentleman, but he did not have an estate, and he was being forced to support himself. Ever since, the Bennets have received letters and threats from the Collinses. It had not been an issue until this generation when father did not have a son."

Kitty and Lydia began laughing at such foolishness, but their mother burst into the room, interrupting them. "What are you doing in here? Mr. Collins is downstairs waiting for you to return."

Quick to defend her sisters, Jane said, "Do not fret, Mama, they were just coming to check on me and keep me informed of the goings on."

Shaking her head, Mrs. Bennet fussed, "You need to be resting, Jane. I cannot have you losing your beauty, and the rest of you girls need to go down there now."

Elizabeth followed her sisters down the stairs with a sinking feeling in her stomach, which only intensified after her mother said, "My girls were checking on their ill sister. They are all so compassionate and caring. Any of them would make the most wonderful clergyman's wife."

Nodding, the man looked at his cousins, asserting, "They are all beautiful, Mrs. Bennet. I never imagined meeting so many comely ladies when I undertook my trip to Longbourn. I am certainly glad I decided to offer an olive branch to my cousins."

This caused Mrs. Bennet to smile and preen. Elizabeth knew that her mother saw any compliment to her daughters as a compliment to herself. Always looking to marry her daughters off, Elizabeth suspected she was also probably happy to hear about the olive branch he offered.

Elizabeth encouraged Kitty and Lydia to sit in the far corner. They should not have to deal with Mr. Collins if they did not have to. She and Mary sat on a settee facing Mr. Collins and their mother. Their father sat in his customary chair, the one he reserved for the rare occasions when he chose to join the women in his family. While he held a book and appeared to read, Elizabeth had seen his gaze dart to Mr. Collins too many times for it to actually be so.

Picking up her bible from the side table, Mary saw Mr. Collins take a deep breath and decided to circumvent a diatribe by asking, "How long have you been ordained, Mr. Collins?"

His brows drew together slightly for a moment before puffing himself up and saying, "It has been a year since I received my ordination, and for the past seven months, I have served as vicar to her gloriousness, Lady Catherine de Bourgh. She has very much honored me with her magnanimity."

Mary compressed her lips before saying, "Mr. Collins, you have referred to Lady Catherine de Bourgh as both having gloriousness and omniscience. Throughout my extensive exploration of the bible and religious texts, I have yet to discover any instance where the church condones the use of those words for anyone other than God. I am curious to hear how you excuse yourself for those actions."

Elizabeth watched as Mr. Collins's eyes widened and then turned hard. Huffing, he replied, "As a mere girl, you cannot fully comprehend the intricacies of the church as much as you may try. Lady Catherine herself explained to me that her role as lady in Kent is simply an extension of the monarch's right to rule. As the daughter of an earl and the wife of a baronet, her wishes and dictates are holy gifts from God."

In her spot next to Mr. Collins, Mrs. Bennet tittered. "Oh, poor Mary, she is so eager to delve into bible study, but it's clear she could benefit from the guidance of a learned man like yourself."

Elizabeth and Mary looked at each other in shock. The heir to Longbourn was a heretic and a fool. What was worse was that their mother was evidently trying to dangle any of her daughters that she could in front of him. Their father was laughing at the whole situation. Elizabeth could see his shoulders shaking with his repressed merriment.

After glaring at Mary for a moment, Mr. Collins turned to their father. "Cousin Bennet, I have been curious to hear of your interactions with your tenants. How frequently do they make their way to you, proffering their tithes and displaying the proper respect befitting your role as lord of the manor?"

Biting back a cry of outrage, Elizabeth rubbed at her forehead. The heir was more than a fool and a heretic—he was dangerous. If he came to Longbourn with the expectation of being treated like a deity by their tenants, he would soon reduce Longbourn to ruins. Yet there was nothing she could do to stop it, and still her father laughed.

Chapter Fourteen

WHILE IT COULDN'T COMPARE to the Peak District, the little hill that he had been directed to offered quite a view of Meryton. Darcy got off his horse and wrapped his reins around a branch before sitting down on one of the large stones nearby to watch the sunrise. The golden light painting the rooftops of the buildings that dotted the landscape captivated Darcy as he looked out at the valley.

A feminine voice from behind him cut into his contemplation when it said, "I have always enjoyed watching the sunrise from Oakham Mount."

Turning, it startled Darcy to see Miss Elizabeth standing beside him, watching the view. Her face glowed with an inner light as she reveled in the awe-inspiring view. Something about seeing her made the breath catch in Darcy's throat. She completely captivated him, drawn in by the mesmerizing sparkle in her emerald eyes and the enchanting curve of her smile.

With a swallow, Darcy found himself saying, "It is certainly a marvelous sight to behold."

Turning, Miss Elizabeth said, "I have been coming up here for years and it never ceases to take my breath away. It is never exactly the same. There is always something new to see."

"This is the first time I have enjoyed the view, but I cannot but agree with you." Looking past Miss Elizabeth, he saw a footman standing at a discreet distance, but no horses, so he asked, "Did you come on foot?"

Laughing, Miss Elizabeth said, "When I was at Netherfield, I know I told you I prefer walking. It is not so far from Longbourn to make it impossible, surely closer than Netherfield. Though I see you came not on your own two feet, but four."

With a chuckle, Darcy replied, "Yes, I relied on Thunder to aid me."

Walking over to his horse, Miss Elizabeth held her hand out for him to sniff it. "He is a magnificent beast, Mr. Darcy. Almost something out of an Arthurian legend. He seems ready to ride off on an adventure to fight a dragon."

"Yes, Thunder is one of the larger horses to come from my family's stables." Smoothing his hand down Thunder's golden mane, Darcy added, "I find it humorous that you describe him as if he belongs in an Arthurian tale, as it brings back memories of my youth when I would ride my pony and indulge in fantasies of embarking on heroic adventures to fight dragons and rescue maidens."

Miss Elizabeth gazed at him, her head tilted, before saying, "I suppose I can picture you thus. Did you ever have any friends that went on these quests with you?"

Darcy sighed, not eager to explain but also not wanting to lie. Eventually, he said, "Though I enjoyed spending time with my cousin Richard whenever he would visit, I spent most of my free time with a boy named Wickham."

"It is a pity that you lost a friendship that started out so well."

Shocked at her response, Darcy croaked, "What do you know of Wickham?"

Grimacing, Miss Elizabeth said, "While I would have known something had soured in your relationship from your expression, your sister confided in me about being betrayed by a man who she had thought was a friend named Wickham."

Darcy bit back a groan. His sister's unexpected revelation about her near disaster caught him off guard, prompting him to consider either escaping or minimizing the potential damage to her reputation. Then he looked into Miss Elizabeth's kind eyes, and his panic ebbed.

Reaching out, Miss Elizabeth laid her hand on his clenched fist and explained, "Miss Darcy is my friend. I would never betray her confidence or do anything to hurt her. More than that, I would like to believe that we are becoming friends and that you can learn to trust me."

Darcy could only nod as he found his throat too clogged to say anything. How was it that his sister had found such a remarkable person? "Miss Bennet, I find I like the idea of us becoming friends. I always seem to enjoy our conversations, even if they leave me pondering the ramifications of your words."

"It brings me joy to hear that you feel that way. I have also enjoyed our conversations. Though I have a question, if you will forgive my intrusion. Can you tell me what happened to the dastard?" Miss Elizabeth then anxiously demanded, "Please tell me you have dealt with him."

Laughing mirthlessly, Darcy reassured her. "My cousin Richard found a very poetic punishment for Wickham. The scoundrel found himself press-ganged and will likely never see the shores of England again."

"It seems appropriate for him to realize that he must work hard or face consequences." Looking over his shoulder at the position of the sun, Miss Elizabeth sighed. "Alas, our conversation must come to an end for now, Mr. Darcy. If I do not begin my journey back home, my sisters will miss me, and I would not want Jane to worry."

Nodding in understanding, Darcy was quick to ask, "Would it be permissible for me to walk back with you?"

"As long as Thunder does not mind trailing after us like a well-trained dog, I would be happy to continue our conversation," answered Miss Elizabeth with a laugh.

Darcy reached out to take hold of Thunder's reins, ready to follow Miss Elizabeth on the trail. However, the footman accompanying her kindly offered to lead the horse instead. With a grateful thank you, Darcy hurried to catch up with Miss Elizabeth's swift progress and asked, "Are you hurrying back home because you are eager to participate in something? I would hate to think that you are regretting your permission to accompany you."

Chuckling, Elizabeth shook her head and said, "No, with what is waiting for me back at Longbourn, I am in no great hurry. However, you will find that I have become accustomed to walking swiftly wherever I go. How else would I make up for not riding a horse? I have places I must be and not the time to dally."

Darcy found himself intrigued by Miss Elizabeth's brisk, purposeful steps, a striking contrast to the affected, mincing steps of high-society women. However, he overlooked that to ask, "What is it that is waiting for you back at Longbourn? Nothing bad, I hope."

Sighing, Miss Elizabeth hopped gracefully over a small log that blocked the trail before answering, "My father's heir, a Mr. Collins, has come for a visit. In order to find the connection between us and him, one must delve four generations into the past. Our involvement with him is due to our estate being entailed to the male line, and unfortunately, with the devastating loss of my brother in infancy, Mr. Collins has become my father's rightful inheritor."

Darcy could only imagine the devastation. Not only had her family lost a son and brother, but they had also lost all hope of remaining in their home when Mr. Bennet passed. "You have my condolences on the loss of your brother," murmured Darcy.

"Thank you, Mr. Darcy. I was only five when my baby brother died, but I can remember his faint smile." Miss Elizabeth's eyes turned misty as she remembered before turning to him to explain, "He was Lydia's twin brother, but regrettably, he was never healthy. When he passed away, my mother's grief turned into anger towards Lydia, unable to understand why her daughter lived while her son did not. In the end, Jane and I did all we could to care for her with the aid of the nursemaid, as Mother would have nothing to do with her. It was only recently when she recognized Lydia's burgeoning beauty that she put Lydia out, saying that she could at least be useful and find a husband that would care for her mother."

Darcy was at first outraged and then astounded at Miss Elizabeth's story. He could not understand a mother being angry at a baby for something so out of their control. Then he latched onto the fact that Miss Bennet had become a mother figure at possibly six or seven years of age, and Miss Elizabeth at only five helping as much as she could. The more he learned about Miss Elizabeth and, by extension, her sisters, the more he was in awe of her.

Attempting to turn the subject to one less depressing, he asked, "What have you learned of this heir that is visiting? Is there a chance he will take care of Longbourn and any of your family in need when the time comes?"

Elizabeth considered for a moment what she might say in response to Mr. Darcy's understandable question. At first, she considered dissembling, but their conversation thus far had been so open that she did not want to taint it with lies. So, taking a deep breath, she answered, "Mr. Collins is a fool, and I fear very much for the future of Longbourn."

Elizabeth did not look up into Mr. Darcy's face but she heard concern in his voice when he said, "I am sorry to hear that, Miss Elizabeth. What concerns you about this Mr. Collins?"

Chucking bitterly, Elizabeth said, "What doesn't concern me? Within five minutes of his arrival at Longbourn, I realized he was not only a heretic, but also possessed a lecherous and foolish nature."

With an audible gasp, Mr. Darcy admitted, "I do not know what part of that sentence has me more concerned, Miss Elizabeth."

As Elizabeth mustered the courage to glance at him, she observed his subtle tilt towards her and the sincere worry etched on his face. This gave her enough reassurance to say, "Only imagine how I feel. My father's heir only stops staring at my person when he wishes to extol the virtues of his grand patroness, Lay Catherine de Bourgh and her sickly daughter, the rose of Kent."

Coming to an abrupt halt, Mr. Darcy's hand swiftly extended to lightly grasp Elizabeth's arm, his voice carrying a tone of shock as he asked, "Your father's heir is Lady Catherine de Bourgh's vicar?"

Studying him with concern, Elizabeth nodded. "Yes, he said that she chose him as her rector about seven months ago."

Shaking his head, Mr. Darcy let go of her arm and ran his hand through his hair. Turning back to her, he exclaimed, "It is inexplicable. Lady Catherine de Bourgh is my aunt on my mother's side."

Eyes widening, Elizabeth said, "That is inexplicable." Then, frowning, she added, "Mr. Darcy, I apologize, but the information I have gathered about Mr. Collins and his remarks about her lead me to believe that she is not effectively handling her estate. It seems like she is overseeing everything as if she were a lord in a feudal system. She has him saying that her dictates are the will of God. His enthusiasm for her leads him to break canon law without hesitation."

Wincing, Mr. Darcy offered her his arm, and they resumed walking down the trail. It was not long before he said, "That is sad to hear, Miss Elizabeth. At one time I would visit my aunt once a year to help review the books and advise her on various aspects of running the estate, but two years ago she attempted to force me to wed her daughter, and I swore to never return. So it has been some time since I have been there. It is sad to hear that she has fallen so far."

"Mostly, I fear for the tenants," Elizabeth admitted. "Mr. Collins speaks of her demanding them to pay obeisance to her and pay her the tithes that are justly owed to the church. At the very least, they receive no benefit from his role of vicar. He is proud to preach the sermons she writes for him from the pulpit."

"When I get the chance, I will consult with my uncle, her brother, and see if there is anything to be done." Darcy halted, aiding

Elizabeth over a fallen branch, and then questioned, "Is Mr. Collins conducting himself appropriately when he's with your family?"

Smiling at Mr. Darcy's consideration, Elizabeth answered, "While he is not overt in his actions, I would call none of his actions correct. For example, he moves about the house, evaluating everything we own and commenting on how he is glad that it will be in his possession when he takes control of the property."

"Is he unaware that the entailment doesn't cover your belongings, only the estate and specific items mentioned in the original entailment?" asked Mr. Darcy.

Shaking her head, Elizabeth sighed. "I do not think he understands much anything about the entail. Mr. Collins does not understand anything about anything. Despite my best efforts to explain the nuances of estate management, he stubbornly rejected my input, asserting that my gender rendered me incapable of comprehending matters of such significance. To make matters worse, he spent the entire conversation with his gaze decidedly below my face."

Elizabeth's eyes met Mr. Darcy's as he emitted a disgusted sound, his furrowed brows revealing his disapproval. He questioned, "Has your father taken any measures to shield you and your sisters from his inappropriate conduct?"

Frowning, she said, "My father finds the whole situation comical and is most often pretending to read a book while enjoying Mr. Collins's foolishness and his daughters' discomfort. Really, I have always known that my father was indolent and uninterested in exerting himself for any reason, but Mr. Collins's visit has opened my eyes to just how little he cares for his family."

They only walked a few paces before Mr. Darcy asked, "Has your mother been able to help the situation at all?"

Elizabeth snorted in a very unladylike way, retorting, "My mother is so desperate to secure a comfortable future that she is throwing all of her daughters in his path except Jane, hoping he will ask to marry one of us. I was the one who assigned two footmen to him so that at the very least, he cannot importune one of us. I have also encouraged Kitty and Lydia to spend time in the schoolroom studying to escape his presence as much as they can."

They walked for quite some time before Mr. Darcy responded to her comment. In fact, they had almost reached the gate where she would enter Longbourn's back garden. He looked down at her, his expression strangely kind in some way, and he said, "You are a very remarkable woman, Miss Elizabeth. Your character goes beyond kindness and compassion; you have consistently showed strength and dedication in caring for your sisters, even when others shirk their responsibilities. That you have done so since you were young amazes me. I am grateful for the opportunity to have gotten to know you better."

CONCERNED BY THE STRUGGLES of Miss Elizabeth and her sisters, Darcy had suggested to Bingley that they call on the Bennet family. Not only could they check on Miss Bennet's recovery, but he could also check out Mr. Collins. They arrived just at the start of visiting hours and even with Miss Elizabeth's warning, Mr. Collins's absurdity surprised Darcy.

Upon being announced, Mr. Collins interrupted Mrs. Bennet's greeting by loudly proclaiming, "How grand of you to come to pay your respects to the future master of Longbourn, gentlemen! It is very magnanimous of you both."

The gentleman in question was surprisingly short. Shorter, in fact, than anyone else in the room by a good few inches. He had a decided paunch and his eyes, to Darcy's view, were beady and avaricious. Still, he would have given the man a chance had he been amiable, but even the first sentience put Darcy off. Then, too, he already knew of Miss Elizabeth's concerns.

Darcy glanced at Bingley, who, for the most part, was willing to overlook the faux pas of others and saw that he was just as startled by Mr. Collins's presumption. What did one say to such a comment, exactly? Bingley shrugged before moving to Miss Bennet's side where she sat near the fire, a colorful shawl wrapped around her shoulders. He smiled in greeting before asking, "Miss Bennet, are you fully recovered from your earlier illness?"

Looking up at him warmly, she answered, "I am much recovered, Mr. Bingley, thank you. Please sit down." Bingley quickly sat in the nearby seat and took up a quiet conversation with Miss Bennet.

Turning his attention back to the group, Darcy's eyes searched out Miss Elizabeth when Mr. Collins huffed, "Yes, I suppose you should sit down."

Darcy wondered if Mr. Collins arrogantly presumed that it was his prerogative to invite the guests to take a seat. Choosing to overlook the conundrum that was Mr. Collins, he chose a spot near Miss Elizabeth, who shared a settee with Miss Mary. Focusing on Miss Elizabeth, he said, "I am glad to hear that Miss Bennet's health has improved. I know Bingley has been concerned for her well-being."

Miss Elizabeth opened her mouth to say something, but Mr. Collins interrupted her. "Truly, it was unwise for Cousin Jane to become ill. It is not at all comely for a young lady to have a weak constitution. My blessed patroness herself is rarely ill and condemns those who do not do as they should to remain healthy. She sees it as a moral failing to fall ill." Looking across the room at Miss Bennet, he sighed. "Truly, Cousin Jane would have been my first choice of bride. Her beauty would have been a compliment to my position as vicar and heir to an estate, but Lady Catherine would never approve of her with such a weakness of character."

Darcy knew his mouth must be hanging agape, but truly, he could not have imagined such a man as his aunt's vicar. Miss Elizabeth's furrowed brow and Miss Mary's tight-lipped expression made it clear that they were both displeased with Mr. Collins's pontification. He couldn't believe his eyes when he saw their mother completely unfazed by Mr. Collins's speech, and instead casually flipping through a fashion magazine and humming a tune. When Miss Elizabeth had said that her mother was encouraging a match with the weasel of a man, Darcy had not known what to think. The woman's situation was rather desperate, but such an indifference to his insults to her daughters was inexcusable.

"I seem to recall, Mr. Collins, that you once remarked on the delicate health of your patroness's daughter, and yet praise her as someone to aspire to while you deride my sister for becoming ill. I must admit to some confusion over the contradiction," questioned Miss Mary.

Glancing at Mary with a look of disdain, he explained, "As I have said before, Cousin Mary, you are only a female, so you cannot understand the intricacies of the world at large. Though Miss de Bourgh is of a weak constitution, she is of the nobility and so is in a different class than you and your sisters. Where she is lauded for her delicacy, you will never be. Your common standing requires you to be hardy. To be less is an insult to your betters."

Miss Mary and Miss Elizabeth looked at each other before looking back at Mr. Collins. Darcy understood their silence. There really was not much one could say to counter such outright stupidity. Darcy had been trying to come up with something to contribute to a more convivial discussion, but Miss Elizabeth beat him to it. "Mr. Collins,

I know you had the opportunity to meet the steward yesterday. Tell me, did you enjoy the tour of the property?"

Mr. Collins looked at Miss Elizabeth with an oily smile, his gaze not quite making it to her face and instead remaining on her chest. Darcy found himself becoming decidedly nauseous and could only imagine what Miss Elizabeth must feel about Mr. Collins's perusal of her person. Leaning closer, Mr. Collins purred, "Your solicitude is too kind, Cousin Elizabeth. I met with the man, but I did not partake of the tour. It is the steward's responsibility to see to the lands, not the master of the estate. And as for the tenants, they will need to come to me, not the other way around. Waiting for them to pay me homage is my right, just as it is my duty to assess their requests for aid and decide whether to show my benevolence or offer them advice on how to do better." Reaching out, he grasped Miss Elizabeth's hand and added, "I know you have not learned the proper course, but do not worry, you will find that I am a kind, if firm teacher, and it will be my pleasure to show you the way a true lady behaves."

From her spot perusing the fashion magazine, Mrs. Bennet said, "You will find, Mr. Collins, that my Elizabeth loves to learn."

Darcy found himself astounded that the woman was paying enough attention to the goings on to encourage a match between her daughter and the idiot heir, but had not lifted a finger when he had insulted them all. He was glad that Miss Elizabeth was intelligent and determined enough not to fall for her mother's manipulations. Such a match would be a degradation.

Eager to divert the man's unwanted attention away from Miss Elizabeth, Darcy said, "Mr. Collins, I find that I must correct your presumption of how the master of an estate interacts with his tenants and steward. We are no longer in medieval England, and you will not be a lord ruling over serfs tied to the land. Successfully managing an estate in today's world requires a conscientious approach, ensuring that tenants are well taken care of and treated with respect. Tenants are no longer required to pay homage to their liege lord. Then, too, it is always wise to investigate the word of your steward, else you run the risk of being swindled."

Enraged, Mr. Collins shifted his attention from Miss Elizabeth to face Darcy. Darcy was happy to see Miss Elizabeth use the distraction to remove her hand from Mr. Collins's grasp and wipe it surreptitiously on her skirt. Meanwhile, Mr. Collins said, "I have learned how to manage an estate from my patroness Lady Catherine de Bourgh, whose excellence is a veritable gift from God. You, sir, may do as you wish in whatever small estate you manage, but I will do as I see fit, and God will bless me for doing as he wants."

Darcy and Bingley, having stayed as long as was proper, soon left Longbourn. As he rode Thunder back towards Netherfield, anxiety consumed Darcy's thoughts, both for Miss Elizabeth's well-being and the dire circumstances that awaited Longbourn at the hands of such a despicable individual. He was glad at least there were a few upcoming events that he could see Miss Elizabeth at and be able to assure himself that she was well. They were friends, after all.

Chapter Fifteen

Georgianna sighed as she looked down at only her brother's letter on the platter brought in by one of the footmen. Taking the letter with thanks, she held it with a certain amount of trepidation. It had been longer than she would like since she had heard from Elizabeth and while she hoped everything was well, she feared it wasn't. Maybe her brother would give her the information she was hoping for.

Netherfield, Meryton

Dearest sister,

I hope this letter finds you well in London. While I look forward to your arrival here in a few days, I hope you are still enjoying the music lessons that you have left before you journey here.

It might surprise you to hear that Miss Bingley has left Netherfield and returned to London with her sister and Mr. Hurst. So you will be free of her here, though I worry she may descend upon you in London.

So be warned. Though it is possible that I will have angered her so much that she will completely ignore you.

You may be proud of me or ashamed of my behavior when you learn that I finally snapped and told her exactly how I felt about her cruel behavior. I also informed her I would never, under any circumstance, marry her. Needless to say, she was not happy with my declaration and has left to find a more suitable object to pursue. I can only say that I hope whoever she targets is either strong enough to resist her or enough like her to be happily married.

I have enjoyed my time here more than I thought I would, though I will admit that I have enjoyed it more since Miss Bingley left. The town of Meryton has been welcoming despite my early blunders at the assembly. I must thank you again for pointing out my need for change. I cannot believe the difference I have found in interacting with people while attempting to assume the best of them. Perhaps it is because Meryton and its residents are so distant from the concerns of high society, or maybe I have never truly observed those around me, but I am astounded by the number of people who genuinely wish to engage in conversations about enjoyable subjects, with no deference to my status.

Among all the enjoyable experiences I've had, the time I've spent with Miss Elizabeth stands out the most. If she is the sort of woman to be found at the London Ladies Society, then I may need to venture there with you. Though truly I do not believe there is anyone one like her in all of England. I have met her at one or two other social gatherings, but what I have enjoyed the most is when I stumble upon her on the trails. I can understand how you became such close friends with her so quickly. There is just something about her that draws you in. I have shared more of myself with her than perhaps anyone, save you and Richard.

Though I must admit that I am becoming more and more unsettled by her situation at Longbourn. Did you know that I have learned from the tenants of Netherfield that she has seen to their needs when the absentee landlord could not be bothered? They have also said that Miss Elizabeth is the one that manages Longbourn with the aid of the steward. Then two of the Bennet sisters are the ones who see to the tenants as the mistress should. I do not know what either of her parents do at all between all the work their daughters have taken up.

More than that, the heir to Longbourn is visiting. He is an absurd little man who, surprisingly, is our Aunt Catherine's vicar. The words that pour forth from his face, resembling that of a conniving weasel, are a venomous blend of heresy and personal affronts to Miss Elizabeth and her sisters. He is full of his own pomposity and worship of our aunt, who he holds akin to God. He deserves a good thrashing, but sadly, I am not in the position to give it. I am simply thankful that his small brain has not put two and two together and realized that his patroness is our Aunt Catherine. I have no desire to be venerated by such a fool.

If I do not miss my guess, he wishes to marry Miss Elizabeth, and her parents are supporting his suit. Though Miss Elizabeth handles his licentious gaze with grace, I can detect her unease with the man. While I trust her to refuse his offer of marriage quite firmly, I am anxious about how her parents will respond to her refusal.

I know she is anxious to see you and introduce her sisters to you. With the extent of her excitement, I do not know who wants to see you more, Miss Elizabeth or myself. I know you will be here soon, so I will not write to you again before you arrive. I will merely say safe travels.

Your loving brother,

Fitzwilliam Darcy

Georgianna looked down at the page before her with a frown. She knew Elizabeth was a hard worker but to hear exactly to what extent was a little overwhelming. She was always so considerate of others, but Georgianna was worried that she would overextend herself. Did the people who should aid her not see what they were doing to her?

Apart from that, Georgianna was anxious about the possibility of Lizzie's parents arranging a marriage with Mr. Bennet's heir. William's portrayal of the man left a foul taste in her mouth. Georgianna recognized the risks of being forced into a marriage through deceitful tactics or compromising situations. After all, Lizzie was not of age and her parents held much power over her. Just thinking of it made Georgianna shudder.

For the longest time after she became an orphan, Georgianna had wished for parents. She did not particularly care what sort of parents. She had been an infant when her mother died, and her father had little to do with her at any point in her life. Georgianna dreamed of having parents who would at least occasionally want to be with her and lovingly care for her. She had never once considered that maybe sometimes no parents were better than negligent parents.

Her last lesson with Master Rossini was supposed to be Thursday, but perhaps she could have it on Wednesday and she could leave first thing Thursday morning. Folding up her letter from William and putting it with the others he had sent, Georgianna went in search of Mrs. Annesley. Georgianna was determined to get to Netherfield as soon as may be.

Miss Elizabeth needed support, and Georgianna was determined to give it. She would not be the sort of person who just took from others without giving in return. She only hoped she would arrive in enough time to help.

"I JUST WISH THAT there was something I could do to help you, Lizzie," cried Jane.

Elizabeth sighed from her spot by the fire in the schoolroom. As time went by, it was becoming more and more evident that Mr. Collins was planning to ask Elizabeth to marry him. No matter what she did, nothing seemed to dissuade him. It did not help that her mother was constantly assuring that Elizabeth would be the perfect bride for him.

Glancing at Jane, Elizabeth shook her head. "There is really nothing that you or even I can do. He has decided you are unsuitable, which I am very thankful for, and he is angry at Mary for calling out the heresy that he cannot see in himself. Really, all I can do is refuse him once he finally proposes and hope that will be the end of that."

Mary asked, "Do you truly believe that will be the end of it? You know Mother will not accept your refusal easily."

Running her hand down her face, Elizabeth tried to find the words to respond. She knew her refusal would not be the end of it. Her mother would certainly not let go of the picture she had in her head of Elizabeth, her most troublesome daughter, married to the heir, saving them all from the hedgerows. She only hoped that her father would support her decision. Though lately Elizabeth had become less sure that he would.

He seemed to find so much entertainment in Mr. Collins's poor manners and foolish ideals, and even how he pestered his daughters. Elizabeth truly did not know if he would do the right thing. Elizabeth's growing fear was that the only reason her father would support her was because he might find entertainment in watching his wife and heir fret over her refusal.

Mary sat in the chair across from Elizabeth, her hands deftly moving the knitting needles as she crafted a cozy scarf for one of the tenants. Grimacing, she finally said, "I have to hope, Mary, otherwise I do not know what I might do." Forcing herself to smile as she looked over at Jane, she said, "Enough of my problems. I saw you chatting with Mr. Bingley for some time at Lucas Lodge. How are things progressing for you?"

It was nice to see her sister's joy in the face of her own struggles. Elizabeth sometimes needed the reminder that everything was not all bad; the happiness of her sisters was a comforting balm to her soul. Nestled in her shawl, Elizabeth curled up with her knees tucked under her chin, marveling at the sheer delight emanating from her sister.

Giggling, Jane said, "Mr. Bingley is everything that a gentleman should be. He is interested in what I think of situations and has asked my opinion on how some of his tenants might be helped through the winter. Unlike many of the men I have come across, he expects there to be more to me than just my pretty face." Her cheeks blushing, Jane let out a sigh and confessed, "Whenever he looks at me, it's like the world aligns itself, even if my stomach is filled with butterflies."

Smiling wistfully, Elizabeth said, "Then all is as it should be." Though her sisters continued chatting, Elizabeth grew introspective. She always tried to stay positive and not dwell on the difficulties in her life. In a household with four sisters, there was never a dull moment, as one of them would always have something to be happy about, even if it was something as simple as a new ribbon or as grand as love. She could also enjoy looking at the world around her. There was so much goodness in the world if one just looked for it. It existed in the breathtaking colors of a sunrise, the carefree frolicking of a spring lamb, and the uncontainable happiness on a child's face when surprised with a treat.

Still, in moments such as these, with so many things pressing in on her at once, she sometimes wished for a different lot in life. When she was younger, Elizabeth had once found solace in her intelligence. Her mother's constant disregard for her looks made Elizabeth glad she had at least something to offer the world. It was that very intelligence that led her to recognize that there were so many things around her home that needed doing.

Seeing that no one else was stepping up, Elizabeth decided to take on the responsibility and do what needed to be done. So she worked with the steward and aided the tenants, which then expanded into helping the tenants of Netherfield when problems arose. With every season, it seemed that her responsibilities grew. She would often ask her mother and father to do tasks that were clearly their responsibility, but the outcome was always the same. They would always say something like, "But Elizabeth, you are so strong! It would be significantly more challenging for me to accomplish that task, so please just continue doing everything as you are."

Her sisters had recently been taking over some responsibilities that she managed with the tenants and the manse, but there were many tasks that they simply could not do. So Elizabeth had a constant stream of things to keep her busy. She was not one to sit idle, so normally Elizabeth enjoyed staying busy. Though when she was low, it was difficult to watch her sister's joy in her newfound love and not want some of it for herself.

Beneath all her strength, she was quite romantic and desperately yearned to look at a man and just know that all was right in the world. Even if that came with a stomach full of butterflies. In the deepest recess of her heart, Elizabeth wished for love, though she feared she would never find it.

Forcing her mind from the strange aching in her heart, Elizabeth tried to listen to all Jane said about her relationship with Mr. Bingley, and all they had shared with one another. Something about her tale seemed oddly reminiscent of something, but Elizabeth was too tired to put her finger on it. As they bid each other goodnight and went their separate ways, Elizabeth had a sudden realization that the discussions Jane had with Mr. Bingley bore a striking resemblance to her own interactions with Mr. Darcy.

Crawling under her covers, Elizabeth chuckled at the thought that friendship had a lot of similarities with love. She had never really thought of it before, but it seemed a couple in love would do well if they were also friends, sharing all that was in their hearts and in their lives. She fell asleep with a smile on her lips, thinking that if she could not have love, at least she had a friend in Mr. Darcy.

DARCY SIGHED. HE HAD not met Miss Elizabeth in his morning rambles as he had hoped to, but all was not lost. He had plans to visit the bookshop in Meryton that morning, and it was possible that he might meet her in town.

Even a few months ago, Darcy never would have imagined missing the company of someone the way he did with Miss Elizabeth. Their developing friendship was a previously unknown source of happiness. Something about the lady drew him like no woman ever had. Their occasional debates about literature and philosophy were invigorating, but there was something more than the intellectual connection they shared.

The realization hit him unexpectedly—he cared more about Miss Elizabeth's well-being than any other lady, with the exception of Georgianna. Darcy was not a stranger to the gossip that seemed to be the currency of the ton. It seemed every season there was talk of certain ladies being persuaded to marry against their wishes. It had never moved him. They were not ladies connected to him, and while he would not be so heavy-handed with Georgianna, he would not speak out against families who acted in what they felt was their best interests. Everything changed when he witnessed Miss Elizabeth's distress when dealing with Mr. Collins.

Finding the need to distract himself, Darcy picked up the letter that had recently arrived from his sister. He was happy to hear from her despite her arriving two days hence. Sitting down in the nearest chair, letter in hand, Darcy loosened the seal and began to read.

Darcy House, London
Dear Brother,

Brother, I have decided that I cannot wait any longer to come and see you. Master Rossini has kindly agreed to move up my last lesson, freeing me up to arrive earlier than expected. I plan to leave as soon as it is light Thursday morning and should arrive in time for an early tea. Do not worry—Mrs. Annesley and I will travel with plenty of the burly footmen that you have hired specifically for when I travel.

Will you forgive me if I say that I am rushing to Meryton, not for you, but for Elizabeth? I am worried for her, Brother. I have only received one letter from her recently, and it was evident that something was off. They might have only been words on paper, but her normally cheerful tone was not there.

That combined with the information in your most recent letter, I am determined to be there as soon as I may. Elizabeth saved me from my melancholy, and she helped us to grow closer together, even if only indirectly. I won't abandon her now that she confronts her own difficulties.

Despite my reasons for hastening my arrival, I look forward to seeing you soon.

Your loving sister,

Georgianna Darcy

Darcy could only chuckle as he read Georgianna's letter. She had changed so much in the last few months. Gone was the once timid girl, and a much more resolute young lady had replaced her. Darcy found he was not at all disappointed that she was rushing to Miss Elizabeth's side. It would make it easier for him to offer his help.

Tucking the letter away, he left his room and went in search of Bingley. Hopefully, they could leave for Meryton soon. Maybe he could persuade Bingley to expand the Netherfield library. He really should have more material on estate management to use for referencing.

In his study, Bingley sat with a cup of coffee, his eyes scanning a letter laid out before him. Seeing his friend, Bingley put the cup down and said, "Good morning, Darcy. How was your ride with Thunder?"

"The weather is growing colder, but I still enjoyed it.," Darcy replied, taking a seat. "The sight of the Websters' roof, fully repaired, was a relief."

After taking another sip of coffee, Bingley grinned and said, "I am glad. The weather will turn harsh soon and they have several young children and an elderly grandfather that I would not want getting sick because of a leaky roof. Do you have any plans for the day?"

Not quite comfortable explaining his hope that he might catch a moment with Miss Elizabeth, Darcy only explained, "I would like to spend some time in town. The book I ordered should have arrived at the bookshop by now, and you really should expand the very sad library here at Netherfield."

Laughing, Bingley remarked, "You and your books. I should have known. I know it is too soon to return to Longbourn. I would not mind going to the bookshop, though I would not know the first thing about what sort of books I should have in my library. You know I was not the intellectual you were back at Cambridge."

"What can I say? I have always loved the classics and a good debate about their content," mused Darcy. Realizing that he should warn Bingley about his sister's earlier arrival, he added, "I have received a letter from Georgianna, and she said that she is coming a day earlier than expected. She should be here midday tomorrow."

"I will be happy to have your sister and Mrs. Annesley here. They will certainly be easier to get along with than my sisters." Looking down at the letter on the desk in front of him, Bingley sighed. "My sisters are not returning, but are certainly not happy with their current situation. I have told the various people they shop with that I am no longer covering their overspending. They have written to complain that they cannot possibly find Caroline the sort of husband she deserves without purchasing a completely new wardrobe."

"Stand firm, Bingley," advised Darcy.

Putting away the letter, Bingley commented, "I might consider paying for a wardrobe if I thought she would choose something other than that dreadful orange hue and it would actually see her married."

Getting to his feet, Darcy dismissed the matter with a wave of his hand. "Put it out of your mind for now, Bingley," he said. "The books are calling us."

Chapter Sixteen

Elizabeth had thought she would have been able to escape Mr. Collins for at least one morning, but she was wrong. Mr. Collins was not fit and as she and Mary set off to walk into Meryton and visit the shops, she couldn't help but hope he would choose to stay at Longbourn. While Elizabeth and Mary walked at a comfortable pace, he lagged behind, huffing and complaining, despite having the option of staying with the rest of their family at Longbourn.

By the time they arrived at the apothecary, he was drenched in sweat and gasping. He had used his cravat to wipe ineffectually at his face. Linking arms with Mary, Elizabeth put on a brave face, refusing to let Mr. Collins's stalking behavior deter her from entering the shop to restock their family's headache powders. It was not surprising really that they had run out at such a time. Everyone was suffering from Mr. Collins's presence.

They strolled in and out of several shops, chatting with the friendly shop owners and making purchases. They managed without issue until they arrived at the bookshop. By that time, Mr. Collins had finally caught his breath, though he still looked bedraggled. Knowing how much they both adored the bookshop, the sisters deliberately left it as their final destination. The bonus was that they would not have to carry any books they acquired throughout the town with them as they shopped.

Elizabeth scanned the spines of the various titles, hoping to spot something new, while Mary perused the sheets of music at the front of the store. She had just drawn a book from the shelf when Mr. Collins disturbed her peace with his blathering. "Cousin Elizabeth, I believe you are in the wrong section."

Taking a deep breath, Elizabeth turned to the poor excuse for a man and said, "What ever can you mean, Mr. Collins? I have been in this bookshop hundreds of times. I know exactly what section I am in."

"Miss Elizabeth, this section holds *novels*. You cannot possibly be thinking of purchasing one of them." Mr. Collins's voice trembled with horror, his pale complexion hinting at his shock or possibly the toll of his earlier exertion.

Looking around the room, it relieved Elizabeth that only the proprietor Mr. Ellis was present, and he would never hold Mr. Collins against her. As Elizabeth turned to confront him, she clutched the novel tightly, her hands trembling with the desire to use it as a weapon. "Yes, Mr. Collins, I was attempting to find a new novel to purchase. Reading novels has been a cherished pastime for my sisters and me. Perhaps you might like to join us as we take turns reading it aloud one of these evenings." Elizabeth knew her comment would upset Mr. Collins, but she couldn't tolerate his pompous behavior any longer. It made her want to needle him.

Without warning, he yanked the book away from her, treating it as if it were a lethal instrument, and let it crash onto the floor. He clutched her arm, his grip unyielding as he tried to forcefully remove her from the store. He would have been more successful if she was not wearing her boots, or had he not been so much shorter than her.

Shocked by his actions, it took Elizabeth a moment to for her to form a protest. "Mr. Collins! Unhand me this instant! What can you be thinking of manhandling me so?" Despite Elizabeth's efforts to resist being dragged, Mr. Collins persisted in tightly clutching her arm, his fingers digging into her flesh.

It was a relief to hear the deep, resonant voice of Mr. Darcy saying, "Mr. Collins, I find that I must second Miss Elizabeth's question. What are you thinking to be handling a lady so roughly?" Turning slightly, Elizabeth saw Mr. Darcy standing in the doorway to the shop, his expression thunderous.

Fuming, Mr. Collins glared fiercely at Mr. Darcy. He snapped, "It is obvious that Cousin Elizabeth is incapable of choosing her own reading material, so I am removing her from the temptation. I would thank you for moving out of our way."

Ignoring Mr. Collins's show of anger, Mr. Darcy's voice gained a sharp edge as he commanded, "Let go of Miss Elizabeth, Mr. Collins. Now."

Jerking Elizabeth in response to her attempt to break free, Mr. Collins shook his head. "You can have no say in the matter, sir. She is my cousin. I am a man of God and a representative of Lady Catherine de Bourgh. Thus, you will not stop me."

Stepping closer to Mr. Collins, Mr. Darcy's voice became even more dangerous. "Mr. Collins, none of those excuses can justify your actions. In fact, they make your behavior even more disgraceful. If you do not release Miss Elizabeth immediately, I may have to break your arm."

Finally, realizing the danger he was exposing himself to, Mr. Collins released her arm and took a step back, his eyes widening in alarm. Stepping forward, Mr. Darcy offered Elizabeth his arm, and she gratefully accepted it and the protection he offered. With a gentle smile, Mr. Darcy covered her trembling hand on his arm and inquired, "Miss Elizabeth, were you looking to purchase something before returning home?"

Clearing her throat, Elizabeth said, "I had been hoping to purchase that novel on the floor."

It surprised Elizabeth when Mr. Bingley, who had gone unnoticed until now, swiftly maneuvered past her and Mr. Darcy to retrieve the novel. He brushed off the dirt and handed it back to Elizabeth, offering her a warm smile and sending a pointed glare towards Mr. Collins.

Huffing, Mr. Collins jerked on his mussed waistcoat and proclaimed, "It is my responsibility to guide my cousin and intended away from the sin of reading inappropriate material, such as novels. I would have you know that Lady Catherine often decries the habit of young ladies to read novels, and I will not allow Elizabeth to corrupt herself so. She is due for a rigorous lesson in her place in the world, and what I expect of her. I will thank you for leaving the matter to me."

Elizabeth could feel Mr. Darcy stiffen beside her. If she wanted to rail at the pompous fool, she could only imagine Mr. Darcy's reaction to the fool that was her father's heir. Coming up with a response to Mr. Collins's ridiculous statement proved challenging for Elizabeth. Just what should she address first? Regardless, she would need some of the headache powders she had just bought by the time that they returned home.

WHEN HE HAD COME into the bookshop and seen Mr. Collins accosting Miss Elizabeth, Darcy had to restrain himself in reacting in a violent manner. Though he had successfully separated her from Mr. Collins, it had not cooled his ire in the slightest. Darcy clenched his jaw, suppressing the urge to strike the diminutive man in front of him.

Beside him stood Miss Elizabeth, who was remarkably calm despite being accosted in so outrageous a fashion. Though he could feel the slight tremor in her hand where it rested on his arm, her voice was firm when she said, "Mr. Collins, you are not my father, and he has not given you any such position of power over me. I seek neither your council nor that of your patroness, so I will thank you for desisting."

Mouth dropping to reveal discolored teeth, Mr. Collins asserted, "My patroness Lady Catherine de Bourgh—"

Darcy cut him off by sternly by saying, "Mr. Collins, your patroness is far removed from here and can have nothing to do with anyone in this town or its environs. You are acting worse than the crudest of laborers disrupting the peace of this shop." Then, with a disdainful shake of his head, he added, "You may be the heir to an estate, but you have not earned the distinction that you seem to think comes with that position. Your actions are not those of a gentleman, but a brute. I suggest you think hard about what you need to do to earn the respect of the people in Meryton. You have done little thus far."

Mr. Collins looked at the shop owner, clearly surprised to see his angry glare. Eager to remove Miss Elizabeth from the situation, Mr. Darcy said, "Mr. Ellis, I believe that Miss Elizabeth was desirous of purchasing something."

Turning his back on the disgruntled vicar, Mr. Ellis rushed to Miss Elizabeth's side. "My dear, I am so happy to hear that you found something you were interested in." The transaction between them was swift, and Darcy suspected they had developed a good relationship with as much as Miss Elizabeth read.

Darcy saw Bingley offer his arm to Miss Mary, who seemed affected by the confrontation as well. He and Miss Elizabeth followed them out. They all walked together to where the gentlemen had left their horses and, gathering their reins, they began walking toward Longbourn in silence. Mr. Collins followed behind them, his animosity palpable.

They had not gone far when Miss Elizabeth spoke up, though she kept her voice low so as not to be overheard. "Mr. Darcy, thank you for helping me handle Mr. Collins. I do not know how I might have handled the situation on my own."

"I am sure that you would have found a way, Miss Elizabeth. You were wearing boots, after all," smiled Mr. Darcy. His admiration for her had been growing for a while, and observing Miss Elizabeth's resolute response to Mr. Collins's abuse only strengthened his conviction.

Chuckling, Miss Elizabeth said, "I have pictured kicking him a time or two." Then, looking up at him, she asked, "Would you have thought it unladylike if I kicked him in the shin?"

Laughing at the image her words had created, Darcy said, "Not at all. Would you think me gentlemanly if I admitted to wanting to punch him in the face?"

When Miss Elizabeth looked back down the path before them, the angle of her bonnet prevented him from seeing her expression when she said, "No, Mr. Darcy, though I suspect at least a few of my sisters would have been sorry to have missed such an action."

They walked in companionable silence until Darcy remembered the news he had for her. Excitedly, he exclaimed, "Georgianna has moved up her arrival and will reach Netherfield by teatime tomorrow."

Casting a quick glance back up at him, Miss Elizabeth smiled. Darcy savored her smile while she said, "I have longed for your sister's company, and I am genuinely thrilled to spend time with her once more."

"I know she is looking forward to spending time with you as well," responded Darcy. Then, after a slight hesitation, he said, "I hope that you and maybe Jane might take tea with her and Mrs. Annesley tomorrow?"

"Of course I would have to check with Jane, but I can see no impediment to our visiting tomorrow," answered Miss Elizabeth with enthusiasm.

Darcy smiled, glad that he had arranged the treat for his sister so easily. It was disappointing to realize that they had nearly arrived at Longbourn, and he would have to leave Miss Elizabeth in the company of the odious man trailing behind them. As if sensing his unease, Miss Elizabeth said, "Do not fret so. Once I arrive home, I will complain of a headache and remove myself to my room. I am certain my sisters will help me avoid his company, at least for tonight, and tomorrow I will get to come see Georgianna. I have much to look forward to."

Startled by her reassurance, Darcy pondered aloud, his voice filled with curiosity. "I have often wondered what it is about you that effortlessly captivates people. The way you decipher my thoughts so accurately, it's as if you have some magical insight into my mind."

Laughing at his comment, Miss Elizabeth shook her head, and Darcy was glad to see the return of her usual effervescent spirits. "It's not magic," Miss Elizabeth chuckled, her voice full of laughter. "I'm just a keen observer and can draw conclusions from what I see. From your frequent glances back at Mr. Collins and the perturbed expression on your face, I can tell that his proximity to me displeases you."

It made a certain amount of sense, though it startled Darcy to think that he had been so easily read. "That is only too true," he grumbled, adding, "if I had my way, he would be heading off to some foreign country full of bugs and safely away from you."

By the time that the carriage was rolling down the drive to Netherfield, Georgianna was practically bouncing in her seat, she was so excited. Looking out the window, she commented, "Netherfield seems to be a lovely property."

"Indeed it does," Mrs. Annesley agreed. She smiled indulgently at Georgianna before saying, "Though I can well understand your excitement, it will not do for your brother to see you act less than the young lady you are."

Giggling, Georgianna assured her companion, "Do not worry, Mrs. Annesley, I will act with the utmost dignity and grace when I meet my brother and Mr. Bingley. No matter how much I will want to do so, I will not jump or squeal and shame you."

In no time at all, Georgianna was being handed down from the carriage. She walked sedately up the steps and greeted her brother with all the grace and dignity that her position of Miss Darcy deserved. It was her brother that leaned down and, taking her up in his arms, swung her about. If she could not help but giggle at such a display, she assumed everyone might have to forgive her. It was her brother's fault, after all.

Setting her back down on her feet, William greeted Mrs. Annesley and escorted them in. Mr. Bingley was hanging back, smiling at the reunion. Once inside, he stepped forward and introduced them to the housekeeper, Mrs. Nichols. She seemed a happy woman eager to please, though possibly less foreboding than Pemberley's own housekeeper, Mrs. Reynolds.

"If I might say, both gentlemen have been looking forward to your arrival. We have you in the suite of rooms across from your brother, Miss Darcy. You and Mrs. Annesley shall share the sitting room that connects the two." As Mrs. Nichols spoke, she escorted the two weary travelers up to their rooms to refresh themselves. As she opened the door for Georgianna, she kindly informed her, "Downstairs, we have a special tea waiting for you. There's no need to rush, as nothing cannot wait for your arrival."

Georgianna thanked the woman kindly before walking into her room to find it well appointed in pleasing green tones with the occasional pop of pink and deep rose. Settling into the chair in the corner, Georgianna took a moment to look around with a smile. She hurriedly completed her toilet, aided by her maid, who had arrived with her luggage. As she changed into a new, less dusty outfit, she felt a sense of eagerness to return to her brother alongside Mrs. Annesley.

As soon as Georgianna took a seat, William wasted no time in instructing a maid to offer her a refreshing cup of tea, while inquiring, "Did everything go smoothly during your journey?"

Glancing at Mrs. Annesley, Georgianna smiled. Her brother was always so solicitous to those he cared for. After taking a sip of the tea to quench her thirst, Georgianna answered, "Our journey went well. We left London just as the sun was rising, though all the smog about the city kept us from truly enjoying the sight."

Mr. Bingley, sitting in the chairs across from her, said, "It seems that you made good time coming from London. I am surprised you arrived as early as you did."

Smiling, Mrs. Annesley explained, "Miss Darcy was very determined to arrive at Netherfield as soon as possible. I believe she had everything packed and ready to go by yesterday morning."

Chuckling, Georgianna said, "What can I say? I was keen to see William."

"As much as I would like to believe you, little sister, I suspect you were not looking forward to seeing me as you were to someone else. Say someone who lives in the area?" joked her brother.

Georgianna looked at William closely. As much as their relationship had been improving, it was still odd to see him so lighthearted and joking. In the past, even with Bingley in the room, he had always been more reserved. However, now that she thought about it, Miss Bingley was normally present as well, and her presence would always create an uncomfortable atmosphere for both of them. Was the whole difference the lack of that horrid woman?

Either way, Georgianna was glad to see her brother more at ease. Taking another sip of her tea to hide her hesitation, Georgianna answered, "I will admit that I am eager to see Elizabeth again and meet the sisters that she spoke so fondly of."

"Then I am glad I presumed to invite guests, though you only just arrived." Gesturing with his chin for her to look behind her, her brother grinned.

Turning, Georgianna saw Lizzie being led in by a footman and being followed by an elegant blonde. Setting her teacup down carefully, she rushed over to greet her friend that she had not seen for so long. There was a lot of hugging and laughing before she was introduced to Miss Bennet, Elizabeth's older sister. Linking arms with Elizabeth, Georgianna moved back to the settee and gratefully noticed that Mrs. Annesley had switched seats so that she could sit with her friend. Miss Bennet had sat near Mr. Bingley and was casting furtive glances his way.

Georgianna smiled at Elizabeth, whispering, "You did not let me know about that in any of your letters."

Accepting the cup of tea that Mrs. Annesley served her with thanks, Elizabeth replied in another whisper, "I did not want to share any confidences until my sister was more certain of her feelings and his. My sister is often the focus of gentlemen, but she often hides her feelings in fear of being hurt." Glancing back over at her sister who was chatting softly with Mrs. Annesley and Mr. Bingley, Elizabeth added, "I hope that she has finally found the man who will respect and love her as she deserves."

"How exciting. Although I don't know your sister well, she gives off an aura of goodness and appears to have a strong rapport with Mr. Bingley. I have always known him to be a cheerful gentleman, though I know he has had trouble finding a lady who might accept him despite his unfortunate relations." Georgianna found it hard to keep a straight face despite her comment about Miss Bingley. It might not have been the nicest thing to say about the lady, but given the countless occasions she had to spend time with her, it was difficult to hold back.

Chuckling, Elizabeth said, "I suppose we all have family members we would be happy to do without. I know I have a few I fear might become an impediment to an advantageous match."

Georgianna observed a subtle change in her friend's expression as she discussed the pursuit of a beneficial match, a fleeting shadow crossing her face despite the smile. She knew her brother had been concerned about the visiting heir. Was it possible Elizabeth was worried as well?

Chapter Seventeen

Darcy fixed his gaze on his sister, captivated by the sight of her animatedly chatting with Miss Elizabeth, her happiness palpable. Their friendship had brought her so much joy and comfort, serving as a balm for her wounded heart after the disappointment with Wickham. He would forever be grateful that Miss Elizabeth came into both of their lives.

Though they were speaking loudly enough that he could hear them converse, he had paid no notice to the words, merely letting them wash over him, until he saw Georgianna's expression turn to one of concern. Wishing that he had been paying better attention to the conversation until that point, he asked, "So do either of you have any ideas of what you will want to do while Georgianna is staying at Netherfield?" Hopefully he could understand what had disturbed his sister if he joined the conversation.

Miss Elizabeth and Georgianna shared a meaningful glance, and then Georgie spoke up, confessing, "Aside from wanting to spend as much time together as possible and meet your sisters, I didn't really have any specific plans."

Shrugging her shoulders, Miss Elizabeth said, "I did not have any plans either, though it might be best to limit your visits to Longbourn where possible."

Georgianna frowned as she asked, "Why would you not want me to come to Longbourn?"

Blushing and stammering slightly, Miss Elizabeth hesitated before speaking. "With my father's heir visiting, it might be best that you not come, at least until he returns to Hunsford to his parish next week," she explained.

After his poor behavior the day before, Darcy could easily understand why Miss Elizabeth might want to protect his sister from spending time with so discourteous a man. Part of him wanted to ask if Miss Elizabeth was all right after her experience but did not want to embarrass her, so he only said, "I doubt he would behave badly while Bingley and I are there, and I am sure that Georgianna would put up with him if only so that she might meet the rest of your sisters."

Darcy watched as Miss Elizabeth rubbed her fingers along her right arm and anger flared in his chest. He could only assume that there was a bruise beneath the fabric of her dress. Though Miss Elizabeth smiled, he could tell that it did not reach her eyes when she said, "I suppose that will be fine." Locking eyes with Georgianna, she went on, "Although I don't want to prevent you from meeting my other sisters, I feel obligated to warn you about Mr. Collins. He is by far the most outrageous individual I've ever come across, and it is not a pleasant experience to spend time in his company. In fact, I would never presume to label him a gentleman."

Georgianna's attention shifted from Miss Elizabeth to Darcy, her eyes filled with intrigue and a faint crease forming between her brows. It seemed his sister had caught on to Miss Elizabeth's unease. As their gazes locked, Darcy felt a familiar sense of understanding with his sister, knowing she would approach him to talk about it once the Miss Bennets were gone.

Grimacing, Darcy decided that a change of topic might be best. So regarding his sister, he said, "It might surprise you to know that Mr. Collins is our Aunt Catherine's vicar. That she would choose such a man to see to the people of her estate says much about our aunt. I have tried to keep him from discovering our connection to her, fearing he might try to win my favor in his oddly servile and obsequious manner."

Eyes widening, Georgianna exclaimed, "Oh my." Turning, she patted Miss Elizabeth's hand and said, "I will take anything he says with a grain of salt, and I will not hold him against you or your family. It is not as if you could choose your father's heir. Just like I cannot choose my aunt. Only you must promise me that if you ever meet Lady Catherine that you do not hold it against me."

Regaining some of her humor, Miss Elizabeth chuckled. Then, sighing, she said, "I will not hold your aunt against you, and you will not hold Mr. Collins against me, and we will have a pleasant time chatting with my sisters about hats and ribbons and lace. We will have such a jolly time that we will drive your brother and Mr. Bingley to distraction."

Having overcome the slight hurdle to their easy enjoyment, their conversation turned to common topics about preparations for the winter months and what they all enjoyed doing during the colder months. Time passed quickly and soon the ladies had to return home, but not before Georgianna and Elizabeth made plans to meet up the next day to spend time together, just the two of them. Elizabeth had promised to look over the medicinal garden with Georgianna and Mrs. Annesley to see if there was anything that might be collected and used for the benefit of the manse or tenants of Netherfield.

Georgianna saw them off with much enthusiasm, but as their carriage pulled away, she turned to her brother and demanded, "What exactly has Elizabeth so out of sorts? She was almost timid when it came to the mention of that man!"

Groaning, Darcy rubbed his forehead before gesturing her and Mrs. Annesley back through the front door. "That is best discussed away from prying ears," he explained.

In short order, they had all moved into Bingley's study, and Georgianna was looking at him with an expectant gaze. When he glanced over at Bingley sitting behind his desk, he couldn't help but notice the subtle shrug and the peculiar frown that creased his face. Directing his attention back to the ladies in the room, he said, "I know I mentioned in my letter that Miss Elizabeth's family seems to encourage a match with her father's heir. As such, he feels he can direct Miss Elizabeth however he might want to correct her behavior."

Huffing, Georgianna exclaimed, "What can he have to correct? Elizabeth is everything that is good!"

"He is a fool, brimming with an unwarranted sense of superiority and blindly following our aunt's misguided advice. Things came to a bit of a head yesterday when he realized that Miss Elizabeth was looking over the novels in the bookshop. Not only did he castigate her for such a choice and knock the book out of her hands, but he also attempted to drag her out of the store by force. Bingley and I happened to be at the shop and had to step in and aid Miss Elizabeth and her younger sister, Miss Mary."

Bingley blurted, "Poor Miss Mary was shaking like a leaf, watching him mistreat her sister and being unable to do anything to stop him. He went so far as to say that as a man of God and a representative of Lady Catherine, we could not stop him from manhandling her."

While Georgianna gave a short sort of shriek, Mrs. Annesley's eyes turned equal parts hard and concerned. "What could he have been thinking?" she demanded. "I hope he didn't injure Miss Elizabeth."

Looking away, Darcy clenched his fists, trying to contain his anger. He finally said, "He gripped her arm so tightly, I'm almost certain it left bruises."

As Georgianna got up, a sense of restlessness filled the room. She paced back and forth, the sound of her footsteps creating a rhythmic pattern. Then, with a sudden stop, she spun around to face him, her voice filled with indignation as she said, "I cannot like it that Miss Elizabeth's parents would push her toward a match with such a despicable man. I know she will refuse any proposal, but she cannot be comfortable in such a situation. Is there anything we might do to help her?"

Everyone in the room looked around at each other with various expressions of frustration. They all knew that there was not much that they could do. Society did not give women much autonomy besides refusing a gentleman's request to marry her. They would have little choice but to wait and see how things progressed.

Finally, Mrs. Annesley said, "We shall be there for her, Georgianna, and give her the support that she needs at such a difficult time. Should anything in the situation shift, we will be available to offer any aid she may require."

FANNY BENNET LEFT HER husband's study unhappy with his flippant reaction to her concerns. She couldn't help but notice that he considered his negligence towards her and their children as revenge for her role in forcing him into the marriage, leaving her with a strong sense of frustration. It became clear to her long ago that her mother's notion of gentlemen swiftly recovering from compromises was completely misguided.

The life she had envisioned for herself, one filled with comfort and security, was nowhere to be found. Instead, the constant reminder haunted her that she would be left destitute and abandoned once he breathed his last at Longbourn. Despite her second daughter's insistence that she would do better to save, Fanny saw her many daughters as her route to financial stability once her husband died.

While Jane and Lydia would certainly have wealthy husbands, she had other daughters to consider as well. Kitty would most likely do well for some friend of Lydia's husband. She was pretty enough and men often like subservient wives, and she was such a follower that following her husband's dictates would be nothing to her at all, or so Fanny assumed. Mary and Elizabeth were different, however. They were not like her, but that did not mean she would not use them. She would not waste any of her money once her husband died to support any of her daughters. They would marry or find their own ways in the world.

Mr. Collins's arrival had proved a godsend. He was looking for a bride and she had plans to shift his attention to either Elizabeth or Mary. While Mary would be better at the role of a vicar's wife, with her moralizing and bible reading, it was obvious from the start that

Mr. Collins had fixated on Elizabeth, which she supposed was just as well. With one of her daughters as the heir's wife, she would maintain her ability to stay on at Longbourn, whatever ended up transpiring.

She had always assumed that Jane or Lydia's husband would invite her to live with them. She also liked the idea of staying on at Longbourn as mistress to continue her position as one of the leading ladies. Yes, Elizabeth would marry Mr. Collins and Fanny could stay on when Mr. Bennet died and really, good riddance. So what if she trapped him into marriage? He needed a wife and had shown no interest in any other lady beforehand. He could not have gone on forever without marrying. She was an excellent hostess and had kept her figure even after five pregnancies. What did he expect of her? She had followed her mother's advice and had not even been unfaithful to him.

Moving down the hallway in a huff, Fanny smiled when she spotted the unctuous little toad that was her husband's heir. He was disgusting but easily led if you knew how to do it. "Oh, Cousin Collins, I am so happy to see you," she gushed.

Smiling at her in his aloof way, he nodded. "Mrs. Bennet, lovely to see you. I have been looking for your daughters so that I may once again expound to them on the evils of reading on the feminine mind."

Forcing herself not to roll her eyes at his commentary, Fanny answered, "Mr. Darcy's sister and her companion have finally arrived, and they cordially invited Jane to join them for tea. Elizabeth, serving as a chaperone, accompanied her. Mary should be around here somewhere unless she is once again bringing aid to our tenants. The younger girls could be anywhere, but I do not know that you wanted to see them."

Shaking his head, his expression crestfallen, he murmured, "I shall simply have to save my speech until after dinner this evening. Perhaps then more of them will partake of Lady Catherine's wisdom."

"Yes, I am sure," Fanny spoke as she planned her escape for that evening. Perhaps she could develop a headache? No, that would not work. She could not force her daughters to pay attention to the man if she were absent. Mentally shrugging, Fanny figured she would think of something.

Deciding to get her plan in motion, she looked down the hall to see if they might be overheard. Then smiling, she stepped closer to Mr. Collins and, laying her hand softly on his arm, said, "My dear Cousin Collins, I know you lost your mother and so might not have the ability to turn to an older lady for advice. You may have your patroness, but I know that there are some things you could not speak with her about."

Looking down at her hand on his arm briefly, he tilted his head slightly before saying, "You are not wrong, madam."

"As part of your family, if only distantly, I would like to help you. You are interested in finding a wife to share your life with. I worry you might hesitate to act for fear of offending someone or saying the wrong thing."

Frowning, Mr. Collins agreed. "I have been instructed by Lady Catherine de Bourgh that it is not right for a vicar as important as myself to remain unwed. She sent me off commanding that I come back either engaged or married. However, I hesitate to act as I am uncertain how my words will be received. Then, too, I have not spoken with your good husband."

"May I assume that because you wish to speak with my husband, you wish to pick one of my daughters as your future life mate?" asked Fanny, knowing full well where his attention lay.

Grinning, he replied, "Yes, I have set my attention on Cousin Elizabeth as my future wife. Not only is she the heartiest, but she would also benefit from my instruction the most out of all her sisters."

"How wonderful! If I might suggest a few things to smooth your way?" Fanny waited until she saw his nod before continuing, "You do not know how it is for young ladies to wait in suspense, wondering when a man will propose. I suggest you put an end to the suspense and ask her at the first opportunity tomorrow."

THE PRESENCE OF MR. Collins sadly diminished the excitement Elizabeth felt about seeing Georgianna and Mr. Darcy later that day. At that moment, she regretted not returning from her walk earlier because now she had to watch him partake of his meal. She had only taken a few bites of her toast and eggs when he started in on his own plate like a hog at a trough. Elizabeth brought her serviette to her mouth in an attempt to hide her disgust.

He had piled his plate so high that Elizabeth wondered that there was any left for the rest of her family to have. Barely breathing in his gluttony, he shoveled food into his mouth in such a way that it defied explanation. Her father watched him, eyes dancing, and Elizabeth could only wonder at his attitude. Mr. Collins was the man that would take his place as master of Longbourn and instead of being concerned, he found the situation comical?

Even though she had lost her appetite, Elizabeth cautiously took small sips of her tea, doing her best to block out the sound of the man slurping and masticating across from her. Just as she thought it couldn't get any worse, he let out a thunderous belch, a satisfied smile playing on his lips as he greedily continued to stuff his maw.

The memory came rushing back to her, and she vividly recalled his account of being invited to partake in a meal with his patroness at her house, an opportunity that had come his way only once. It made even more sense now, observing his complete lack of table manners. Though she wondered why such an autocratic woman would not have demanded he improve or rather gain some table manners.

Throwing down her serviette in disgust, Elizabeth stood and said, "I find I have lost my appetite. I am going to get ready for a day of visiting the tenants."

As she moved to quit the room, Mr. Collins called out, his mouth full of half-chewed food that sprayed the table as he said, "Oh, but Miss Elizabeth, I wanted to have a word with you this morning. You cannot leave Longbourn before I have had a chance to talk with you."

Turning, Elizabeth faced him with a flat sort of smile. "I doubt you can have anything to say to me that I would want to hear. Or rather, you may not want to hear my response."

Having said as much, Elizabeth turned and fled the room. Such a man would not importune her in her own home. Not if she could help it. However, her mother's hand on her arm stopped her abruptly as she walked down the hall to her room.

Face florid in her anger, Mrs. Bennet declared, "Elizabeth, I insist you give Cousin Collins a moment of your time. I am sure he has something very important to discuss with you. You will hear him out and, of course, agree to whatever he asks of you."

Refusing to wince at the strength of her mother's grip, Elizabeth replied, "You may insist all you want, but I will not be obliging you."

Elizabeth had always known that her mother's fits of nerves had been a ploy for attention and to get her way, but it was never more evident in her fury at that moment. Her mother exhibited no weakness or nerves when drawing her daughter closer with a jerk. She hissed, "You stupid, hateful girl. Do you think you will get a better offer? You have not half of Jane's beauty or Lydia's liveliness. With your bluestocking pretensions and hoydenish behavior, the only husband you might catch on your own would likely be a tenant farmer."

Shaking her head, Elizabeth willed her tears not to fall. She had always known that her mother thought very little of her. More proof of it would not truly change anything. Focusing on her anger, Elizabeth ground out, "I care not what you think of me and my prospects. I still will not wed that man."

"You will marry him and save our family from the hedgerows. I will not lose my position as mistress of Longbourn to some unknown chit!"

With her soft soled slippers offering little resistance, Elizabeth's mother forcefully pulled her back to the breakfast room. To Elizabeth's surprise, her mother demonstrated a greater ability to pull her along than Mr. Collins had shown. Mrs. Bennet flung open the door and forcefully thrust her smaller daughter into the room. Elizabeth crashed into a chair, knocking it over before she caught herself on the edge of the table. Continuing her rant, Mrs. Bennet exclaimed, "Cousin Collins, Elizabeth is here and ready to hear whatever you wish to say."

The sight of laughter in her father's eyes only served to amplify Elizabeth's shame, as he seemed to find her mother's rough treatment of her as something to be entertained by. Elizabeth found she could no longer view her father as intelligent if this was how he behaved. In his relentless search for amusement, he had forsaken his intellect and any compassion he had ever owned. If he could not comprehend or care about the distress she was experiencing, understanding the great philosophers of the past meant nothing.

Mr. Collins, for his part, only put down his fork and asked, "Is there something wrong with Cousin Elizabeth?"

Mrs. Bennet laughed, "No, my dear Mr. Collins, she is merely clumsy this morning. I am sure you will find that she is not always so."

Ignoring the smear of grease on his chin, Mr. Collins tugged at his waistcoat absentmindedly before saying, "Well, then, Cousin Elizabeth, almost as soon as I entered the house, though I recognize your need for firm guidance, I singled you out as the companion of my future life. But before I am run away with by my feelings on this subject, perhaps it would be advisable for me to state my reasons for marrying."

Elizabeth refused to hear anything else. Instead of letting him have his say, she spoke over him, crying, "Mr. Collins! You may have chosen me as the companion of your future life, but I urge you to look elsewhere. Because believe me when I say that I will not marry you under any condition. You may stop your prattle and return to the trough that you have created for yourself."

Elizabeth's delight at witnessing the astonishment on Mr. Collins's face was short-lived, as her mother immediately intruded, violently seizing her and administering a sharp slap to her face. Cradling her aching cheek, Elizabeth looked to her father, hoping that finally he might step in. It was horrible to realize that he was chuckling at the display before him. Though they locked eyes for a moment, he only looked away.

"Dear Cousin Collins, do not mind my daughter or her false words. I fear her father has long let her have her way in things and it is time for her to understand her place. Her father and I will talk with her now and I am sure we can help her understand the inappropriateness of joking so with her intended." Mrs. Bennet propelled Elizabeth back towards the door before adding, "Mr. Bennet, it is time we speak with your daughter in your study." Grumbling, Mr. Bennet stood from his seat, leaving his paper and half-eaten breakfast, and followed his wife and daughter from the room.

Chapter Eighteen

Elizabeth caught sight of Mrs. Hill watching the tableau with sad eyes as she was being manhandled down the hall. They both knew that despite caring for those at Longbourn as the housekeeper for decades, Mrs. Hill was powerless to protect Elizabeth in that moment, no matter how much she wanted to. Still, Elizabeth took comfort in Mrs. Hill's desire to help, especially when she had lost all trust in her own parents' love and protection.

Jerking her arm out of her mother's grip, Elizabeth walked down the hall to her father's study with her head held high. Her parents could act however they wanted to. She was going to proceed with dignity. Once in the small room so filled with books and memories of a better time, Elizabeth stood before her father's desk, her gaze looking past where he sat and out the window.

It was not long before her mother began her rant. "I blame you, Mr. Bennet, for allowing her to develop airs and take up manly interests. Look at her now, so full ideas that she has become blind to the realities of life and what she owes us." Rounding on Elizabeth, she continued, "All the work I put into seeing you out in society—the dresses, the lessons, and the fretting and worry—and this is how you repay me? Despite all the care, feeding, and clothing we've provided for you throughout your entire life, how can you not show us gratitude and do what we ask?"

Facing her mother, eyes hard, Elizabeth let go of the tight lid she had been maintaining on her frustration. She retorted, "Mrs. Hill cared for me. Mrs. Anderson fed me. In fact, Jane and I took over the responsibility of planning meals for the family years ago. So I ensured that *you* were fed, and I created the budget that kept Longbourn afloat. As for clothes, yes, you saw me dressed, but never did you ask my opinion or my preferences when you chose my clothes, and you added so much lace I looked ridiculous. Aunt Gardiner taught me to manage a household, and I taught myself to manage an estate when my father's inattention risked the well-being of the estate we all rely on for support. Who exactly should be shown gratitude?"

On a roll, Elizabeth interrupted her mother's attempt to reply, her words laced with defiance. "You claim I am blind to life's realities, Mother, but I question if you truly comprehend the situation. If you somehow contrive my marriage to Mr. Collins and father should pass away, then I would be the mistress of Longbourn, not you."

Mrs. Bennet looked nervous, but she managed to say, "Obviously you would give way to me. I am your mother, and I have more experience running a household."

Laughing coldly, Elizabeth dispelled her mother's misconceptions by saying, "If you were to trap me in a life of torment with that man, I would make sure to repay the favor at the first opportunity. Think, Mother, that man is a fool. I could easily have you evicted from Longbourn the moment Papa died. As you have never sought to save for such an outcome, I wonder how you will manage on two-hundred pounds a year, which is all you will get in the interest of your dowry."

Turning to her husband, Mrs. Bennet cried, "Thomas!"

Throughout the whole confrontation with her mother, her father had only watched as if enjoying an on-stage drama. When his wife seemed to ask for his help, he only laughed. "She has you there, Fanny. If our daughter marries Mr. Collins, she will be mistress of Longbourn and able to act as she sees fit."

"But! I am her mother. She has to do as I say," wailed Mrs. Bennet.

This only made Mr. Bennet laugh harder. Once he could bring himself back under his control, he said, "Leave us, Fanny. Your daughter and I must talk."

Looking between her daughter and her husband, seeing that neither were doing as she wished, she began to cry and fled the room. As soon as her mother had left, Elizabeth faced her father, knowing the coming confrontation would be no easier. She began by saying, "It seems that you wish me to marry your heir."

Shrugging, he leaned back in his chair. "Why not? Someone must marry him, and it would be nice to have an actual Bennet at the helm."

Sighing, Elizabeth said, "I only wonder why you spent so much time educating me, allowing me to step in and run things."

"I have long known that my heir was a fool and would be incapable of managing Longbourn. In fact, without help, I am sure he would run it into the ground within two years. You are smart enough and have proven yourself these last few years. With you married to him, Longbourn has a future."

Aghast, Elizabeth cried, "I have essentially been the lamb, unknowingly groomed and fed for an inevitable sacrifice."

Placing his hand on his chin, Elizabeth watched as he pondered her words before smiling and saying, "That is a very apt analogy."

For a moment, Elizabeth hoped that there was something of her beloved father in the man before her, but then she saw his smile and she asked, "You would actually have me marry that man? Mate with that man? What of my happiness and self-respect?"

"It has been a long time since I have been happy. I do not see why you believe yourself better than me." Eyes starting to harden, Mr. Bennet continued, "And as for marrying that man, and mating him as you so aptly put it, you will have to marry and mate someone. Why not my heir? It's unrealistic to have higher expectations."

Shaking her head, Elizabeth said, "Just like my mother, you have missed understanding something vital. Though women have few rights the world over, in England we have the right of refusal. You can force me to the altar, but I have the power to say no once I get there."

Smiling, he countered, "Oh, but you do not reach your majority for another six months. That is a long time to resist your mother's insistence. I will allow her to proceed however she wants to get you to comply or force the issue. At the very least, I am sure it will be a merry battle of wills."

Had the man she had known throughout her childhood been a lie? A carefully crafted act to arrange things as he wanted them and at his least inconvenience. Had he never loved her? "I am surprised at you, Father, willing to wager Longbourn on such shaky odds. You know I will not comply and if by some slim chance I am forced, I will not be kind to Mother and I am unlikely to have any control over that buffoon. What then? What of Longbourn and Mother then?"

Shrugging, Mr. Bennet said, "I will be dead and certainly beyond caring."

Feeling suddenly cold, Elizabeth turned to leave without another word. She got as far as the door before he commented, "If you think to leave and seek refuge with your aunt and uncle in London, know that I will just command your return from your Uncle Gardiner. As I said previously, you are still six months shy of your majority. I would suggest that you think before you act. The world is not a nice place, and it is not as if you have any friends among the great and good." As she looked over her shoulder, Elizabeth caught her father's gaze and heard him say, "Though if you choose to cast your lot away from Longbourn, I am sure you may find some form of worthy employment. I saw to your education, after all."

It did not take long for Elizabeth to make it to her room and mechanically open her top drawer. She could not stay, not even to search out Jane. If she waited, her parents might realize what she was about and lock her in her room. As she collected all the money that she had kept on hand and shoved it roughly into her reticule, Elizabeth clamped down on her emotions. She could cry later. At the moment, she had to flee. Most of her savings were in an account with her Uncle Gardiner, but she would have enough to cover a few expenses, and she would not leave it behind with everything else.

She found she wanted nothing that her mother and father had so begrudgingly given her. Not the boots or the books or any of the clothes sewn with too much lace. She would leave it all. Only taking the time to grab her heavy shawl that had been a gift from her Aunt Madeleine, she left without even taking one last look around the room that had housed her for so long. After all, it was not the shelter she thought it was—it had just been the pen to keep her in until her parents were ready to lead her in the way they chose. A sacrifice on the altar of her parents' selfishness and derision.

GEORGIANNA SAT ON THE stone bench with her head tilted back so she could soak in the sun's rays. It was a beautiful autumn day, though chilly, and the little garden running alongside Netherfield was delightful. Taking a deep breath, she smiled at the sweet smell of it. It smelled of damp earth and fallen leaves and Georgianna could not get enough of it into her lungs. After spending so much time in London, with its smog-filled sky, Georgianna was relieved to breathe in the fresh air and cleanse her lungs of the city's pollution.

"If you keep doing that, Miss Darcy, you are likely to faint," commented Mrs. Annesley.

Giggling, Georgianna turned to her companion, replying pertly, "If fainting is the price I have to pay to get London out of my lungs, so be it."

Reaching out, Mrs. Annesley replaced the shawl that had slid down Georgianna's shoulder in a motherly fashion. Gazing out over the garden and fields beyond, she asked, "Your brother will be done discussing matters with Mr. Bingley and his steward soon. Do you know what you would like to do with him?"

Smiling up at the sun, Georgianna murmured, "I do not really know. Maybe I will ask him to give me a tour of the garden or some of the nearby lanes. Though it is getting rather cold to be out of doors for any length of time. Regardless, Miss Elizabeth is supposed to be coming this afternoon. I long for an extended discussion with her, where we can openly address the sadness that was clear in her eyes yesterday, and I hope she will feel comfortable confiding in me."

Turning to Mrs. Annesley, Georgianna worried her lip before continuing, "Do you suppose she might consider me too young to confide in?"

Patting Georgianna's knee, Mrs. Annesley answered, "No, my dear, if she has any hesitation confiding in you, it will not be because of your age."

Eyes widening, Georgianna leaned forward, concerned by the implication that Lizzie might hesitate to confide in her. "Why do you think Elizabeth might not want to confide in me?"

Georgianna watched as Mrs. Annesley sighed, looking off into the distance for a moment before saying, "Miss Elizabeth is the type of person who is so used to being the one that others rely on that it might be difficult for her to accept help from others. It is not uncommon for individuals in such circumstances to measure their worth based on their deeds for others, mistakenly viewing vulnerability and seeking help as signs of weakness and failure."

"Oh, but Lizzie could never be a failure!" cried Georgianna. "She does so much to help so many people. Just look at how much she has helped me and William!"

A melancholic half smile tugged at the corner of Mrs. Annesley's lips, her eyes filled with an unmistakable sadness before she said, "It is not about what kind of person she is; it is about how she sees herself."

Though what Mrs. Annesley said made sense to Georgianna, it only deepened her curiosity about the source of her wisdom. Turning to face her companion fully, she asked, "Where did you come by such wisdom? Not that I doubt you by any means. I am just curious."

"It is a hard-earned knowledge, Miss Darcy." Mrs. Annesley paused, and Georgianna wondered if she had asked too much of her.

But then looking over Georgianna's shoulder at nothing much at all, Mrs. Annesley continued, "I married a gentleman who, as a third son, had little in the way to support himself, let alone me, but we were in love and thought little of the hardships we faced. He joined the regulars in order to support us and I was determined not to be parted from the man I loved, so I followed him to the continent. It is how I met your cousin, the colonel, actually. I saw many things during my time with the troops and I came back a changed woman and a widow, but what is relevant now is that I often saw people who, like your Miss Elizabeth, took much on themselves. The issue with this kind of behavior is that it gradually becomes unbearable, and when everything inevitably crumbles, the weight of their perceived failures can overwhelm people. I saw it several times in soldiers who believed that their unwavering determination and tireless efforts could rescue every single person. My husband was such a man."

Leaning over on the bench, Georgianna wrapped her companion in a hug and said, "Oh, Mrs. Annesley, I am sorry. I knew you were a widow, but I am sorry to admit that I had never thought how it came about." Pulling back, she looked Mrs. Annesley in the eye and clasping her hands in her own, she added, "I do not know if it is exactly proper, but I want you to know that if you should ever want to talk about your husband, I want to listen."

Smiling, albeit through a haze of tears, Mrs. Annesley said, "That is very kind of you, Miss Darcy. I will not hesitate should I feel the need."

Georgianna hugged Mrs. Annesley again, glad to have learned something about the very compassionate woman. It was no wonder that she seemed so wise. Mrs. Annesley had seen more of the world than probably most women and yet somehow, she had not let it drag her down into the darkness.

After releasing Mrs. Annesley and giving her some space, they sat together on the bench in peaceful silence. Georgianna relished the tranquility of nature and the gentle presence of the sun on her face. However, something drew her attention to the distant field.

Brows drawn in concern, Georgianna stood and moved a few steps toward the distant figure. "There is someone coming this way, and I think they may need help."

Following Georgianna's lead, Mrs. Annesley moved closer, shielding her eyes from the sun and agreed, "Yes, I believe you are correct. Go tell a servant to fetch your brother and Mr. Bingley. They should probably be made aware. I will see if I can be of aid."

ELIZABETH REGRETTED NOT CHANGING into her walking boots. It was all well and good to want to have nothing to do with what her parents had given her, but walking to Netherfield in her soft-soled shoes had been eminently foolish. She had not made it one mile before she had begun limping.

Still, Elizabeth had not stopped. She had trudged ahead. At that moment, all she knew was that she wanted to see Georgianna. She had promised that she would see her that day, and so she would. Elizabeth found herself at a crossroads, unsure of what to do about moving forward. However, she remained determined to honor her commitment before escaping her parents' schemes.

Ignoring her throbbing feet, Elizabeth moved one foot after another, knowing that she would reach Netherfield soon enough. Somewhere in the back of her mind, Elizabeth knew she was not thinking logically, but that part of her mind that should have cared was damaged.

Elizabeth could not worry about what she would do after she saw Georgianna. She could not determine how she might circumvent her parents from harming her and her sisters. The part of her that used to strategize and push forward with determination seemed to have disappeared. She had no choice but to put one foot after another and move forward in the only way she knew how.

She walked until suddenly she was stopped by hands on her shoulders and a firm voice drawing her back to herself. It took Elizabeth a moment to hear her name. "Miss Elizabeth!"

Blinking away some fuzziness, Elizabeth realized that Mrs. Annesley was before her saying something. Was she already at Netherfield? Again Mrs. Annesley spoke, and this time Elizabeth could understand her when she said, "Miss Elizabeth, look at me now, my dear. Have you walked all the way from Longbourn?"

Feeling like a broken doll, Elizabeth nodded. Part of her wanted to explain what had happened, but another part wanted to stay numb. Staying numb meant she did not have to face the anguish of her parents' betrayal and the question of what she was going to do.

Elizabeth felt Mrs. Annesley wrap an arm around her shoulders and lead her onward. Looking around her, it bewildered Elizabeth to realize that she had reached Netherfield. It felt like only moments before she had walked through her old home and shut the door behind her for the last time.

Then Georgianna was there in front of her with tears on her face and something inside of Elizabeth shuddered. Elizabeth hated it when those she loved cried. It always made her want to help someone or hurt someone, depending on what was required.

Blinking again, Elizabeth heard Georgianna say, "Oh, Lizzie, whatever happened to you?"

Licking her numb lips, Elizabeth felt the need to reassure Georgianna. Her voice was oddly rough when she said, "I am all right, Georgie."

As Elizabeth started feeling more like herself, she took in more of her surroundings. They were not quite all the way to Netherfield, still in the grassy field that ran alongside the gardens. While it relieved Elizabeth that she had almost reached her destination, she wondered what she would do once she got there. Should she ask for help to get to London? Even if her father demanded her returned to Longbourn, her Uncle Gardiner could squirrel her away somewhere. He had contacts all over the world. Surely, he could help her. Elizabeth would go almost anywhere as long as it was not with that fool, Mr. Collins.

Elizabeth could feel Georgianna's arm on her waist, adding her support to Mrs. Annesley's. She was just about to tell Georgianna that she was fine when she stepped on an uncomfortably sharp rock. The pain that went shooting up her leg would have sent her to her knees if not for the steady support from both of them.

"Miss Elizabeth," Mrs. Annesley suggested, "perhaps we should wait for assistance to arrive?"

Elizabeth had always liked how capable she was, heading everywhere under her own power, but she knew she was going to have to stop soon. Her feet were constantly throbbing now, and it took most of her concentration to put one foot in front of another. Looking to the garden with the convenient bench, Elizabeth judged it to be possibly ten yards away. Surely, she could make it that far.

Glancing over at Mrs. Annesley, Elizabeth tried to smile but found it oddly painful. So instead she said, "If you will help, I think I can make it to the bench just over there."

Elizabeth could tell that Mrs. Annesley was not particularly happy about her suggestion, but despite the notch between her brows, she nodded and said, "All right, Miss Elizabeth, let us make our way to the bench."

It seemed to Elizabeth that she struggled more in those last few yards than she had for the rest of the miles she had traversed to get there. She would never go walking out of doors without a sturdy pair of boots again. Elizabeth realized it was foolish of her to have not changed into her boots out of spite, but she could not go back and change it, so she pushed herself forward one step at a time.

Elizabeth finally reached the bench and sank onto it, feeling an overwhelming sense of gratitude as the weight lifted off her aching feet. Georgianna immediately sat down beside her, wrapping Elizabeth in a warm embrace and crying, "Oh, my dear friend, what has left you so altered?"

Leaning into the comfort that Georgianna offered, Elizabeth sighed, murmuring, "My parents happened."

Chapter Nineteen

Darcy hurried out to the garden. He and Bingley received information about an issue and someone needing help. With the meeting with the steward swiftly wrapped up, they wasted no time in embarking on their quest to uncover the source of the issue. He felt a sinking sensation in his heart, and he prayed his sister was all right. He attempted to convince himself that Georgianna was unharmed, but still there was an odd stuttering in his chest.

As he came outside with Bingley at his heels, he saw his sister and Mrs. Annesley huddled around someone sitting on the bench. As he approached, Mrs. Annesley broke away and, coming towards him, said, "It is Miss Elizabeth. She came all the way by foot. It seems she has fled Longbourn."

Fled? What could have happened that would have caused Miss Elizabeth to flee her home? Darcy knew that her mother had been encouraging a match with that foul Mr. Collins, but beyond that, he knew of no danger she might be facing. Putting his questions out of his mind, Darcy rushed past Mrs. Annesley, only to halt as he took in Miss Elizabeth's disheveled appearance.

The sight of Miss Elizabeth, with her usually impeccable brown curls now in disheveled strands falling around her pale face, only emphasized the haunted look in her green eyes. She wore a delicate morning dress that offered little protection against the chilly autumn wind. The worst part was the visible bruise on her cheekbone, its dark hue contrasting with her pale skin.

Dropping to his knees, Darcy's anguished voice filled the air as he cried, "My God, Miss Elizabeth, what on earth could have occurred to leave you in such a state?"

From beside Miss Elizabeth, Georgianna spoke up, her voice thick with tears. "She said her parents had something to do with it."

Sighing, Miss Elizabeth said, "My mother was unhappy when I refused Mr. Collins. My father is supporting her attempt to dissuade me from my refusal."

There was a hollow quality in Miss Elizabeth's voice that made Darcy ache. Miss Elizabeth was light and enthusiasm. She was a gift to everyone around her, and the fact that her family had brought her so low was so horrendous. It pierced his heart in a way that hurt him and enraged him. He might not know the details of what had happened, but he knew in that moment that someone was going to regret hurting Miss Elizabeth. He would see to it.

He could not look away from the tears in Miss Elizabeth's eyes, but Mrs. Annesley put her hand on his shoulder. "Mr. Darcy, we must get her inside and away from prying eyes. We certainly cannot help her out here."

Nodding, he said, "You are right, Mrs. Annesley, we must get her inside."

Standing, Darcy began to offer his arm when Georgianna said, "She wore her slippers walking here and has hurt her feet, William."

Looking at his sister, Miss Elizabeth murmured, "Georgie, my feet do not hurt that badly. I am sure I am well enough to make it into the building."

Shaking her head, Georgianna said, "But you do not have to." Turning to Darcy she said, "Carry her, William. She should not be walking."

Without hesitation, he obliged his sister's command. His muscular arms encircled Miss Elizabeth, lifting her effortlessly and cradling her against his chest. When he heard Miss Elizabeth release a small gasp, he had to strengthen his knees and force himself to walk with purpose.

He had almost forgotten that Bingley was there until he saw his concerned expression as he hovered next to him. Realizing that it was important to prevent gossip, he said, "Bingley, clear the path so that the servants see nothing."

He strode silently through Netherfield, Georgianna and Mrs. Annesley trailing after him. As he stopped at the top of the stairs, trying to decide where he should bring Miss Elizabeth, Georgianna said, "Take her to my sitting room, William. My maid will not say a word. Lizzie will be safe there."

Once again, following his younger sister's instructions, he walked and if anything had been able to make him smile at that juncture, it was at that moment when he realized how much his sister had grown. She was giving orders like the grand lady she would someday be and all because she had been strengthened by her friendship with the wounded woman in his arms. Together, they would see her returned to her previous effervescent nature.

In no time at all, he was putting Miss Elizabeth down in his sister's sitting room. When she hobbled the last few steps and sunk down onto a chair with a sigh, Darcy frowned, realizing just how injured she truly was. After everyone was in the room and Georgianna's maid had been sent off to bring back tea, he sat down.

As he glanced at Elizabeth sitting in the chair across from him, Darcy couldn't help but notice her carefully blank expression, prompting him to conclude that something had shifted in her world. A shift had occurred in his world as well. Carrying her changed everything, and in his heart and mind, she was no longer just Miss Elizabeth. She meant more than that to him now. He did not know what that meant yet, but he was not about to let it go without finding out.

The silence stretched out like an expectant pause before them all. Darcy wanted to know what had happened. He wanted to know all the details and wanted to identify every person responsible for the bruise on Elizabeth's cheek. And yet it hurt him to think of her being so injured and so he held back, afraid to ask what had happened. But then into the silence, Elizabeth spoke.

"I suppose I have known for some time that things would come to a head, but in my foolishness, I hoped that if I ignored it or rather tried to circumvent the coming proposal, things would be well. I was wrong." With a sigh, Elizabeth ran a hand down her face and winced as her fingers grazed the tender bruise on her cheek.

Around the room, four pairs of eyes watched her in obvious concern, but no one spoke. Elizabeth knew that they all wanted to know why she had shown up so out of sorts and bedraggled. So, gathering her fortitude, Elizabeth took a breath and continued, "After my walk this morning, I found myself stuck at the table with my cousin and my parents. Unable to bear witness to his horrendous table manners any longer, I excused myself, only to have Mr. Collins say that he wished to speak with me. With a firm voice, I told him I was certain he would not wish to hear my response to anything he had to say, and without waiting for a reply, I swiftly left the room."

Georgianna, who had taken a seat beside her on the settee, took her hand in her own and squeezed it reassuringly. Elizabeth smiled gratefully at Georgianna before saying, "My mother stopped me in the hall and commanded me to return and agree to his proposal. When I refused, she dragged me back into the room and practically threw me at Mr. Collins's feet. After a few sentences of his inept attempt at a proposal, I interrupted him. I told him in no uncertain terms that I would never marry him under any circumstances. Needless to say, my mother was not happy, though my father thought it was humorous. They escorted me to my father's study where I learned that my mother believed she would remain mistress over Longbourn until her death if I married Mr. Collins. I quickly dispelled her misconception, sternly warning her that if she dared manipulate me into such a vile predicament, I would ensure she was thrown into the very hedgerows she dreaded the moment my father died."

The memory of her mother's shock at the news was, now that the moment had passed, quite comical. Elizabeth pressed a hand to her lips to stop herself from bursting into unaccountable laughter. It was just all so ridiculous. Looking over at Georgianna, who still held her hand, Elizabeth saw sorrow while Mr. Darcy and Mr. Bingley's expressions were harder, as if they wore twin masks of granite. Mrs. Annesley's gaze held a gentle understanding, mirroring the comforting kindness Elizabeth saw when confiding in her Aunt Madeline.

Determined to complete her story, Elizabeth pushed through the pain in her heart and disclosed the remaining details. By no means was she going to leave her father out of the tale. "My father dismissed my mother and revealed that my marrying his heir had long been part of his plan. He knew that Mr. Collins was foolish and incapable of taking possession of Longbourn without destroying it. He taught me and allowed me to manage things with the thought in mind that I could run Longbourn or at least mitigate the damage done by Mr. Collins. I've effectively run Longbourn for three years, reinforcing his perception that sacrificing me would be the best solution to the problem at hand. In the end, he pointed out that if I fled to my family in London, he would only have me brought back as I am not of age. He was looking forward to watching the struggle between myself and my mother as she would have free rein to force the issue in the ensuing months. He said that if I choose to forsake my family, at least he had allowed me to learn enough to take a position that was at least remotely respectable.

"So I left. I took the money that I saved and left everything behind. I was afraid that if I staid any longer than necessary, I would be locked in my room." Turning to Georgianna, she squeezed her hand and said, "I promised that I would see you today, so I came here. I do not know where I will go from here, but I wanted to at least say goodbye to you all and ask that you let my sisters somehow know what has happened. Otherwise, they will be terrified that I have gone missing."

Gripping both Elizabeth's hands in her own, Georgianna said, "Nonsense. You are in no shape to travel somewhere, nor are you prepared for it." Looking across the small sitting room, Georgianna looked at the gentlemen and declared, "Elizabeth shall stay here with me, and we will do what we must to see her through. If that is not something you are prepared to do, I shall take her with me, and we will either go to Darcy House or Pemberley."

Standing, Mr. Bingley exclaimed, "Of course Miss Elizabeth shall stay. Though we shall have to be careful that word does not spread that she is here, else her father may insist upon her return."

Mr. Darcy also stood but instead of saying anything, he stalked closer to Elizabeth, then kneeling before her, said, "I think that you have left something out of your tale."

Confused, Elizabeth's eyebrows drew together, and she shook her head ever so slightly before asking, "What do you mean, Mr. Darcy? I explained everything important." Elizabeth could feel his gaze shift and focus on her sore cheek, the warmth of his attention causing her to blush. Self-consciously, Elizabeth reached up, hovering near the bruise that had so much of Mr. Darcy's attention.

Mr. Darcy's voice turned soft and yet somehow urgent when he inquired, "Who hit you?"

Wide eyed, Elizabeth licked her lips at the power of Mr. Darcy's presence before she could say, "My mother hit me, Mr. Darcy, and my father laughed."

As Darcy paced around Bingley's study, an image came to him of a panther that he had once seen caged in a menagerie in London.

Its pacing had intrigued him, its steps measured and filled with a sense of danger. Its motions had mesmerized him. They were calculated and controlled, exuding an air of menace. It was not until that moment that Darcy understood the animal's predicament. The panther wanted to get out of its confinement and hunt and tear and rend, but it was impossible, so it paced.

Making another circuit of the room, Darcy looked back at Bingley who sat at his desk, though he was certainly not calm. Turning to face Bingley, Darcy barked, "I cannot allow this to stand. Something must be done about Mr. and Mrs. Bennet."

Darcy recognized the hardened expression on Bingley's face, similar to the one he wore during their fencing sessions. He was planning a strategy of attack. Tapping on the table with his forefinger in a rapid beat, Bingley said, "I agree. Miss Elizabeth's parents' actions have been repugnant, and we must, of course, protect her however we can. Though now that I am thinking about the matter, I am worried about Miss Bennet and her other sisters. What is to say when they realize that Miss Elizabeth is well and truly beyond their control that they don't just turn their focus on one of their other daughters?"

The sound of Darcy's footsteps echoed through the room as he returned to his angry pacing. The moment that Darcy had seen Elizabeth's condition, he had known that he would have to see to it that her parents regretted their actions. Realizing that he had to protect Elizabeth's sisters as well only moved up the timeline. The fact that Mr. Collins hadn't touched Elizabeth again was the only reason he wasn't on his way to Longbourn to confront him.

The Bennets would find that he was not the sort of man to make an enemy of. Though he rarely used his connections, he had them in abundance. His uncle was an earl who was prominent in the house of lords, and that was only the beginning. Darcy had connections to various members of the upper gentry through blood and friendship. His cousin Richard was a colonel, facing off against Napoleon. Through Richard, Darcy had connections all over England with various retired military men. As far as Mr. Collins, well, he would quake at the knowledge that Darcy's godfather was the archbishop of Canterbury.

"Darcy, I am going to go over to Longbourn. I know Jane will be worried about her sister, and who knows what her parents might be up to."

Sitting down across from Bingley, Darcy said, "I know you are concerned for your lady love. You should make your way to Longbourn and see her for yourself. We want to make it clear that we are fully committed to taking care of her sister, and perhaps extend an invitation for her to join us for tea tomorrow with Miss Mary." Eyes narrowing, Darcy smiled, "While you are there, see if you can observe anything that might help us protect Miss Bennet and her sisters. I am going to get to writing a few letters that I want to send by express. I have a few ideas about how we might handle things, but I will need to consult with a few people."

With a nod, both gentlemen stood and left the room, Bingley to get ready to leave and Darcy to seek his room and his desk so that he could write his letters. As he made his way up the stairs and to his room, Darcy saw Mrs. Annesley coming out of the sitting room that she shared with Georgianna. Hurrying to her side, he asked, "How is Elizabeth?"

Frowning, the woman said in a low voice, "I put a little laudanum in some wine and encouraged her to drink it. She was in quite a bit of pain from her poor feet."

"Her feet?" asked Mr. Darcy.

"Walking here wearing her slippers did not do her any favors and severely blistered and bruised the soles of her feet. She also has bruising on both of her arms, probably from such rough handling." Sighing, Mrs. Annesley continued, "Really, all of this morning was too much of a shock for her, and I hope that a good rest will help her regain her equanimity."

Pausing, she looked back at the door that she had just left before adding, "Though I fear such a betrayal will be difficult to overcome."

Darcy could well imagine what Mrs. Annesley had said was true. Hadn't he suffered when his father failed to hear him, when he warned him about Wickham's duplicity? Still, how much worse was it to have a cherished parent want to sacrifice you because they were too lazy to care themselves? Knowing Mrs. Annesley was waiting for a response, Darcy said, "I am going to my room to write a series of letters. I have an idea or two about how we might rectify the situation and protect Elizabeth and her sisters. Please summon me if there is any need at all."

As he turned to go, Mrs. Annesley stopped him, saying, "Mr. Darcy, I know you are a man used to ordering everything in your life at your own will, but I would hate you to do something to hurt Miss Elizabeth unknowingly. Keep in mind that beneath the shock she has had, she is an intelligent woman, and she most likely has her own ideas about how things might be best handled. How would you like it if someone directed your life without your consultation? Whatever you do, do not move forward with any plans without consulting her."

Running a hand down his face, Darcy let out a weary sigh. He wished he could take away the pain that Elizabeth was sure to feel when she woke, both physical and emotional, but he knew that would not be possible. He had only ever felt this way when he had seen Georgianna's tears, the raw pain and betrayal etched on her face. It made him want to do something, anything, to help, but Mrs. Annesley was right. He needed to consult with Elizabeth before he acted.

It was odd realizing that he felt so strongly about a woman he had only recently met. Georgianna had talked of Elizabeth for some time before they had met. Until that point in his life, Darcy's two closet friends were Richard and Bingley, and he had not even felt this strongly when either of them had needed his help. Was the experience of being friends with a woman significantly different from that of being friends with a man?

Chapter Twenty

Elizabeth woke up with a feeling of all-encompassing dread. The night before had been a hazy mix of pain and tears. Between the ache in her feet and her heart, Georgianna and Mrs. Annesley had not left her alone and were constantly plying her with tea or wine laced with laudanum. She was determined that she would handle everything that day without the aid of the laudanum. She did not like the way it made her feel and had heard stories of people becoming far too attached to the substance.

On a normal day, she would have gotten out of bed and gone for a long walk to help her sort through the turbulence in her mind, but that was out of reach for the moment. Her error in not changing into her boots the day before had left her feet bruised, battered, and blistered. When Georgianna caught sight of Elizabeth's feet, she immediately considered summoning the apothecary. However, the urgency of maintaining secrecy dissuaded her from doing so.

They had undergone the painful process of cleaning and bandaging her feet themselves, and Elizabeth had to admit that she was grateful for the laudanum. She had little expectation of seeing much improvement that morning. Wiggling her toes beneath the covers, Elizabeth attempted to gauge the extent of her discomfort. It was not as bad as she thought it might be, but it was certainly not comfortable.

Looking over, Elizabeth spotted Georgianna asleep in the bed next to her. Despite feeling slightly guilty for imposing, Elizabeth found it endearing that her friend was so willing to sacrifice her privacy and share her bed. Unable to lie there any longer, Elizabeth sighed and, sitting up, swung her feet over the side of the bed. Surely, she could make it at least to the sitting room so that she could sit up and maybe read.

Elizabeth had often thought it impossible to think over serious matters while laying down. The longer she lay there, unable to escape her swirling thoughts, the more she felt the urge to give in to her emotions, potentially resulting in rash actions such as crying or screaming out against her frustration. Biting her lip, Elizabeth let her right foot come to rest against the floor and slowly brought her weight to bear. Breathing deeply through her nose, Elizabeth changed her destination to the chair in the corner of Georgianna's room. Perhaps she could make the five or so steps it would take to get there.

By the time she reached the chair, Elizabeth felt an overwhelming desire to express herself more forcefully than simply saying it hurt. She wondered if the origin of the phrase "curse like a sailor" was rooted in the fact that sailors often injured themselves. It made sense that they would want to find a more expressive way to cope with their pain. It might have nothing to do with that, but it certainly helped to take her mind off the pain in her feet and allowed her to chuckle.

Elizabeth sat there breathing deeply for a few minutes before she looked around and spotted a small stack of books on the side table. As much as she wanted to read and forget all her worries, Elizabeth knew she could not. As kind as everyone had been, it was not as if she could stay at Netherfield indefinitely. She would have to leave sooner rather than later. But where would she go?

She could not go to the Gardiners in London. Her father would simply demand her return, and she did not want to risk them getting in trouble somehow. Just a mere six months older, and things would be so much easier, but then again, she would not be in this situation if she had already reached her majority. Elizabeth could have just gone to stay with her aunt and uncle in London and be done with her parents.

The daunting task of evading her father's detection for the next half a year loomed before her, and she couldn't devise a single plan to accomplish it. Elizabeth had put some funds aside, hoping to be of use as a small dowry, but she was uncertain if she could arrange all that would be necessary. She would need to find a companion and a small cottage somewhere to wait until her father lost his hold over her. The thought of being forced home after what had occurred was too much.

Her biggest fear of being forced to return home was the possibility that her mother or father might stage a compromise. Not only would that ruin her, but her sisters as well, if she did not comply to their wishes. Marriage was for life and if God did not strike Mr. Collins down for his heretic ways, her life would not be worth living.

Elizabeth looked down at her feet in frustration. If there was ever a time to pace, this was it. She knew she might take a position as a companion or possibly a governess, but both options had their drawbacks. If she took employment, she would give up her societal status and any hope of ever marrying well, if at all, would be gone. Despite her reservations, Elizabeth had consistently believed that she would be happier working rather than being trapped in a loveless marriage that lacked respect.

Still, Elizabeth hesitated to consider employment to solve her current problem. Her father's last cutting comment about having prepared her for a life of employment made her resist such an option. Elizabeth knew him well enough to understand that he found the notion of her debasing herself by seeking employment rather than obeying his desires and becoming the mistress of Longbourn quite comical. The thought of doing something he would be happy to laugh at made her sick to her stomach.

For all her thinking, when she finally heard movement from the various preparations for the day, Elizabeth had not come to any conclusions besides the fact that she felt like an orphan, and she would refuse to acknowledge either parent as such again. They were to be Mr. and Mrs. Bennet when she addressed them, even in her thoughts. Never again would she say the words mother and father or any of its derivations.

Somehow, it did not surprise Mrs. Annesley to find Miss Elizabeth awake and pensive so early in the morning. She first saw her hobbling into the sitting room from where she had slept with Georgianna. Mrs. Annesley hurried to her side, helping her settle on the settee. Concern etched her face as she asked, "What were you thinking, trying to walk about?"

Taking up one of the nearby pillows, Mrs. Annesley propped up Miss Elizabeth's feet and looked at her with concern. It was easy to note the lines of pain around the young lady's mouth and eyes when she said, "I just could not sit quietly any longer and I did not want to wake up Georgianna. I stopped and rested for a while in the chair in Georgianna's room."

Tsking at Miss Elizabeth, Mrs. Annesley knelt near her feet and examined the bandages she had put in place the day before. They looked well enough. At least there was not anything seeping through.

Rising, Mrs. Annesley moved to sit in a nearby chair and said, "I would have preferred to have summoned the apothecary to look at your wounded feet, but as we cannot, you really must stay off your feet. I really do not know what we might do if they get worse."

Sighing, Miss Elizabeth ran a hand down her face while being careful to avoid her bruised cheek. Looking back at Mrs. Annesley with weary eyes, Miss Elizabeth said, "I understand, but it will be a struggle. Whenever I'm feeling unsettled, the urge to go for a walk always takes hold of me. It brings me a sense of peace, and as I tire myself physically, I also find that my thoughts become more organized and focused."

"I can only imagine the conflicting emotions that must be swirling within you, having gone through so much hardship and simultaneously being deprived of the pastime that used to bring you solace." Mrs. Annesley watched as Miss Elizabeth nodded.

It was sad to see Miss Elizabeth brought so low, but Mrs. Annesley knew from experience that life was often unfair. Mrs. Annesley almost wished that she would have a good cry instead of trying to be so strong and self-contained. It was wiser to sway with the storm rather than risk breaking under its force.

Finally, speaking up, Miss Elizabeth said, "Mrs. Annesley, I feel lost and unsure of what to do with myself. I cannot tell if I want to cry or scream and as I cannot do what I would normally do, I am growing weary from the struggle of trying to maintain my composure."

"I realize this may not align with societal expectations for women, but I believe a good cry is exactly what you need right now." Leaning forward, Mrs. Annesley focused on Miss Elizabeth, waiting for her to look up before she continued. "I do not think that trying to maintain your control will help you in the long run, and you will find that I am a good listener. Let me be there for you as you have been there for others in the past."

Having said what she wanted to, Mrs. Annesley waited. Waiting quietly often led others to fill the empty space with words. It had helped her to learn many things in the past. After waiting for only a few minutes, Miss Elizabeth said, "I really cannot understand how I feel, or rather, I am feeling too many things at once to sort through them." Miss Elizabeth hesitated, appearing as if she was about to sit up and swing her legs around, but then halted and huffed in frustration. Cradling her head in her hands, she muttered, "One of the chief things I am feeling is frustration at this moment."

Then, after waiting even longer, Elizabeth admitted, "I have always tried to be a good daughter. The only thing I ever do for myself regularly is take my morning walks. I give, and I give, and I give, and when I finally come to a line that I cannot cross—that if I cross, I will be no more—I say no. I finally say no and what do I get? A slap in the face and condemnation. I am told that I am reprehensible and that I should be glad that I have a chance to sacrifice my joy, my sanity, and my very virtue on the altar of my mother's happiness and security."

Breathing heavily, Miss Elizabeth rubbed at her eyes, her voice turning weak when she said, "Who I am and what I can do is not enough for them." Looking at Mrs. Annesley, she begged, "Why is who I am never enough? What did I do to deserve such treatment from both my parents?" Glancing over at Mrs. Annesley with tears glistening on her lashes, "Have all my sacrifices been for nothing?"

Shaking her head, Mrs. Annesley said, "I could never understand why people are so driven to mistreat others. Though you might be able to answer the reverse. Why do you treat other people well?"

A surprised "oh" escaped Miss Elizabeth's lips, but her demeanor quickly shifted to a more serious one. Taking a moment to consider, she said, "The sight of a smile on someone's lips is much more pleasing to me than the sight of a frown. Knowing that I have lived a privileged life compared to others, I cannot fathom why I would ever want to exacerbate someone's circumstances instead of working towards making them better." Blinking, Miss Elizabeth glanced at her clutched hands for a moment before looking back at Mrs. Annesley and adding, "It is simply not in my character."

Mrs. Annesley had known her answer would be something of the sort. Hoping to provoke further thought, she asked, "I know you have worked hard not just to be kind but to care for the poor and Longbourn's tenants. Were you seeking any personal gain from your actions?"

Shaking her head, Miss Elizabeth quickly explained, "When I knew that no one else was doing what needed to be done, I took up the reins myself. I have worked tirelessly at Longbourn because I couldn't bear to see tenants suffer without offering my help. I did not do it in hopes of any sort of compensation."

Mrs. Annesley smiled warmly at Miss Elizabeth, admiring her kindhearted nature. She knew that living in a small hamlet, Miss Elizabeth had yet to experience the vastness of the world. She was, however, realizing how dark it could be. So she counseled Miss Elizabeth by saying, "In this world, there are individuals who navigate through life solely driven by self-interest, always on the lookout for what they can take from others, including their own family. There also exist individuals similar to you, who possess the ability to perceive the hardships of others and possess a deep desire to bring happiness to their lives. The key, Miss Elizabeth, is to choose to not let those who are selfish and who take from others to stop you from being the sort of person who gives. It is not always easy, but I think you are capable of doing it."

Watching her closely, Miss Elizabeth nodded in thanks. They had little time for any other conversation before Georgianna woke and joined them. Soon Miss Georgianna's maid brought up an overly burdened tray of breakfast foods for them to break their respite. As they ate together, the three of them, Mrs. Annesley hoped that Miss Elizabeth had been able to settle her heart somewhat.

DARCY LOOKED OVER HIS shoulder to confirm that Mrs. Annesley was sitting in the corner of the room to maintain propriety. Though she smiled briefly at him, she went back to the embroidery project that she always seemed to work on. He was grateful for her apparent inattention. There was a long list of topics he needed to discuss with Elizabeth, and he knew it would be an emotionally charged conversation. Hopefully, they could make some plans before Georgianna finished practicing her piano.

Moving to sit near Elizabeth, he could not help studying the bruise on her cheek. The bruise on her face had darkened during the night, becoming an unsightly blemish on her otherwise beautiful face. Clearing his throat, he addressed Elizabeth by saying, "Elizabeth, thank you for agreeing to discuss matters with me this morning. I know the last twenty-four hours have been difficult for you, but it is important we act swiftly."

Though Elizabeth smiled, it did not reach her eyes, and her shoulders were drooping. After licking her lips, Elizabeth said, "Recent experience has proven that it is best to confront a problem head on rather than try to avoid it." Then, after grimacing, she continued, "I must admit that I have been thinking of nothing but what I might do since I awoke this morning and have come up with a few satisfactory ideas."

Without being able to rely on someone for aid, a young lady like Elizabeth would have little recourse in such a situation. The fact that her father had to know that only made Darcy madder.

Fortunately, Elizabeth was not alone. Her goodness had attracted friends like himself who would ensure her safety and discourage those who sought to harm her from benefiting from their cruelty. Darcy hesitated, unsure exactly how to explain his plan to Elizabeth, but after a moment he said, "I want you to know you are not alone in this, Elizabeth. Bingley, Georgianna, Mrs. Annesley, and I are all eager to lend a helping hand. I only ask that you let us."

Elizabeth's eyes widened, and he observed her struggle between appreciation and self-reliance. "As lovely as it is knowing that you are all so willing to help, I cannot let myself become a burden on you. Though it would be wonderful if you could provide transportation for me, I have yet to decide on a destination," she responded.

Darcy somehow knew that she would be so self-effacing, and he wondered if a life under her unappreciative parents had caused her to lose sight of her worth. With determination in his voice, Darcy said, "Will you deny us the opportunity to reciprocate your kindness?"

Shaking her head, Elizabeth protested, "I have only done what I should have, helping where I could. There was nothing spectacular about anything I have done."

Reaching out, Darcy lay his hand over Elizabeth's. He knew he was acting beyond the bounds of propriety, but he needed her to know how much what he was about to say meant to him. "What you have done both for me and Georgianna may not have been spectacular, but it was significant. How many people had seen my sister as she suffered from her harrowing experience from earlier this summer before you stepped in and befriended her? Have you seen how much she has blossomed since meeting you? What you have done means the world to me and those who love her. We had tried to bring her out of her despair and yet we failed where you succeeded. Not only that, but drawing closer to my sister has also allowed me to make positive changes in myself."

Tilting his head so that he could hold her gaze, Darcy added, "You are worth protecting, even if your mother and father cannot see it, and I think I have found a way to do so."

Elizabeth blinked away tears, her voice trembling as she agreed. "I suppose I must accept your help to avoid seeming ungrateful." When she managed a smile, Darcy saw the sparkle in her eyes that seemed to have been missing since everything horrible had begun.

Smiling in response, Darcy said, "Yesterday, Bingley went to Longbourn and paid a call on your sister. He went for two reasons. Above all, he wanted to convey to Miss Bennet that you were here at Netherfield and well cared for. Another reason was to ensure the well-being of your sisters and confirm that your parents weren't trying to shift Mr. Collins's attention to one of them."

Fright spread across Elizabeth's face as she attempted to stand, crying, "I cannot let them force Mr. Collins on one of my sisters in my stead. I cannot believe that it never crossed my mind. If they were so cruel to me, of course they would behave no better to my sisters."

Standing, Darcy pushed gently on her shoulders to keep her from getting up. He knew from Mrs. Annesley how badly she had injured her feet, and he would hate for her to hurt herself further in her panic. Looking down in her tear-filled eyes, he crooned, "They are safe. Do not worry. I will not allow them to be harmed by either your parents or Mr. Collins."

Blinking, Elizabeth questioned, "How can you know that? They are at Longbourn, away from your attention."

Sitting back down, Darcy answered, "My valet went to Longbourn with a message for Mrs. Hill. If necessary, she will get word to us before anything happens. In fact, she sent me a message letting me know your parents did not even realize that you were missing until well after dinner last night and she overheard them discussing the plans to go to London to retrieve you in a few days. They wanted to wait until Mr. Collins had left. So it seems we have time to put a plan into place to protect you and your sisters from their selfish machinations."

"How can you promise to protect my sisters from him in the long run?" asked Elizabeth.

Grinning, Darcy said, "That is where my plan comes into play."

Chapter Twenty-One

Elizabeth listened as Mr. Darcy explained his plan. Frankly, she was glad someone had a plan that might work. The only plans she had come up with were fleeing or returning to sacrifice herself for her sisters' safety. So she paid close attention to Mr. Darcy as he explained, "My godfather is the Archbishop of Canterbury. He was actually good friends with my father back when they went to Cambridge."

Holding up her hand to ask him to pause, she asked, "Truly, the Archbishop of Canterbury?"

Looking at her askance, Mr. Darcy replied, "Yes. Though I have not been able to spend much time with him since my father's funeral, I have always been fond of him."

Elizabeth couldn't resist a chuckle as she clarified things for Mr. Darcy, who was clearly puzzled. "My father told me that I did not have any friends among the great and good, and implied that any attempt to flee his plans for me could not possibly succeed. Yet you speak of being the godson of the Archbishop of Canterbury. My father doesn't know how wrong he is."

Mr. Darcy chuckled with her for a moment, and Elizabeth was grateful. She reveled in the joy of rediscovering her authentic self, casting aside the shackles of sorrow, if only for a moment. Smiling, she asked, "So how does your godfather come into play?"

"I understand your concern about the potential of either you or one of your sisters being coerced into marrying Mr. Collins. I think getting him out of the picture will be a simple matter, though it might take some time." Pausing, Mr. Darcy settled more comfortably into his chair before continuing, "We both know that Mr. Collins has no business being a man of God—almost anything he does could get him removed from his position at the very least, or even excommunicated. I plan on writing to my godfather and telling him of what is going on at Rosings. Most likely he will remove any control my aunt has over picking her vicar and put a much better person in place to truly help the people."

It was a wonderful idea. Mr. Collins should not be allowed to hurt the people of Kent, and neither should Lady Catherine de Bourgh. Elizabeth couldn't help but feel a pang of guilt for neglecting to think of notifying Mr. Collins's superiors earlier. Though she reasoned that Mr. Darcy's extensive network would undoubtedly grant him a more receptive audience than she ever could. Curious, she asked,

"How would acting so affect Mr. Collins's removal? Do you think he would be punished or sent elsewhere?"

Tapping one of his fingers on his armrest, Mr. Darcy continued explaining, "I am uncertain of what exactly might happen, but I thought of possibly asking that he be sent off as a missionary or be forced to serve under someone who would keep him in line and on a short leash." Grinning once more, he added, "I personally like the idea of sending him off to live among the natives in Africa."

"That again?" Elizabeth looked at Mr. Darcy with an eyebrow quirked. Giggling slightly, she asked, "Didn't you say that you wanted him far away in a place full of bugs?"

Shrugging, he said, "What can I say? I can only assume that he would do well to learn some humility and diligence, as my impression of him has been less than favorable."

"I am starting to believe that you might not like insects. Why else would you want Mr. Collins to have to deal with them?"

Grimacing, Mr. Darcy rubbed at his eyebrow before saying, "I will admit to a certain amount of distaste when it comes to insects. My cousin Richard has long known that he can unnerve me with tales of the insects that afflict foreign lands. I think it started when I was a child hearing of the ten plagues. The thought of a multitude of gadflies and locusts invading to the point where they obscured the sun's rays was nothing short of horrifying."

Elizabeth's fascination with such stories caused her imagination to run riot. However, she could empathize with how a child of a different temperament might have been negatively impacted, especially if he had cousins who took pleasure in teasing him about it. Sensing Mr. Darcy's unease, she steered the conversation away from insects, opting for a different subject.

"So we are removing Mr. Collins from the equation, at least for now," mused Elizabeth. "His absence doesn't change the fact that I can't imagine going back to Longbourn. My parents would make it unlivable for me there."

There was a flash of something in Mr. Darcy's face that he quickly hid from her and though Elizabeth wanted to ask, she did not want to push. So instead, she said nothing and waited for him to speak his mind. "I have an idea about that as well." After only a brief hesitation, Darcy continued, "My sister once had her own establishment in London. After the earlier issues with Mr. Wickham, she moved back to Darcy House, but I believe it might be feasible for you and Georgianna to move there with Mrs. Annesley. In such a way, you could avoid the detection of your family and remain out of their power until you reach your majority."

His willingness to go so far to help her astounded Elizabeth, causing her to sit up straight and carefully study his expression. From what she could tell, he was in earnest. Still, Elizabeth said, "I would not want to put yourself and Georgianna out in such a way."

Chuckling, Mr. Darcy answered, "Do not be ridiculous. Georgianna would be upset if she found out that I could have procured your company for her but failed. So great is her attachment to you."

Elizabeth smiled at the thought of how Georgianna would react if she knew they might get the chance to live together for months. Could she take advantage of his generosity in such a way? Did she have any options even half as palatable? Biting her lip, Elizabeth summoned her inner resolve and made the bold decision to place her trust in Mr. Darcy's offer, believing it held the promise of deliverance. Her only genuine worry was that his act of generosity would somehow sour the friendship that she had come to rely on so much. "If you are certain about offering your assistance in such a manner, I would be immensely grateful."

As he stood up, Mr. Darcy's smile radiated with genuine warmth, reassuring Elizabeth that he made his offer wholeheartedly. "I will begin sending letters immediately then, to alert my godfather and open Primrose Place. I am uncertain when we will have everything in place so that we may move you and my sister to London." With a nod towards Mrs. Annesley, he mentioned, "In the meantime, Mrs. Annesley will be there to support you in any way you need during your recovery."

Elizabeth watched him go, feeling a sense of loss that she did not understand. Granted he was quite the most handsome man she had spent any time with, but she did not think that she was becoming distracted by his looks. Was it possible because he was so chivalric coming to her aid the way he was? Surprisingly, she recalled their conversation, where he mentioned being captivated by tales of knights. Had the idea of chivalry become ingrained in him as a boy? Was that why he was helping her? Elizabeth simply did not know.

ELIZABETH'S SISTERS ARRIVED AT Netherfield shortly after Georgianna had finished her piano practice. She was excited to see them both despite the situation that brought them to there. Georgianna quickly showed them both into her sitting room, where she watched them rush to Elizabeth's side and kneel next to her on the settee. Miss Bennet wept while Miss Mary's face turned hard. Georgianna stood back and let them console each other however they could.

After many tears, Elizabeth's sisters had gotten up off the floor. Jane settled into a chair, pulling it as close as possible to Elizabeth. Taking a seat on the settee, Mary lifted and cradled Elizabeth's legs, resting her feet on her lap. Georgianna settled into her seat near the group, but soon rose to her feet as the tea service arrived. Smiling at the maid, Georgianna thanked her before setting about to get everyone a cup of tea.

Georgianna noticed the look of concern on the maid's face as she watched Elizabeth, so she offered her a reassuring smile. Nodding, the maid left, returning to her other tasks. It had been interesting to learn that Mrs. Nichols had suspected something was going on and after approaching Mr. Bingley, she assured him that there were several staff members who would take Miss Elizabeth's secret to the grave. There would be no whispers of Elizabeth's presence there. It was those staff members who would see to the various needs of Miss Elizabeth and Georgianna during their stay. Georgianna was not at all surprised to learn that Miss Elizabeth's reputation in Meryton was exceptional, and there were those that wanted only the best for her.

The first person to talk was Miss Mary, who said, "Mother and Father both acted as if nothing was amiss, that you had merely gone on a walk. I had no notion that I should be worried about you until Mr. Bingley showed up. What could Mother and Father be thinking of treating you so?"

Miss Bennet's lips pursed, her eyes blinking away tears repeatedly before she spoke. "When Mr. Bingley came and said that you had taken refuge at Netherfield, I did not know what to think. I wanted to believe it was just a misunderstanding," she confessed, her voice heavy with realization, "but seeing you confirms otherwise. Can you ever forgive me?"

With a sigh, Elizabeth said, "Of course! You wanted to believe the best of Mrs. Bennet and Mr. Bennet, Jane. Even I was not expecting them to behave so badly, and I am much more skeptical than you."

Turning to Georgianna, Miss Mary said, "Thank you for providing a refuge for our sister, and for all the care you are providing for her, Miss Darcy."

Fighting a blush, Georgianna said, "She is my dearest friend in the world. I could do nothing else, Miss Mary."

"There is no need for such formality, Miss Darcy," Miss Mary replied, wrinkling her nose slightly. "I would be pleased if you would call me Mary."

Miss Bennet added her own request, saying, "Yes, and I would be happy if you were to call me Jane."

With a wide grin, Georgianna said, "I will, but only if you promise to stop referring to me as Miss Darcy and start calling me Georgianna."

After taking a delicate bite of a scone and taking a sip of tea, Elizabeth asked, "How has the family reacted to my absence?"

Jane and Mary glanced at one another for a moment before Jane said, "We sisters had been concerned about your absence until Mr. Bingley visited and let us know you were safe, discreetly, of course."

Mary took up the story as her sister stopped, saying, "At first, Mother and Father acted as if all was well, but then as it grew later, they both seemed agitated, but still said nothing about your being gone. Mr. Collins was quite upset and muttered about the lack of respect shown to him." Taking a sip of her tea, Mary seemed to ponder something before adding, "This morning, Father announced you had gone to London to help our aunt with her lying in. He went so far as to say that they needed you urgently, which is why you left so early in the morning."

Grimacing, Jane confessed, "Mama even said that once you returned, we could announce your engagement to Mr. Collins."

Making a face, Mary said with disgust, "Mr. Collins seemed thrilled about that. Though I will tell you that there was just something about his expression that sent a shiver down my spine." As Mary's eyes remained fixed on Elizabeth, she confessed, "In the beginning, I entertained the thought of subtly persuading Mr. Collins to develop feelings for me. My spiritual inclination had always led me to believe I would enjoy being a vicar's wife. However, it is my firm belief that he is not suitable to be a vicar, and marrying him would pose a potential danger to any woman."

Reaching out, Elizabeth patted Mary's hand and said, "I do not know if this is something I should share, but Mr. Darcy will soon put an end to Mr. Collins's position of power in Kent by removing him from the role of vicar."

Eyes widening, Mary asked, "How is he going to manage that?"

"He must be reaching out to his godfather, the archbishop," guessed Georgianna.

Smiling, Elizabeth agreed with Georgianna, saying, "Yes, he said he was going to contact his godfather and let him know of the heretical beliefs and behavior Mr. Collins is guilty of. He suspects that Mr. Collins will either have to work under someone who could control him or be assigned to minister alongside one of the missionaries in a foreign country. That is, if he is not excommunicated."

Nodding with a smile that spoke of relief, Mary pronounced, "I am happy that I no longer have to worry about his poor flock in Kent any longer. I can only imagine what they have endured with that man as their spiritual leader."

Setting her teacup down on the end table beside her, Jane said, "Though I am glad that Mr. Collins will not be a problem for much longer, I am still concerned about your welfare, Elizabeth. You cannot just hide here at Netherfield. Are you coming back home to Longbourn once Mr. Collins leaves?"

The hopeful look on Jane's face saddened Georgianna. It was obvious to Georgianna that Jane wanted her sister back with her and for things to return to normal. However, given the circumstances of Elizabeth's shattered relationship with her parents, it was highly unlikely that such a thing could occur.

Frowning, Elizabeth looked at her older sister and gently murmured, "I doubt I will ever return to Longbourn, Jane. Not after what happened and how I learned how little they respect and care for me." The sisters locked eyes for a moment and though a few tears ran down Jane's cheek, eventually she nodded, and Elizabeth added, "I know I cannot stay here indefinitely; I cannot even go to our aunt and uncle in London because Father would just demand I return home. I am fairly certain that is where they think I am, but Mr. Darcy and Georgianna are putting things in place to provide me with a safe place out of his reach," explained Elizabeth.

Understanding the sisters' disappointment, Georgianna clasped her hands together to contain her excitement as she explained, "I am going to take Elizabeth back to London with me and we are going to stay together until she reaches her majority at Primrose Place."

"Primrose Place?" questioned Mary.

Leaning forward in her chair, Georgianna explained, "Primrose Place is my own establishment in London. I have been staying at Darcy House of late, but Primrose Place is a townhouse that was left to me by my father. Though I am sorry you will have to do without your sister, I am glad for my sake because we are going to have so much fun together."

IN THE END, DARCY was able to do much in a brief period of time. He had already heard from his godfather, who had been outraged by all Darcy had conveyed. There would be an investigation taking place soon after Mr. Collins arrived back in Kent. Despite knowing it was wrong, Darcy couldn't help but feel a slight satisfaction at the thought of Mr. Collins finally facing the consequences, not the least for his treatment of Elizabeth.

Mrs. Chambers, the housekeeper in charge of Primrose Place, said that everything would be in order for Georgianna to resume living there by the end of the week. The woman's letter implied her excitement about catering to the young miss and her friend for the foreseeable future, even though she didn't explicitly state it. Darcy knew that Georgianna and Elizabeth would be well taken care of, but he would add several burly footmen to the staff. He wanted to ensure that they were both completely protected from any threats. Darcy did not trust Mr. Bennet, and should he learn of Elizabeth's location, he wanted to make sure that he could not just come and take her without some sort of resistance.

Not that Darcy planned on being taken by surprise by Mr. Bennet. He already had two of his men in London looking into Mr. Bennet and his finances. Darcy did not know if he was anything but a horrible father and a negligent landlord, but he would appreciate finding some leverage with which to protect Elizabeth.

Darcy had not stopped to ponder the depths of his loyalty, even to someone he considered a friend. He was kept busy with letters and pretending that Elizabeth was not hiding at Netherfield. He still had to go out and socialize at gatherings, and if it was a suitable setting, even Georgianna attended. It was the reason he was at the Lucas's home that evening.

Georgianna had stayed home pleading a headache, but he knew she preferred Elizabeth's company to that of a bunch of strangers. Scanning the room, he easily spotted Bingley in quiet conversation with Miss Bennet. It seemed even from this distance that she was not doing well. According to Bingley, the oldest Bennet daughter was finding it difficult to cope with the current situation in the Bennet home.

Closer to him, Mrs. Bennet was talking with Lady Lucas. "Had it not been for the need to assist my sister-in-law during her lying in," she mused, "I'm quite certain Mr. Collins would have proposed, and my Lizzie would have been thrilled by it. As it is, she will not be back home before he has to leave."

Lowering her voice, she added, "Still, there is a certain understanding between them before she had to leave."

"I wouldn't have thought that Miss Eliza would have taken to such a man as your husband's heir," commented Lady Lucas.

"Well, Lizzie knows she is not even my second most beautiful daughter. Really, what options are available for her here in Meryton? Besides, she knows it is her duty to protect her family by marrying Mr. Collins," Mrs. Bennet finished with a huff.

It was difficult for Darcy to restrain himself from going over to Mrs. Bennet and denouncing her cruelty and lies. The ease with which Mrs. Bennet publicly disparaged her own daughter disgusted him. All the Bennet ladies were beautiful in their own way, and, to Darcy, Elizabeth was the most beautiful of them all.

Some might say that Miss Bennet was the most beautiful of the sisters, but Darcy did not agree. His lack of attraction to blondes meant he didn't find the oldest Miss Bennet's angelic looks particularly appealing. Still, he would never say she was not comparable to any of her sisters, especially in public. Darcy walked across the room, knowing that he would not be liable for what he said if he heard Mrs. Bennet say anything else derogatory about Elizabeth.

Not knowing many of the men present, it satisfied Darcy to skirt the edges of the conversing groups. He ended up near Elizabeth's youngest sisters, who were chatting with Miss Maria Lucas. It was fascinating how similar and yet different their conversation was in comparison to the conversation between their mothers' conversation.

"No, Maria, Lizzie would never agree to marry that man. She declared more than once that she would leave home and take up employment rather that bind herself to such an oaf," declared Miss Lydia.

Her brows drawn quizzically, Miss Maria questioned in a whisper, "But your mother is telling everyone that they have an understanding and will get engaged once she returns from helping your aunt."

Glancing around, Miss Kitty explained, "I am afraid my mother is trying to force Lizzie's hand. Even if Lizzie had to leave in a rush to help our Aunt Madeline, she would have said goodbye to at least one of us, if only by leaving a note. Lydia and I are afraid that Lizzie had to leave to avoid being forced to marry Mr. Collins."

Mouth dropping open, it took a moment for Miss Maria to respond. "But why would your sister go against your parents' wishes and run away like that?"

Sighing, Miss Lydia looked at Miss Maria askance. Reaching out and laying her hand on Miss Maria's arm, Miss Lydia said, "Maria, marriage is forever and refusing a gentleman is one of the few rights we ladies have. Any man you marry will have the right to treat you however they wish to, so it behooves us to choose wisely. Mr. Collins has proven himself foolish, heretical, and worst of all, cruel to those under his power. He is the sort of man that no woman should consider marrying."

Miss Maria's eye grew ever wider in her face, and she became slightly pale as Miss Lydia spoke. She stammered, "But the bible says we must obey our parents."

Miss Lydia's response surprised Darcy in its reasoning when she said, "The bible also says fathers should not provoke their children. I hold the belief that there is a line that parents should not cross in what they ask of their children, a line in which obedience is not required by God. This implies that parents should be mindful of their requests, ensuring that they do not infringe upon their child's rights or compromise their well-being."

After that, the conversation turned to fashion and fripperies, but Darcy had a lot to consider about what he had thought about Elizabeth's sisters. There was more to them than he had originally supposed.

Chapter Twenty-Two

BECAUSE OF THE SUPPORT of the staff, who had been outraged at Elizabeth's mistreatment, Elizabeth could go sit in the garden in the morning, even if she still could not walk around because of her injured feet. Mr. Darcy had been kind enough to either carry her himself or arrange for one of the groomsmen in the know to help her. Despite not being atop Oakham Mount, she still found solace in immersing herself in the beauty of the sunrise.

"How are your feet feeling this morning?" asked Mr. Darcy.

Elizabeth glanced at him sitting next to her and smiled. Mr. Darcy was always so attentive to her and her care. He even made sure a maid was available to accompany her outside for propriety's sake. It was a welcome change from what she had experienced at home. "They are very much improved, Mr. Darcy. I believe I could make my way around with little pain."

Clearing his throat in a way that Elizabeth suspected he was repressing laughter at her comment, Mr. Darcy said, "Ah, but I would hate for you to set back your healing."

Nodding in understanding, Elizabeth turned her attention back to the riot of colors painting the frosty morning sky. Pulling the warm blanket closer around her shoulders, Elizabeth asked, "How did you enjoy the evening at Lucas Lodge?"

Mr. Darcy leaned back and braced himself on his hands to look straight up at the sky above them that was still dark and dotted with the fading light of stars. After a moment's contemplation, he began, "I have never felt comfortable in crowds of people I do not know, but Sir William was very welcoming and, on the whole, the evening was enjoyable."

"That is good. Sir William has always been welcoming. It was, in part, the reason he was knighted," commented Elizabeth. "Besides Sir William, who did you talk to?"

Still speaking towards the sky, Mr. Darcy said, "Being hesitant to join conversations, I lingered on the outskirts, catching fragments of various conversations."

There was something about what Mr. Darcy said that made Elizabeth truly sad. What kind of existence was that to never being comfortable to reach out and speak with people, always on the outside and watching others socialize and enjoy himself? She asked, "Did you overhear anything interesting?"

Turning to face Elizabeth, Mr. Darcy said, "Actually, I overheard your younger sisters talking with Maria Lucas and I was quite surprised by what they said."

"What did you overhear that surprised you?" asked Elizabeth.

"Your mother is spreading the story that you and Mr. Collins have an understanding but are not engaged because you are in London helping your aunt with her lying in. Miss Lydia and Miss Kitty are likewise spreading the tale that you would never have an understanding with a fool like Mr. Collins and that you had vowed to leave Longbourn before being forced to take part in such a misalliance." Stopping, he rubbed at his forehead before continuing, "I had never realized how well reasoned your youngest sister is. She has always struck me as... as well, somehow not very mature."

Shaking her head, Elizabeth sighed, saying, "Do not be upset by your wrong assumptions. You fell into the trap that my sister created to counter my mother's plans."

His head flinching back slightly, Darcy asked, "Trap?"

Looking back at the ever-brightening sky, Elizabeth explained, "Mrs. Bennet insisted Lydia come out in Meryton at fifteen. She is convinced that Lydia is pretty enough to catch a very rich husband. Though at fifteen, Lydia is far too young to be getting married, which is why she behaves immaturely whenever there is a chance of attracting a potential suitor. She cannot stop Mrs. Bennet from dressing her up in mostly inappropriate dresses, but she can make people think she is foolish and not worthy of their attention."

"But what of her chances of a good match once she is old enough? Won't everyone think poorly of her by the time that she wants to marry?" questioned Darcy.

Shaking her head, Elizabeth explained, "Everyone in town understands it is an act. They can see how she acts when she is not at an assembly. They know she is too young to be out, but that she really has no choice to be there." Pausing, Elizabeth smoothed out a wrinkle in her dress before adding, "If she continues to act the same after she is, say eighteen, they may react badly, but for now, her youth protects her. I am glad that she and Kitty explained everything to Maria Lucas. She is almost as good at spreading gossip as her parents. Hopefully, it will protect my reputation if people doubt Mrs. Bennet's blathering."

Nodding, Mr. Darcy said, "Your mother is trying to back you into a corner. If it is common knowledge that you have an understanding with Mr. Collins even should you return after you are twenty-one, you may still encounter some difficulty. Despite that, your sisters are trying to thwart your mother's plans. They are quite clever to do so."

"Sadly, my sisters and I learned the power of gossip at a young age by watching our mother use it against those in our community. Had my parents acted against another one of my sisters, I would do something similar." Elizabeth could imagine the information she would spread to protect one of her sisters. She would not stop until her parents could no longer hold their heads up in town.

Mr. Darcy looked at Elizabeth, his eyes searching, before he said, "I believe if your parents hurt one of your sisters in such a way, you would do more than spread gossip to protect them. You would take decisive action to protect them, ensuring their safety and emotional well-being."

Blushing, Elizabeth had to agree with Mr. Darcy. "Yes, I am rather protective of those I care for, as well as slightly vindictive."

"Your sisters are lucky to have you," commented Mr. Darcy.

Elizabeth smiled warmly and spoke words of gratitude. "We are truly blessed to have each other. I will miss them when we leave the day after tomorrow."

"So, you will stay here at Netherfield and continue your courting of the eldest Miss Bennet and monitor things while I return to London, escorting my sister and her companions," stated Darcy. They were to leave in the morning, and Darcy wanted to make sure that nothing would disrupt his plans to protect Elizabeth.

Sitting across from him in front of the fire and enjoying his coffee, Bingley reassured him, saying, "Do not worry about it, Darcy. No one will suspect that Miss Elizabeth is leaving with you. You will leave early and travel through Meryton with the curtains drawn. Miss Elizabeth's escape is all but accomplished. While I remain here, I will keep my ear to the ground and watch Mr. and Mrs. Bennet. If anything seems amiss, I will write to you and send it by express."

Staring into the fire, Darcy mused out loud, "I know we have everything arranged, but I cannot help but worry. The memory of that morning when she arrived, her body battered and her eyes filled with pain, keeps replaying in my mind. I want to make sure that her family cannot hurt her like that again."

"Your passion for justice has always been a defining characteristic, drawing you in and fueling your actions. Even in Cambridge, you could not abide the mistreatment of the boys from less spectacular backgrounds. It is part of the reason our friendship bound us together so firmly," responded Bingley. Taking another sip of his coffee, he added, "I fear that there will be many here who will regret Miss Elizabeth's parting. Her sisters will miss her, of course, but so will all the tenants that she sees to in her parents' stead. I know her sisters will attempt to fill in the gaps, but they are not all as equally skilled at what is required."

In agreement, Darcy stated, "She takes on the responsibility of balancing the books for both the household and the estate, while also making sure that all necessary supplies for planting and harvesting the crops are secured. Beyond doing what her father should, she helps her sisters do what her mother should do by helping to run the household and providing aid to the tenants. I know heirs of grand estates who do not work half as hard."

Bingley smiled as he watched his friend's enthusiastic recital of Elizabeth's accomplishments. He commented, "It sounds as if you are almost in awe of Miss Elizabeth. At the very least, you respect her a great deal."

"She is a remarkable young lady, unlike any I have ever met before. I am truly glad that my sister met her." Darcy averted his eyes from Bingley and fixated on the dancing flames of the fire. After a moment of silence, he broke it by saying, "It's remarkable how much she has already altered our lives, and yet it seems like there is an even greater transformation on the horizon." Darcy could feel the strength of Bingley's stare but did not look back at him. He knew Bingley would want more of an explanation and he did not have one. All he knew was that things were going to change somehow and though he was normally one for pattern and routine, he looked forward to what was coming.

ELIZABETH LOOKED AT HER sisters with misty eyes. They had all come presumably to take tea with Miss Darcy before she returned to London, and this would be the last time she would see them presumably for at least six months. Of all of them, she was the most concerned for Jane, who appeared paler than usual.

Jane's inability to handle discord made it especially difficult for her to cope, knowing that Elizabeth would leave because of her parents' actions, and the strain was taking a toll on her. Elizabeth knew than Jane wished Elizabeth would simply return home and overlook her mistreatment, but it was not something that she could do. Not after that horrid morning that she had seen the people that her parents truly were. While Jane held onto hope that Mr. and Mrs. Bennet regretted their actions, Elizabeth saw their indifference to her all too clearly.

"Thank you, Georgianna," said Mary, as she accepted a cup of tea and a few biscuits. Elizabeth smiled at her next youngest sister as she stirred her tea and putting her teaspoon aside, she took a sip with a smile. Mary, in contrast to Jane, had stepped up into the breach, showing her strength and resilience. Elizabeth was proud of how far Mary had come. She suspected that realizing their mother's opinions were obviously flawed had helped Mary to relax slightly. Mary had even started to dress however she wished and not to spite their mother's comments about being plain.

Turning to Kitty and Lydia, Georgianna asked, "You will have to forgive me. I do not know how either of you take your tea."

Giggling, Lydia replied, "Do not worry, Miss Darcy. We haven't had the chance to have tea together enough for you to learn our habits. We both take our tea with cream and sugar and as many biscuits as we can get away with." Sitting beside Lydia, Kitty nodded vigorously with a broad smile. Kitty might never be as bold as her younger sister, but Elizabeth was glad that her shyness did not keep her from responding all together.

As Georgianna set about preparing the last two cups of tea, Mary drew Elizabeth into a conversation when she said, "Mrs. Hill helped me to secret a trunk of your things away from Longbourn this morning. I know you have made do with borrowed dresses and those few items we could sneak to you."

Elizabeth leaned forward and said, "I would hate for you to be caught doing something so risky."

Shaking her head, Mary patted her sister's hand. "Do not worry. Mrs. Hill is our stanch supporter and, sadly, our mother is quite foolish. The day before yesterday, Mother must have realized that one of us might become suspicious if we realized you did not take anything and directed Mrs. Hill to pack up your belongings saying that you would need them sent to you as you had only taken a few items with you. Then she told her to put the trunk out of the way and our father would see that it got sent to you." Pausing, Mary tilted her head, saying, "We both know they cannot send it to you, but regardless, Mrs. Hill used the opportunity to back two trunks and we are sending one with you. She will keep the other on hand in case Mother and Father remember they need to send it to you."

Elizabeth did not know if she should be happy to hear of Mrs. Hill's forethought and concern for her or disappointed by her mother's underhanded tactics. Shaking her head, Elizabeth focused on the goodness of Longbourn's longtime housekeeper and said, "Mrs. Hill has always been rather clever and has shown much concern for us all. Please thank her for me when you can."

"I will," Mary assured Elizabeth. Then, pulling a small book out of her reticule, Mary handed it to Elizabeth. "I did not want you to leave without a gift from me to remember me by. It is a book of Psalms, and I have marked several passages that you might find encouraging if you are finding your situation difficult."

Elizabeth looked at Mary and her slight blush in gratitude, exclaiming, "Thank you! I will cherish it." With a bittersweet feeling, Elizabeth leaned over and embraced her sister in a tight hug. The weight of their impending separation hung heavy in the air. More than missing her sister, Elizabeth worried about what Mary would face when she left Meryton behind.

As if sensing Elizabeth's concern, Mary murmured, "Do not worry about us while you are gone. You have handled so much nearly on your own, we four should be able to manage for a few months. If we should truly need help, we have systems in place to get aid." With a smile, she leaned back and remarked, "Let's not dwell on these sad thoughts. We still have tea to relish and conversation to enjoy before we depart."

Elizabeth smiled back at her before she shifted her gaze back to Lydia and Kitty, who were chatting with Georgianna about what she enjoyed doing in London. It was nice to watch the younger girls just be girls for the moment and not have to worry about anything more serious than modistes, Hyde Park and Hatchards. Lydia exclaimed with a giggle, "While I would love to experience the elegance of a fancy dress fitting in London or take a leisurely stroll in Hyde Park during the fashionable hour, I don't mind waiting a few more years."

"Truly?" Georgianna asked, her eyes wide. "That is all anyone at the school I attended would talk about. Though, to be honest, I would prefer a trip to the symphony over Hyde Park. I dislike the idea of people just there to look at me."

Nodding, Kitty, her voice soft and introspective, confessed, "I've never been comfortable with too much attention. I prefer to blend into the background and watch everyone else."

"Maybe one day several years in the future we shall all go to Hyde Park and sit and watch everyone else, or should you both still dislike the idea, we shall go together to the symphony," laughed Lydia.

Her smile widening into a grin, Georgianna declared, "I say it is a plan." Looking back and forth between Lydia and Kitty, she continued, "Let's make a plan to visit London together in two years and do all the things we've been talking about."

Looking at one another, Kitty and Lydia turned in unison and said, "It is a plan!"

They spent a considerable amount of time chatting about different subjects, but eventually ran out of tea and biscuits. They all knew that it was time for the Bennet sisters to return to Longbourn, except for Elizabeth, who would stay behind. After hesitating, Elizabeth straightened her shoulders and said, "I believe it is time for you to go home. Now come and give me a hug and do not fret. I will see you all before you know it."

Everyone stood and, after walking silently to the entryway, the last of the hugs begun. It would, after all, be months before Elizabeth saw any of her sisters again. Though they had thought of a way to pass letters back and forth as long as they were careful. Georgianna was about to become a regular correspondent with the Bennet ladies.

Kitty and Lydia embraced her first and at the same time making Elizabeth chuckle. Lydia looked at her sister and said, "Do not let what is going on make you forget to have fun while you are in London. I want you to promise to visit Hatchards and go to go shopping for a new bonnet at least once."

Resolved not to cry, Elizabeth instead smiled while responding, "I promise. I might even find a way to get you a bonnet, though it might just take a while for me to get it to you."

Next, Mary gave her a hug, but no words were said, just a look of love and acknowledgment. They had already said what needed to be said. Besides, they would write to one another. To Elizabeth's surprise, the chaos in her life had brought her and Mary closer together, which she found to be a wonderful benefit despite the remaining sadness.

Lastly, Jane stepped forward and Elizabeth could not help but worry about her older sister. Jane had always been the serene one, smiling and kind. It hadn't occurred to Elizabeth just how much Jane's serenity had relied on the blinders she wore to shield herself from the troubles of the world. Elizabeth held onto faith that Jane would stand strong and not allow what she had learned to overpower her.

Chin wobbling, Jane gasped, "I do not know how I might carry on knowing what I do about your situation and what our parents have done. However, I do know I love you and I will miss you."

"I love you too, Janey." Taking her sister by the shoulders, Elizabeth looked deeply into her eyes and said, "I do not want you to let this destroy you. While there is darkness in the world and in our parents, it's crucial to remember that there is still light to be found. Besides, I will not be gone from your life forever."

Jane embraced Elizabeth in a hug that was almost bruising in its strength before stepping back and being shepherded away by Mary. Elizabeth's heart sank as she peered through a tiny crack in the curtains, witnessing the departure of her beloved sisters from Netherfield and their ascent into the awaiting carriage. Elizabeth could not even wave goodbye in case someone they did not trust should see her and tell tales.

Despite the difficulty of being separated from her sisters for the next six months, Elizabeth recognized the necessity of the situation. Though she was uncertain about the specifics, she held onto the belief that the events to come would somehow shape her future happiness. Certainly staying behind would only lead to her destruction.

Chapter Twenty-Three

Darcy climbed into his carriage, his mind awhirl with conflict. So much had happened the last five months. For the most part, the plans he had started had been working well, but still he felt unsettled, and he did not want to admit why. So instead he stared out the window, trying to distract himself from what concerned him the most.

The carriage came to an abrupt halt, causing Darcy to startle and glance around, only then realizing that he had reached his club where he was supposed to meet Bingley. Nodding to his footman in thanks, Darcy descended the steps and walked rapidly inside, finding Bingley drinking a cup of coffee and reading one of the latest treatises on crop rotation. Seeing Darcy, Bingley stood and said, "Darcy, it is good to see you after so long." Clapping Darcy on the back, he added, "How are you? How are things?"

Smiling, Darcy answered, "I am well, my friend, and as for things, perhaps we can retreat to one of the less used rooms and talk over our meal."

Eyes alert, Bingley nodded and finishing off his coffee, Bingley moved with Darcy to a room where they could eat unbothered by people eager to overhear them. They chatted about inconsequential things until their food had arrived and they were left alone. Watching the retreating back of the server, Darcy asked, "How is everything in Meryton?"

Smiling, Bingley answered, "Not a lot has changed since my last letter."

Chuckling, Darcy said, "You realize I can rarely read more than half of your letters. Though I congratulate you on your engagement to Miss Bennet."

Bingley grinned, chagrined, as he rubbed the back of his neck. "I keep meaning to work on that," he admitted. Then brightening, Bingley exclaimed, "Thank you, Darcy. I am truly happy to have Jane as my future wife."

Darcy was happy to see such a look of joy on his friend's face, but then Bingley's smile faded as he said, "Jane is still quite distressed over the rift in the Bennet family. Actually, she has asked to postpone our wedding until Elizabeth may attend, though I do not understand how we might manage that without extreme distress to Miss Elizabeth. What do you think? Would it be possible for Miss Elizabeth to attend our wedding?"

Leaning back into the cushions of his chair, Darcy pondered the question. Elizabeth remained firm on never stepping foot in Longbourn again. Knowing that she wished to be present at her sister's wedding, he acknowledged that she would have to find accommodation away from Longbourn. It was possible, but would not be easy.

Taking a sip of the claret that had been served with the meal, Darcy sighed before saying, "I think she would love nothing more than to be at her sister's wedding, but she will not set foot on Longbourn land while either of her parents remain. Your wedding would have to be after she reaches her majority and she will have to stay somewhere else, possibly Netherfield. Still, I would hate for her parents to make a fuss at your wedding."

"I had assumed it would be difficult for Miss Elizabeth to return to Longbourn. Still, we will plan for the wedding to take place a week or two after Miss Elizabeth reaches her majority. That way she can attend if we can manage it." Then, turning more serious, Bingley asked, "How has everything that you were handling gone?"

Cutting into his pheasant, Darcy said "Dealing with Mr. Collins was certainly easier than I thought it would be. Obviously, the church investigated him and found that he not only broke canon law regularly, but he had been taking advantage of the people of the perish with Lady Catherine's blessing. There had been some hesitation as to whether or not they should excommunicate him and be done with it or handle it in a different manner."

Putting down his glass after taking a sip of his claret, Bingley asked, "So what did they decide?"

Chewing contemplatively, Darcy swallowed before saying, "My godfather and his associates decided that Mr. Collins should not be excommunicated as they felt a sense of responsibility towards him and believed they could exert more influence over him if he remained associated with the church. Mr. Collins found himself at a crossroads, where he had to make a tough decision. He could either accept excommunication and the responsibility of repaying the tithes he had collected, as well as making reparations to the families he had wronged, or he could embark on a journey to India as a curate, assisting a rector in establishing a missionary school."

"What did he decide?" questioned Bingley.

Darcy could not but help smile when he said, "Mr. Collins is currently in India under the thumb of a very strict taskmaster being forced to help others."

Nodding, Bingley said, "It seems fitting. He had obviously been taught the wrong things. Perhaps he will learn to do better." Bingley's eyes widened, and he questioned, "What about your aunt, Lady Catherine? She was the one who caused so much of his bad behavior."

Darcy nearly spewed his wine when Bingley asked about his aunt. Once he regained control of himself, he explained, "My aunt was severely displeased that her toady had been taken away from her. She was even more displeased to learn that she would no longer have the ability to decide who was to be given the position of vicar near Rosings. She went so far as to make her way to London to call on the assistance of her brother, the earl." Chuckling, he finished, "Which turned out to be a bad idea."

Sitting forward in his seat, Bingley asked, "What did the earl do?"

"My uncle, the earl, was more than displeased when he understood the extent of his sister's depravities and forced her to move to the dower house," Darcy explained. "The only thing Lady Catherine is in control of now is her wardrobe."

After enjoying another bite of his meal, Darcy added, "It has been amazing for my cousin, Anne. Lady Catherine's iron grip on Anne's life has hindered her from gaining any knowledge or independence. To address this, plans were made to revitalize Rosings and give Anne the opportunity to flourish."

Both men chuckled at the fate of Lady Catherine for a moment before focusing on their meals for a time. That did not mean Darcy's mind was idle; in fact, his thoughts were racing at an overwhelming pace. In the five months that Elizabeth had been living with his sister, the daunting task of figuring out how to bring justice to her parents for the harm they had caused had consumed Darcy. He was certain that Elizabeth was far more forgiving than he was proving to be. He knew he should take his cue from her, but he had simply not found a way to let the harm to her go. Darcy knew Elizabeth longed to stay as far away as possible from the couple who had raised her, while he was determined to make them rue their actions.

Darcy had never been vindictive toward anyone in the past except for possibly Wickham and that was because he had harmed a person he loved. That very morning, as Darcy contemplated his thirst for revenge on behalf of Elizabeth, he stumbled upon a shocking revelation. He had fallen in love with Elizabeth Bennet and that was why he wanted so desperately to protect her.

To say it had been a shock had been an understatement. It made him remember the conversation he had with Bingley so many months ago when Bingley had said, "When you do finally find love for yourself, it will blindside you." Bingley had been right. He was blindsided, and it made things so much more complicated.

ELIZABETH LEANED INTO GEORGIANNA as she giggled. Things could have been so much more difficult for her when she had to leave Longbourn if it was not for Georgianna and her brother, Mr. Darcy. She could have had to use up all of her savings to get by or even been alone and looking for employment. Yet here she was giggling at the absurdity of a novel with her friend that had become like a sister to her.

Getting control of themselves, they both sat up and Georgianna asked, "Do you think the author intended that scene to be taken that way or was it written to be satirical?"

Elizabeth pondered the question for a moment. She was not an author and rarely thought about the process that went into creating the novels that she so enjoyed. She glanced across the room to see if Mrs. Annesley had any input, but the woman only smiled indulgently and continued to work on her latest project.

So Elizabeth said, "I would hope that the author was being satirical. It's a sorrowful notion to think that someone who possesses the ability to express themselves so coherently would hold the belief that the world operates in such a narrow fashion." Then, smiling again, she added, "Either way, I have enjoyed reading it out loud with you."

Closing the book in her lap, Georgianna said, "I have enjoyed it as well. Before you came to stay with me, it was not a pastime I had ever thought to try. It is no wonder your sisters enjoyed it so much."

"As much as this has been entertaining," Mrs. Annesley sighed, "I fear it is time for us to get ready to go to the modiste. I know you do not want to be late." Saying so, she put down her watch fob and put away her supplies of embroidery threads.

With a smile directed at Georgianna, Elizabeth inquired, "Have you given any thought to what you might want made?"

Standing, Georgianna smoothed out the wrinkles in her dress and replied, "I would like to use that lovely fabric your uncle gifted me for an evening gown. I know I am not out yet, so it will have to be simple, but I would like something new for the next time William takes us to the theater or the opera."

Elizabeth could easily imagine such a gown and said, "I think that is a lovely idea. That light peach fabric would look wonderful as an evening gown."

Bustling about, the three ladies were able to get ready to leave in practically no time at all and soon enough, they were in the carriage that Mr. Darcy had provided for their use. Elizabeth had never truly enjoyed visiting the modiste with her mother and sisters, but she had found that without the chaos that her mother produced in her wake, attending with Georgianna was actually enjoyable.

Upon entering the shop that Georgianna frequented, the proprietress quickly greeted them. "Welcome, ladies. It is a pleasure to once again to have you in my shop. We have everything ready for the two of you."

Suspicious, Elizabeth glanced at Georgianna, who looked the other way as she responded to the shop owner. "Madame Genevieve, you are too kind to fit my friend and I into your schedule at the same time. Of course, my dress will have to be sedate as I am not out yet, but I would like my friend Miss Elizabeth to look marvelous the next time we go to the theater."

Not wanting to embarrass Georgianna in front of the proprietress, she waited until they were alone, looking over some fashion plates with a cup of tea and some delectables. Once they were alone, just the three of them, though Mrs. Annesley was studiously avoiding their confrontation, Elizabeth said, "Georgie, did you forget to tell me something?"

Biting her lip for a moment Georgianna said, "I knew you would insist on having the fabric your uncle gave you made up in something rather more practical at the modiste that you see. But really, Lizzie, that fabric is meant for something so much more that an adequate dress." Setting her shoulders firmly, Georgianna continued, "Besides, I have always wanted to have a dress made up with you, and it is my treat! You would not want to see me disappointed, would you?"

Raising an eyebrow at Georgianna's pathetic expression, Elizabeth shook her head at her friend's manipulation but knew that she would not gainsay her. With a huff, Elizabeth picked up a fashion plate before saying, "Fine, but I am putting my foot down when it comes to lace. I cannot abide the stuff." Staring intently at Georgianna, Elizabeth's severe expression left no room for doubt as she stated firmly, "Lace will not be tolerated."

This set them both off into a round of laughter, and even Mrs. Annesley was chuckling when Madame Genevieve returned. Looking between them all, she asked with concern, "Is there something amiss, ladies?"

Attempting to keep a straight face, Georgianna explained, "My friend Miss Elizabeth was just explaining the depth of her disdain for lace. It is not something she will tolerate on her dress." Georgianna could barely get her words out before she broke into another snicker.

Nodding sagely, Madame Genevieve said, "Yes, I can understand the hesitation, Miss Elizabeth. The emphasis on using lace as a display of wealth often overshadows the importance of true style for many women." Smiling at Elizabeth, she added, "I can see that it will be a pleasure to dress you. In fact, I think I have just the pattern that will go with the fabric that Miss Darcy sent over in advance of your arrival." Going towards a table nestled in the corner, she carefully examined a stack of fashion plates and eventually returned with a chosen one.

Handing the plate to Elizabeth, she added, "Now that I have seen you and know the sort of look you want, I think this would suit you well."

Taking the fashion plate, Elizabeth studied it and knew immediately that the woman was right. It was simple but extremely elegant, and there was not a speck of lace on the design. The dress would be perfect for the moss green silk her uncle had given her. And yet...

Elizabeth pressed her palm into her stomach. The thought of wearing such a dress and accompanying Mr. Darcy to the opera or the theater filled her with nervous excitement, causing her to swallow convulsively. Refusing to focus on the butterflies in her stomach or the reason for them, Elizabeth swallowed again before saying, "I think it is perfect."

WHILE GEORGIANNA HAD NEVER been happy that her friend had so much go wrong in her life, having Elizabeth stay with her had certainly improved her own life. For example, her dinners with her brother had always been stilted at the very least. Now they were nothing but delightful.

"Of course, Lydia's mouth and hands were stained purple, so our cook had no problem figuring out who had eaten the blackberries she had saved to make tarts," Elizabeth recalled, chuckling at the memory.

William was quick to say, "Growing up with so many siblings so close together in age was quite entertaining."

Smiling across the table at William, Elizabeth replied, "I did not realize it at the time, but yes, I quite enjoyed my childhood with my sisters."

Smiling at Elizabeth's story, Georgianna took another bite of her food, just happy with how her life had improved in the last year. Not only had she met Elizabeth and obtained her first genuine friend, but then that friend had moved in with her and they had become even closer. Just that morning she had gone with Elizabeth to the modiste, and they were able to chat over the dresses that they were having made. Even though she was tired, the joy she experienced made every moment worth it.

Buttering a roll, Georgianna watched as her best friend and her brother talked of one of the books they had both read. She grinned as Elizabeth said, "That was not it at all. Taking the first passage into account completely alters the meaning of the passage you are referring to."

Without having read the book, Georgianna observed as they engaged in a lively debate, passionately discussing the different elements of the story. Most times that her brother came for dinner, he and Elizabeth got into some form of discussion or debate about something intellectual.

Georgianna found it quite entertaining to watch the two of them. Though their words may have hinted at disagreement, the smiles on their faces revealed their underlying harmony to Georgianna. Taking a bite out of her roll, Georgianna froze in mid-chew as she looked more closely at Elizabeth's smile. There was just something about her smile, or was it the look in her eyes?

Georgianna's eyes narrowed as she closely examined Elizabeth's face. There was just something about the way her friend's eyes sparkled as she watched William. Somehow, it added to the strength of her smile. Was Elizabeth in love with William? Somehow, Georgianna thought it was possible. What was more, Georgianna suspected that Elizabeth herself did not know of the depth of her feelings.

Smiling, Georgianna looked across the table at where Mrs. Annesley sat, curious to see if she had noticed, but it seemed that she hadn't. Georgianna rather liked being the only one who knew of Elizabeth's feelings. More than that, she thought it was going to be highly entertaining to watch things unfold.

She did not know what her brother felt for Elizabeth; he was much more difficult to read. Georgianna hoped he would return

Elizabeth's feelings, at least eventually. The longer she thought about it, the more she realized how perfect they were for each other. While they were both intelligent and loved reading and expanding their horizons, it wasn't just that. Elizabeth would infuse William's life with brightness and joy, while William would push Elizabeth to discover more about herself and the world around her. Even Pemberley would be better for them working together.

Georgianna was still contemplating having Elizabeth for an actual sister when she realized her brother had asked her a question. Blushing at having been caught out, she responded, "I am sorry, I was woolgathering. What did you say?"

Smiling, William said, "I am sorry we got so involved in our debate. I was just asking you if you had any plans for the week."

In a flurry of quick thinking, Georgianna's mind whirled as she attempted to concoct a scheme to orchestrate a romantic encounter between Elizabeth and her brother. "I do not think we have anything specific planned, though I was just thinking it would be nice to go do something fun one of these evenings, maybe see a play?"

Smiling, William glanced briefly at Elizabeth before saying, "That sounds like a good idea. There is a farce that is getting excellent reviews. Would you ladies enjoy going to see it on Friday evening?"

"I think that would be lovely. Don't you think so, Lizzie?" Georgianna questioned her friend, knowing that she was never one to pass up the chance to go to the theater.

With a nod, Elizabeth gracefully wiped her mouth with her serviette and replied, "I find the idea of going to the theater and watching the new play quite enchanting."

Georgianna felt like clapping in excitement. Now all she had to do was make sure the dresses that they commissioned were ready to wear Friday. She would send a note around to Madame Genevieve in the morning and offer an incentive to have them both ready in time.

Chapter Twenty-Four

Darcy was happy to visit Bingley at his home without having to worry about Miss Bingley being there to pop in and bother him. He smiled at the butler as he showed him to Bingley's study. Making himself at home, he sank into one of the luxurious, overstuffed chairs near the desk.

Looking up from his papers, Bingley grinned and said, "Thank you for visiting me here before I head back to Meryton in the morning."

"I do not mind at all. Did you sort out the settlement paperwork?" asked Darcy.

Nodding, Bingley answered, "I have everything together. Whatever the future holds, Jane will have what she needs. Though I resent the need to bring the papers to Mr. Bennet to sign. I already know that he cannot be trusted to see to his children's best interests."

Grimacing, Darcy said, "Miss Bennet is of age. She could sign the documents herself, I suppose."

Bingley sighed and shook his head, his voice filled with resignation as he said, "Jane wants her father to sign the papers. She thinks it is the right way to go about things. Despite her initial struggle, she has handled the situation more effectively and still holds onto hope that her father will eventually make the right choice. She hopes he will show his love for her and her sisters somehow." Pausing, a ghost of a smile crossed Bingley's face. With a slight tilt of his head, Bingley shrugged and remarked, "It is one of the reasons why I am so deeply in love with her—her endless optimism. She looks to see the best in everyone."

Darcy nodded, understanding that when you loved someone, you had to take the bad with the good. It wasn't necessarily a negative trait to be optimistic, and Miss Bennet's unwavering positivity had its advantages, despite the occasional letdown. Deciding he would leave Bingley to his concerns regarding his affianced, Darcy attempted to change the topic of conversation by asking, "Did I see an announcement about your sister's marriage in the paper? I had thought you might have mentioned it."

Darcy's heart sank as he saw the smile disappear from Bingley's face upon mentioning Miss Bingley, hinting at an underlying tension. Darcy had hoped to change the conversation; he had not thought to crush his friend's spirit. He was quick to apologize. "I am sorry Bingley, you do not have to talk about it if you do not wish to."

Waving him off, Bingley said, "I was going to tell you eventually, but yes, Caroline married Sir Jasper Wilton in a small ceremony last week."

Darcy knew Bingley was hopeful that his sister would get married sooner rather than later, so he had assumed that Bingley would be happy about her marriage, but he wasn't. Understanding that there must be something off about the marriage, Darcy questioned, "Was there something about the match that you disapprove of?"

Slumped in his chair, Bingley's voice conveyed deep concern. "I advised Caroline against marrying the baronet," he revealed. "However, she was resolute in her belief that a title and the respect it would bring among the ton were worth any sacrifices she might have to make in her personal life."

"Was what you learned about Sir Jasper so terrible?" asked Darcy.

Expression turning dark, Bingley explained, "In a partner, Caroline sought both a title and a primary residence in town. While Sir Jasper met both of her qualifications, she did not care about my concerns. If it was only the fact that the man was some thirty years older than my sister, I would not have said anything. However, Caroline is Sir Jasper's third wife. His first wife died birthing his fourth daughter and after a suitable waiting period, he remarried. His second wife died shortly after her marriage to the baronet in a fall down the stairs that was quite suspicious. Faced with the need for an heir, he set out to find a third wife, who ended up being my sister."

Running his hand through his hair, he continued, "All reports say that he is often in his cups and his servants have whispered about being mistreated when he is drunk. I fear for Caroline, but she is of age and there was nothing I could do."

Shocked at the revelation, he attempted to commiserate with his friend and said, "I am sorry to hear that, Bingley."

Shrugging, Bingley said, "What can you do? My sister has made her choice, and I can only hope that the outcome won't be as disastrous as I fear." Then, sitting up straighter, Bingley picked up his ever-present cup of coffee and, after taking a sip, he declared, "I no longer want to discuss something gloomy. How are your sister and Miss Elizabeth doing? You know Jane will ask the moment I return to her."

Smiling at the image Bingley's words conveyed, Darcy said, "Elizabeth and Georgianna are both doing well. I think their time together in London has done good things for both of them."

Quirking an eyebrow, Bingley inquired, "Elizabeth, is it?"

Realizing his mistake, Darcy hoped that the room was dim enough to hide his slight blush. Understanding the need to talk with someone about his dilemma and knowing that Bingley was the ideal person, Darcy affirmed, "Though she has been Elizabeth to me for a while, it was only this morning that I grasped the true reason behind my strong inclination to shield her and revel in her company. I had thought we were just friends."

Chuckling, Bingley remarked, "I had always assumed love would knock you about when it finally found you. I am not even surprised by your falling in love with Miss Elizabeth. She seems like the perfect match for you—intelligent, well-read, and hardworking. Moreover, she's kindhearted and outgoing, which I think you could use in your life. She will help you get out of your shell, so to speak." Studying his friend for a moment, Bingley sat forward slightly and asked, "Being in love is not a bad thing, you know. What has you worried?"

"The moment I realized I was in love with Elizabeth, I wanted to rush to her and propose," began Darcy.

"Not an uncommon reaction," commented Bingley.

Rolling his eyes at his friend, Darcy said, "I hadn't taken two steps before I began to worry. What if she only accepts my proposal because she feels she must? I have helped her, wanting nothing in return, but my love for her complicates matters. I only want her to marry me if her heart truly beats for me, as I couldn't bear the thought of my love causing her any pain." Scrubbing at his face with both hands and thoroughly mussing his hair, Darcy groaned, "What makes it worse is that I came up with the perfect idea for how to deal with Mr. and Mrs. Bennet and Longbourn once I realized I was in love, but it only works if Elizabeth and I are married. I just hate to think that she might misunderstand my intentions."

"So what are you going to do?" asked Bingley.

Looking at his friend in annoyance, Darcy grumbled, "I do not know. I may know how to run an estate and balance ledgers, but I am clueless when it comes to matters of the heart. You have always been more in tune with your emotions, and you are currently in love with Elizabeth's sister. What do you think I should do?"

Smirking, Bingley took a sip of his coffee and Darcy wanted to throttle him for all that he was taking his sweet time to respond. Bingley placed his cup on the table, a mischievous grin spreading across his face before he spoke again. "My suggestion is to have confidence in Miss Elizabeth and to share your thoughts and feelings openly with her. Let her know that your support is not contingent on her saying yes. You never know, maybe she has feelings for you but has said nothing for similar reasons. What have you done to show her you care so far?"

Disarmed by the question, Darcy sputtered, "Ahh, I...um, nothing so far?"

"Darcy my friend, you have had months with the lady.," Bingley teased. "If you continue to move this slowly, you will both be old and gray by the time you act. Or worse, some other gentleman will swoop in and sweep her off her feet." Laughing, he added, "Then too, there is the possibility that if Lydia finds out her sister loves you and you break her heart through inaction, she will have your head."

Darcy furrowed his brow, feeling a mix of confusion and concern. "Is there something about Elizabeth's feelings for me that I'm unaware of?" he asked, rubbing his forehead.

"Not explicitly, no. Based on my observations, Miss Elizabeth spends a considerable amount of time in your presence. If she had no feelings for you whatsoever or disliked you, she would undoubtedly find a means to limit her interactions with you. As I have continued to visit, I have become acquainted with most of Jane's sisters, and it has become clear to me that Miss Lydia is fiercely protective of all her sisters." Bingley's smile had grown as he spoke, and Darcy could not help feeling as if his friend was enjoying his struggle.

Despite the temptation to grumble, Darcy controlled himself and opted to respond, "I have plans to go with her and my sister to the theater tomorrow."

Nodding, Bingley said, "That is a great beginning. You do not have to declare your undying love, but at the very least, show her some extra attention or something. Sit next to her, offer her your arm, talk to her about something I would find boring and that the two of you find interesting."

As ELIZABETH CLIMBED THE steps at the theater, she felt a familiar thrill coursing through her veins. Although she had some prior experience attending plays, it paled in comparison to the unforgettable experience she had while watching from the Darcy box. This evening was even more special.

This evening, Mr. Darcy had offered her his arm and while it was a polite gesture, it felt special somehow. Normally, he offered his arm to Georgianna, which was only right. Georgianna was his sister, after all, and Elizabeth was merely his sister's friend. Elizabeth couldn't help but feel that the subtle shift in his behavior held significance, and she wasn't the only one who picked up on it. Georgianna had grinned widely before a look from Mrs. Annesley had encouraged her to stop.

Mr. Darcy had always been a gentleman, but now it seemed like his courtesy was directed solely at her. Moving through the crowd, he shielded her, and it was a lovely sensation to be so thoroughly looked after. When they finally got to their box, Darcy sat her next to him and asked, "Did I tell you yet how lovely you look?"

Elizabeth hoped that the light was dim enough for him to not see her blush when she answered, "Thank you. The dress is new."

Georgianna chimed in, saying, "We visited the Gardiner's warehouse to look at fabric and we found the fabric for both of our dresses. Her uncle was kind enough to gift me the fabric for my dress, so I insisted on taking Elizabeth to my modiste to have her fabric made up along with mine. I think the results are quite flattering on her."

Elizabeth acknowledged, "It was incredibly generous of your sister, but I couldn't say no to her desire to share the experience of going to the modiste together to get the dresses made."

Their chatter stopped as the lights dimmed, and the play began. Elizabeth's attention was pulled towards the stage in anticipation of the coming drama. She had always loved reading Shakespeare's plays and even though the play that evening was to be a farce from a lesser-known artist, she still expected to enjoy it.

With her attention thus diverted, Elizabeth was taken aback when Mr. Darcy leaned close, his warm breath tickling her ear as he whispered, "I think the seamstress did a remarkable job on your dress, but sadly, the dress cannot rival your inherent beauty."

Mr. Darcy, having said his fill, turned and smiled as the curtain rose, immersing the audience in a visually stunning set and a cast of uniquely attired characters. Sadly, Elizabeth found she could not quite concentrate on the play with Mr. Darcy's words echoing in her mind. Mr. Darcy thought she was beautiful.

Never before had Elizabeth been told she was beautiful by someone who was not one of her sisters. In fact, she had often been told by her mother that she would never hold a candle to Jane or Lydia. Elizabeth couldn't help but be swayed when a gentleman praised her beauty. Elizabeth suspected that Mr. Darcy would have encountered at least several seasons' worth of stunning beauties, and yet he said she was beautiful. She knew Mr. Darcy well enough to know he would not lie to her and so he must believe what he said was true. It gave her a thrill that she did not quite know what to do with. So with a determined air, she focused on the play. She refused to let herself be thrown off by Mr. Darcy's words and was determined to enjoy the enchanting night.

If only paying attention was as easy as she would have liked. Every time Mr. Darcy shifted in his seat, Elizabeth was aware of it. Still, she enjoyed what she saw of the play, even laughing at the antics of the characters. She did so love to laugh and was glad that they were attending something comical rather than sad.

All too soon it was the intermission, and the lights came up. Standing, Mr. Darcy asked, "Would you ladies like me to get you some refreshments?"

Elizabeth looked at Georgianna, her brows raised in question, and her friend answered, "No, you do not have to fight the rush on my account."

Adding her own denial, Elizabeth said, "I am certainly fine with no refreshment."

They had only begun discussing the characters in the play and the interesting costumes when the first of their callers arrived. Elizabeth had her back to the entrance talking with Mrs. Annesley on the way the play alluded to various royal families throughout history when she heard a slightly nasal voice greet Mr. Darcy.

"Mr. Darcy, when I saw your box was occupied, I just had to come say hello. After all, our families have been friends for so very long," cooed Miss Caroline Bingley.

Turning, Elizabeth spotted Miss Bingley on the arm of a much older gentleman in all her orange glory. Mr. Darcy had not yet responded to the greeting beyond a nod when Miss Bingley seemed to spot Elizabeth. Miss Bingley's eyes flashed in anger and her lip curled in spite before her expression relaxed and she declared, "Miss Eliza! I never would have expected such a quaint country girl to be in

London attending the latest play and with the Darcys, of all people. You must feel so out of place so far from home."

The woman had changed little at all since she had last seen her. Putting on her best smile, Elizabeth said, "As you can see, I am in London, and I am quite enjoying the play. What character have you enjoyed the most so far, Miss Bingley?"

Tittering in response, Miss Bingley said, "Oh, you are droll, Miss Eliza. No one comes to the theater to watch the play; they come to see and be seen." Snuggling up to the older gentleman beside her, she smiled condescendingly and said, "You must have missed the announcement. I am no longer Miss Bingley; I am Lady Wilton now and you should address me as such."

"Then congratulations are in order," responded Elizabeth. She couldn't help but notice that Caroline's husband, who was standing beside her, didn't inquire about being introduced. He was just as puffed up with himself as the new Lady Wilton was.

WHILE DARCY ENJOYED HOW Elizabeth handled the new Lady Wilton, he had focused much of his attention on Sir Wilton. Despite his well-groomed appearance, the older gentleman's stylish waistcoat failed to fully conceal his noticeable paunch. The man's hair was graying around the temples, but he still seemed to have most of it. The most disturbing thing about the man was the way his pale blue eyes lingered on Elizabeth. Moving to stand closer to Elizabeth, Darcy attempted to convey his protection without having to confront the baronet.

Her voice snide, Lady Wilton asked, "However did you end up sharing a box with Mr. Darcy?"

Smiling, Elizabeth glanced at Georgianna before responding, "Although she favors symphonies over theater or opera, Georgianna couldn't pass up the opportunity for a night out at the theater and was kind enough to insist that I come along. Georgianna and I have both enjoyed her brother's magnanimous efforts to keep us entertained."

Darcy was quick to note the brittle expression on Lady Wilton's face when she said, "Really, Miss Eliza, I would have thought that even someone from the country would know better than to use Miss Darcy's Christian name in such a setting. I have known Miss Darcy for years and still haven't been graced with that privilege."

That was when Georgianna cut in, saying, "Do not think you need to chastise my friend, Lady Wilton. I gave Elizabeth permission to call me Georgianna long ago. In fact, I asked her to call me Georgie, though she still insists on only using it privately." Pausing, Georgianna looked at Elizabeth in a puzzled manner before saying, "Elizabeth, I thought you told me you preferred the name Lizzie to Eliza. Did I misunderstand?"

Darcy could see Elizabeth's struggle not to laugh in the way she pressed her lips together before answering, "No, I actually dislike the name Eliza. I only allow my good friend Charlotte and her family to use the name, as it is a small joke between us. Though some individuals insist on using the name Eliza without ever being given permission to address me so informally. I far prefer Lizzie when among friends."

Darcy could not help smiling at how Elizabeth and Georgianna were handling the confrontation with the new Lady Wilton with grace and aplomb. Lady Wilton was growing even angrier, and it only got worse when Lord and Lady Matlock entered the box and, after ignoring the Wiltons, greeted his group.

Embracing Georgianna, the countess said, "It is so good to see you, my dear!" Then she embraced Elizabeth as well before kissing her on the cheek. "I see you are once again helping my niece and nephew to get more culture, Elizabeth. What have you thought of the farce thus far?"

Smiling fondly, Elizabeth replied, "I have found it quite entertaining thus far. Though some of the happenings have been quite ridiculous, I think that has been the point. The costumes have been quite stunning. What is your opinion of them, Lady Matlock?"

"Darling girl," Lady Matlock tapped Elizabeth with her fan before playfully saying, "I've asked you before to call me Aunt Margaret. And I agree the costumes are delicious with all those lovely fabrics." As she spoke, Lord and Lady Wilton retreated from the box with a disgruntled huff. Darcy assumed they did not appreciate being ignored by the earl and countess. That his aunt, the countess, was asking Elizabeth to call her Aunt Margaret was probably the last straw.

Darcy missed the rest of their conversation as he was drawn into one of his own with his uncle. The Earl of Matlock chuckled and said, "Your aunt has always wished for daughters, and it seems she's found a way to fulfill that longing by attaching herself to your sister and her friend."

Watching the three ladies chat, Darcy smiled and said, "They both seem to revel in her maternal affection."

Nodding in agreement, his uncle said, "I think it is good for all three of them."

Darcy had informed his family of the shoddy way that Elizabeth had been treated by her own family and, after meeting her and seeing the way she got along with Georgianna, they had welcomed her into the fold wholeheartedly. Curious to know if there had been any fresh developments with his other aunt, Darcy asked, "Have you heard from Lady Catherine since her dethronement?"

Sighing, the earl muttered, "My sister has done nothing but castigate everyone and write censorious letters. Thankfully, my staff is in place at the dower house, and I pay them well. They have forwarded me all the letters she attempts to send, and I have been able to prevent her from attempting to spread scurrilous lies about the family in an effort to get back at us."

"I had wondered why I had stopped receiving letters from her," commented Darcy. Then, seeing his uncle's look for further explanation, Darcy shrugged and added, "There has been a longstanding order to burn anything she sends as soon as it arrives, but my staff would still tell me that she had written."

"It makes sense, I suppose," his uncle said, a smile playing at the corners of his lips. "I knew you had stopped communicating with her years ago."

During the entire conversation with his uncle, Darcy had been observing Elizabeth with furtive glances. The longer he knew her, the less he could spend time out of her presence comfortably. There was just something about her that drew him.

It seemed that his glances had been less furtive than he thought because his uncle said, "So when are you going to do something about bringing that lovely girl into the family?"

Darcy jerked his head back to face his uncle so quickly that he might have hurt himself. Even his uncle knew of his feelings? Rubbing at the now twinging muscles, Darcy attempted to find the words to adequately express himself. "I do not want her to enter into anything with me out of obligation. Nor do I wish for anything I say or do to ruin her relationship with Georgianna. I am moving slowly."

Clapping Darcy on the shoulder, his uncle said, "No, son, you are barely moving at all. Starting with a trip to the theater is commendable, but if you want to get her to fully grasp your intentions, you'll need to make a greater impression."

Slumping slightly, Darcy grumbled, "I was afraid that you were going to say something like that."

"It is not your fault, my boy. Your father was quite the same way and did not know how to go about courting Anne for all that he was madly in love with her. Thankfully, my sister noticed the signs and found his fumbling endearing," reassured his uncle.

Chapter Twenty-Five

Elizabeth stretched as she sat on the side of her bed. Standing, she walked over to the chair by the fireplace and picked up her dressing gown and put it on distractedly. Looking about the room, Elizabeth smiled. It took five months of living at Primrose Place, but now her room and bed felt like a true haven, no longer just a guest room in a grand house.

No, her discomfort was not from where she was, but her unexpected thoughts about Mr. Darcy. The first thought she had on waking up had been about her friend's older brother and how she hoped to see him later that day. Startled, she shot up in bed, her heart racing against her ribcage. Just when had the mere thought of Mr. Darcy possibly visiting begun to fill her with such joy and excitement?

Pacing, Elizabeth attempted to decipher her feelings. Yes, she enjoyed her conversations and even debates with Mr. Darcy. Yes, she looked forward to seeing him when he came to have tea with Georgianna and herself. But was it more than just friendship? Would she be feeling such a strong sense of unease if their relationship was solely based on friendship?

Elizabeth came to a sudden halt, her breath catching as she confronted the startling realization that her feelings for Mr. Darcy had transcended mere friendship or even familial affection. Stumbling to the chair by her fireplace, Elizabeth cradled her head with her hands. What had she done? How had she developed feelings for a man so far out of her reach?

She could not possibly take advantage of his and Georgianna's kindness by putting herself forward in any way. They had done so much for her. There had been visits to plays and the opera with Mr. Darcy, Georgianna, and Mrs. Annesley. They had even invited her aunt and uncle to dine at Primrose Place quite often.

Elizabeth had been invited to dine at the Matlock's house and eaten with the earl and countess. She had met their two sons, Phineas and Richard, who were a viscount and a colonel, respectively. Remarkably, they were a kind family who accepted her into their circle without hesitation, despite their position in society. In particular, Elizabeth found Richard hilarious. He enjoyed teasing Mr. Darcy and coaxing him to relax whenever he became tense about something. There was something about the way they interacted that Elizabeth found heartwarming.

Forcing her mind from the path that it was traveling, Elizabeth sighed. She could not risk what she already had for what she was just realizing that she wanted. Standing, she set her shoulders and moved to the bellpull to summon the maid who would help her dress. She could not face her revelations on an empty stomach.

In no time at all, she was dressed and sitting at a table with a plate of food before her, finding it difficult to actually eat anything. It turned out that realizing she had developed a romantic attachment to someone left her feeling slightly queasy. Turning away from the eggs, Elizabeth took a bite of her toast.

"Good morning, Elizabeth. How are you doing today?" asked Georgianna as she walked into the room.

Elizabeth tried to swallow the toast that seemed to be lodged in her throat before croaking, "I am fine." Then, choking slightly, she added, "How are you?"

Looking over her shoulder at Elizabeth from where she stood filling her plate, Georgianna questioned, "Are you sure you are all right? You are not coming down with anything, are you?"

Taking a sip of her chamomile tea and hoping that it would calm her frantic mind, Elizabeth assured her friend, "Do not worry, I only swallowed wrong."

Nodding, Georgianna filled her plate before sitting across from Elizabeth at the table. Elizabeth attempted to act normal and take another sip of tea. She knew that she could not yet attempt to eat anything else on her plate.

It seemed that she had not succeeded in acting normal because Georgianna put her fork down and demanded, "No, something is wrong. I can tell. You have barely touched any of your food, which could suggest that you are unwell, but there seems to be another reason. I have sat across from you at breakfast for months now and you are never this fidgety."

Sighing, Elizabeth fought against irritation. She had become ever closer to Georgianna over the last five months, possibly as close as she was with any of her sisters. They had confided in each other a lot over in the many quiet moments that they had had together. Georgianna now knew her moods, and she was not in any kind of mood to pretend that she was fine.

Realizing that she could not get away with anything else, Elizabeth told Georgianna the truth, or at least part of it. "I had a startling realization this morning, and I am still coming to terms with it. That is all."

"Is it dawning on you that you've developed feelings for my brother?" Georgianna's face was guileless and seemingly unsurprised.

Georgianna's question left Elizabeth speechless, her mouth hanging open in disbelief. All she could say was, "How?"

"I've been seeing flashes of it for the past few weeks," Georgianna said, shrugging one of her shoulders. "I knew it was only a matter of time before you realized." Georgianna shifted her focus to her plate, taking a bite, while Elizabeth grappled with the blow she had just been dealt.

Coming to terms with what Georgianna just said, Elizabeth inquired, "What flashes of love did you see?"

Looking up, with a full mouth, Georgianna swallowed and then, taking a sip of tea, answered, "You have been more eager to see my brother than I have of late. You also smile differently when you look at him."

Dropping her head into her hands, Elizabeth groaned, "How could I have missed it for so long?"

Sitting back in her chair, Georgianna said, "You were the one that said we often miss that which is right in front of us."

Not being the first to realize she was in love made Elizabeth feel strangely out of place. Taking a moment, Elizabeth closed her eyes and attempted to think about what Georgianna had said. From the moment Elizabeth arrived at Primrose Place, she found solace in knowing that Mr. Darcy was close by. There were also several footmen stationed about the house, ensuring her safety from any potential danger posed by her parents.

It was impossible for her to determine the exact moment when her emotions transformed from comfort and respect to romantic love, but there was no denying that it had blossomed. As she reflected on her encounters with Mr. Darcy, she distinguished a familiar warmth from the vicinity of her heart that accompanied his entrance into the room. Elizabeth realized how deeply her love for Mr. Darcy had begun to wind itself around her heart, but with a gasp she said, "Are you not upset that I have fallen in love with your brother? You have already helped me so much. It is not as if I can expect more from either of you. Please know I am not planning on acting on any of my feelings."

With a loud clatter, Georgianna set her teacup down, her eyebrows knitting together as she leaned forward in her chair. Her tone demanding, she asked, "Why would you choose to do nothing about it?"

Surprised by Georgianna's vehemence, Elizabeth explained, "I come from a humble background, with no family of note or influential connections, while your brother is exceptionally wealthy and well-connected to important figures in society. Your brother could never want me for anything more than a friend."

"That is almost as foolish as the time I believed every word that came out of George Wickham's mouth." Georgianna pressed on in her attempt to convince Elizabeth, questioning, "Can you honestly believe that my brother desires a vapid socialite as his wife, rather than a capable partner or, even better, a loyal friend to navigate the ups and downs of life with him?"

Elizabeth might not have been ready to think that Mr. Darcy reciprocated her feelings, but she found solace in the faint possibility that there was still a flicker of hope for her love. Gazing carefully across the table at Georgianna, she asked, "You would want me for your brother?"

"And have my very best friend as my sister?" After the smallest of pauses, Georgianna added, "Of course!" With a shake of her head, she lifted her teacup to her lips and took a sip, her eyes twinkling with delight.

For the first time that morning, Elizabeth smiled. She might never have the man she loved, but she had a friend who loved her so much she wanted her for a sister. Elizabeth picked up her fork and said, "Thank you for liking me so much that you would want me for a sister."

"Thank you for reaching out to a sad girl lost in a dark world." Taking a bite of her pastry, Georgianna chewed it contemplatively before swallowing and saying, "So, how are you going to get him to fall in love with you?"

DARCY HAD NOW BEEN told by two people that he needed to put in more effort to show Elizabeth how much he cared for her. He spent a substantial amount of time analyzing how the evening at the theater had gone as far as wooing Elizabeth went. He wanted to think that it had gone well, but if he was at all adept at romance, he would not be second guessing himself so much.

The only real snag had been the former Caroline Bingley and her new husband. It had seemed to Darcy that the gentleman had wanted to feel superior and so did not ask to be introduced to Darcy and his party, but it rebounded on him. They had both given every indication of being quite put out when his aunt and uncle came in and ignored the interlopers.

Feeling the need to continue his pursuit of Elizabeth, Darcy called on Primrose Place to see if Elizabeth was available to go for a walk at one of the nearby parks. He was aware of her affinity for spending time outside, so being away from the country was hard for her. Hopefully, she would enjoy some time in peaceful surroundings. Furthermore, he pondered that leaving his sister behind could serve as a way to communicate to her that his affection for her surpassed the boundaries of friendship.

Hopping down out of his carriage, Darcy made his way up the few quick steps and was about to knock when the footman opened the door. He was a frequent enough visitor that he was often recognized as he approached. It did not hurt that Darcy actually employed the footman. With the animosity against Elizabeth from her family, Darcy enjoyed having an extra layer of protection in place for her.

Darcy waited while the footman announced his arrival, and soon enough, Georgianna and Elizabeth were making their way into the entryway, with Mrs. Annesley following at a more sedate pace. Georgianna reached out, giving him a hug as she said, "I did not know that we were to expect you this morning. Is everything all right?"

Shaking his head, he hugged her back, reassuring her he answered, "No, there is nothing wrong. Only it is such a lovely day out and we get so few lovely days in London, I thought I would ask if Elizabeth was free to go for a walk in the nearby park." Turning to Elizabeth, he noticed her slight blush but forged ahead adding, "I know it is not Hyde Park but that in itself has its advantages. What do you think? Would you be able to come out with me, or do you have other plans?"

Biting her lip in a way that sent Darcy's pulse racing, Elizabeth murmured, "I am rather fond of walks, and it is a lovely day. Only—"

Georgianna cut in by saying, "Do not worry, Lizzie. I know you thought you had lost your best spencer, but I noticed it only this morning in my wardrobe. I shall get it for you." Turning back to Darcy, she added, "It is such good timing. I was just going to start some lessons with Mrs. Annesley and Elizabeth was going to be left to her own devises. Be sure to take your time on your walk. You know how much Lizzie loves a pleasant walk."

Georgianna was gone in a flash, hurrying up the stairs, presumably after the spencer for Elizabeth. Darcy could not help smiling as she rushed away. He was uncertain if Georgianna knew what he was about, but she was certainly helping him. If her assistance helped him with Elizabeth, he realized he would owe her a token of gratitude. Maybe she would like a new bonnet?

In no time at all, Georgianna was back with the spencer, a bonnet, and a maid that would accompany him and Elizabeth on their walk. Offering Elizabeth his arm, they stepped outside, and Darcy was reassured to glimpse a smile coming from Elizabeth. Pausing at the bottom of the steps, he asked, "Would you like to walk to the park or take my carriage?"

Smiling up at him, Elizabeth answered, "It is not so great a distance. I would be pleased to walk."

So Darcy walked with Elizabeth on his arm the short distance to the park and the maid trailing behind them at a discreet distance. He had accomplished his one goal for the day and worried about what to do next. He was not the best with words. What should he say?

Thankfully, Elizabeth stemmed his worry when she said, "I quite enjoyed the play the other night. How did you feel about the performance?"

Happy to have something to talk about, Darcy said, "I did, though I think I am more fond of the Bard's work than some of the more modern playwrights. I found it much more entertaining than some of the pantos that have been so popular."

"Yes, I prefer a good monologue or soliloquy to all the pomp and fanfare that accompanies a panto." After a slight pause with no conversation, Elizabeth continued by saying, "It was so nice of you to take us to the theater. It still feels like such a treat to me. Before I came to stay with Georgianna, I had only ever seen a few plays and been to the opera once. You have blessed me with the opportunity to enjoy a far wider exposure to the world than I was formally capable of. I want you to know how grateful I am."

Darcy placed his hand over Elizabeth's, feeling the warmth of her touch on his arm. "I did not invite you for your gratitude, Elizabeth," he blurted, his voice filled with sincerity. "I was blessed to have your company. It should be I thanking you."

Elizabeth looked up at him, her mouth forming a little o, before she smiled at him and nodded. As they resumed their walk, Darcy could feel her grip on his arm become firmer and less perfunctory and he hoped it meant that his feelings were starting to reach her. Even without any immediate conversation, Darcy found himself satisfied. Walking along the gravel path of the park, a simple endeavor in itself, had been amplified by the treat of having Elizabeth on his arm as he walked.

When Georgianna had first maneuvered things so that Elizabeth was backed into going for a walk with Mr. Darcy on her own, Elizabeth had been quite upset. However, with every step that she took on Mr. Darcy's arm, she found she could no longer be angry at her friend. Georgianna knew Elizabeth had recently voiced her worries about being with Mr. Darcy, and she anticipated that Elizabeth might say no if she didn't take action.

With a gentle breeze rustling her skirts, she couldn't help but feel grateful as she walked arm in arm with Mr. Darcy. They had engaged in brief conversation but had lapsed into companionable silence. With the silence, Elizabeth could contemplate some of Mr. Darcy's actions.

At the theater, he had offered her his arm and said she was beautiful. Now he said that he was blessed to have her company.

Was it possible that he had developed feelings for her just as she had developed feelings for him?

In all her musings over her what was in her heart, she had never imagined that Mr. Darcy would return her feelings. Such a thing had been almost unimaginable, but now Elizabeth had a new sort of hope. A hope that made her wonder if she should be bold. All things considered, she had always held her head high, unafraid and ready to face any challenge that came her way. So what if the challenge was the fear of declaring her love?

Mr. Darcy was a logical man if he did not return her feelings the way she suspected—the way she hoped—they could surely muddle their way back to friendship, right? Elizabeth had moved on to trying to decide how to find out if he loved her back when Mr. Darcy said, "I am sorry that the former Miss Bingley interrupted our evening at the theater. Though you seemed to hold your own along with Georgianna."

Chuckling, Elizabeth remembered how they had worked together to put the harpy in her place. Smiling up at Mr. Darcy, she said, "Do not worry about Lady Wilton's visit. I have always recognized her pernicious nature for what it was—insecurity and jealousy." Tilting her head and scrunching her nose, Elizabeth continued, "Though I fear my stay with Georgianna has allowed some of my impertinence to rub off on your sister. I will apologize if you wish."

Stopping in his tracks, Mr. Darcy turned towards her, gently cupping one of her hands in his. With sincerity in his eyes, he declared, "I would never want you to apologize for helping my sister to blossom into someone who is confident enough to defend a friend as well as herself."

Gazing up into soulful eyes, Elizabeth said, "Then I will not apologize." Mr. Darcy's deep brown eyes locked with Elizabeth's green ones, and she felt a sudden rush of emotions, making it hard for her to breathe. With the moment stretching out before her, Elizabeth mustered up her courage, fueling it with a flicker of hope. Finally, she resolved that the moment had arrived to act.

She licked her lips nervously, her voice barely above a whisper as she asked, "Is there even a slight possibility that you could reciprocate my feelings?"

It was fascinating to watch Mr. Darcy's reaction to her words. Upon first glance, his gaze was empty as he stared at her, but then his eyes widened, and a broad grin transformed his strong, sculpted face. Time seemed to slip away as he moved closer, his words a soft melody in her ear, "If you speak of love, then yes, I reciprocate your feelings with vigor." Shaking his head as if in wonder, he continued, "You cannot know how wonderful your words have made me feel. I have been trying to find a way to ask you that very question for some time."

Blinking her misty eyes, Elizabeth responded with a sense of relief, "Then I am glad I have finally put an end to our suspenseful wondering."

Shaking his head, Mr. Darcy said, "I had been worried that you would feel beholden to me and somehow you would not truly reciprocate."

"And I felt you had already done so much for me. I did not want to presume on your friendship."

His smile widening, Mr. Darcy looked down at Elizabeth, his voice gentle as he said, "I am glad that we have come to know better. I want to laugh and embrace you, but the circumstances don't allow it." Then, looking to the path they traveled, he asked, "Do you want to keep walking along?"

Smiling up at him, Elizabeth nodded, "Yes, I would like to continue walking and perhaps we might discuss what our discovery means to us moving forward."

For a time, neither said anything, and they walked along the path at a leisurely pace. Elizabeth was grateful for the quiet moment of reflection because it meant that she could fully take in the magnitude of what had happened. Not only had she admitted her newfound feelings for Mr. Darcy, but he returned them. With this realization, she knew that her life was about to undergo a profound transformation, shattering all her previous expectations.

Only two weeks ago, she had thought that once she turned twenty-one, she would move to her aunt and uncle's house on Gracechurch Street. Elizabeth had assumed that she might find a husband among her uncle's associates. The moment she acknowledged her feelings for Mr. Darcy, thoughts of spinsterhood and the necessity of seeking employment flooded her mind. She knew she could never marry another while her heart was otherwise engaged.

Now she knew that neither option would take place. Mr. Darcy would never express feelings for someone without intending to follow through on those feelings and asking her to marry him. The thought of a lonely life no longer haunted her, for she knew she would always be a part of his world. Whether in London or Pemberley, their love would keep them together. Though there were no specifics, Elizabeth was happy with what was to come.

So she was not completely surprised when Mr. Darcy, once again, stopped and faced her, his eyes searching her own as he said, "This may be premature or even presumptuous, but I find myself compelled to ask. Will you marry me? Or, if your feelings for me are still fledgling, would you consent to a courtship?"

Chapter Twenty-Six

Darcy waited with bated breath, hoping against hope that he had not just completely harmed his burgeoning relationship with Elizabeth. Every moment that she did not respond, his heart thudded painfully in his chest. In a move that left him breathless, Elizabeth slowly licked her lips before saying, "I am aware that it might seem sudden, but I truly believe I know my own feelings, and those feelings are telling me to say yes."

"Yes?!" Darcy felt dizzy with relief at hearing her softly spoken words and as he could not pick her up and swing her around in the park under the watchful gaze of passers-by, he contented himself with squeezing her hands.

Grinning mischievously, Elizabeth tugged him along on the path, the sweet smell of blooming flowers filling the surrounding air. Soon she was saying, "Mr. Darcy, I have had the pleasure of knowing you for quite some time, and during our acquaintance, I admire your remarkable qualities. Why would you question my acceptance of your proposal?"

With a chuckle, Darcy shook his head and responded, "I can't believe you're able to say that, considering how badly I fumbled our initial encounter."

"Yes, that was rather badly done, but you quickly atoned for your ill-mannered behavior," she snickered. Then, hugging his arm slightly as they walked, she said, "Do you need to understand why I feel comfortable committing myself to you? First of all, your diligent stewardship of your estate is clear in how you tirelessly assist those who require aid. Even from a distance, you are constantly busy seeing that everyone and everything is cared for."

Darcy declared, "I've only acted in accordance with my responsibilities. There is nothing so remarkable about that."

"Think about where I come from, Mr. Darcy. My father has many responsibilities that he does not take care of, instead he foists them on others. Knowing that you are not such a man is more than reassuring. I find it oddly attractive. In fact, it is almost as attractive as the fact that I know you respect me and enjoy knowing my thoughts on a wide range of topics, from crop rotation to the philosophies of Aristotle," Elizabeth explained with heartfelt vigor.

For Darcy, who had never felt that he would have what a woman of society would want in a husband, it was reassuring to know that Elizabeth appreciated what he had to offer. Her statement also reminded him of why he wanted to lash out at Mr. Bennet as

Elizabeth was the one who most often ended up having to take up her father's responsibilities.

He had grown quiet when Elizabeth spoke up, once again saying, "I still haven't told you how you have made me feel protected and even cherished in a way that I never felt before." Then, almost whispering, she added, "I have always known I was loved by my sisters and even my Aunt and Uncle Gardiner, but having your attention when I was suffering was something else. You carried me when I could not walk on my own. I have never encountered someone so attentive to my needs, anticipating them even before I ask for assistance."

Looking down at the woman who held his heart, Darcy said, "I have to help you without your request, or have you not noticed that you rarely ask for help? I suspect that when you finally do ask for help, it is only because you are far beyond what you are capable of handling. You take so much on to yourself. I will be glad when we are married, then I will be able to step in and help you whenever I want and not have to step back and leave someone else to the task."

As they turned along the last bit of path before they would have to walk back to Primrose Place, Elizabeth said, "It will be something to get used to, not having the weight of the world on my shoulders."

"You are not Atlas, my dear, and that your father thought you should be, in my opinion, is a crime." Darcy gritted his teeth to refrain from saying more against Elizabeth's father and ruining their lovely moment.

"And that," she murmured, her voice filled with affection, "is just one small part of why you mean the world to me, Mr. Darcy."

Having completed the circuit around the park, Darcy paused and asked, "Would you like to continue walking or should we return to Primrose Place and share our news?"

"Although a part of me wants to make Georgianna wait, considering how she practically pushed me out the door with you, I cannot contain my happiness. Let us return and share our news." Then, sighing, she added, "We can even begin making plans if you want to. I know getting married to me will be on the more complicated side."

Arm in arm, Darcy and Elizabeth strolled back to Primrose Place, their conversation turning to wedding plans. Darcy said, "Most ladies I know would be thrilled to be about planning their wedding, yet I do not think you are going to be the sort to go mad over linens and lace."

Chuckling, Elizabeth laid her head briefly on Darcy's shoulder before saying, "No, I quite despise lace. I suppose it comes from my mother constantly trying to dress me in the stuff when I knew that the money would be better spent elsewhere. Besides, her taste in fashion was not at all like mine."

"I will admit that some debutantes I've seen remind me too much of fancy tearoom pastries with all the lace layered about their dresses. So I am not unhappy that your taste leans in another direction," commented Darcy.

Elizabeth's voice turned soft, almost melancholy as she said, "I think I would enjoy the thought of planning my wedding more if I knew that my sisters could be part of the joy. Without them, I think I will settle for something simple." Then, looking up at Darcy with a brave sort of smile, she added, "The only thing I really want is to be married to you. I do not need some grand affair."

Darcy's heart turned over at the strength of Elizabeth's words. He knew he did not care how their wedding took place as long as it happened, but he wanted more for Elizabeth, and he had an idea of how to accomplish it. Elizabeth had learned to ask for less from the world, but in his opinion, she deserved everything the world had to offer, and he would see that she got it.

GEORGIANNA PEEKED OUT THE window while trying to move as little of the curtain as possible. She could finally see William and Elizabeth coming down the street arm and arm and from what she could tell, they appeared rather involved in their conversation. Turning, she glanced back at Mrs. Annesley, exclaiming, "They are on their way back! Do you suppose they have realized what we have already known for some time now?"

Shaking her head disapprovingly, Mrs. Annesley paused her stitchwork to scold her. "You are well aware, Miss Darcy, that it is not proper to spy on your friend and brother. Come sit with me and take up your project. Didn't you tell your brother I was showing you something?"

After one last glance, Georgianna moved away from the window and sat down next to Mrs. Annesley with a sigh. She wanted so much for Elizabeth and her brother to realize that they were perfect together, but she knew that beyond pushing them together and a few encouraging words, she could not do much to help matters. Picking up her embroidery hoop, she studied the pattern of roses twined around a gate. She hoped to give it to Elizabeth as a gift once she became her sister in truth.

When she heard the commotion at the door of William and Elizabeth being admitted, it took everything she had in her not to bounce up and demand how their walk had gone. Still, as they came into the room, she knew that it had gone well, if only from the glances they kept sharing and the smiles splitting their faces. When she could not wait any longer, she said, "So?"

Chuckling, Elizabeth crossed her arms and said, "I do not know if I should tell you what you want to hear after the way that you practically threw me at your brother."

Standing, Georgianna looked back and forth between William and Elizabeth, studying their faces. They were playing with her, which she assumed was a good sign, so she said, "You know you wanted to go with him. You were just nervous. Now tell me about whatever it is that has you so happy."

William and Elizabeth exchanged a meaningful look before her brother excitedly announced, "I asked Elizabeth to marry me, and she accepted!"

Georgianna did not know who to hug first, but since Elizabeth was closer, she grabbed her and hugged her for all she was worth. Squealing with joy, she said, "I have long known that you were perfect for each other, but I thought it would take much longer for you to come to such a realization." Moving on from Elizabeth, she hugged her brother, whispering, "Thank you for choosing such a wonderful woman to be my sister."

Smirking, her brother replied, "It's good to know that you're pleased with my choice, but I must confess that my chief priority wasn't necessarily to make you happy."

Georgianna was astounded to see her brother's happy smirk. Elizabeth was already helping her brother to have a happier life. Her moment of thoughtfulness allowed Mrs. Annesley to come to their merry group and add her congratulations.

Hugging Elizabeth, to whom she had grown close in the last few months, Mrs. Annesley said, "I am so happy for you!" Then, standing back and holding Elizabeth by the shoulders, she admonished, "I told you that you were not destined to be a governess."

Chuckling, Elizabeth said, "I still say that I could have been happy as a governess." Then, looking back at William, she added, "Though

I believe I will be happier united with Mr. Darcy than I ever could have experienced as a governess."

Looking at her brother, Georgianna exclaimed, "Why is Lizzie still calling you Mr. Darcy? She is going to be your wife. Shouldn't she be able to call you William, at least in private?"

The reaction of the pair was quite comical to Georgianna. Elizabeth blushed and croaked, "Georgie!"

Her brother said, "Georgianna, we only just became engaged. We have had very little time to discuss anything, let alone my desire for her to call me William."

Blushing even more, Elizabeth turned to her new fiancé and inquired, "Would you prefer me to address you as William?"

William extended his hand towards Elizabeth's, intertwining their fingers as he pulled her closer. Softly, he spoke, "I want you to address me in whatever way makes you feel most comfortable." Then, barely audible, he whispered, "Though I must admit, I'm curious to hear how William sounds on your lips."

In a moment of awe, Elizabeth's mouth opened into a rounded shape, her eyes widening and her blush deepening as she breathed out, "William?" She seemed half-uncertain, and half-delighted. Georgianna wanted to squeal at how cute they were but knew that doing so would ruin the moment.

As Georgianna shifted her focus to William, she was met with an expression of unadulterated adoration. They stayed like that, their gazes locked unmoving, somehow affirming their emotions without a single word spoken. The effort to restrain herself had Georgianna bouncing slightly on her toes.

Mrs. Annesley laid a calming hand on Georgianna's shoulder, and with a tilt of her head, they returned to their seats. After a few more moments of the couple's unspoken conversation, Mrs. Annesley cleared her throat and said, "I believe some tea may be in order."

Standing, Mrs. Annesley went to the bellpull to summon a maid and doing so disturbed the loving couple who blinkingly came out of their love-fueled trance. Noticing that she had William and Elizabeth's attention, Mrs. Annesley told them, "I am going to have them bring up a tea service so we can discuss things over a nice cup of tea and perhaps a biscuit."

Nodding, albeit distractedly, William walked with Elizabeth over to the settee where they sat down together. There was little conversation until tea had been served and everyone had taken a few sips of tea. Then, unable to wait any longer, Georgianna asked, "So when is the wedding going to be?"

First looking at William and then back to Georgianna, Elizabeth said, "I have no desire for a long engagement, but without my father's approval, I cannot marry before I gain my majority."

"You will reach your majority in a little less than a month. Is a month from today a short enough engagement? Or is it too short?" Shrugging, William added, "I must admit, I have never paid attention to these sorts of things."

Georgianna and Elizabeth both looked at each other and then Mrs. Annesley before Mrs. Annesley said, "I am sure a wedding could be arranged in a month without any sort of issue."

With a grin, William eagerly exclaimed, "Then I believe I've come up with a splendid idea."

LOOKING OVER AT MR. Darcy—*no, William*, she corrected herself—Elizabeth asked, "What idea is that?"

Putting down his teacup, William smiled. "I know you have long wanted your sister to be a part of your wedding. Bingley says that she wants the same. What if your aunt and uncle encourage your parents to have Jane and possibly Mary shop for her trousseau in London? While they are here, you could shop with them for your own trousseau. Then, prior to their departure for Meryton, they could attend our wedding. Miss Bennet could even be your maid of honor."

William's suggestion sparked a flurry of thoughts in Elizabeth's mind. It would be the perfect arrangement if they could somehow convince her mother to stay behind at Longbourn. Encouraged, she said, "It would all be ruined if Mrs. Bennet came with them but... If Mr. Bingley expressed his disapproval of the shopping excursion, if Mrs. Bennet neglected her duty of overseeing the wedding arrangements or something similar, it might just work."

"I think we can make that work," William said, his smile filled with encouragement. "Bingley told me that Mrs. Bennet is quite determined to make sure the wedding goes off without a hitch and is keen to keep him happy."

Elizabeth pressed a hand to the butterflies in her stomach. It seemed she might get more than she had ever hoped for. First, she had realized that she had fallen in love with a wonderful man. Then, despite her fears, she had learned that he loved her in return. Now she was engaged to him and there was talk of having their wedding and the miracle of miracles, her sisters might be able to attend the ceremony.

Eyes narrowing, she turned to William. "You cannot tell me that you only just thought of how to bring my sisters to London to attend our wedding."

Rubbing at the back of his neck, William offered her a sheepish smile as he answered, "I will admit to considering how to bring at least some of your sisters to London for a visit for some time. That it happens to coincide is just glorious serendipity."

"Serendipity?" Elizabeth asked, an eyebrow raised.

Georgianna was soon giggling uncontrollably at the remark, but William only spared her a single glance before stating, "I always had a secret desire for us to get engaged and eventually get married, but I never foresaw you reciprocating my affection so swiftly."

Reaching out, Elizabeth clasped William's hand where it lay next to her on the settee. "I will choose to believe you."

Returning to her tea before it grew cold, Elizabeth took a sip as Georgianna, overcoming her fit of giggles, asked, "So when do we get to start shopping for wedding things and Lizzie's trousseau?"

With a sigh, Elizabeth pulled her teacup away from her mouth and shook her head before murmuring, "I have very little saved for shopping excursions."

Rolling her eyes, Georgianna turned to William. "William, tell her we will provide the funds for her trousseau. If it is unseemly for some reason, I will fund our shopping with my pin money. You know I can never use it all." Turning to Elizabeth, she explained, "You will have to understand that my brother is extremely generous in all he does, whether it is towards those in need or those he loves. You will never lack for anything."

Elizabeth looked at the siblings and knew that she would not win the battle. William, his voice gentle, said, "Georgianna is correct, Elizabeth. We Darcys have much more than we need. You will be a Darcy in thirty-one days or so. Why should I wait to make sure you have what you need for a month when I can provide for you now?"

"Fine," Elizabeth reluctantly gave in, before adding, "but let me be clear. I don't want anything flamboyant or ostentatious, even if you're helping me pay for my trousseau."

Nodding, Georgianna said, "Yes, I know exactly how you feel about lace. There will not be one speck of lace more than necessary."

Joining in the conversation, Mrs. Annesley looked at Georgianna and said, "There will be a lot to coordinate in a month. We should contact your modiste about fitting Elizabeth into her schedule. There is much that will need to be completed within the next month."

Worried, Elizabeth said, "Surely I do not need much more than a wedding dress?"

Smiling kindly at Elizabeth, Mrs. Annesley said, "While the wedding dress is one of the first things I would suggest she work on, you will also need at least a few dresses for around town and warmer wear for when you journey to Pemberley. As Mrs. Darcy, you will be much observed by those who wished to have the coveted spot next to Mr. Darcy. It is easier to hold your head up and stare them down when you are wearing something on par with your new station in life."

Elizabeth could understand the need for a new wardrobe, even if she did not like the idea of having to pick it out. Sighing, she turned to William and said, "Do you see how much I love you? I am willing to endure the discomfort of being measured, pricked with needles, and judged for you."

Lifting Elizabeth's hand to his lips, William kissed her knuckles and said, "I am eternally grateful for your love and all you do. Would it help at all if I promise to take you to Hatchards for books after every fitting?"

Giggling, Elizabeth freed her hand and flung her arms around William's neck. "You know just how to treat a girl."

William joined in on her laughter and remarked, "Most ladies would be happier to receive a wardrobe than a few books, but you are not most ladies. And that is one of the countless reasons why I adore you."

Chapter Twenty-Seven

Darcy felt it was important to talk to the one man in Elizabeth's family he could like now that they were engaged. So he had arranged to meet with Mr. Gardiner and discuss matters with him. He had met Mr. Gardiner on several occasions, and he had always seemed an amiable man who showed much affection for his niece. Darcy took comfort knowing that Mr. Gardiner exhibited more common sense and diligence than both his sister- and brother-in-law combined.

Though now, as he rode towards the man's home, he wondered if Mr. Gardiner would give him a hard time when he told him of his engagement to Elizabeth. The man had seemed quite protective of his niece. When Mr. Gardiner had learned of what Elizabeth's parents had put her through, it had been difficult for Elizabeth to restrain him from going to Longbourn and confronting them.

Darcy hoped that everything would go well. It was possible that he could even discuss his thoughts of bringing about some comeuppance on the Bennets. He had learned things through his investigators that would put him in a position of power. The question was whether he chose to act on it.

With the realization that he had reached his destination, he carefully disembarked from his carriage and walked up to the door, giving the knocker a firm knock. A well-dressed footman answered and greeted him by saying, "Mr. Gardiner has been expecting you. I will bring you to his study."

Before he knew it, he was facing a gentleman not so much older than himself who looked slightly like Elizabeth. He could see the family resemblance in the line of his brow and the sparkle of intelligence in his eyes. It was possible the intelligence had not been inherited but rather learned from the man. Either way, it was something Mr. Gardiner had in common with Elizabeth.

"I must admit, Mr. Darcy, I was taken aback when you requested this meeting," Mr. Gardiner remarked, unable to conceal his curiosity.

Eager to make a good impression, Darcy said, "I know you are a busy man, Mr. Gardiner. Thank you for agreeing to make time to see me."

"No need to thank me. Setting aside time to meet you was a simple task." Smiling, Mr. Gardiner added, "Now that pleasantries are out of the way, it seems you have something important you want to discuss with me. As you are vital to the care of my beloved niece, Elizabeth, I am anxious to hear what you have to say."

It felt as if a heavy stone had lodged itself in his stomach, but Darcy managed to say, "I have fallen in love with Elizabeth, sir, and once I realized that she returned my feelings, I was moved to propose to her."

"I assume that you are here because she said yes," stated Mr. Gardiner, his expression offering no reassurance of his approval.

Darcy had not felt so uneasy since he was giving an oral report to his most difficult professors at Eton. Swallowing hard, Darcy managed to confirm Mr. Gardiner's assumption without choking on the weight of his anxiety. In the empty silence while Darcy waited for a response from Elizabeth's uncle, he realized why he was such a successful businessman. By keeping his emotions hidden, he could manipulate any negotiation to his advantage.

Finally, after the suspense made Darcy think he would do something ridiculous like begging for his blessing, Mr. Gardiner smiled. An unsteady breath burst from his lungs as Mr. Gardiner said, "Having seen the two of you interact, I had assumed this would happen eventually. In fact, I was half glad that you would be given so much time in one another's company. Despite your differences, there were certain similarities that made me fear you wouldn't realize how perfectly suited you were for each other without sufficient time."

Attempting to force his muscles to relax from their anxiety-fueled knots now that he knew that Mr. Gardiner was accepting of his suit, Darcy said, "I am just glad that I recognized my feelings before someone else recognized how amazing she is."

As if just realizing that Darcy was still standing, Mr. Gardiner exclaimed, "Sit down and so we can discuss matters."

Taking a seat in front of Mr. Gardiner's desk, Darcy murmured, "Thank you." After crossing his legs, he spoke, "Although I understand you can't grant me the permission to marry Elizabeth, I wanted to seek your blessing because of how much she loves and respects you."

"Thank you for the consideration. I know Elizabeth will be of age soon and so you will not need permission for long. When is the happy day to be?"

"Actually, two days after her majority. My godfather is going to help me get a common license." Leaning slightly forward in his chair, Darcy said, "Actually, Elizabeth and I were hoping you could help us arrange things so that some of Elizabeth's sisters could attend our wedding. The plan we have come up with would involve having Miss Bennet and, possibly, Miss Mary come up to shop for Jane's trousseau. Elizabeth could join them in shopping, and then, before they return to Longbourn, they could attend the wedding. It would be best if you offered for them to stay here for the plan to work."

Grinning, Mr. Gardiner said, "That is a splendid idea! Madeline was going to invite Jane up anyway, but I am certain she would love to be a part of the plan to include Elizabeth's sisters in the wedding."

"I had hoped it would not be too difficult to arrange. I know how close Elizabeth is with her sisters. Actually, I have been wondering about the possibility of attending Bingley's wedding with Elizabeth once we are married. Mr. Bennet would have absolutely no sway over her at that point." Rubbing at his forehead, Darcy wondered if Elizabeth would feel comfortable staying at Netherfield so that she could at least attend her sister's wedding.

Mr. Gardiner's lip curled slightly as he commented, "I am still so disgusted at my brother-in-law over his treatment of Elizabeth. I have never been fond of the man, but I never supposed that his indolence would bleed over into cruelty. If only there was a way to make him understand the consequences of treating others poorly."

Fighting the desire to tug at his cravat, Darcy said, "Actually, I have had investigators learning about Mr. Bennet and they have found that he purchased several rare books using a loan he had obtained from a friend from Oxford. Mr. Bennet was paying the friend back in increments as he could, but he had not been able to pay anything since Elizabeth had left. Things became less productive at Longbourn without Elizabeth's continued attention and Mr. Bennet refuses to put forth any effort to improve matters."

Eyebrow rising in intrigue, Mr. Gardiner asked, "You would not be considering buying his debt and putting my brother-in-law in debtor's prison, would you?"

Pressing his lips together in a hard line, Darcy thought for a moment before saying, "I am not sure if it is something I want to do. Though it would certainly be something that could make Mr. Bennet feel the sting of his actions."

Nodding, Mr. Gardiner said, "You would have to speak with Elizabeth about it before you did anything." Then, after a pause, he added, "For that matter, what about Longbourn? My sister could never manage that place; her husband hasn't done much either, so it's doubtful she would make things any worse."

"As for Longbourn, I have an idea. What do you know about common recovery?" asked Darcy.

"Enough to know that we will have to discuss everything with Elizabeth and plan our next moves carefully.

Two days from now, let's gather for dinner. Madeline will send round an invitation, including Elizabeth, your sister, and Mrs. Annesley. It will give us an opportunity to discuss matters." Standing, Mr. Gardiner said, "I hate to show you out so quickly, but I have a meeting with investors that I need to prepare for."

Darcy stood as well and assured Mr. Gardiner by saying, "There's no need to worry about it. I know you are a busy man, and I need to meet with a few other people today myself." Turning, Darcy made for the door but stopped and, looking back at Mr. Gardiner, said, "Thank you, Mr. Gardiner, for being so supportive."

"Call me Uncle Edward or if that feels too informal, you could try Gardiner," the man replied with a smile. "We are soon to be family, after all."

LOOKING OUT THE WINDOW of the carriage, Elizabeth saw that they were almost there, and she barely restrained herself from bouncing up and down on her seat. Elizabeth had already had a wonderful day, and now she was heading towards her aunt and uncle's home for dinner. Despite having to start her day being poked and prodded at the modiste, William met her at Hatchards afterwards. They had spent a lovely bit of time discussing various books and he had insisted on treating her to three books that caught her eye. After perusing the bookstore, they headed over to Gunther's, treating Mrs. Annesley and Georgianna to ices as a thank you for their patience.

She was looking forward to speaking with her aunt and uncle about her wedding. She wanted both of them to be a part of her wedding day. There were so many things that she knew her aunt could help her with and, as for her uncle, she hoped he might walk her down the aisle.

William had told her he had spoken with her uncle about their engagement and had gotten his blessing, which meant a lot to her. He had even asked about having Jane and Mary come up so they could sneak them to her wedding. Elizabeth did not want to be rude, but she hoped to make plans while they were there.

Soon enough, William was helping her down from the carriage and she was escorted into her aunt and uncle's home. Elizabeth had barely handed her wrap to the footman when her Aunt Madeline enveloped her in a bone-cracking hug, exclaiming, "I am so happy for you, Lizzie!"

Leaning back, Elizabeth smiled at her aunt and replied, "I am glad then that is not just me, for I could not be happier to marry William. Please say you will help me with the planning and shopping for what I will need to weather a Derbyshire winter."

"Of course, my dear, of course." Aunt Madeline, wrapping an arm around her waist, said, "Welcome, everyone. You will have to forgive me for my lapse in hospitality. I have been so excited for our Lizzie."

Shaking her head, Georgianna said, "I completely understand. I have been at sixes and sevens knowing I will get Lizzie as a sister."

With a smile, Aunt Madeline gestured everyone into the drawing room where they could wait for dinner to be announced. Turning back to Elizabeth, she said, "I have already sent a letter inviting all your sisters up for a shopping trip. I have worded it in such a way that I do not think your mother will become suspicious. I offered to gift each of your sisters something for the wedding and make sure Jane has everything she needs to hold her head up as Mrs. Bingley. Now I do not know if all of your sisters will manage to come, but we can hope."

Sitting on a settee, Elizabeth smiled at William as he sat next to her, but did not interrupt her conversation with her aunt. She was quick to thank her, saying, "I cannot thank you enough for helping to arrange that. I would give anything to have at least some of my sisters at my wedding."

Waving her off, Aunt Madeline said, "Do not give it a second thought. I know how close you are to your sisters." Hesitating, she lost some of her smile before asking, "Have you considered attending Jane's wedding? I understand your wish to be by her side and by that point, you will already be wedded, leaving your father powerless to do anything to you."

Biting her lip, Elizabeth considered her aunt's words. She wished to be there for Jane, but she had such a visceral response to the thought of returning to her childhood home. Looking up at William, she asked, "I do wish to be there for Jane, but I do not think I could step foot in Longbourn and have a civil conversation with either of my parents. What do you think, William?"

Reaching out, he took her hand in his from where it had sat on the settee between them and said, "I do not think you should avoid your sister's wedding if it is somewhere you want to be. Bingley has offered for us to stay at Netherfield if we should wish to come to the wedding. We could potentially attend the ceremony and sidestep the inevitable confrontation at Longbourn by skipping the wedding breakfast. There will be a time to confront your parents, but it will not be at your sister's wedding."

Seeing the logic of what William said, Elizabeth nodded. There was no reason that her parents should be able to keep her away from her sister's wedding. Taking a breath, she said, "Yes, that sounds like a good idea. You are actually right on both accounts. I want to be there for my sister when she gets married, and I should not let my parents stop me. I also think that I will have to confront my parents sooner rather than later."

Glancing over at her uncle, William hesitated before saying, "I actually have an idea about that, but as we are about to be shown into dinner, what do you say we talk about that afterwards?"

When Elizabeth studied the two men who were most significant in her life, she realized the evening would be more complicated than she had previously assumed. There was going to be something hard to be discussed later. As both men were in agreement over whatever it was, Elizabeth decided she would hear them out later without hesitation. She trusted them to have her best interests at heart. She knew that in the meantime, she could indulge in a delicious dinner that was bound to be scrumptious, surrounded by some of those closest to her.

DARCY HAD NOTED ELIZABETH'S concern when she realized that there was going to be a discussion that would surely make her uneasy. His heart had gone out to her, but she seemed to put her worries aside and enjoyed the dinner with her family. She had even taken time to visit her nieces and nephews, taking pride in showing him her newest little niece, Beth, who seemed to be so tiny.

Watching her hold the small bundle and coo at the bright-eyed baby did something to Darcy. He couldn't resist the urge to rub his chest where his heart thudded forcefully. Darcy had never thought of having children before that moment, not really. He had known he would have to have an heir, but the concept had always been something ephemeral.

Watching Elizabeth changed that. Now, he yearned for children—not just any children, but children he could raise and cherish alongside Elizabeth. He craved it with a sudden fierceness. He longed to watch her cradle their child and coo at them. Darcy did not know how long he watched Elizabeth before Gardiner clapped him on the shoulder, saying, "It hits you kind of hard. Believe me, I know."

Hoping he was not blushing, Darcy nodded. He had no words to express what he was feeling, or at least nothing coherent, so the nod was all he could offer. Unable to take his eyes off Elizabeth, he watched as she kissed baby Beth's forehead and handed her back to her aunt.

Then, after saying something to her aunt, she came over to him and her uncle, a grim smile on her face. Setting her shoulders in a way he recognized, Elizabeth said, "I believe, gentlemen, that it is time that we get to that discussion you mentioned."

That was the thing about Elizabeth. When faced with an issue, she did not run away; she didn't hide; she set her shoulders and faced it. Even when it was an insurmountable problem, even if it should not have been her problem, if she saw something that needed doing, she would do all she could to take care of the issue.

Darcy loved it about her. The willingness to work hard and face issues head on. Only he did not want her to have to face things alone anymore. He wanted to be there for her, standing at her side, offering her aid and lending her his strength.

So, offering her his arm, he said, "Shall we?"

Smiling, she took his arm, and they all walked into her uncle's office together. After settling into the small grouping of chairs before the fireplace, she said, "I take it you have come up with a way to handle Mr. and Mrs. Bennet, but you are hesitating to act."

Grateful that they were sharing a settee, Darcy took her hand in his with a hope that he could offer her comfort in what was sure to be a difficult discussion. Taking a deep breath, he said, "Since you left, things have grown worse for Longbourn and its coffers. You had been keeping your mother from overspending, but without your influence, she has been far exceeding any sort of budget. She has had several fancy dinners and redone her favorite sitting room. There is also your father's negligence, which has influenced two of the tenant families to leave for greener pastures."

Darcy knew that she had been close to all the tenant families, so it was probably a blow to her to learn of their desertion. He watched as she bit her lower lip slightly in a way that made him swallow hard. Forcing his eyes away from her mouth, he listened as she said, "I hope whoever left will be treated as they deserve, wherever they have gone. With two families gone, that would be roughly twenty percent of the Longbourn profits. Though, really, it will most likely be closer to thirty or thirty-five if the situation is bad. He cannot expect to get the same amount of rents from the remaining tenants. If Mrs. Bennet is overspending as badly as I fear, the coffers will be dry."

The smallest of smiles flickered across his lips as he listened to Elizabeth. She had understood the depth of the problem in no time at all. "To make matters worse, your father borrowed money in order to buy several rare books and can no longer make his scheduled payments."

Rubbing at her forehead, Elizabeth sighed. "I had wondered how he always found the funds for those books." Shaking her head, Elizabeth continued, "They are ruining Longbourn before Mr. Collins can even get his hands on it. What happens if the person he borrowed from wants his money back and Mr. Bennet cannot pay it?"

With a heavy sigh, Darcy glanced at Gardiner. When Darcy remained silent, Gardiner finally spoke up. "It's a very real possibility that Mr. Bennet will be thrown into debtor's prison."

Darcy found it difficult to watch Elizabeth's face pale as her uncle spoke, but before he could console her, she interrupted, her voice filled with concern, "I don't want to shield Mr. Bennet—he deserves to face consequences for his actions—but what about my sisters and Longbourn? Is there any way to protect them?"

Once again, Darcy glanced at Gardiner, though this time he spoke up and replied, "There is, though it will take finagling. Actually, I think it is quite fitting, but I will not act if you do not fully support my idea."

Looking him in the eyes, Elizabeth squeezed the hand he still held and said, "I know you are trying to protect my sisters and Longbourn. I will not get upset if you tell me your idea."

With her encouragement, Darcy felt a weight lift off his shoulders, allowing him to speak with a newfound confidence. "I must confess," he began, "along with my powerful urge to shield the innocent in this predicament, I desire retribution for what your parents did to you."

As she linked her arm through his, Elizabeth leaned on his shoulder, her voice filled with determination. "I will admit to wanting a certain amount of retribution as well," she confessed, before adding, "tell me your plan, William."

Taking a deep breath, Darcy plunged ahead with his idea. "I know who your father owes money to, and I have asked that he not act against Mr. Bennet until after your sister marries Bingley and they leave on their wedding trip."

Smiling, Elizabeth said, "Thank you for that. I do not know if Jane could handle such a dramatic event up close. It is best that she be told about it at a later time."

Taking back up his explanation, Darcy said, "With your father in debtor's prison and his heir in India as part of a punishment from the church, it gives me the ability to use common recovery to take control of Longbourn."

"I will admit that I am not so very knowledgeable about legal matters. What is common recovery?" asked Elizabeth, looking back and forth between her uncle and Darcy.

Here Gardiner picked up the explanation by saying, "With both your father and his heir proving themselves irresponsible and unsuitable to manage the family estate, Darcy can tell the court that he wants to preserve it for your second son or even a daughter. He could even set up something that would say that it goes to the first son of the Bennet daughters who does not inherent his own estate. Really, it depends on the judge that handles the case."

Adding his own thoughts on the matter, Darcy said, "It is the best way that I can come up with to protect the land and the tenants that you care for, not to mention your sisters."

Biting her lip again, Elizabeth seemed to consider what they were saying. Then, closing her eyes, she took a breath and after opening her eyes she asked, "Once we wrest power from Mr. Bennet and Mr. Collins, what happens to my sisters and Mrs. Bennet?"

Darcy was quick to reassure her. "Without Mr. Bennet in the picture, I will have the right to oversee Longbourn as it deserves to be, and I was considering offering your mother a cottage to live in with a servant or two. Your sisters would have a choice of where they would want to go. I would be more than willing for them to stay with us at Pemberley."

"I know Madeline and I would be completely willing to take in your sisters as well. It will be their choice, though," added her uncle.

Darcy felt a wave of relief as Elizabeth once again hugged his arm, her touch providing reassurance that she understood the depth of his contemplation. "I can tell you have given this a lot of consideration," she acknowledged. "I also sense your apprehension over my reaction to your plan, but it really is the most effective way to protect the people I care about. That Mr. and Mrs. Bennet will have to confront the repercussions of their behavior is a minor source of delight for me."

Darcy was relieved when he heard Elizabeth chuckle and added, "I do not know who will be affected more—Mr. Bennet, going to debtor's prison, or Mrs. Bennet, no longer being able to play the lady of the manor. I think it is a splendid plan, and we should move forward with it."

Chapter Twenty-Eight

It was an odd sort of let down to realize that all the plans she had gone over with William and her uncle would not see any kind of traction until after her wedding. Elizabeth tried to shrug off the odd sort of anticipation and dread that came with waiting for something so significant and emotionally charged. So she focused on the plans that were underway for her wedding. Thankfully, there was no need to argue over lace—a situation that would have surely arisen had Mrs. Bennet been involved.

The high note was that she had a small collection of books from Hatchards, as William still insisted that he meet her there after every shopping trip. He had even added her to his account, which seemed to thrill the proprietor. Actually, she had been added to quite a few accounts. There was the modiste that Georgianna and Lady Matlock frequented, as well as all their favorite shops. William had really been quite thorough trying to make sure she would have access to everything she might need or even want.

Now she was waiting for her sisters at her aunt and uncle's home on Gracechurch Street. Elizabeth hoped that her mother would have let all her daughters come to London, but she was still unsure who would get out of the carriage when it arrived. Her most recent letter from Mary smuggled through Georgianna said that Mrs. Bennet was intending to only send Jane and Lydia *because they were the most deserving of such a treat*. William had assured her that Bingley would try to convince her mother to send all the girls.

To prevent Jane from having to hide anything from their parents, she made the choice not to disclose to her that they would have a chance to spend quality time together. So it would be quite the surprise when Jane entered the parlor and saw Elizabeth sitting there. Elizabeth had wanted to greet her in the hall with her aunt, but as a precaution, she stayed in the parlor. Mrs. Bennet was supposed to be staying back at Longbourn, but if she should arrive with Jane, Elizabeth would be told, and she could sneak out the back.

Happily, that was not the case, and Elizabeth soon heard the happy chatter of her sisters in the hall. The moment Elizabeth came into view, her sisters rushed towards her, engulfing her in a chaotic mix of hugs and tears, their emotions overwhelming any coherent words. Lydia was the first to speak and said , "Lizzie, what a fantastic surprise!"

Mary was next to speak, having waited to hug Elizabeth until her other sisters had received their fill. "I had hoped that we could contrive to see you while we were here, but I had not expected to see you so soon," Mary exclaimed while hugging her tightly.

Kitty merely hugged Elizabeth while saying she was glad to see her older sister, and Elizabeth smiled kindly at her shyest sister. Turning her attention to Jane, who seemed unable to speak through her tears, Elizabeth led her over to one of the settees and encouraged her to sit. Hugging her older sister to her, Elizabeth let her cry while she listened to her mumbled talk about how hard it had been to be separated from her.

Eventually Elizabeth leaned back and, taking Jane by the shoulders, she said, "Come now, you cannot spend our entire time together in tears. From tomorrow onwards, Aunt Madeline has planned appointments for you at a modiste and various other shops, where you can find all the essentials for your trousseau. I'm looking forward to cherishing our time together, but not if you cannot stop crying."

Hearing her words, Jane seemed to pull herself together and after wiping her face with a handkerchief. Finally, she smiled and said, "You are right Lizzie, I cannot carry on like this. It is a time of celebration and joy." Clutching Elizabeth's hands, she continued, "I promise that I have not been moping the entire time you have been away. I have been so happy planning my life with Charles. Really, the only sliver of upset has been that you have not been there to join in my joy."

"And I have missed being there for you, though I have been there for you in spirit," consoled Elizabeth. Looking at her other sisters, she said, "I am so happy you have all come to London. I was afraid Mrs. Bennet would not let you all come."

Mary smiled and explained, "Mother was going to keep Kitty and myself at home, but between Lydia and Mr. Bingley, she really had no choice."

With a giggle, Lydia exclaimed, "I made a scene, demanding Kitty and Mary's help in carrying my packages. Mr. Bingley, however, intervened and convinced Mama she would be more efficient in planning the wedding without our distracting presence. He has gotten very good at manipulating her. I think it is because of his experience with his sister, but Jane won't hear it."

Grabbing Elizabeth's hand in the way that only younger sisters do, Lydia said, "Forget being sad. I want to know where you got this gorgeous ring, Lizzie."

Blushing, Elizabeth allowed Lydia to study the ring that William had gifted her as an engagement present. It had been in the Darcy family for generations. It was passed on from one Darcy bride to the next, and Elizabeth felt honored to wear it. Clearing her throat, Elizabeth said, "That is part of my surprise." Looking around at her sisters' curious stares, she said, "I have not told you all everything that has been happening here in London like I promised. It was just too personal to put in a letter. I wanted to tell you in person. I am engaged."

Her sisters' faces displayed a range of shock, while Mary, with a knowing smile, said, "I had sensed a growing connection between you and Mr. Darcy before you left. When did you realize your feelings for one another?"

Feeling slightly embarrassed despite the kindness behind the question, Elizabeth couldn't help but blush as she answered, "Actually, it was not something we realized so long ago, only about three weeks."

After a flurry of hugs and congratulations, an excited Lydia asked, "So have you started planning the wedding? Do you think we will be able to come?"

Elizabeth's response came out as a hesitant yet enthusiastic "Yes, and yes," as she couldn't contain her nervous excitement to open up about everything with them after so much time. Taking a breath, she looked at them all and said, "William and I are getting married this coming Friday, two days after I reach my majority, and you are all invited to be there. We arranged things so that you could attend."

The strength of Lydia's hug almost bowled Elizabeth over. After hugging her back, Elizabeth turned to Jane to say, "I don't want you to think I am trying to overshadow you and Mr. Bingley. I know you are going to be getting married a little more than a week later, but it was the best way we could think that we could attend each other's weddings."

Lighting up, Jane said, "So you will attend my wedding?" Jane reached out to grip Elizabeth's arm before adding, "Charles said he thought you could come, but I still worried." With a sense of immense happiness, the two sisters locked in a warm and comforting hug, grateful for the opportunity to be there for one another, just as they had always yearned for.

Kitty looked around at the excited faces and asked, "Does this mean we have to shop for two weddings? When do we start?" The sisters all laughed until they cried.

DARCY KNEW HE WAS spending half the time with Bingley distracted, but he could not help it. As usual, his mind was on the woman he loved. He wondered what Elizabeth was doing with her sisters and Georgianna on her last night away from him. Tomorrow marked the beginning of a new chapter, one where they would no longer have to endure long periods apart. Not if he could help it.

Bingley seemed to be good natured about it though, not commenting on the many times Darcy would fade out of the conversation. Looking back at Bingley, Darcy valued his pleasant smile as he requested, "All I ask is that you don't comment if I become disinterested in your presence during my wedding."

With a nod and a smile, Darcy acknowledged his distraction. "I'm sorry for not being fully present."

Waving him off, Bingley took a sip of his brandy. It was unusual for Darcy to see him drinking something besides coffee, but they were celebrating his coming wedding, and brandy seemed more appropriate. Putting down his glass, Bingley asked, "What are you thinking about?"

Turning his own glass in circles on the desk next to him, Darcy contemplated the question, before saying, "Over the last several weeks, months even, I have grown to crave time with Elizabeth. After tomorrow, propriety will not keep us apart. I will savor all the precious moments we have together, making the most of the time we are given."

"I can well understand the frustration. Recently I have become exasperated by having to limit my visits to see Jane to visiting hours and always in the presence of others." Taking a sip of his drink, Bingley seemed lost in thought before finally uttering, "I long for the simple joy of unhindered conversation, where I can freely discuss my thoughts and concerns without fearing interruption by her mother."

Wincing, Darcy could not help but be grateful that his courting Elizabeth had not been done under the greedy eye of her mother. "I am sorry, my friend. I had not thought of how difficult it would be to court Miss Bennet while in the company of her mother."

"This situation has been quite challenging, mainly because of my knowledge of how she harmed Miss Elizabeth and the hurtful remarks she makes about Miss Elizabeth, Miss Mary, and occasionally Miss Kitty," sighed Bingley.

Darcy found it hard not to want to leave and confront Elizabeth's parents just knowing they were still being cruel, even without her presence. Then a thought occurred to him, and he asked, "Have they ever acknowledged where Elizabeth went? I know at first, they said she was helping her aunt in London, but they had to have given that up if they agreed to have her sisters stay with their aunt. The story would have fallen apart easily."

Bingley shrugged and replied, "At first, they said that Elizabeth had an understanding with that buffoon but was in London to help her Aunt Madeline. The town, however, did not receive their story well." Chuckling, he added, "Miss Lydia spread her own tale of her leaving to avoid the pressure her parents were putting on her to marry Mr. Collins because of his cruelty. The bookshop owner supported her story by saying that he had been horrible to her and abusive just before she disappeared. Lydia excitedly shared with everyone that Miss Elizabeth had accompanied a newfound and wealthy friend from her volunteering days in London. This friend had kindly extended an invitation for Miss Elizabeth to stay until she reached her majority, thus escaping her parents' manipulation."

Darcy could not help but smile. "At first, I did not like Miss Lydia much, but she has since won me over. She has proved very protective and much wiser than I first thought. What happened after that?"

"Mrs. Bennet lost some creditability with her friends when Miss Lucas revealed she had a letter from Miss Elizabeth confirming Lydia's tale. Then she told everyone that Miss Elizabeth had fled Longbourn, and her family wanted nothing to do with her anymore." Laughing, Bingley added, "It was not the best idea to say that because Miss Elizabeth was well respected in the community. These days, Mrs. Bennet is seldom included in social gatherings, and I believe it's for the best, even though I haven't expressed this sentiment to her to avoid upsetting Jane."

Rubbing at his forehead, Darcy said, "Miss Bennet seems to be upset when there is discord."

"Yes, but she has grown stronger," commented Bingley, his voice filled with admiration. "Of late, when Mrs. Bennet says something about one of her sisters, Jane has begun to tell her mother that it is not something she wants to hear and that she needs to stop, or she will leave with her sisters to spend time elsewhere."

"That is good." Making a snap judgment, Darcy said, "After you leave on your wedding trip, I am going to confront Mr. and Mrs. Bennet, and I think you may find a very different Longbourn when you return."

"Somehow, I am not surprised," responded Bingley. "If someone had treated Jane the way they did Miss Elizabeth, I do not know what I would do. You are already the most chivalrous man I know. The thought of witnessing a lady you love being mistreated by her own family, or anyone for that matter, is something you would never tolerate standing unanswered. Just let me know if there is anything you need my assistance with."

Nodding at his friend, Darcy lifted his glass to his lips and sipped at his brandy, thinking of how things might go when he confronted Elizabeth's parents. He was looking forward to the confrontation, but not nearly as much as he was looking forward to being married to Elizabeth. Smiling, he said, "I will let you know if I need any help, but that is for later. My focus right now is completely on tomorrow, when I will finally marry the love of my life."

To Elizabeth, it seemed that the week with her sisters had gone by in a flash. It had been enjoyable, but she was more than glad to shift her attention to the man she was about to marry. The next few minutes would mark a profound moment in their lives as she made a lifelong commitment to the man who held her heart.

Looking over, Elizabeth smiled up at her uncle, who stood beside her. At any moment, someone would give a signal, and she would walk into the chapel on her uncle's arm. It was not at all as she had pictured as a little girl, but she was happy to have him there for her. Her Uncle Gardiner had been fully supportive of her even against his sister- and brother-in-law's wishes. He was exactly who she wanted to walk her down the aisle.

Then, suddenly, they were walking down the aisle. Though she knew both of their families were there, she did not see any of them. She only had eyes for William. As if in a lovely trance, she said her vows and listened to his but knew she would never be able to remember all he said, only the power of the moment. A moment that was cemented by his lips, warm and supple on hers, binding them in them in the most primal of ways.

Elizabeth clasped William's arm, cherishing the feeling of their connection as they made their way down the aisle, surrounded by the joyful voices of their loved ones. They hugged people in the vestibule, and Elizabeth finally realized that there were more people there than she had realized. The gathering was a grand affair, with all of her sisters, aunt, uncle, and his family in attendance. The earl, countess, and both his cousins were there, along with his sister, Georgianna. In fact, the man who had married them was none other than his godfather, the archbishop. They all embraced them in hugs before agreeing to meet them back at Matlock House, where their wedding breakfast was to be held.

After what seemed like an eternity, she and William were in the carriage alone together—really alone for the first time since they had accidentally run into each other back on Oakham Mount. Soon they were kissing again, this time more passionately than ever before, and Elizabeth was quite happy that her aunt had told her that her passion for her new husband was not something to be ashamed of.

Out of breath, they broke apart and William panted, "Please tell me that we do not have to stay at the wedding breakfast long."

Chuckling, Elizabeth leaned her forehead against his shoulder and, after breathing in his scent that somehow seemed woodsy, it took a moment for Elizabeth to remember that she was supposed to be answering him. Clearing her throat, she said, "We will probably have to stay longer than either of us prefers, but once we leave, I promise we will be able to hide from them all back at Darcy House for at least a week."

Nodding, William reached out to push a pin back into Elizabeth's hair, where it seemed to have come loose. Then, leaning back against the cushions of the carriage, William breathed deeply before saying, "I will hold you to that promise, Mrs. Darcy."

Reaching out, he held her hand, running his thumb along her skin in a way that made it difficult for her to slow her heartbeat. It did not help that he had called her Mrs. Darcy; the way the title rolled off his tongue resonated deeply with her. A hidden part of her, unknown until now, seemed to have been yearning to hear it for a while.

They were not far from Matlock House and Elizabeth did not want to show up looking a mess and out of breath. It would be too embarrassing. So she distracted her new husband and herself by saying, "I love hearing you say Mrs. Darcy, but I wonder if that is what you will call me all the time, or are you going to come up with pet names for me?"

A smile spread across William's face as he glanced over at her, his voice filled with warmth. "Pet names?" he questioned. "I had not thought of any pet names. I am just happy that I can call you Elizabeth without shocking people now. Would you like a pet name?"

Elizabeth couldn't help but blush at the overwhelming love conveyed in his words. With a newfound confidence, she whispered,

"I would not have thought so, but the title of Mrs. Darcy caught me off guard, but in the best possible way. I am not entirely certain what I would have you call me. Regardless of the name, as long as it's spoken with love, I have a feeling that it will have the same impact on me."

"What impact would that be?" asked William, a smug sort of glee now settling into his eyes.

Elizabeth resisted the urge to pout in response to that smugness, opting instead for honesty. "Hearing you say Mrs. Darcy sent a tendril of delight coursing through me. I am thrilled to have you acknowledge me as the woman who holds your heart, the one who brings warmth and love to your home. Being Mrs. Darcy is a role that encompasses not only being your wife but also being the woman you trust to oversee the well-being of your staff and tenants. I am grateful for the pride you show in me by giving me your name."

As Elizabeth observed her new husband, she couldn't help but feel a sense of satisfaction as she saw his mouth slightly part and the smug expression on his face fade away. She waited for him to say something, but for a while he did not. He only stared at her.

William opened his mouth and then closed it before finally saying, "I am the one honored by your agreeing to marry me. I do not know what I could have done to be gifted with your attention and love." Leaning in, he kissed Elizabeth, his lips brushing against the soft skin of her cheek.

Gasping at the sensation he was creating, Elizabeth said, "William, I cannot understand how you could doubt your ability to garner my love. You saw me in distress, and you befriended me. You saw me in pain, and you came to my aid. If our lives had unfolded centuries ago, people would have hailed you as a gallant knight, William. You would be my knight."

Sadly, when William attempted to capture her lips in response to her words, Elizabeth said, "William, my love, the carriage has stopped. We need to get out and attend our wedding breakfast."

William let out a groan of frustration as he rested his head on her shoulder. He took a deep breath, then exhaled slowly before saying, "We'll be leaving as soon as we can get away with it, Mrs. Darcy."

Chapter Twenty-Nine

It was fascinating to Georgianna to watch her brother with Elizabeth. Georgianna hadn't laid eyes on them in a week, as they had confined themselves to Darcy House after their wedding. It wasn't until they arrived to collect her and Mrs. Annesley for their trip to Netherfield that she finally saw them again.

Somehow, the newlyweds found a way to always stay in contact with one another. Oh, it was nothing indecent; rather, it was cute. From start to finish, they never let go of each other, constantly holding hands or leaning into one another, or even doing both simultaneously.

When they stopped to water the horses, her brother had even kept his hand on the small of Elizabeth's back as they walked into the back room and were served tea. Their constant care for each other's needs made her smile, appreciating the depth of their bond. Still, she felt a need for conversation as they sipped their tea, so she said, "It will be good to see your sisters again, Elizabeth. What time is Jane's wedding going to be tomorrow?"

Seeming to draw her gaze away from William's eyes with difficulty, Elizabeth looked at Georgianna and said, "The wedding will be held at ten tomorrow with the wedding breakfast held at Longbourn shortly thereafter." Looking back at William, who rubbed her back and nodded in an encouraging fashion, she continued, "But we will not be going to the wedding breakfast at Longbourn."

Georgianna could understand why she would not want to return to her home after what she had endured at the hands of her parents. It was probably a good thing that they would not be attending the wedding breakfast because she would certainly be tempted to say something to Elizabeth's parents, and if she didn't, then her brother would, and a wedding breakfast would not be the time or place to do so. She liked Jane too much to want her wedding breakfast to be ruined in such a way.

It galled her that Elizabeth's parents were getting away with being so horrible to her closest of friends. Possibly seeing her expression, William spoke up. "Once Bingley and his new wife leave on their wedding trip, Elizabeth and I will be going over to Longbourn to confront her parents together. Actually, we may be here a few days after the wedding while we handle matters, but Bingley has said that we may stay at Longbourn as long as we need."

Nodding, Georgianna was glad that Mrs. Annesley was able to change the conversation to something lighter, because her mind was focused on what her brother meant by handling matters. Curiosity consumed her as she wondered what plans William had in store for Mr. and Mrs. Bennet, but she knew she would have to wait patiently for a few days to find out. Before she knew it, her tea was gone, and Georgianna found herself back in the carriage, on her way to Netherfield, and she was one step closer to seeing how her brother would handle things.

Sitting with Bingley the night before his friend's wedding, Darcy couldn't help but feel a touch of irony about the situation. Just a week or so previously, their situations had been reversed, but he was still the distracted one of the two of them. Luckily, Bingley did not seem to be upset by his continued distraction.

The last week was spent primarily in Elizabeth's company and even spending a few hours with his friend made him miss her presence at his side. It did not help matters that Elizabeth was becoming more and anxious about the upcoming confrontation. He just hoped that he could make it through the ceremony in the morning without punching his father-in-law.

"You know," Bingley drawled, "he had asked for money."

Focusing back on his friend, Darcy asked, "Who asked you for money?"

Shaking his head, Bingley took a sip of his coffee with a grin. "You might just be worse than before you got married." Chuckling, he pushed a lock of hair off his forehead before answering, "Mr. Bennet asked me for a thousand pounds yesterday."

Leaning forward in his chair, Darcy stared at his friend in shock before saying, "I did not expect that of him. Though I know that the man he borrowed from was going to come to Meryton so he could confront Mr. Bennet soon after the wedding. Maybe Mr. Bennet heard he was here and realized that he was running out of time. What did you tell him?"

Running his hand through his reddish locks, Bingley said, "I asked him what the money was for, and he became uncooperative. He ended up complaining that he was giving me his daughter to marry, and I should be grateful he was not standing in my way. I pointed out that most daughters of Jane's station would have a dowry of at least five thousand pounds and yet I had not asked him for anything, and he had already signed the marriage settlements. He demanded I leave his study after that."

"He must be more desperate than I thought," Darcy exclaimed, his eyes widening. "Do you think he will make a scene during the wedding?"

Bingley frowned down into his coffee cup, before looking back up and saying, "No, and even if he does, Jane is of age, and he has signed the settlement papers. There is nothing he can do to stop it. If he tries, he will just make the town dislike him even more. If I have to, I will lay his issues bare to the whole town."

"And I will support you, whatever happens. Though, I would hate for the man to detract from your wedding for his daughter's sake." Darcy sighed. There was just so much about Mr. Bennet that annoyed him. It would have been nice to have a father-in-law that he could respect, but he would have chosen no one besides Elizabeth.

As he leaned back in his chair, he couldn't help but glance at the shadowed ceiling, pondering how Elizabeth's remarkable qualities flourished despite Mr. Bennet's dissipated nature. Was she so amazing because of or in spite of how she was raised? Whatever it was, he was glad that he had Elizabeth as his helpmate.

Wanting to focus back on his friend, Darcy asked, "So, are you ready to be forever bound to Miss Bennet?"

Grinning, Bingley exclaimed, "I was ready weeks ago but as you know, Jane wanted to wait until Elizabeth could come."

"Well, your wait is almost over, my friend. Come morning, you will marry the woman you love and then flit off to spend weeks alone with her, enjoying each other's company." Pausing, Darcy's smile turned wry before he said, "Though I warn you now, the wedding breakfast will seem interminable. I know mine was, and I did not have Mrs. Bennet's bragging and effusions of delight."

"I doubt I will pay Mrs. Bennet any mind. My attention will be solely on the loveliness that is my Jane." Bingley took a swig of his coffee and, putting his cup down, said, "By the way, thank you for letting us stay at Darcy House before we continue on to Bath."

"Do not worry about it. My staff knows to treat you well, not that they would do anything else. Besides, you are letting us stay here at Netherfield while I manage everything."

"I know you want to go find your wife, but before you leave, I want you to know how grateful I am that you will stand up with me tomorrow." Bingley expressed his gratitude with a genuine appreciation that touched Darcy's heart.

Standing, he moved to clap his friend on the shoulder, and said, "I am glad that I will be there as well. I am relieved that we could find a solution that accommodates both the women in our lives, not to mention being there for you."

"Go find your wife," Bingley instructed, "and I'll catch up with you in the morning, my friend."

Nodding, Darcy left the room and went in search of Elizabeth. Although it wasn't particularly late, he had a feeling she would be curled up with a book in the sitting room they shared. He didn't rush to find her, but the urgency in his steps as he ascended the stairs hinted at his deep longing for his wife's company.

He found Elizabeth as he thought he would, curled up in a chair by a crackling fire, a book in her hands that she was completely engrossed in. As she read, a single wayward curl danced against her cheek, adding a touch of drowsy beauty to her appearance. His fingers ached to play with the curl, but he hesitated to approach her.

He watched her for a moment in silence, memorizing her beauty in that moment, wanting to remember it always.

Darcy must have made a sound or alerted her somehow because Elizabeth looked up, her attention diverted from her book as she slipped a finger into the pages to hold her place. Her smile was instant as she saw him at the door and she asked, "Did you enjoy your time with Mr. Bingley?"

With her awareness of his presence shattering the moment, Darcy felt compelled to close the distance between them. He moved towards her, his hand reaching out to capture the loose curl at Elizabeth's cheek, relishing the way it wrapped itself around his finger. After only a short time enraptured by the curl, Darcy said, "Yes, I enjoyed talking with my friend, but I missed being with you."

Elizabeth picked up the ribbon that she used to mark her page and, placing it in her book, she said, "And I have missed you. What are you going to do about it?"

ELIZABETH COULDN'T SHAKE THE feeling that it was wrong for her to be sitting on Mr. Bingley's side of the church, but she refused to move closer to her parents. Jane understood and had smiled brightly when she saw her sitting on the front row next to Georgianna. As Elizabeth observed the joy radiating from her sister's face, she pushed aside the strain she felt from being in such close proximity to Mr. and Mrs. Bennet.

Something must have let Georgianna know she was struggling because she reached out and took Elizabeth's hand in both of hers, offering strength in such a difficult time. Elizabeth would have liked to turn to William for support, but he was standing next to Mr. Bingley at the altar. It was odd seeing Mary standing next to Jane, but she did not begrudge her the honor. Mary had worked hard and grown closer to Jane in Elizabeth's absence. Besides, it would have been a nightmare if Mrs. Bennet had discovered Jane was in contact with Elizabeth and wanted her to stand up with her.

The ceremony itself was over in a flash, and then Jane was at Elizabeth's side, hugging her tight. Eventually she managed a teary, "Thank you for coming, Lizzie. I know how hard it must be for you to be here."

Hugging her back, Elizabeth said, "I was not about to let Mr. and Mrs. Bennet stop me from being here for you if I could help it."

"I have to leave for the wedding breakfast soon and we are leaving for our wedding trip from there, but hopefully we can see you when we get back somehow." Jane blinked tears out of her eyes as she looked at Elizabeth. "Charles says that you will confront our parents after we leave. Promise me you will be all right."

Kissing Jane's cheek, Elizabeth wiped away a tear before she said, "William will be with me, so I will be fine. Do not worry about me. I want you to enjoy her time with Mr. Bingley."

Laughing, Jane said, "You know he said that you can call him Charles."

With a shrug, Elizabeth replied, "I will eventually, but it does not feel natural. Even William calls him Bingley."

Having finished talking with William, Mr. Bingley came over to collect Jane so they could face the other well-wishers together and Elizabeth said, "Take good care of my sister, Mr. Bingley. Make sure that you enjoy yourselves and not worry about anything while you are away."

With a brief hug and a nod to Elizabeth, they moved off into the crowd. Elizabeth felt relieved knowing that William was right by her side as they walked away. She looked up at him and, in an attempt to stay positive, she said, "It was a beautiful ceremony."

If they weren't in public, William would have wrapped his arms around her in a warm hug. Instead, he held her hand, squeezing it and offering silent support. Of all people, he knew how much she struggled. Grateful for his ever-present support, she smiled up at him. They had already decided to wait until everyone left before they made their exit.

Neither of them wanted Mr. or Mrs. Bennet to make a scene if they spotted her. So far, it had not been a problem, as Mrs. Bennet was completely oblivious to her presence thanks to the excellent selection of her large bonnet. Now Mrs. Bennet was rushing outside to crow about how marvelous it was to have her eldest daughter married to such a wealthy man. Elizabeth shook her head as she could hear the woman from all the way in the chapel.

Unexpectedly, Elizabeth was approached by Charlotte, who embraced her warmly. "I had hoped you would come."

Blinking her eyes rapidly to stop her tears, Elizabeth hugged her good friend back. Then, leaning back, Elizabeth said, "I am glad to be here, and I am glad to be able to see you. William and I are going to be staying at Netherfield for a short time."

"William, is it?" Looking between her friend and the man standing next to her, Charlotte said, "I had wondered about the two of you. May I assume this is a recent development? You only just reach your majority."

Nodding, Elizabeth said, "Yes, we married two days after my birthday."

Looking back over her shoulder at the dispensing crowd, Charlotte said, "I will have to call on you before you leave. I want to know how you have been doing since you were forced to flee your home."

Nodding, Elizabeth replied, "I would love to spend time with you as well, but tomorrow we will be busy at Longbourn."

A knowing look crossed Charlotte's face as she exclaimed, "Bearding the lion in its lair, I see! I wish you every success."

After she left, William looked down at Elizabeth and asked, "Is the lion Mr. or Mrs. Bennet?"

Seeing the humor in his comment, Elizabeth managed a weak laugh. Shaking her head, she said, "I hear that a male lion is a rather lazy creature when compared to his female counterpart. He allows her to hunt for food while he defends the territory. It may be that they are both the lion in their own ways."

Offering her his arm, William said, "It is a good thing you say I am a knight if we are going to confront a pair of lions tomorrow."

"A good knight would never allow a pair of lions free to harm those he is determined to protect," replied Elizabeth. She had become quite fond of their little game. His chivalrous nature had not gone unnoticed by her, and she felt the urge to give him a genuine compliment, carefully concealing it to avoid embarrassing him too much. Looking around, she realized no one was paying them any attention, so she reached up on her tiptoes and kissed his cheek.

Gazing down at Elizabeth, William's eyes seemed to smolder as he said, "How can a knight not protect his fair lady when she has given him such a token of her esteem?"

They hurried out of the chapel after that and made their way back to Netherfield. In such a religious location, she thought it was best not to linger on the thoughts that had been provoked by the power of William's gaze.

Chapter Thirty

Darcy had never been one for confrontation. He preferred to manage things by talking them out with people and convincing them of a better action. The idea of using force to control others, like his father did, never appealed to him. Despite that, Darcy felt like he would have to restrain himself in the coming confrontation.

Mr. Porter, the man Mr. Bennet owed money to, graciously permitted Darcy to accompany Sir William to Longbourn with him. Both gentlemen knew that Darcy had a strong interest in the well-being of the Bennet family. He only hoped that he could maintain a cool head if Mr. Bennet behaved badly or insulted Elizabeth.

Looking over at Elizabeth, who sat next to him in the carriage, he was reassured to see her smile as they made their way up the Longbourn drive. Elizabeth had insisted on coming with him and confronting her mother after he dealt with her father. She would stay with the carriage and wait until her father was taken away. Darcy did not want her to have to be around the man if he could help it.

Taking a deep breath, he hopped down from the carriage but gazed back at Elizabeth. Still smiling, she said, "Take down the lion and ye shall get another token of my affection."

Darcy appreciated that she was attempting to inject some humor into such a tense situation. Dipping into an excessive bow, Darcy answered, "It shall be as my lady wishes."

Turning around, Darcy positioned himself alongside the other gentlemen, and together they were led into the house by Mrs. Hill. Darcy exchanged a smile with the helpful lady who had been his informant, silently indicating the direction of Mr. Bennet's study. It was time to face the inevitable confrontation.

Mr. Porter did not knock when he reached Mr. Bennet's study. He simply opened the door and marched in. With a scowl, Mr. Bennet looked up from his pages and glared at them all. He couldn't help but complain, "Not only did you disregard my housekeeper, but you also didn't have the courtesy to knock." Having said his fill, Mr. Bennet ignored them and turned back to the book he was studying.

Speaking up first, Sir William said, "Bennet, I believe you should listen to what these men have to say. If you do not, it will only get worse for you." This only earned Sir William a huff and a roll of his eyes.

Next, Mr. Porter stepped forward and his hard voice broke the silence. "You may not recognize me, but my name is Mr. Porter. Two years ago, you borrowed a large sum of money from me in order to make a purchase. It has now been four months since you have made a payment. Per our agreement, I have come to demand the payment of the reminder of the loan in full, along with the accumulated interest and additional fees for nonpayment."

Looking up from the book on his desk, Mr. Bennet began to look uneasy. After closing his book, he directed his attention towards them, puffing up his chest in a manner reminiscent of a rooster's attempt to intimidate its rivals. His voice dripping with condescension, Mr. Bennet said, "Mr. Porter, if you will recall, I did inform you that I would recommence payments once the situation at Longbourn normalized. I am currently looking for a new steward as my last one left recently, but I am sure that once I find a new steward, things will improve, and I should be able to resume some form of payment after harvest."

Mr. Porter flicked at a remnant of lint on his coat, seemingly unfazed by Mr. Bennet's attitude, before explaining, "You may request something, Mr. Bennet, that is your right, but I do not have to grant that request. I told you when we struck our bargain that I would come to collect the entire amount if you missed payment for more than three months in a row."

"But I am a landowner," Mr. Bennet declared proudly. "Surely you can trust me to keep my word, and I have told you that I will pay you when my funds become available." His voice had turned to a whine as he tried to reason with Mr. Porter.

Shaking his head, Mr. Porter said, "I have known too many landowners, Mr. Bennet, to ever trust one again. You are just another man who has extended himself too far and I want my money. Pay now or face the consequences."

Fluttering his hands about the desk, Mr. Bennet came to rest on the book he had been reading when they had entered the room. With a sigh, he said, "I do not have the money you want. My coffers are bare, and I will most likely need to sell something just to keep us afloat until after the harvest. But I can offer you the books I used your money to buy."

"What use do I have with a bunch of old books? I am a man of business, not barter. Either give me the twelve hundred pounds that you owe me, or I will have you taken to debtor's prison." Mr. Porter watched the color leech out of Mr. Bennet for a moment before adding, "I am not all bad, though. I will give you the choice of Coldbath Fields Prison, King's Bench Prison, and Marshalsea Prison. Which do you prefer?"

Darcy watched as the man who had hurt his Elizabeth struggled, his mouth opening and closing in a futile attempt to speak. Despite the scene, Darcy found himself incapable of mustering any sympathy. If Mr. Bennet had possessed some sympathy for his daughter all those months ago, things might have been different, but they weren't.

Mr. Porter snapped and the hulking men that Mr. Porter had brought with him entered the confined space, making it feel much smaller with all their bulk. When Mr. Bennet still did not manage to say anything, Mr. Porter's expression turned hard. "Do not make this more difficult on yourself than it must be. I can either have these men drag you out of your home like a criminal or if you cooperate, I will allow you to have a bag packed so that you have a few necessities to take with you."

Mr. Bennet turned to his old friend with a look of panic on his face. "William, you are the magistrate for Meryton. You cannot allow him to treat me this way."

Shaking his head, Sir William said, "I am here because I am the magistrate, and he has every right to take you away for nonpayment. He has all the paperwork in order to forcefully remove you if you refuse to cooperate with him." Drawing closer, he placed his hand on Mr. Bennet's shoulder and said, "I would do what they ask, my friend."

It seemed as if Mr. Bennet deflated at his friend's words. His assurance that nothing could touch him bled from him, along with the color in his face. It did not take long for the butler to be asked to pack a small back with a change of clothes and some toiletries. All the while, there was a tense standoff in the study as Mr. Bennet gathered books to his chest.

It was when he was handed the small bag of his things, and he was trying to stow away as many of his precious tomes as he could, that Mr. Bennet realized just who Mr. Darcy was. He stood completely still, his gaze fixed on Darcy, as if he held the key to his only chance at salvation. As a meaty hand with scarred knuckles clamped down on his shoulder, Mr. Bennet said, "Mr. Darcy, you would have the money to pay off my debt." With a desperate tone, he tried to draw closer and pleaded, "Please, you know my family. You know I am a gentleman. Pay this man and we can come up with some sort of agreement."

As Mr. Bennet tried to draw closer to Darcy, he was held back by Mr. Porter's man. Which was probably a good thing because Darcy knew that his answer would not be well received. Looking at the desperate man before him begging for help with disdain, he said, "You say you are a gentleman, but I see no evidence of it. A gentleman cares about the state of his tenants and servants. He wholeheartedly involves himself in his family's affairs, going above and beyond to shield them from harm and prioritize their needs. I know for a fact that you are indolent and imperious, not to mention cruel. You derive humor from situations by sacrificing others, unconcerned about the harm caused as you laugh. No, sir, you are not a gentleman, and I will not help you."

Furious at his words, Mr. Bennet tried to take a step forward but was prevented from doing so. "Then why are you here?" he demanded.

"I have a vested interest in protecting your family, or rather, your daughters. I know you cannot be trusted to act as a parent should and I promised Bingley his new sisters would be taken care of while he was away."

"You should be grateful, Mr. Bennet," explained Mr. Porter as he directed his men to take Mr. Bennet out of the house. "Mr. Darcy was the one who gave you an extra month. He did not want your being dragged off to debtor's prison to ruin his friend's wedding."

Mr. Porter's words seemed to be some sort of tipping point for Mr. Bennet because he struggled in earnest. Because of his indolence, he lacked the physical strength required to escape or pose any threat to his guards. Mr. Bennet's futile struggles were almost amusing to witness, and if Darcy had possessed even a fraction of his father-in-law's humor, he would have found it hilarious.

OPTING FOR A RESPITE from the carriage, Elizabeth sought refuge on a bench in the shade, biding her time until William emerged with her father. Standing at attention nearby were Gregson and Reed, her two large footmen. They would stay with her until William returned and even then, they would be nearby in case there was a need.

Over the months away from Longbourn, she had come to know both men, and their presence brought her comfort as she waited. Between William and her two footmen, she felt safe, regardless of what happened with Mr. and Mrs. Bennet. So when Mr. Bennet was pulled out of Longbourn kicking and screaming, it did not surprise Elizabeth that Gregson took a step closer to her while Reed moved between her and Mr. Bennet.

The movement caught Mr. Bennet's attention, causing his already roused anger to focus on her. He shouted, "What are you doing here? It has been over six months. By now, you should have found some way to support yourself." Casting his gaze around, he couldn't help but notice the seething anger in Mr. Darcy's expression, prompting him to mock, "Did you bring your mistress when you came to my home, Mr. Darcy? And you said *I* wasn't a gentleman."

Elizabeth was certain that the only thing holding William back from taking action before her was the distance between him and Mr. Bennet. Fueled by her long-standing anger, she launched a rapid attack on Mr. Bennet, catching everyone off guard as she delivered a resounding slap across his face. He attempted to retaliate but was held fast by the guards at his sides.

"Never again," she warned Mr. Bennet, her eyes blazing with anger, "will you dare to malign my husband! While you may have felt inclined to condemn me, William is the most remarkable man I have ever known, and I won't tolerate any insinuations against his character."

Fury burned in his eyes as he shouted, "Husband? You cannot marry him. I forbid it! I told you, you are meant for my cousin, the buffoon."

Coming to stand beside her, his hand on the small of her back, William said, "Once Elizabeth was of age, she could marry anyone she chose. You are the buffoon if you ever thought to bind any of your daughters to that man, let alone someone as brilliant as Elizabeth."

Turning to Mr. Porter, he said, "No one wants to hear what he is liable to spew. Might he be gagged as well as bound for his journey?"

Offering his arm, William smiled down at Elizabeth and they both ignored the man who she once thought of as her father. They walked toward Longbourn as he was bound and gagged, then shackled and thrown into the back of a cart. Elizabeth nodded to both Mr. Porter and Sir William as she walked. She paid no attention to Mr. Bennet's muffled complaints as she walked away, leaving him behind. Mrs. Bennet was her next opponent, and it was time to confront her.

Elizabeth's grip on William's hand tightened as she crossed the threshold of her childhood home, overwhelmed by a mix of emotions and the familiarity of the surroundings. Breathing through her rising anxiety, Elizabeth attempted to focus on what she knew was going well. Mary, Kitty, and Lydia had gone to visit Charlotte and Maria Lucas, so they were not present for Mr. Bennet's downfall. Nor would they be present for her coming confrontation with Mrs. Bennet.

They had made their way into the main portion of the house when Mrs. Hill came around the corner and, seeing Elizabeth, she burst into tears. Hurrying to the woman who had done so much for her in the course of her life, Elizabeth embraced her as she cried, "Oh, Miss Elizabeth, I am so sorry. I wish that I could have done something to protect you from your parents all that time ago. I worried endlessly until I discovered that Mr. Darcy and his sister had been keeping you safe."

Leaning back, Elizabeth said, "No, I am sorry. I thought about telling you that I was leaving, but I did not want to make you lie to Mr. and Mrs. Bennet."

Wiping her face with the corner of her apron, Mrs. Hill said, "Oh pish. I would lie for you in a heartbeat. Those people are not worth the respect their position deserves." Pausing, she tilted her head and said, "Now stand back and let me take a look at you."

Nodding, Mrs. Hill smiled, and Elizabeth asked, "Do I meet with your approval?"

She smiled first at Elizabeth, her eyes sparkling with warmth, and then turned her attention to William, a playful grin on her face. "It seems that being married to Mr. Darcy has certainly done you a bit of good," she remarked teasingly.

With a slight blush coloring her cheeks, Elizabeth met William's eyes and spoke with unwavering conviction, "I don't mean to diminish Mr. Hill, but I honestly believe that my William is the embodiment of goodness and chivalry and the absolute best husband any girl could hope for."

"Feeling such admiration and love for one's husband is a rare gift, Miss Elizabeth. You are indeed a lucky woman," imparted Mrs. Hill. Then, becoming serious, she said, "I suppose you are here to deal with Mrs. Bennet."

Elizabeth nodded, asking, "Do you know where she might be?"

Mrs. Hill grumbled disapprovingly, "She is lazing about in her sitting room. She quite overdid it yesterday with all her effusions of joy."

Elizabeth could quite imagine how Mrs. Bennet had behaved, exclaiming her good fortune to have Jane married so well. Not that the woman cared about the fact that Mr. Bingley was a good man who loved her daughter. No, she only noted his wealth and her daughter's pin money. Elizabeth sighed and met William's gaze, realizing they couldn't delay any longer.

Before they left in search of Mrs. Bennet, William explained, "Mr. Bennet is gone and should not be back anytime soon, if ever. I have already petitioned the courts about common recovery and to give me control over Longbourn due to the circumstances. Regardless, if you need help or would even just like to relocate, please feel free to reach out to me."

Mrs. Hill nodded in agreement. "I will do that. You just take care of my girl there," she replied, her words filled with trust.

Gazing down at Elizabeth, he replied, "I could do nothing else."

Chapter Thirty-One

Dangling her foot over the edge of her chaise lounge, Mrs. Bennet couldn't help but feel a deep sense of satisfaction with the way Jane's wedding had unfolded. She had just loved the look on Lady Lucas's face when she had crowed about having the first daughter to be married. Jane had chastised her for it, but it was worth it. She dug around in her bag of chocolates, enjoying the anticipation of the next treat as she felt the smooth surface of each piece before savoring the way the sweet flavor melted on her tongue.

With Jane married to a well-to-do man, she would be able to put her other daughters in front of wealthier men than they would normally have access to in Meryton. Once they returned from their wedding trip, she would visit Netherfield and make sure Jane was doing everything she could to bear her husband an heir, as well as running the estate properly. Jane was sure to want her to become a semipermanent fixture in her home, and it would become Fanny's route to get back in the good graces of the townspeople.

Things had started to run downhill ever since that ungrateful second daughter of hers had left. Fanny's plan had been foolproof, yet Elizabeth had chosen to defy her. Then her friends somehow uncovered the truth about Elizabeth's disappearance, and from that point on, everything began to crumble. Invitations to gatherings had slowed to a trickle, and whispers and gossip surrounded her when she went into town.

Jane's wedding was the key to regaining her status and reputation. Her daughter's beauty had not been in vain, as it had attracted the attention of a wealthy man who had chosen her to be the mistress of the largest estate in the area. Everyone would once again have to invite her or else they would insult Jane. Once things settled back down to as they should be, she would spread the rumor that Elizabeth had become a maid or something else demeaning and the townspeople would recognize that Elizabeth got only what she deserved.

Fanny indulged in another chocolate, licking a smudge of chocolate off her thumb. Her smile faded into a frown as she recalled the one sour note on an otherwise delightful wedding breakfast. The new Mrs. Darcy had been on everyone's lips. She had only glimpsed the woman in the chapel. The brim of the woman's bonnet was too deep to allow her to see her face.

The most annoying thing was that was that none of the Darcy party bothered to attend her wedding breakfast. She had thought that Mr. Darcy was Mr. Bingley's closest friend. The man had stood up with her new son-in-law but had not come to the wedding breakfast. It just made little sense to her. It must have been the new wife's fault.

With a heavy sigh, Fanny leaned back against the pillow behind her and directed her gaze towards the ceiling. Its dull, off-white color did nothing to lift her spirits. Surely the austere couple would not be in the area long and she would not have to deal with them. While stuffing another chocolate in her mouth, she realized things had been mostly perfect and were sure to get better.

Hearing the door open, she turned her head to yell at whoever had come in; she had told them she was not to be disturbed. Her mouth dropped open in shock when she saw the people in the doorway, and a trickle of melting chocolate escaped from the corner of her mouth. She clenched her jaw shut, swallowing hard and fighting the urge to choke.

ELIZABETH'S GAZE LINGERED ON the woman who had played a significant role in her life. She couldn't help but notice the chocolate dribbling down her chin and staining her dressing gown. She had been celebrating yesterday's success by eating an entire bag of chocolates.

When Elizabeth saw the woman who was her mother, she felt a wave of nervousness wash over her, causing her to stumble over her words as she greeted her with a hesitant, "Hello, Mrs. Bennet. It's been quite some time."

After choking for a moment, Mrs. Bennet jumped up from her languid position, shouting, "How dare you show yourself here, you ungrateful child! You disappear for months without a word and all because you did not want to obey your parents as you should!" Taking a step forward, she continued, "I should box your ears for such ill behavior. As it is, do not think you will get out of being locked in the nursery until it is time for you to marry Mr. Collins. We will send for him today and I will pay for the common license myself if it means I can see you married to him tomorrow."

Elizabeth could feel the muscles in William's arm tense at her mother's verbal attack. Patting William's hand soothingly, she calmly responded, "I do not think so, Mrs. Bennet."

Halting, Mrs. Bennet looked at her askance, as if uncertain of her daughter's bold reply, and Elizabeth wondered if Mrs. Bennet had become used to being able to bully people around in her absence. Straightening her shoulders, Elizabeth stood strong and asked, "Have you forgotten that I am now of age?"

Parroting her words, Mrs. Bennet said, "Of age?"

"I know you hardly ever remembered my birthday, Mrs. Bennet, but still you should know that now that I have come of age, I do not have to do anything you say."

Elizabeth smiled up at William as she finished her statement, feeling a sense of empowerment as she declared, "I am my own woman, or I was until I became Mrs. Darcy."

With a tender gaze, William looked down at Elizabeth and said, "You are still as much your own woman as you ever were. Being married could not change that. It is more that we belong to each other in all the best ways."

This only served to fuel Mrs. Bennet's rage. As she came forward, her voice rang out with fury, "You are the new Mrs. Darcy? How dare you! You do not deserve such a marvelous match!"

Moving to block Mrs. Bennet's approach, William stood firm, his voice hard. "Elizabeth deserves much more than you were ever willing to give her. If you ever think to harm her again, be aware that I will not hesitate to press charges against you."

Looking at William for the first time, she scoffed, "You would never want it known that you had your mother-in-law charged with something. It would not look good to all your wealthy friends."

Shrugging, William responded, "What makes you think that? I just watched your husband being forcefully taken away, and now he is being transported to debtor's prison. If I was not about to stop that, why would I hesitate to have you charged? Besides, it would help them know that I do not tolerate attacks against the people I love."

Taking a step back, Mrs. Bennet's face took on an ashen pallor. Feeling behind her, she reached blindly for the chaise so that she could sit down. After a period of silence, Mrs. Bennet asked, "But who is to manage Longbourn? We do not even have a steward."

Elizabeth's voice betrayed no weakness when she answered, "While I would have been able to manage Longbourn even without a steward, I know that is something that you could never do. And before you think to pressure any of my sisters to take up the mantle, know I will not allow it. My husband has kindly arranged for an under steward in his employ to come to Longbourn to take over, but it will come at a price."

Shoulders drooping, Mrs. Bennet said, "Of course there is a price. You were always a spiteful girl."

Ignoring Mrs. Bennet's biting words, Elizabeth continued, "Things will change at Longbourn. There will no longer be any overspending, you will be given a strict budget for the running of the household, and it will not include the funds to host all the lavish gatherings that you enjoy. If you want to throw a party, you must use your pin money, which will be two hundred pounds a year—exactly what it should be according to your marriage settlement."

This elicited a muffled shriek as Mrs. Bennet's hands instinctively covered her mouth. However, Elizabeth pressed on, determined to make her point. "I know you would never think to care for my sisters properly, so they will no longer be your concern. My husband's aunt, the countess, has invited them all to stay with her for the next several months at the Matlock estate."

Sitting up straighter, Mrs. Bennet actually smiled and said, "If the countess would like to spend time with my daughters, surely she would want me to—"

Elizabeth cut her off right there. "No. You are not invited, and you will not be able to connive an invitation. Should you attempt to make your way there, you will be turned away." Taking a deep breath, she said what she had specifically come to say. "You are a selfish woman who only sought to use her children to better her own life. I know that you often complained that Mr. Bennet did not treat you better, but I think you deserved each other. Neither of you are capable of caring for anyone but yourselves and what you want. Your actions were not just wrong, but cruel, when you disparaged me during my formative years and then tried to coerce me into marrying Mr. Collins. From this day forward, I will have nothing to do with you."

As Elizabeth stared at the woman she had once considered her mother, a newfound sense of liberation washed over her, knowing that she was no longer under her control and had finally had her say. While she may provoke pity from another individual, Elizabeth would never extend that kind of sentiment towards her.

Taking out a handkerchief, Mrs. Bennet dabbed at her eyes, sniffing in a familiar effort to gain pity. Elizabeth and William turned to leave, only to have Mrs. Bennet shout, "But what about Mr. Bennet? Those debtor's prisons are rife with illness and violence. Surely, he will die soon. Mr. Collins will throw me into the hedgerows the first chance he gets. He was not at all happy you backed out of your engagement. What will become of me then?"

Turning back over his shoulder, William remarked, "Mr. Collins has been sent to India for crimes against the church and the people in his parish. I am petitioning the court to enact common recovery. Longbourn will go to our second son or oldest daughter. And you, Mrs. Bennet, will not be going to the hedgerows. I will allow you to use the cottage on the property as your home when your husband dies. With your two hundred pounds a year, I am sure you can afford a few servants and whatever else you may need."

As a unit, Elizabeth and her husband left her mother's room. They had only moved a few steps away from the door when the sound of shrieking and breaking glass reached their ears. Sighing, Elizabeth shook her head and looked up at William. "It seems Mrs. Bennet will learn the hard way that I told the staff not to cater to her whims or her tantrums. They are not nursemaids, and she will have to learn to behave like a grown woman." Then chuckling, she added, "At least this way she will not have to pack much when she ends up moving into that cottage."

Chapter Thirty-Two

Climbing into his carriage, Darcy let out a weary sigh, feeling the weight of the day on his shoulders. But when he caught sight of Elizabeth, his exhaustion melted away and he couldn't help but break into a broad smile. The last few days had been trying, but he had Elizabeth at his side, and they were finally leaving for their wedding trip. Sitting next to her, he took her hand in his before knocking at the roof of the carriage and they pulled away from Netherfield.

Their week alone at Darcy House had been lovely, but he had been wanting to show Elizabeth the Peak District and eventually Pemberley. The last few days with her sisters, Mary, Kitty, and Lydia, along with his sister, had been filled with constant chatter and giggles, leaving little time for him to be alone with his new wife. Then too, he had been acquainting his steward with Longbourn and its remaining tenants. Mrs. Bennet had been difficult, but not anything he could not handle. He couldn't help but feel disappointed that his time with Elizabeth had been cut short.

But now they were free from everything that was holding them back. Running his thumb back and forth along Elizabeth's palm, Darcy asked, "Are you excited about beginning our adventure?"

Humming under her breath, Elizabeth replied, "Yes, I cannot wait to see all the marvelous sights you have told me about. We will see things during the day and in the evening, and we can read before a fire. It is going to be lovely."

"I hope you will spend time with me now and then," Darcy murmured, a slight pout evident in his voice, if not his expression.

Looking up at Darcy, Elizabeth playfully cooed, "Is my chivalrous knight feeling ignored?"

Shaking his head, Darcy kissed Elizabeth's temple before saying, "Not neglected, no. It is only that I have had to spend so much time away from you of late taking care of matters that I find I greatly miss your company and our time alone together, just the two of us."

Nestling against Darcy's side, Elizabeth whispered, "You valiant soul, you battled the lions of Longbourn for my sake, yet fate conspired to keep us apart, delaying my chance of expressing my gratitude. Being a knight errant is a thankless job."

Smiling, Darcy said, "Have I become a knight errant without noticing?"

"Well, it seems that you were not just satisfied with helping one damsel in distress. You helped all four of my sisters and waited to take our wedding trip until after your aunt safely collected the youngest three."

"My aunt will love having your sisters with her. They will be pampered and given the training they need to join a higher society, and she will be able to spend time doing all the girl things she has missed out on by only having sons."

Chuckling, Elizabeth continued, "So there is another woman you have helped—your aunt. You even agreed that Mrs. Bennet should have a place to live despite everything she had done." Elizabeth leaned away from him, her gaze fixed on Darcy as she spoke. "I believe a knight errant is a man who selflessly seeks out wrongs to right and performs chivalrous acts without expecting any personal gain. You have given up what you wanted, namely, to spend time with me, so that you might help those in need, even those undeserving. You are a knight errant."

Elizabeth snuggled back into his side, wrapping one arm around him and murmuring, "*My* Knight." Her voice was filled with affection.

Leaning in to kiss her temple once again, he whispered, "And you, my love, will forever be my lady."

So THE KNIGHT AND his lady went off on their adventure. Their life was a beautiful blend of highs and lows, just like any other person's, but what set theirs apart was the unwavering bond between the knight and his lady. They faced whatever came their way together, their love binding them tightly and seeing them through it all.

When children eventually came their way, their favorite fairytale always began with the line, "In a land far away, there lived a knight whose heart was courageous, but his charm with ladies left much to be desired..."

And it ended, "...and they all lived happily ever after."

Acknowledgements

Before you go, I'd like to express my gratitude to all those who assisted me in bringing the Bennet sisters' stories to the world. I'd like to start by acknowledging and thanking the people closest to me. It was thanks to my sister Megan's encouragement that I began writing. Then there is my mother, who serves as my alpha reader and sounding board for fresh ideas. My sister Chelsea's support is invaluable, just like the inspiration I find in my nieces and nephew for my younger characters. If you haven't had the pleasure of debating with a one-year-old who can articulate their thoughts in complete sentences, you're missing out. It is an absolute delight!

Additionally, I would like to extend my appreciation to my Beta readers and the people who show support through my newsletter. Doris, Debra, Carol, and Frankie, working with you to bring my stories to the world has been an honor. The encouragement and feedback I get from you helps me more than you know.

Lastly, it has been an utter pleasure working with my editor, Tayler. Your feedback not only helps me ensure that my story flows and my characters shine, but I also thoroughly enjoy reading your comments. I always love seeing your emojis in the comments, especially the ones with heart eyes!

Most importantly, I would like to thank you. It's been a joy to create this work of love, but without readers, it would be an exercise in futility. The fact that you chose my book to read is an honor. Thank you for taking the time to finish my book, I hope the characters and their stories resonated with you.

If you enjoyed reading this book, please consider leaving an honest review on your favorite site. It does not have to be very long, but I would really appreciate the feedback.

About the Author

My journey with words started out as a painful one. The letters on the page seemed to taunt me, and I spent countless hours with my mother trying to decipher their meaning. Our reading journey started with Little House on the Prairie and continued with other books, mostly in the historical fiction genre. Slowly but surely, I started reading independently, advancing from historical fiction to fantasy and science fiction.

The stories I found in the books I read held me captive, and I often lost track of time. The realization of the true power of the written word inspired me to pursue writing. Unfortunately, I had to put it on the back burner in order to deal with pesky things like paying for food and housing. Then a dare from my sister brought back memories of my passion for writing in high school. It was a passion that I was determined to rekindle.

When I got back into writing, I turned to my latest reading addiction for inspiration, Pride and Prejudice Variations. My mind was fixated on the regency era and the romance of Elizabeth and Darcy, making it hard to write anything else. So I went with it and here we are.

Visit jaimemariewrites.com to delve into my world of words, or find me on Instagram @jaimemariewrites for a glimpse into my creative process.

A Free Gift For My Readers

Have you ever wondered how Pride and Prejudice would change if Elizabeth had an Irish wolfhound? I know I did. Thus, *Pax, the Canine Cupid*, was born. My newest series, the Elizabeth and Darcy True Love Multiverse, has its first story, and it is yours for free if you follow the link by clicking on the cover below. You won't receive duplicate copies of my newsletter if you're already subscribed. But if you haven't and you want to receive my newsletter, along with exclusive updates on my upcoming releases and other exciting content, I'd be thrilled to have you follow me on my writing journey.

Part of the
Elizabeth & Darcy
True Love
Multiverse
Pax,
the Canine
Cupid
A Pride and Prejudice
Variation
Jaime Marie Lang

Books by Jaime Marie Lang

The Bennet Ladies Liberation Series

Darcy's Gallant Gambit

Kitty Catches Kismet

Mary's Daring Demand

Jane's Fragile Façade

Lydia Acquires Adoration

Elizabeth & Darcy True Love Multiverse

Murdered on a Wednesday: A Pride and Prejudice Mystery

Darcy, Knight Errant

Access my linktree account by scanning this QR code and discover the different places where you can find my books.